RADIANT

One

KATIE M LEBLEU

This book is dedicated to my husband. Thank you for always inspiring me and never letting me give up on my dreams.
To my two amazingly smart kids, I love you. You will always be my sunshine.

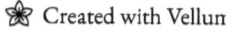

Radiant One

THE SAVIOR SERIES
BOOK ONE

KATIE M. LEBLEU

Chapter One

W renna was curled up in bed, looking through narrowed eyes at her latest book. She had her unwashed blanket pulled up to her chest, unbothered by the piles of dirty clothes strewn across her bunk room floor. Wrenna could lay here for hours if only her father allowed it. There were stacks and stacks of books that lined the walls and covered her tiny desk. So much clutter, it almost completely concealed the large golden bird cage that housed her pet raven, Isha. Her room was dark. Only a small lamp shed just enough light allowing Wrenna the ability to see as she read. She felt at peace with the disarray, unlike her father, who demanded order and neatness. Throughout her life, she found herself shuffling through many different hobbies, never sticking to one for much time. Like learning to crochet and then rapidly losing interest and moving on to something new. Wrenna's brain craved new things. She loved to learn and grow, but she unfortunately lacked motivation and focus, finding herself quickly giving up on her new interest and moving on to the next. Stuck in an endless cycle of searching for something to satiate her purpose, her calling, so to speak. Something other than what was already written out for her, her inherited future. A future planned precisely by her father. A future that Wrenna thought at one time she would enjoy, but like everything else, that interest quickly dissipated. Losing herself in books was the one time she found true focus. She found solace in leaving her predictable life behind for hours at a time, jumping into a fantasy story written by someone she had never met before. Stepping out of this world and into another was when Wrenna felt best at home.

As time ticked by, Wrenna decided with dread it was best to get out of bed. She pulled back the warm covers and tossed the book she was reading called *Creatures of the Lost City* onto the floor. The book was full of mythical creatures, ones conjured up throughout history. Creatures that the Fae were told never existed but were just written in stories to keep kids entertained. Wrenna didn't know for sure which she believed, but she hoped that at least some of these amazing creatures could have been real at one time. Either way, Wrenna repeatedly found herself dreaming of what it would be like to live among these stories, getting to encounter and experience these mythical life forms.

Crawling off the bed, Wrenna stumbled through the dark into her small washroom. She splashed cold water onto her face and patted down her frizzy, wild hair. She checked her reflection in the mirror, feeling she looked good enough to meet with her father. She looked around her dark and pocket-sized bunk room, searching for her backpack, and said a quick "namaste" to Isha, who then replied with a loud squawk. She flung her heavy backpack over her shoulder and turned to the door with a sigh, reaching for the cold doorknob. Not looking forward to the speech she knew she would have to endure shortly, she then exited her bunk room. Her father had told her to meet him in his office at twelve o'clock p.m. for lunch. He wanted to discuss her upcoming welfare work that she had been assigned to do. Glancing down at her watch, she saw it was currently twelve fifteen p.m. She was late as usual. She quickly headed down the hallway to her father's room, rubbing the sleep from her eyes and trying to straighten her disheveled clothes. She took in another deep breath as her father's door came into view.

As Wrenna pushed the door open, she found Chief Thain sitting behind his long desk, peering out the window at the city of Shambhala. His food was probably already getting cold, and his patience looked to be wearing thin as he turned his furrowed brow and eyes towards Wrenna. Chief Thain was quite a substantial man, with broad shoulders, rosy cheeks that shone through his pale, iridescent skin, dark eyes, and salt-and-pepper hair. His ancestral markings flowed up his neck and down each arm. They had been getting darker in color with each year's passing, but he always wore them with pride. Their representation held a great deal of meaning in the Fae culture. He was a strong male, with plenty of battle scars to prove it.

Growing up, Fae never let Wrenna forget how brave her father was and what a strong leader he was for their city. As an adolescent Fae, Wrenna began to notice that she looked nothing like her father, assuming she had inherited her red, thick curly locks and her olive-green eyes from her mother. Wrenna's father never spoke of her mother, and there was no trace of her existence to be found. After years of questioning by Wrenna, her father finally divulged bits of her mother's story. She learned that soon after her mother died, just days after Wrenna's birth, her father had burned and destroyed every sliver of evidence that her mother even existed. The only thing Wrenna did have that was her mother's was Isha. Chief Thain ordered everyone in the city to never mention her or her untimely death ever again. She had always assumed it was too painful for her father, and this was his way of coping with her loss. When Wrenna was a small girl, she would often wonder what her mother was like. When she asked her father then, he would say, "She's gone, been reincarnated into something else, something better. You will see her again one day." He completely sideswiped her questions, trying to change the subject before she was ever able to get a full answer. Wrenna often wondered what having a mother was like or what her mother would be like today. She knew for sure she would have the same pointed ears and iridescent skin like the rest of the Fae but for the other details, she could only imagine.

Chief Thain's booming voice pulled Wrenna from her thoughts as he said, "Well, it's about damn time. I don't understand why you can never just be on time."

Wrenna pulled up the chair just next to her father, where her food sat cold. "Sorry, I got wrapped up in this book I'm reading. Have you heard the stories of these creatures? They shed their skin and regrow completely new skin, like three or four times a year. They can even move super fast across the ground, but they don't have arms or legs! Isn't that so interesting?"

Her father, rubbing his temples, looked at her with annoyance in his eyes. "Wrenna, dear, you need to get your head out of those books. You're living in a fantasy world. You're twenty-five years old, and it's time you begin focusing on the real world and your responsibilities. I need you to find your focus. The city is relying on you."

Wrenna rolled her eyes and let out a breath. "Boring!" she said as she reached for her fork and poked at her food.

This was the same speech he had given her time and time again. Wrenna could almost repeat him verbatim. *"This city is relying on you." Well, they will be waiting for a long time.*

Chief Thain always criticized Wrenna about not taking her role more seriously, not taking the initiative to take on more responsibility as his daughter. Now that she was older, Chief Thain hounded her about her lack of drive more and more. When Wrenna was growing up, she was often left alone in their massive compound with only the maids and groundskeepers to take care of her. Her father seemed to always have business to attend to back then, whether it be within the city or sometimes even outside the walls of the city. This always left Wrenna wondering because she never got to leave the city. No one, at least not regular citizens, ever left the city. It was forbidden. Only the patrol units and Chief Thain had permission to travel outside the city's walls.

"Yes, Father," Wrenna finally said with sarcasm as she turned to stare out the window.

Chief Thain continued lecturing her about growing up, that she one day would be in charge of this city and she needed to start taking it seriously. Wrenna had absolutely no interest in running a city, telling Fae citizens what to do, signing documents all day, and going to snotty dinners with even snottier Fae people. That life was definitely not something she desired to have as her future. When she was eighteen, she had attended a few meetings with her father. He wanted her to start learning the ins and outs of things. After sitting through three grueling hours of some pompous Fae city official blabbering on about the geothermal engineering he had successfully installed, Wrenna confirmed to herself that was not the life she wanted.

After her father finished his incessant ranting, he assigned Wrenna her welfare work for that week, being sure to reaffirm the importance of doing her best. Wrenna pushed her chair back, stood up, and headed towards her father's office door.

"Oh, and Wrenna, no more sleeping in until whenever you like. From now on, I want you up by seven a.m. Do I make myself clear? You are sleeping the day away! You better start getting used to rising early," Chief Thain said, quickly turning back to his plate.

"Yes sir. Namaste, Father," Wrenna said as she walked out the office door. "Gods, I could use some coffee right about now," Wrenna said to herself as she turned down the long hall towards the stairs.

She hadn't eaten any of the disgusting healthy "food" her father had waiting for her, so her belly was now rumbling. She descended the stairs and walked past the unmanned front desk and out the huge double exit doors. Wrenna took her normal route, heading straight for her favorite place in the city. She enjoyed the walk there, only a few blocks. The fresh air was always nice. Most of the people in her city recognized her and knew she was the future leader, so smiles and "namastes" were given as she traveled the city walkways. These walkways opened up into many different shops, businesses, and houses. There were benches strewn about and open areas for Fae to gather. Several Fae were seated in a semi-circle atop a large rolled-out blanket. Each sat with their eyes closed, legs crisscrossed, deep in their afternoon meditation. As Wrenna swiftly passed, she had only one thing in mind: her favorite place to get her own dose of serotonin, with the bonus of caffeine simultaneously.

The House of Books had a grand storefront with giant stone doors and large rocks stacked on either side. The owner was a very eccentric old Fae female. She dressed much differently than the average citizen, which made Wrenna like her even more. Huge earrings dangled from her pointed ears. Bracelets ran up and down her arms, making her ancestral markings barely visible, and layers of necklaces swayed to and fro as she turned towards the opening door.

Zelda greeted Wrenna. "Namaste, Wrenna, what sort of knowledge are you searching for today?"

Zelda was always reshelving books. She thought when things stayed in the same spot for too long, the energy of the space became stagnant and negative. Wrenna scanned the books on the dusty shelf in front of her, not really looking for anything in particular.

"I need some coffee before anything. Especially after listening to my father ramble on for the last hour," Wrenna said as she headed towards the messy counter near where the moka pot awaited, holding the source of Wrenna's search for fuel.

Zelda insisted the best brew came from a super old moka pot, one that she said had been passed down for generations in her family. Wrenna really didn't care how the coffee was made; she was just thankful for the taste of it on her tongue. For a while, the city had been completely out of coffee. There was none at all to be found. Wrenna had felt like she was suffering from withdrawals at one point. The horticulturist in the city could not figure out the proper environment for growth of the coffee bean. Eventually, the patrol units returned from one of their expeditions beyond the wall with crates of supplies: different herbs, medicines, and most important of all, coffee. Wrenna had assumed they made some sort of trade with the other territories, but at the end of the day, she was just thankful to have coffee back in her life. After pouring a cup and mixing in several different additives, she began sifting through a large pile of books on the counter. Most were pulled from the shelves by Zelda, some light reading in her free time. Others were books patrons decided against at the last minute.

Soon the coffee was hitting the spot, sending that beautiful surge of familiar energy through Wrenna's body, a surge of energy that would help her power through her afternoon run. Wrenna had read somewhere that exercise was the best medicine. Ever since then, she tried to make it part of her daily routine, along with practicing yoga. Growing up, she had gone to school at The Moksha Academy, where they taught about the Fae history, directing young Fae towards liberation and freedom. They also taught basic studies and incorporated practicing yoga and meditation daily. She had continued doing yoga even after graduating from the academy, feeling a great connection with the practice.

She exited the bookstore, yelling to Zelda in the back that she would see her soon. Zelda just grunted and turned back to the dust-ridden shelves. Wrenna tightened the straps of her backpack and headed down the walkway, preparing for her run. She always wondered to herself why she lugged her heavy backpack all over the place, even when she ran. She justified carrying it because she needed a place to store her passkey to the front entrance door of the municipal building. Plus any books she wanted to possibly read at some point in her day and any other random items she felt she could need, like an extra hair tie, rose hip oil for her always dry lips, those sorts of things. Wrenna slowly began to pick up the pace in her steps, giving her body a few minutes to warm up. Jogging never came easy but every time she finished, she felt better, more focused.

It must be all the endorphins.

Wrenna always took the same path through the city, avoiding others walking with bags and buggies, taking in the sounds as she ran past. Her run consisted of a wide circle, staying close to the city, never venturing too far out. The city itself was surrounded by a walkway that weaved in and out amongst the buildings. Branched off from that walkway was another unbeaten path used by maintenance and the patrol units. This path ran alongside the giant wall that surrounded the city and was said to be more than twenty miles long. Wrenna had little desire to run that sort of distance, so she stuck to the well-maintained walkways. Not only did the thought of running that far seem unbearable, there was also the recent missing Fae to take into account. The city had experienced its first odd occurrence in many years, and the thought of that kept Wrenna on edge as she ran. Chief Thain assured Wrenna that these so-called "missing" Fae were not actually missing, that they had chosen to leave on their own. He told her not to worry about it, that nothing bad ever happened in Shambhala.

On the outer edge of the walkway, large boulders had been scattered, creating a barrier between the city and the vast dry, barren land. In school, Wrenna had learned of a place located near the far edge of the city's wall called the Badlands. It was said to be a desolate place. A place no one went or wanted to go to. Wrenna found stories of the Badlands in a few books over the years, but the stories never gave much information as to why this place was avoided.

She had asked her father if he had even been there before. His response was, "Well, of course, Wrenna. I know every inch of this city and the areas around it."

"Then why do Fae say to stay away from that place? What's out there?" Wrenna asked.

"There are places for citizens, and there are places for leaders. One day, you will learn what's there, but until then, don't fret over it," Chief Thain had said, keeping his answers, as always, vague and open-ended.

Other than the tightly kept secrets of beyond the wall and the Badlands, Wrenna loved the city she had grown up in. She never really witnessed any crime or any Fae acting out of sorts. Everyone there was pretty calm for the most part. The city's name itself meant "place of peace, tranquility, and happiness," and it definitely lived up to that name. The Fae dressed respectfully, were all very minimalist, and no one tried to stand out much in a crowd. With the exception of Zelda, but she was just a different breed, some would have said. The Fae here all shared the same commonality of interest: keep the city clean, keep peace, don't ask questions, and help the city prosper when and wherever they can.

As Wrenna jogged through the city, she took in the beauty. Nothing was really out of place. It was pristine, manicured, and simple. Between the walkways was golden, glistening sand, small black obsidian stones sprinkled throughout. The general consensus was polished, organized, and nothing out of place. Not at all like Wrenna and her personal vibe, but it definitely reflected that of her father's liking. The Fae here all had the same skin, which was passed down by the ancestors who came before them. Very pale, iridescent skin, almost blue, it reflected many colors depending upon the angle. Their skin was also covered with unique markings of swirls and circles, which resembled wisps of smoke kissing their skin. When the Fae were first born, the colors of these markings were very light, almost invisible, and as they aged, they darkened to almost a black color, which symbolized the completion of their life cycle. The skin color and pointed ears weren't their only characteristics. They each possessed a different sort of unique power. Most awakened powers amongst the Fae citizens were unimpressive. Very rarely was a Fae born with abilities more powerful than the average citizen. Chief Thain always insisted Wrenna was going to be one of those rarities. Fae powers generally began to awaken around the age of six, slowly progressing and advancing in power over the years. A Fae's powers should be fully awakened and mastered by the age of twenty-five. Some

Fae could experience brief glimpses of their future powers even earlier in life.

Wrenna was always nervous about her powers growing up. She had only experienced them a handful of times in her life so far, all of them being bad experiences. Her father, on the other hand, would not stop talking about it, constantly reassuring her that her powers would be a great asset to the city one day. For now, Wrenna was able to steer clear of any conversation about it and hoped to avoid it for as long as possible. She wasn't afraid of her powers being fully awakened. She wasn't worried about that. She was worried that they wouldn't live up to the great expectation her father had for her powers to be something greater than any Fae had ever seen before. The pressure was overwhelming to Wrenna at times, so she hoped she could live her life a bit longer before she potentially became an even bigger failure to her father.

As she continued with her jog, she liked to Fae watch. Seeing the mothers with their little ones, smiling, laughing, playing peekaboo. She always had a bit of jealousy and envy when she witnessed these normal, family-type interactions. As a child, she never had that, especially not with her uptight father, who was too busy running the city to be an actual father. Some of the little ones would periodically lose control of their turbulent, awakening powers, creating water out of thin air or vanishing and reappearing down the block, causing their mothers to panic. Wrenna laughed to herself, remembering a time when her powers showed up unexpectedly and what an epic catastrophe had then unfolded.

She was probably six years old at the time. Her father was having another one of his dull dinners with the city councilmen and their families. Wrenna always hated these dinners. Her father made her put on a dress and always made her promise to be polite to the Fae children. One of those other Fae children in particular had always gotten under her skin. He was a know-it-all who tried to act smarter and more grown than everyone else, even though they all were close to the same age. His name was Stiles Mahon, and his father was her father's lead officer. He was prancing around, demanding all the other Fae children use the proper utensils and keep their elbows off the table, pushing Wrenna's annoyance to an all-time high. She started to feel her anger growing. She was in her own dining room, and this Fae male thought he could tell her what to do. All of a sudden, she began feeling a warmth in her chest. It felt like a massive hot blade had been stabbed in between her ribs. She thought maybe it was the food or all the bubbly drinks she'd had that day. Then, without warning, this beam of orange light blasted from her chest, knocking over the small table they were sitting at, spilling all the food and drinks onto the floor. Stiles turned towards her with a down-turned face and began to cry. Food was running down his perfectly pressed clothes, dripping onto his bright and shiny boots. Everyone in the room was shocked. The other Fae children began to laugh. They laughed at Wrenna for her uncontrolled outburst of power. Stiles soon joined Wrenna in embarrassment when the Fae children laughed at him as well as he stood covered in soggy, green leafy vegetables. After the dinner that night, Chief Thain made Wrenna apologize to Stiles for what happened. Seeing how humiliated Stiles was, Wrenna felt a tiny bit sorry for him. She could tell how important it was to Stiles to keep up his appearance and look his best, and she had made him look stupid in front of everyone. Stiles accepted her apology and from that day forward, they developed a sort of friendship. It was a kind of under-standing between the two. That shared experience had brought them together in a weird way.

Pulling herself from her memory, Wrenna found herself now standing in front of the municipal compound. She had finished her run without even realizing it. Sweat now cascaded down her back and across her brow, but she only felt a bit winded. She turned towards the double doors of the front entrance of the municipal compound that was the home assigned to the chief and his family. Which was a total of two Fae in their entire family. She didn't have any siblings or cousins, nothing. It was just her and her father. Well, and the thirty-something staff members that also lived in the compound. She pulled her passkey from her bag and scanned it at the door. Just beyond the entrance, Ralf was now standing behind the front desk. He was much older than Chief Thain and had worked for him since before Wrenna was born.

He gave her a brief smile and said, "Namaste, Wrenna, how was your run?"

"Oh, same old, same old, Ralf. Sucked as usual," she said. Ralf laughed and turned back to his massive book sprawled open on the desk. Papers were scattered around it, and numerous writing tools littered the space. Ralf was always doing research, but no one seemed to know what exactly on, and no one cared enough to ask. With Ralf's old age, Chief Thain had reassigned him to door keeper, which was better for his aging back and legs. Ralf seemed thankful for his new job, which gave him much more time for his top-secret investigation. She walked towards the stone staircase that led her up to her and her father's living quarters. They had a small sitting area with a stone hearth heating space in the middle. A large window ran along the back wall with a view to the city. On the other side of the room was a small kitchenette area for her to store leftovers or to grab a quick drink. The bigger kitchen area was downstairs, where the staff cooked all the meals and stored all the essential food.

The city acquired one hundred percent of its power from underground hot springs. These springs were then warmed by even deeper lava that flowed all over, coming from Naraka, which their ancestors said was the core of the earth itself. These ancestors created steam-powered turbines that pumped up water that was then piped to nearby houses and businesses. They also used it to cook their food, incinerate any waste, and desalinate water for drinking.

Wrenna walked to the end of the long hallway towards her tiny bunk room. Her father might have been the highest ranked official in Shambhala, but he refused to live large.

He always told Wrenna, when she complained about where they lived, "Take what is truly necessary. No more, Wrenna. We need to set an example to the citizens. Living free from greed, no longer desiring possessions, non-attachment, non-accumulation—this is the way of our ancestors."

He was always preaching different quotes from *The Book of the Sacred Code*. It was the way of the Fae to live, ethical guidelines laid out like a map to guide them to the next life. Within this book, the Gods, or some called them deities, spoke these guidelines, providing the Fae people with instructions on how they should live and treat one another. Some of the most prominent Gods, those that most Fae prayed to daily, were Brockma the Creator, Sanub the Preserver, and Liabe the

Destroyer. These Gods were no longer living, but their teachings were a way of life for most of the Fae people of Shambhala. Wrenna had learned much of their teachings at The Moksha Academy and tried her best to live according to those teachings. They were not the only Gods of the Fae people. *The Book of the Sacred Code* listed over thirty million other Gods, some living and nonliving. The Fae people held *The Book of Sacred Code* to a high standard and continued to share its readings throughout the centuries.

Turning the cold knob to her bunk room, she pushed the door open and jumped as she found someone sitting on her bed. Stiles was sitting on the corner of her unmade bed in his patrol uniform, with a smirk on his face. He was a tall male with blonde hair and dark blue eyes, almost black. He had broad shoulders and plenty of muscles. Pretty much any Fae female's dream of a husband. He was definitely fun to look at, if only he could just keep his mouth shut from time to time. Wrenna and Stiles had been on-again, off-again lovers for the past seven years. He had asked her to marry him and make it official probably a hundred times, but Wrenna just wasn't into labels and definitely wasn't a sentimental type. She had always just figured Stiles had ulterior motives, like possibly being married to the future heir of the city. She didn't see that as her future. Getting married, having little ones, and living happily ever after—it just wasn't her thing. They had grown up together, and there was a time that Wrenna thought she was in love with Stiles, but as she had gotten older, their differences had kept Wrenna from committing.

"What the hell, Stiles? It's super creepy when I come home to you waiting like a damn pet. It's such a turnoff."

"Well, it's the only way to see you. You always avoid me," he said, batting his dark lashes of his even darker eyes.

Stiles was the lead officer of her father's patrol unit, which made him think he was more important and better than basically everyone else. She had spent many nights with him, listening to him ramble on about how amazing he was, how strong he was, and at one time, Wrenna swooned over him. He represented the perfect male. As time passed, Wrenna watched Stiles allow his ego to take over more and more. She began to see who he was becoming. His personality began to twist and change, becoming more and more self-absorbed and conceited. But for some reason, Wrenna kept seeing him, allowing him in her bed. Mostly out of boredom, a way to pass the time, she thought. Stiles was the only Fae male she had been with, not that she couldn't get with another male. She just didn't have the energy to build another relationship with someone else. Things with Stiles were just easier out of convenience. Growing up in the compound, there was no shortage of young male Fae, but she learned really quick to avoid them. She didn't really enjoy being around other Fae. She liked her alone time, her peace and quiet. So when Stiles barged into her room, uninvited, it really started to get on her last nerve.

"I was just about to head down to the kitchen to grab a bite to eat. I wanted to see if you wanted to join me," he said.

Wrenna threw her backpack over her desk chair and said, "No, I'm good, I just had a large coffee from The House of Books. I paid a ton of money for that caffeine boost, and I want to let it ride through my veins for as long as possible."

She turned towards the washroom, so ready to get out of this sweaty top, when Stiles stood up and said, "Well, fine then. You know that coffee isn't good for you, right?"

He always did that, tried to make her feel bad for splurging on coffee. "Yeah, no shit, but that's what makes it so good." She turned and winked at him as she slammed the door of the washroom.

He yelled through the door as he was leaving, "Well, I hope to see you later tonight if you are still up to it?"

Wrenna rolled her eyes. This guy never stopped. "Yeah, that's fine, make it like two a.m. if you can. I have a lot of reading to do."

Chapter Two

Wrenna woke up the next day to her alarm going off. She was supposed to start her welfare work at the greenhouse at eight a.m., and she could not be late. She jumped up out of bed, grabbed the nearest pants, took a quick sniff, decided they smelled decent enough, and put them on. She quickly braided her bright red curly hair and tried rubbing yesterday's makeup off of her eyes. She looked herself over in the mirror. She was plain, freckles sprinkled over her nose and cheeks. Her Fae markings swirled down her neck, across her shoulders, flowing down her arms. She always thought her body was different from the average Fae. She had a much thicker build, more muscular, not like the average skinny Fae seen around the city. Her father always told her she was unique and being different meant she was blessed by the Gods, and she should be thankful for those blessings, knowing others weren't given them. Wrenna didn't care what her father thought or what the expected image was. She was fine with what she looked like and didn't waste time worrying about it. She debated relining her eyes with a kohl pencil—she always liked the way it made her eyes pop—but then that guaranteed she would for sure be late.

"Good enough," she said to herself, grabbing her backpack and walking out the door.

Wrenna didn't meet anyone else in the hallways of the municipal compound on her way out, leaving before the staff had started their day. She headed towards one of the city's greenhouses, a place where they grew most of their food. They had to meticulously cultivate the sand with minerals and Fae power to create the perfect environment for plants to grow. When Wrenna entered the vented stone doors, walking into the large, dome-shaped arboretum, she felt a rush of heat and humidity engulf her body.

"Thank the Gods I braided my hair today," she whispered under her breath.

Wrenna had an insane amount of hair, curly and oftentimes frizzy. Red hair was a rare trait within the Fae, and curly hair was unseen. The other Fae always whispered about it like it was some kind of omen, but no one ever clarified if it was a good or bad omen. All these things she was born with, the family she was born into and her future power, these things made life very confusing at times. Wrenna could feel Fae eyes watching her throughout her life. Alongside her father, they also expected great things from her. These expectations of her were to become someone unlike her current self. More of a leader, a beacon for the citizens of Shambhala to look to. She was far too comfortable, living with zero responsibility, doing as she pleased, to even consider transitioning into this Fae figurehead they all expected her to be.

For now, she would give her time around the city and help where she could. Welfare work was required from all Fae people of the city at one time or another. Those who hadn't established a family yet and whose powers hadn't fully awakened were the ones enlisted first. Each month, a new job was given, and young Fae would oblige, doing chores, helping with the community needs, and learning new skills. Wrenna did it because it was what was expected of her.

Her father would often say, "We must set an excellent example when and wherever we can, Wrenna" when she would complain about doing some of the more dirty jobs.

But working in the greenhouse seemed like something that could be somewhat interesting and possibly enjoyable. She wasn't that upset about it. Learning about these ancient practices always piqued her interest.

She wandered into the front office area, looking for the greenhouse headmaster, only to find him bent over some sort of plant with his butt crack hanging out of the back of his pants.

"Um, excuse me, sir," she said, causing the heavyset man to jump and slam his head on an overhead pipe.

"Oh, hello there, so sorry. I was inspecting the axillary buds on this new herb the horticulturist has fabricated. It seems to be growing well." He then gestured for a handshake.

"We haven't been formally introduced. My name is Arnie. You must be Wrenna?"

She shook his hand and nodded a yes.

Arnie turned back to the plant that he had been examining before and said, "Well, hopefully you aren't afraid to get a bit of sand under your nails?"

Wrenna replied, "No sir."

"Follow me," he said, and he then turned and walked deeper into the jungle of plants that were growing wildly along the walls and up the middle of the massive space. He began showing her how to open different valves, ones that turned on the water that was piped into a massive cistern that stood at the back of the greenhouse. Her first chore would be to inspect all the overhead misters that were strategically placed throughout the greenhouse. Her next job was to go through each plant and look for odd coloring, dead leaves, and check for any fruit or vegetables that may have blossomed. She was to make a note of which plant and give "abundant detail," Arnie said, of what she found on each plant. He explained they were currently experimenting with different formulas of Fae powers blended with minerals. The horticulturist wanted to see which blend produced the best results for each plant. Wrenna's last chore of the day was to sweep the floors and remove any sand that could have fallen out of the large boxes the plants were growing in.

Arnie said, "Cleanliness is next to godliness, kiddo." Wrenna proceeded to do all the chores expected of her, making sure to do them adequately, knowing a full report of her performance would be given to her father.

Finally, walking out of the greenhouse about six hours later, Wrenna welcomed the fresh seventy-degree air. The city always maintained a constant seventy-degree temperature year-round.

They were blessed by the Gods, her father would say.

The citizens of Shambhala hadn't known anything different. It had always been that way since the beginning of time. They used the steam from the geothermal vents in the ground to warm up the greenhouse, which, over time, the Fae learned helped grow the vegetation, helping it produce abundant crops.

Turning towards the walkway in the direction of the compound, she heard someone call to her. "Wrenna, Wrenna, wait. Is that you?" She immediately recognized the voice of a fellow student she had attended the academy with.

Myra Elsher was a snooty female Fae who attended The Moksha Academy alongside Wrenna and Stiles. Wrenna and Myra weren't close friends but did hang out from time to time when they were younger. Her father, of course, worked for Chief Thain. He was another one of the councilmen, so she always saw Myra at the events and dinners she was forced to attend. It had been a few years since they had really talked. They had a falling-out when Myra made a rude comment about Wrenna having commitment issues and that if she planned on leading the city one day, she needed to wake up and get her act together. Wrenna already had her father harping down her throat about this stuff; she didn't need anyone else doing it.

"Myra, oh my goodness, it's so great to see you," Wrenna lied.

Myra looked the same: perfectly ironed hair, dazzling blue eyes, sparkling skin, looking absolutely flawless.

"Wrenna, dear, how have you been? I see you are leaving the greenhouse. Isn't it just lovely? My father helped design and construct the intricate steam system."

"Oh yes, it's just wonderful. You should be so proud of your father. What a wonderful thing he built for our city. We are so blessed by it," Wrenna replied somewhat sarcastically.

Myra slowly looked Wrenna up and down, probably judging her appearance. "Well, we should get together sometime and have dinner. You can bring Stiles and I'll bring Issan; we could have a double date." She smiled and waited for Wrenna to respond.

"Yeah, that sounds like fun. Send a message to the compound and we will set it up. It was so good seeing you, Myra," Wrenna said,

"Oh, you too, Wrenna. You look amazing, by the way," Myra said, returning the sarcasm.

"Thank you." Pressing her lips into a slight grin, she quickly turned and walked away.

There was always a bit of jealousy between the two Fae females. Myra always had eyes for Stiles and didn't think Wrenna deserved him, but honestly Wrenna couldn't care less. A few years ago, Wrenna went with Stiles to the Patrol Officers Ball. It was an event they had each year for the patrol officers and their partners to attend. The staff of the municipal compound put together a great feast. They all dressed up in their best suits and gowns and would spend the evening dancing and drinking. Wrenna went once and never went again. Myra and her friends were always there with their noses upturned, passing judgment and being their usual pretentious selves. That was the night Myra made the rude comments about Wrenna being irresponsible and having commitment issues.

"He deserves better than you. Someone that can devote themselves to him," Myra had added as her eyes jolted towards Stiles and her poor partner, Issan, stood numbly.

Stiles was someone to help her pass the time. They had never put a label on what they had. They never once told each other they loved each other out loud. But for some reason, Myra's comment that night made her angry. She started to rethink her feelings for Stiles. Did she want to be with him? Days later at the municipal compound, Wrenna overheard Stiles yelling at a lower-ranking Fae officer. The way he spoke to him, the lack of empathy or kindness, answered Wrenna's question for her. So she continued to keep him at arm's reach, not sharing too much of herself with him. She kept it only physical, the entirety of their relationship revolving around only one thing.

Wrenna headed towards the compound she called home. Walking several blocks, she saw the walkway was empty of other Fae. Most had already made it home from the day's work. She noticed something out of place, something abnormal lying on the city's walkway a few feet ahead of her. She squinted her eyes, trying to make out exactly what it was she was seeing. On the ground was a stone, but not like the average black obsidian stone that was common in the city. This rock was translucent. It sparkled some and had smooth edges, like someone cut it out with purpose. She bent over to pick it up, looking around to see if anyone else saw what she saw or if someone dropped it, but no one was around. Wrenna held the stone—if that was what it even was—closer to her face to get a better look. It was like nothing she had ever seen before, and it radiated a kind of warmth into the palm of her hand. It was clear with an orange tint but when you looked deep into it, it reflected a variety of colors. Each color seemed to project off the stone and out into the space around it. As she turned it in her hand and looked within the stone, it was like a kaleidoscope of colors bouncing around inside. She was amazed, having no clue what it actually was, but she knew someone who would.

Wrenna burst through the front doors of The House of Books. Knowing Zelda, she had to know what it was.

"Zelda, where are you? Zelda, *hello*?" In the back, she heard a loud bang and what sounded like several things falling to the floor. Zelda mumbled vulgarly under her breath, then stumbled through the beaded curtain that separated her living quarters and the store itself.

"Hang on one damn minute, kid. I'll be right there."

Wrenna watched as the ancient Fae female meandered to the counter, adorned with ample amounts of jewelry as usual.

"What can I help you with, young one?" Zelda muttered. Wrenna held her hand out in front of Zelda as she slowly peeled her fingers back to reveal the stone. Zelda didn't immediately react. She took in a quick breath and blinked a few times, not taking her eyes off the stone.

"I found this outside on one of the walkways. I've never seen anything like it. Do you know what it is?"

Zelda stood almost speechless, which was unusual for her. Taking a few moments, she eventually found the words to speak. "Hmmm, well, I'm not exactly sure if it's what I think it is, because what I think it is hasn't been seen or found for centuries. It's impossible to be what I think it is. They were completely depleted. The Fae used the last of them before I was even born into this world," Zelda responded.

"What is it? I mean, obviously, it's a stone, but I have never seen a stone like this before," Wrenna said with uncertainty.

"It's a stone, yes, but not just any ordinary stone. I believe it is called an opal. Fae mined for them ages ago and fabricated them into jewelry or weapons. They were said to increase Fae powers, even opening realms to other worlds when their power was used correctly. Stories say when these stones' power was used incorrectly, evil and disaster would wreak havoc and kill the Fae who abused that power."

Zelda began walking towards the far back shelves of the store to the lost history section, one of Wrenna's favorite sections. Zelda crouched down to the bottom shelf and pulled a tattered book from the shelf. On the front cover of the book, there was a golden seal, a symbol she had never seen before. It resembled a semicircle shape. Zelda lifted the heavy book and carried it to the front counter of the store. She hustled to the front door, turned the lock, and then dashed back to the book waiting on the counter. She began flipping through pages like she knew exactly what she was looking for, like she had the pages memorized. At long last, Zelda stopped on a page titled "Upala." Zelda scanned the page, running her boney fingers down it. Eventually, she looked up from the ancient, decaying book and smiled.

"This is what I thought it was. It's known as a fire opal or Upala, an ancient precious stone. It reveals the inner truth of your own aspirations, so if you are good, it will bring only goodness and truth. If you are evil and have ill desires, it can destroy you. Fae have searched this world, fought and stole for these. The power it carries is unlike anything we could ever conjure with our own powers. This stone awakens courage, strength, and bravery, and it allows for the release of dormant abilities. It can amplify your cosmic consciousness and stimulates flashes of intuition and visions of the future. It can be used for tremendous good but can also be used for ungodly things. It can give life, and it can take life away. I don't understand how you found this. Where did it come from?"

Wrenna shook her head. "I have no idea; it was just lying in the middle of the walkway. I noticed it out of the corner of my eye."

"Well, you must hide it and tell no one you have it. If this falls into the wrong hands, it could be bad. Do you understand, my dear? You have a very rare, very powerful stone here. Fae have killed for this in the past!" Zelda whispered.

She looked Wrenna directly into her eyes with extreme seriousness and a little fear. She was worried. Her body language and demeanor had changed. Wrenna knew it was a serious matter, and she was almost afraid to keep it, but something was drawing her to it. She felt a pull, a tingle, warmth coming from the stone. Something was calling to her, coaxing her towards the power held within.

Wrenna thanked Zelda for her help, giving her a hug, and decided to head home. After Wrenna left The House of Books with the fire opal buried deep in her pocket, she wasn't sure what to make of it all. She had so many thoughts running through her head, and she definitely felt something new, different, spiraling through her body. Was it excitement from finding such a rare gem or was it something else? She yearned for the chaos of her bunk room where she could have some privacy to think.

After scanning her passkey, Wrenna rushed up the stairs, almost ran down the hall to her bunk room, and quietly closed the door behind her. She tossed her backpack on a nearby chair and jumped onto her bed. She pulled the fire opal from her pocket, wanting to get a better view of it. Just placing her fingers on the stone, she felt a tiny jolt of energy. It was surprising, but she liked it. It was as if something powerful was waiting within the stone, calling to her, enticing her, tempting her. She turned the stone over, taking in every detail. She eventually jumped from bed and headed to her desk in the corner. She flipped on her lamp and placed the stone under the light. Wrenna was mesmerized by the beauty of the stone. As she turned it over in the light, different colors beamed from it. It had an all over color of what looked like red or orange with a million other colors sprinkled in. It was absolutely beautiful. Isha, in the cage on her desk, squawked loudly and flapped her wings as if she sensed the power of the stone as well.

"What is it, Isha? What do you think it is?" Wrenna asked the bird, half expecting an answer.

Eventually feeling satisfied at the examination of the stone, she knew no answers were going to be found tonight, so she placed it in the drawer of her desk. She fell back onto her bed, staring up at the ceiling. So many thoughts began swarming her mind. Should she tell her father about what she had found? What about Stiles? Before she could decide, her eyelids became heavy and she drifted off to sleep.

Chapter Three

A blast slammed into Wrenna's side, throwing her onto the ground. She rolled over, seeing only smoke, hearing cries surrounding her. A battle raged around her, flashing lights and loud explosions making her ears ring. She felt massive pressure on her chest, looking down and seeing what looked like blood on her shirt. She had to get up, she had to keep looking for ways out. Her body couldn't move, no matter how much she tried. Another massive explosion went off, hitting the ground just next to her paralyzed body. The dust and smoke were so thick, and the air smelled like burning flesh and singed hair. She couldn't get a clear visual of what was going on around her. Wrenna squinted her eyes and looked above her through the smoke, seeing what looked to be a bright orange light. She couldn't make out what it was, but the light was getting closer, brighter. She heard a loud sound like nothing she had ever heard before. The sound vibrated all the way to her bones. Moments later, the orange light was just above her, shining deep in her eyes. She couldn't see, she couldn't breathe, and her entire body began to tingle. More explosions went off around her. It was a war zone. Where was she? She could feel her heart pounding in her chest. She found the strength to lift her hands towards her chest, searching for a possible wound. Just above her heart, her hand landed on what felt like an oval stone. It was the fire opal. She clasped her hand around it, feeling a sense of peace, warmth. And soon, blackness took over.

Wrenna sat up in her bed with a jolt. She had awoken from a dream. One that seemed more real than any dream she had ever had. She could feel her heart pounding, her pulse rapid in her throat, and she was even sweating. She reached for her chest, finding only her oversized T-shirt, one she had stolen from Stiles from their encounter that night. No stone. She immediately leapt from bed towards her desk, pulled the drawer open to find the fire opal lying in the same place she had left it the night before. It all felt so real. It was like she could still smell that wretched stench and hear the screaming. Wrenna reached for a day-old glass of water sitting on the desk and chugged it down. She felt like the smoke was actually in her throat, nose, and lungs.

"Why would I have a dream like that? I never dream!" Wrenna whispered to herself.

Wrenna felt dirty, like she was covered in grime—probably sweat—so she jumped in the shower. She scrubbed her body, hoping the smell and feel of those images would wash down the drain. She couldn't shake it. The vividness of the dream began to make Wrenna feel exhausted and extremely anxious. She pulled on a pair of sweatpants and her favorite T-shirt, tossed her hair on top of her head in a bun, and slumped back into bed. She had zero energy to do much of anything today and had that achy feeling in her body like she was coming down with something. Her body was tired, and her mind was buzzing with energy, jumping from one thought to another. She had so many unanswered questions with complete uncertainty as to where to find those answers.

Wrenna was startled when she heard a knock on her door. She yelled, "Come in!" to whomever was waiting outside her door. She hoped it wasn't Stiles. She had no energy for him today. The door slowly opened just a crack, and Ralf poked his head in.

"Oh, I'm so sorry, Miss Wrenna, but when I didn't see you leave for your morning coffee today, I got worried. Are you not feeling well? Is there anything I can get you?"

With a slight smile, Wrenna responded, "Oh, thank you, Ralf, for checking in on me. I'm just feeling a little off today. I may just rest in my room. Thank you for coming up and looking in on me. That was so thoughtful."

"Is there anything I can do to help?" Ralf said.

"If you could ask the kitchen for some fresh water and maybe some of that veggie soup, that would be amazing," Wrenna said.

"Yes ma'am, coming right up. I will get that going for you as soon as possible. Well, I hope you aren't getting sick. Do let me know if there is anything else I can help you with," Ralf said. He pulled the door shut.

Wrenna eventually fell back asleep after devouring the veggie soup and crackers brought up to her by the kitchen staff. She didn't dream, as usual, and when she woke up, she felt well-rested and less drained than before. She pulled the covers off and stepped out of bed. She had to find out more information on the fire opal, but she couldn't let anyone know she had it. She thought maybe she could say she had stumbled upon a story about them in one of her many books. She could just act like an ordinary curious Fae, wondering if these things actually were real.

As she sat debating her next move, something began to distract her. It wasn't a sound or movement but more like a pull. She felt like she had noticed it earlier, but the pull was getting stronger now. It was like a strange energy coiled around her. It was drawing her towards her desk. She stood up and walked to her desk, and the vibrations of energy intensified. She pulled the drawer open. She could feel the energy the opal was emitting from the bottoms of her feet to the top of her head. It was as if it was trying to speak to her, trying to tell her something. Wrenna felt an intense craving begin to gnaw at her. She reached her hand in and picked it up. It was instantly like she was connected to something, that something her body was craving. Once she had the opal cradled in her hand, it was like that craving started to feel satisfied. Wrenna couldn't understand why, but she knew there was something strange happening that she had never felt before.

Wrenna quickly got dressed, deciding to go speak with her father and see if she could learn any information from him inconspicuously. She had a desire to bring the opal with her, so she put it deep into her pocket. Isha ruffled her feathers, chirping a few times as if noticing the change in Wrenna.

"I'll be right back," she said to Isha.

Leaving her bunk room, she walked towards her father's office, hoping he would be there. She quickly knocked on the door. Without waiting for a reply, she entered. He was there sitting at his desk, but he was not alone. His top adviser, Arban, who was seer for the chief, was standing over a stack of papers. They both looked up at Wrenna when she entered the office without invitation.

Her father, Chief Thain, spoke first, looking quite annoyed. "What can I do for you, Wrenna? As you can see, I am in the middle of something."

"Oh, I am sorry, Father. I just wanted to ask you about something, but I can come back when you are not busy," Wrenna replied.

"No, no, go ahead. What is it you need?" Chief Thain responded.

Arban stepped back from her father and waited for Wrenna to ask the question, frustration in his eyes.

"Well, I was just curious if you have ever seen a fire opal or know anyone who has. I was reading a book that mentioned them briefly, and I found the legends behind them so interesting."

Arban's eyes widened, and Chief Thain cleared his throat.

"Well, my dear, I have never seen one myself since they have been completely dissipated by the Fae scavenging the city and surrounding territories to find them," Chief Thain said.

"Why were they so wanted by the Fae people? Were they truly as powerful as the stories say? How come I have never heard of them before?" Wrenna said.

Chief Thain took a moment to answer. "What book did you read this in?" He looked at Arban and back to Wrenna. Reluctantly, he continued, "They were used long ago to help Fae tap into dark powers, but who knows if that is true. We don't really talk about them much because they are only legends, Wrenna. Not everything you read is true."

Wrenna continued to look at her father, hoping her eyes would convey that her questions still were not being fully answered.

Her father continued on. "These opals are said to have energy that calls to you. The power can be so addictive, Fae have been known to kill for them. At least that's what the stories say. As far as I am concerned, I am glad they no longer exist. It seems like only bad could come from them. Nothing good," Chief Thain finished saying, looking towards the large window, looking out into the city.

Arban then decided to share his opinion on the subject. "I personally believe these stones are only legends. Nothing in this world could possibly contain the power they say these fire opals do," Arban said.

Yeah, well, you obviously are the worst seer there is because I have one in my pocket now as we speak! "Okay, well, sorry to bother you. I just was curious about what your thoughts were. Thank you, Father, I will get out of your hair now."

She turned to the door to leave, and her father spoke. "Wrenna, please try to get your head out of those books. Go hang out with other Fae your age. Once Stiles comes back from a perimeter check today, why don't you go see him?"

Wrenna sighed and responded, "Yes, Father."

She kept her responses way shorter than what she actually would have liked to say. She didn't really know anyone her age. A few other Fae females that she had met doing her welfare work and the dreadful Myra, but she never really built a relationship with any of them. She walked out of her father's office and leaned back against the door. There was something he wasn't telling her. It was like he had danced around the questions, not wanting to go into much detail. Maybe he didn't want to talk about it in depth in front of Arban, or maybe he was telling the truth and he really didn't know much about the fire opals. Whatever it was, Wrenna knew there had to be more info out there. Someone had to know something.

Why was it just lying there out in the open? Did someone drop it? She reached in her pocket and encircled the opal within her palm. Something was off; something didn't feel right. Was there something more to be told? Maybe the story was so much bigger or maybe she was totally overthinking it all. Her mind just kept racing. She had so many questions. She decided maybe a run would help her think better, get her thoughts in a more productive order. So she headed towards her bunk room to grab her tennis shoes.

Once she had the proper shoes and bra on, she headed out the front door of the compound, waving towards Ralf.

He yelled out to her, "I'm glad you're feeling better, Miss Wrenna!"

She looked back at him with a big smile of thanks. She took off down the walkway, immediately picking up her pace and getting into a full run. She felt the opal in her pocket bouncing around, knocking against her leg. She ran and ran and ran. Sweat was pouring down her back when she noticed she was no longer on the walkway but running down the maintenance path that ran along the city wall. The realization that she was no longer on the city's pristine walkways made Wrenna's body tense as she became aware of the new forbidden surroundings. She was always told the wall was there to keep random Fae outsiders from just waltzing into their city. With that thought and the "missing" Fae, fear began to slow her steps briefly.

"Some may have ill intent," her father would say.

He believed anyone outside the walls should have to check in at the entrance gate and state their business in the city. Wrenna had never gone this far out. She was surrounded by barren land, no houses or buildings, just sand and rocks.

This is the perfect place for a kidnapping. No one to see, Wrenna thought as she continued on running.

The energy boiling over inside and curiosity kept her feet moving forward. Wrenna looked up at the giant stone wall that hovered over her and saw a numbered sign: MI. 7.

I guess that means mile seven. The patrol officers must use these signs to help with location or areas of the wall that need repair.

Wrenna kept running, feeling like she had a tremendous amount of energy she still needed to burn off. Eventually, she began to slow down, turning to look back at the city. It was smaller, and the details of it were harder to see. She couldn't believe she had gotten this far that fast. She searched for another mile marker sign. MI. 8.

Maybe it was because she was so in her head that time passed quickly. She walked a little further, noticing a pile of rocks that seemed to look like they were formed into some sort of structure. Stacked perfectly together. She got closer and began to hear what sounded like Fae talking or maybe even crying.

"Huh, maybe patrol officers?" Wrenna said aloud.

Are there some officers out here today? My father did mention that Stiles was out doing a perimeter check, so maybe it's him.

She walked closer, stepping lightly because she didn't want them to know she was that far out. Once she got closer to the rock structure, she noticed it was a complete circle, and there was a door built in the side of it being the only way in. She began to walk around the circular structure, listening and looking for any way to see inside, when she heard screams. Fae males were yelling and what sounded like a female was crying and pleading. She recognized one of the male voices: Stiles. Finally, she found a small crack between two of the rocks, and she peeked in. What she saw was shocking and absolutely unbelievable. She peered through the rocks and watched as Stiles pushed a bound female into what she could only see as a dark, smoky pit in the ground.

Chapter Four

This can't be happening.

Stiles had pushed the female, who had her hands tied behind her back, into what looked like a smoldering pit in the sand. Wrenna gasped, quickly covering her mouth with her hand, and stepped back away from the rock enclosure.

"This cannot be real!" Wrenna whispered under her breath.

Her heart was pounding in her chest, and her body was trembling from fear. Laughter rang in her ears, exploding from the male patrol officers. She stepped back towards the small viewing hole, peering in. Shock rang throughout her body, and disbelief at how they could be laughing at such a thing. She continued to watch the males as they headed back to a small room the size of a closet built into one of the rocks. One male pulled the large metal lock back, releasing the door to open. He reached inside towards the sound of screaming once again. He jerked another female prisoner from the small room. She was weeping, covered in filth, hands bound behind her back. She was pleading with them, begging them to let her go. They all just laughed once again. Then the female prisoner said something that Wrenna didn't quite understand.

"Please, I want to go home! I promise I won't tell anyone. Please just take me back. I'll tell you everything I know. Please, I beg you!" the female pleaded.

Wrenna then noticed the female prisoner looked different. She didn't have pointed Fae ears, she didn't have pure, pale, iridescent skin, and she was missing the traditional Fae markings. She didn't look like a Fae at all.

That's weird. Wrenna furrowed her brow, confused.

Stiles grabbed the female aggressively on the arm and pulled her towards the pit. He looked at her with such an evil eye, speaking in such an insulting manner. "You are worthless. There isn't any information you could give us that we don't already know, you stupid human. Look at you. You disgust me. You are willing to give up everything in order to save yourself. Typical human. You have no honor, no integrity."

He slowly pushed her to the edge of the pit, her heels hanging over the rim, looking into her eyes for one last second and then letting go. It felt like time stood still at that moment. Wrenna's heart stopped; she stopped breathing. Everything froze. The female prisoner was no longer visible, and all Wrenna could hear was a gut-wrenching scream and then nothing. Wrenna blinked awake, shaking her head. Soon the reality of the situation began to pour into every cell of her body. She turned toward the city and began to run. Her adrenaline started pumping, and it pushed her to run even faster.

I couldn't have seen what I just saw. How could Stiles do that? What's a human? What is happening? Many questions ran through Wrenna's head.

As the city grew bigger and she got closer, Wrenna slowly began to cry. Tears poured from her eyes. She slowed her pace, and her body stopped moving. She bent over and placed her hands on her knees and wept, quickly realizing she had to get back to the city before Stiles or the other patrol officers caught her out there. They would know she witnessed what they had done. Wrenna stood up, took in a deep breath, and found a jog once again.

The city began to get closer and closer and finally, she was standing outside that big stone compound. Pulling her passkey for her backpack, she opened the door. She blazed past Ralf. He looked at her and noticed her red face, took in her tears.

He bellowed out, "Wrenna, what's wrong? Are you okay?"

"Yes, fine, Ralf. Don't worry, I'm fine."

She continued to run up the stone stairs, taking them two at a time, heading towards her bunk room.

Almost there, almost to safety.

Wrenna gripped her doorknob and turned, feeling slight relief. She was home.

Wrenna slammed her bunk room door and quickly turned the lock. She felt like she wasn't in real life anymore. Her thoughts were a dazed blur, like she had just woken up from a dream. More like a nightmare. So much had happened in the last few days that had her spinning, questioning everything. Witnessing Stiles, someone who she had known for almost twenty years, kill someone so easily, was disturbing to say the least. She had known he had a darkness to him, but this extent was utterly shocking. Yes, Stiles was arrogant, egotistical, and an asshole at times, but she could not believe he was a murderer.

Where are these "humans" from? A nearby city, possibly. How long has this been going on? Are humans the ones that live outside the wall that we are told to fear? Are they responsible for the recent missing Fae? Maybe those prisoners deserve their deaths? Wrenna's mind was shuffling through so many unanswered questions.

They looked innocent enough, but that didn't always mean that they were.

Those humans could have possibly been caught killing the rebels, and maybe my father ordered them punished. Those females had to have done something to deserve that. There's no way they would have killed them for nothing. It could be possible they climbed the wall and committed crimes in the city, and they were caught. Wrenna continued wandering aimlessly through her scattered thoughts.

That was a known law of the city. If people entered without proper papers and did not check in at the gates, they could be punished by death. Wrenna always thought that was a scare tactic to frighten outsiders from trying to enter without permission.

The city of Shambhala was small in size, and the rock wall that surrounded it was put there centuries ago to protect Shambhala and its Fae people. Very few Fae traveled outside the wall, and those that did never spoke about who or what was actually beyond. They just insisted that it was not safe and no one could survive out there without elite powers and weapons training. Most of the average Fae citizens had little desire to leave the city, so going beyond the wall was not something many tried or even wanted to do. The citizens trusted in the words and experiences of Chief Thain and the past city leaders. There was an understanding, and the citizens followed any laws brought upon the city without question. They trusted the leaders, and so had Wrenna.

There was a group of so-called warrior rebels that sometimes left the city, looking for more opportunity, more freedom, but none had ever returned to speak about it. Those warrior rebels lived by outlandish conspiracy theories, believing that the citizens of Shambhala were trapped here without freedom of choice. They were convinced that Chief Thain was corrupt and was hiding very disturbing things from the Fae people of Shambhala. They suspected he was surrounded by dark secrets and was a dishonest Fae leader. Wrenna mostly always ignored these theories. Her father always told her they were just crazy, simple-minded criminals who only wished to live by their own rules. Each time word got out that another group of warrior rebels crossed the wall, Wrenna always wondered what it was they found on the other side. Did they survive? Maybe they found these humans. Was it possible these humans captured them and they are now prisoners, or even worse, they killed them?

Wrenna sunk down into her chair, exhausted, pondering these many new details of her life. She was startled by a loud banging on her door. *Could the patrol officers have seen me running away?*

Wrenna slowly stood from her chair and yelled out, "Who is it?"

"It's the most handsome, strong, brilliant Fae male around." Stiles was at her door.

His tone was relaxed and comical, but Wrenna still worried he had seen her running.

"Stiles, I am not feeling well. Can you come back some other time, please?" Wrenna spoke through the door.

"I really want to see you. It seems like it's been weeks. Please, Wrenna, let me in so I can make you feel better," Stiles replied back with his usual gross, unenticing pick-up lines.

She took a long exhale and turned the lock, opening the door. Stiles was standing there in his perfectly pressed uniform, looking like it was just any regular day. He didn't move or act like he just did what he had done less than thirty minutes prior.

"Stiles, I'm really not in the mood for company." She tried to keep the shake and nervousness out of her voice.

"Babe, I'll make it all feel better."

He pushed past her, making his way into her bunk room.

Stiles took a seat on the bed, patting the space beside him, beckoning her to sit. Wrenna slowly walked to the bed, still feeling fearful that he knew the truth. She sat next to him but not as close as he would like. He then grabbed around her waist and pulled her closer. Wrenna looked down towards the floor, hunching her shoulders over, fear radiating from her body.

"Babe, what's wrong? You seem nervous. Did something happen?"

"I told you, I am not feeling well," she replied.

Stiles began stroking her back with his hand, causing Wrenna's body to become covered in chill bumps. Less than an hour ago, he was killing someone without a second thought, and now he was touching her. She was utterly disturbed, and her body kept telling her to retreat. Stiles's hands made their way up to her shoulders as he rubbed them.

"I bet it's all that damn coffee you like to drink on an empty stomach. I told you a million times that shit isn't good for you," he said.

Seconds later, Wrenna was running to the bathroom and vomiting in the toilet.

"What the hell, Wrenna? If you are sick and you get me sick, I'm going to be so pissed. I have too much work to do, and your father won't stand for me slacking on my responsibilities. Not all of us have it as easy as you do!"

Wrenna's head rested on the toilet seat. She glanced down into the water, and then she heard her bunk room door close. He was gone. He didn't even have the gall to come check on her. Nevertheless, she was thankful he left without a mention of what had happened earlier.

Wrenna took a quick shower and got dressed, needing someone to talk to. She needed answers, and the one place to find them was her father. She put the fire opal into her front pocket and headed down the hall towards her father's office. As she approached, she heard multiple voices coming from within the office. She got a little closer, recognizing the voices as Stiles, her father, and Arban. Wrenna decided to try to listen to see if they were discussing what had happened. She placed her pointed ear against the door.

"Did you get the job done that I asked you to complete?" Chief Thain asked.

"Yes sir, we disposed of the trash like you wanted. All is in order, and we are ready for future departures. Just give me the orders, and I'll make it happen," Stiles said.

Wrenna began feeling her stomach turn once again, nausea creeping in.

"I would like you to take five of your best officers and head above the rim tonight. We are not meeting the demands that have been requested of us. Ready a second ship with an empty cargo hold. I want it packed with prisoners. Do you understand the importance of fulfilling our bargain in a timely manner?" Chief Thain asked.

"Sir, if I might, I suggest we do not destroy all of the prisoners. The more specimens I have to study, the further I can advance in our own personal endeavors. These barbaric acts of disposing of all can no longer continue. It is putting a hindrance on my research and wasteful, if I might add," Arban whined.

"Sir, I am merely fulfilling the bargain we are bound to. If we do not provide as many humans as possible, I fear we will not reach our quota," Stiles answered with a loud voice.

Wrenna pressed her ear harder into the door. Chief Thain slammed his hands down on to what Wrenna concluded was his desk.

"You two will stop bickering and do what I ask. I am your chief. Stiles, tonight, bring back five specimens unharmed, and please refrain from taking it upon yourself of disposing what you deem necessary. We need to learn what we can, even if that means bringing them into this compound so Arban can do his work."

"Yes sir, I will get the officers ready and depart at zero one hundred hours. I will have your specimens in custody and in lockdown chambers by dawn."

Wrenna heard footsteps heading her way. She needed to run so she wasn't seen. She turned to run when she heard Stiles's voice once again from within the office.

"Oh, by the way, what's up with Wrenna? She seems sick. Have you heard anything?"

"She seemed fine earlier today, but I will send someone to check in on her. Thank you for informing me. You are dismissed."

Wrenna ran, diving into a vacant room located in the hallway. Thank the Gods it was dark. She was able to slide against the wall into the shadows as Stiles stomped by. She barely made it, but she had definitely gotten information, even if she didn't understand a word of it. She crouched down in the dark, thinking. *I have to follow Stiles; I have to find out what is happening here.*

She waited for a few minutes to make sure the hallway was clear and headed back to her bunk room where she would wait. She knew something wasn't right. Something was going on right under everyone's noses. Maybe those rebels had been right all along. Maybe her father was evil.

Later that evening, her father had sent one of the kitchen staff to go check on Wrenna. They brought up a broth and some crackers: classic sick Fae food. She told them she was feeling a little better and she would be going to bed early. Wrenna didn't want to be disturbed, not because she was truly sick but because she wouldn't be there, and she didn't want to be questioned about her absence. It wasn't shocking that her father didn't come check on her himself. He seriously lacked any fatherly instincts. Wrenna was used to it but in all honesty, she was glad she didn't see him. She wasn't sure what she would have said to him, knowing what she knew now, what he was hiding. Wrenna decided to put on her black cargo pants and black shirt. She braided her hair back and slid a large black hoodie over her head. She had to be as inconspicuous as possible, so an all-black attire just seemed fitting. She found the opal in her desk drawer where she had left it earlier and slid it into one of her pockets.

The entire compound was dead quiet. All the staff would be in bed at this hour. She assumed her father was fast asleep in his massive four poster bed. She crept down the hall towards the stairs that descended down to the front entrance. Wrenna had only an inkling as to where to begin searching for Stiles and the other officers. They had barracks in the basement for officers in training to stay overnight during their initial enrollment. She had only been down there a few times as a child. Her father didn't want her around the male officers. It wasn't safe for a small Fae female, he would often say. Stiles brought her down there once to show her around and brag about the tedious task he forced the new enrollees to carry out. Wrenna had noticed the cells located in the back, several small rooms with long, tube-like rocks that ran from floor to ceiling and a locking door. The rooms were clearly meant to lock someone inside. Wrenna recalled asking Stiles what the cells were for. He only said for training tactics to teach future officers how to properly treat criminals and keep them in holding cells if ever needed. Wrenna figured that would be the best place to start her search, knowing that was where many officers congregated and seemed to be the most likely place they would be.

She quickly found the massive door that led to the downstairs barracks. Pulling the door open slowly, she listened for voices. She didn't hear anything, so she began her downward climb of the stairs. Once she reached the bottom, she scanned the room full of bunk beds. No one was in sight. It was completely empty; she must have just missed them. Wrenna decided to hide and wait for their return, snooping around to look for more answers for the time being. Wrenna headed past the communal showers and bathrooms to the back where the cells had been. As she scanned the cells, they were all empty, but something caught her eye. Wrenna walked into one of the cells heading towards the back wall, where she spotted what looked like a single drop of blood. She got closer, dipping her finger in, confirming it was in fact blood. Wrenna sensed that something happened here, but as to what, she wasn't sure. She continued examining the cell and beyond, looking for anything that seemed odd or out of place.

Several hours later, she hadn't really found anything that piqued her interest, other than the drop of blood on the wall. She found mostly male clothes, dirty boots, wet towels, and a random smell she could only attribute to male body odor. Wrenna sat on an empty bunk, feeling defeated and unsure as to what to do next, thinking she should just sit and wait for their return, which should be before dawn, according to Stiles's promise earlier. Wrenna propped her elbows on her knees, bracing her chin in her hands, and sighed. She felt like there had to be some shred of evidence down here to point her in the right direction. Her eyelids began to feel heavy as her gaze drifted to the far wall under the stairs where she noticed a glowing orange light coming from the bottom of one wall. *That's strange.*

Wrenna hopped up and walked closer towards the light. As she approached the glowing orange light, she trailed her eyes up towards the ceiling. She found the outline of what looked like a hidden door. There wasn't a knob that Wrenna could find, affirming it was a secret entrance to a possible secret room. You wouldn't have noticed it concealed under the stairs during the day, and you had to be looking just perfectly in the dark to see the orange glow flowing from beneath it. Wrenna raised her hand towards the secret door and pushed. She heard a *click* respond, and just like that, the door swung open.

"Wow, that seemed too easy," Wrenna whispered.

She prayed to the Gods there wasn't anyone inside as she slowly creeped her head within. The entire room had a soft glow of orange, and she wasn't quite sure where it was originating from. This hidden room was currently vacant of any occupants, so Wrenna felt safe enough to step in. There was a large, smooth rock table in the middle of the room; it looked like a medical table. On one end of the table, there were two circular locking mechanisms and two more located at the foot of the table. It looked like something that was made to strap someone down. She looked around the room. Along each wall were shelves filled with what looked like different vials of liquids. Several medical instruments were strewn about on another small table. A knife, what looked like protractors, and scissors. Wrenna walked closer to the back wall where she had noticed the glow was coming from. There was a box with its lid closed, but from each seam, the orange light poured out.

Wrenna reached for the lid and with great apprehension, she slowly lifted it open. She squinted her eyes from the light as she peered down at the contents of the box. There were several circular tubes stacked on top of each other filled with a bright orange substance. The substance emitted a glow like she had never seen before. As she gazed into the light, she began to hear, maybe even feel, vibrations ripple throughout her body. She felt that magnetic pull of energy travel through her body, its final destination, her pants pocket. She quickly realized it was searching out the opal. She reached into her pocket and pulled it out, seeing that the opal was now glowing. It shined so bright, reflecting multiple colors. The glow surrounding the opal grew brighter as she lowered it into the box, closer to the tubes. It was like the two objects were pulled towards one another. They called to each other and sang in response to one another's closeness. The vibrations and strange humming sound began to overcome Wrenna's senses, creating the feeling of anxiety. She closed the lid and stepped away. Her body was warm and covered in sweat, the experience causing her to have physical reactions. Nausea swirled around in her stomach; she felt like she could be sick. Wrenna spun around the room, trying to take in every detail she could. This place felt off. It had a cold, dark feeling, like the things that went on here were nothing but evil. The room looked like a place where medical procedures were performed, but the energy of the room was that of darkness and torment. It was time to leave before Stiles and the officers returned and caught her and before she got sick on the floor. Wrenna headed for the door and stepped back into the darkened barracks room, quickly closing the door behind her. It was fast approaching dawn, so she needed to find a place to hide. She slid under one of the far bunk beds, hoping the cover of darkness would hide her well enough. At this point, the immense feeling of sickness was too much for her to care otherwise. Wrenna rested her head down on the cold floor, rocking it side to side. She welcomed the cold feeling. She needed to cool down and for her nauseousness to subside.

Wrenna jolted awake, hitting her head on the bottom of the bunk bed. *How long have I been asleep?*

Moments later, the source that seemed to cause her to wake sounded more clearly. Loud echoes of boots began approaching. The officers had returned, but they were not alone. She heard muffled cries and males yelling.

Then Stiles's voice came booming in. "Shut the fuck up, you filth. You are lucky you aren't free falling into the pit as we speak. My chief has granted you clemency for now, but I'm sure you will wish for death after the seer gets done looking at your insides."

Wrenna tried to wiggle out from under the bunk bed a little more so she could see better, but she stayed within the darkness to keep hidden.

She was able to see Stiles and several other officers surrounding prisoners. By the looks of it, they were humans just like the ones Stiles pushed into the pit earlier that day. The humans were bound and gagged. They seemed to be covered in grime; she couldn't quite tell in the dark room. There were five humans, just as her father had requested, what looked like two males and three females. The officers began to drag the humans back towards the cells.

One of the Fae male officers spoke. "Why aren't we just tossing them into the pit? Why are we keeping them alive?"

Stiles replied, "Because these are our orders, and we do not question what the chief wants, we just do it. You understand?"

The officer only shook his head in response. The group was now out of Wrenna's range of sight. She could only hear them. The doors of the cells slammed shut, and she heard Stiles yell a few more offensive words and then what sounded like him spitting, most likely at the humans. Wrenna slid as far back underneath the bunk bed as she could and waited.

"I expect to see you all bright and early. We have a briefing in the morning with the chief. Do not be late!" Stiles yelled to the officers as Wrenna heard them ascending the stairs.

All of the officers had left the barracks, Stiles waiting behind, pacing back and forth. Moments later, she heard the large door open and footsteps descending the stairs. Someone else was coming down into the barracks.

A female voice was heard. "Stiles, are you here?"

Myra Elsher. What was she doing here?

"Yeah, I'm here. Come on down, it's all clear."

Footsteps quickly moved down the stairs. "I wish we didn't have to hide to see each other. I hate meeting like this," Myra whispered.

"Myra, enough of your bullshit. I'm not in the mood for it. You should be grateful for what time you do get to spend with me. I'm very busy and I've got needs, so I suggest you get to it."

Wrenna heard boots moving, soon hearing what sounded like the ruffling of clothes, shoes being tossed to the side, kissing, and heavy breathing. She was shocked. She knew those sounds, and they were not something she wished to hear as she quietly placed her hands over her ears.

Wrenna shook her head side to side. *Of course. Why am I such an idiot?*

Wrenna wondered just how long this had been going on. She felt anger begin to well up in her gut, along with disgust. Wrenna couldn't believe that she could be so naive and stupid to not see it. This was totally expected of Myra. She always seemed completely fake, and she definitely always had a thing for Stiles. And in Stiles's defense, Wrenna allowed him to use her in the same way. She was the one who wouldn't commit or make what they had official. Not that that would prevent Stiles from being with Myra on the side anyway.

Soon the sounds were so loud that Wrenna's hands were incapable of muffling them any longer. All she could do was pray to the Gods that it would end as quickly as most encounters she had with Stiles did. Wrenna felt vomit rise in her throat, along with a tingle of warmth in her chest, like the time when she was a child. Anger always seemed to be a catalyst to the stirring of her powers. Wrenna found herself concentrating deeply on her breathing, a technique she had learned in The Moksha Academy when she was much younger. She found when she used her breath as anchor to her body, stepping out of her thoughts, it helped calm the whirlpool of energy in her chest. After what seemed like hours, although she realized it had only been minutes, the sounds coming from Stiles and Myra finally stopped. Wrenna released her hands off her ears and listened.

Myra was the first to speak, her voice breathy. "Stiles, as usual, you do not disappoint. Phew! So when do you think we can do this again? I really wish we could just come out with this thing we have. I don't understand why you are ashamed to be with me."

"Myra, you are ruining my evening with your incessant bitching. I am tired; I have had a long night. I think it's time you head out. We can talk about this later," Stiles said with a monotone voice.

Myra sighed dramatically. "Fine."

The sound of the bunk bed squeaking indicated someone had stood up. Clothes ruffled, and bare feet padded toward the stairs. Myra left without Stiles as much as saying anything more. Wrenna continued to stay as still as possible, keeping her breaths slow and quiet. Stiles's breathing soon began to deepen. Wrenna knew he was asleep already. She had witnessed this many times in her own bunk room during all of their late-night rendezvous. Wrenna was ready to get out of there, and now was the time. She slowly crept out from under the bed, peeking up over one of the bottom bunk beds, getting a better view of where Stiles slept. His eyes were closed, the sheets barely covered his waist, and his arms were flung above his head. She looked at him, completely disgusted, and sickness began to fill her stomach. Wrenna wanted to strangle him in his sleep, an urge that would have to wait, knowing she was most likely not capable of it anyway. Wrenna ran towards the stairs and took the steps two at a time, exiting through the door she had entered hours prior. Exhaustion hit her before she could even reach her bunk room door, and with that exhaustion came grief. She wasn't sad for herself but mostly for the death of the life she had lived for so long. Her life was so carefree and simple just days ago, and now it had been flipped upside down. She felt so ignorant. How could all these lies and secrets have been going on right under her nose? And she was so clueless, she had missed all of it. There was no going back now. She couldn't unlearn what she had learned. She couldn't unsee it. Most of all, she couldn't ignore it. As she slipped off her clothes and drifted into the shower, tears ran down her face, swiftly washed away by the warm water. She cried for the humans pushed into that pit, the humans locked up two stories below her. Wrenna rested her head on the stone shower wall.

"I can't let this continue. I can't just pretend any of this didn't happen," Wrenna whispered.

She straightened her spine and continued to let the warm water fall down her body. She felt a deep longing for answers. The weight of these newfound truths of the things going on around her, unseen, now sat heavily upon her shoulders. Guilt filled her soul. Wrenna knew that her life could not go on as usual. Things were now forever changed. As she stood under the shower, Wrenna lifted her head upward, closing her eyes. These last few days had brought forth a formidable responsibility that only Wrenna could take on. She began to feel acceptance of what it was she would have to now do. It was time for her to become something more than what she had been. It was time she did something that mattered. Wrenna stepped out of the shower, wiped the fog from the mirror, and looked herself right in the eyes as water dripped down her face.

I will not bury my head in books any longer and try to avoid the truth and realities of what is going on around me. It's time to put on my big girl pants and do something outside of my bleak existence. It's time to find the courage to become someone I am proud of. You've always wondered what your true purpose was. Well, here ya go. There's no turning back now.

Chapter Five

Wrenna didn't sleep at all that night after spending most of it crouched under a dark and dirty bunk bed. The sounds of Stiles and Myra together kept repeating in her head, and the thoughts of those human prisoners kept circling her mind. She hoped they were still there in that cell. She prayed to the Gods they hadn't been disposed of in that pit. Stiles had mentioned the seer, Arban, would be visiting the humans. All this time, Wrenna thought Arban was just someone who was gifted in prophecy. Now, finding out that he was also capable of such dark butchery only added to Wrenna's turbulent sea of emotions.

Has he gotten his hands on them yet?

She had to work fast if she was going to be able to successfully complete her plan. A plan that she had not fully come up with at the time, but she knew she had to devise some sort of action. Wrenna sat on the corner of her bed and tried to conjure her next moves. She knew first, of all things, she was going to rescue those human prisoners. She wasn't sure how or where they would go after she freed them from that cell, but she was going to get them out. Wrenna couldn't waste time dwelling on all the details. She just needed to act. She quickly got dressed, placing the fire opal in her front pocket of her dirty pants, ones she had found lying on the bunk room floor. She experienced a sense of calm and ease when the opal was near her. It was as if it connected to her emotions, granting her bravery and giving her the backbone she needed.

Wrenna slipped out her bunk room door and tiptoed down the hallway towards the stairs. It was still super early, and most of the others in the compound were still sleeping. Wrenna stayed close to the wall in the shadow of the hallway, turning towards the stairs. She quietly walked down to the main floor of the compound. Ralf and the staff were nowhere to be seen, still too early for them. Wrenna walked towards the door to the basement floor, listening for any sounds. *If Stiles is still down there, I'll just pretend I was looking for him. I'll distract him somehow and come back later.*

Wrenna reached for the doorknob, turning it gently, trying to avoid any noise. The door opened, and she stopped and listened for any sounds. Peeking her head into the stairwell, she only saw darkness at the bottom, no lights. She took to the stairs, making her way down as softly as she could. Eventually, she had gotten far enough to the bottom where she could bend to look into the room. She slowly hinged at the hips and peered into the barracks. Her eyes went straight for the bunk that Stiles had been sleeping on when she left. It was empty. The room was free of any officers and had only empty beds and quiet. Wrenna continued down the stairs, swiftly heading towards the cells where the humans had been locked up. Just before she reached the cell, she stopped for a moment. She felt a bit of apprehension.

What if these things were dangerous? What if they could possibly hurt her? They seemed scared both times she had witnessed them. They didn't produce any type of power in their own defense, so she hoped she would be okay. Wrenna walked into the space where the humans were clearly visible in the cell. They were all lying on the floor, still bound and gagged, looking to be sleeping. As she crept closer to the cell, one of the humans jolted up, scooting backwards and pressing its back to the far wall. The others lay still, no movement.

"Don't worry, I won't hurt you. I am here to help you," Wrenna whispered, trying not to alarm the others.

Wrenna began looking around the area for keys to the door, hoping the officers had left them nearby. She didn't find them and felt immediate defeat. *Now what?*

She headed back to the cell. The male human was now closer to the outer edge of the cell, looking out to see if Wrenna had found any way to open the door.

"Do you understand me? I am not gonna hurt you, I want to help you. Here, come closer so I can remove that gag from your mouth," Wrenna said.

The human male timidly leaned closer to the cylindrical rocks that separated him from his freedom. He allowed Wrenna access to the gag. She stuck her hand between the rocks and pulled it down and out of his mouth.

"Did you happen to see where they put the keys?" she asked him.

The male human spoke back, his voice dry and raspy. "I didn't see," he said.

"Um, okay, I'll find them. In the meantime, let me get you some water. I am sure you are thirsty." Wrenna went to stand.

"Why are you helping us?" the male said before Wrenna could turn to look for water.

"I'm not sure. I don't know what's going on, honestly, but I do know some of the things I have seen are not right."

Wrenna turned and walked towards the bathroom, looking for a cup and finding one sitting on the counter, then filling it with water from the tap. She quickly headed back to the cell. By then, the other humans were awake. They were all looking at her, their eyes each big, filled with fear and uncertainty.

Wrenna bent down, sending the cup between the rocks, giving the male human access to drink. Wrenna held the cup and tilted it back, pouring the water down the human's throat. "You drink first. I'll get more for everyone else."

The male human gulped down the water and when he had emptied the cup, Wrenna pulled her hand back through the rocks.

"What are you? Where are we?" the male asked.

Wrenna realized the humans probably were just as confused as she was. The characteristics between the two were totally different. Scanning each human, she noticed they each had different shades of skin, none being as pale as she was. They didn't have the common pointed ears of the Fae or the swirling ancestral markings. Their clothes were all very different as well, heavier articles, ones she would sweat to death in. One big trait she did notice that she shared with a few of the humans was curly hair. She was the only Fae in the city that had curly hair, and seeing these humans sharing these features was confusing to say the least.

Wrenna said, "You are in the city of Shambhala. Did you climb over the wall? Is that how you got into the city?"

The human male looked at the others. "No, we were captured. Those officers put us in some sort of craft and brought us here."

Wrenna paused, trying to make sense of what he had said. *Craft?*

Wrenna felt her nerves begin to stir, trepidation returning. She scanned the room and listened for sounds signaling anyone was coming down the stairs into the barracks. She turned back to the prisoners.

"I want to help you all, but I can't find the keys to open the cell. I may have to come back another time. I'm gonna head upstairs and see if I can find anything that I can use to help me open this door," Wrenna said, scanning the faces of each human.

Wrenna quickly took the cup and refilled it several times, allowing each prisoner to drink. She returned the cup to where she found it, not wanting to leave anything out of place.

"I will be back as soon as I can. Let me put the gags back in your mouths so no one knows I was here," she said.

They moved closer to the rocks that secured them in the cell. Wrenna reached in, placing the gags back in their mouths. Before she placed the gag back into the talkative male human's mouth, she asked, "What is your name?"

The human male responded, "My name is Abel, and yours?"

Wrenna answered, "My name is Wrenna. It's nice to meet you." She placed the gag back in his mouth, staring into his eyes, noticing they were deep brown with sprinkles of gold throughout. She quickly got up and raced towards the stairs, leaving the humans behind in the cell.

Wrenna's mind was racing and searching for some sort of answer to all the questions that now plagued her. She immediately thought about the only person she could trust: Zelda. She had to go see her and see if she could help her figure all this out. First, Wrenna went to her bunk room to look in her desk to find a possible tool or something that could help her pick the lock to the cell. She had never picked a lock in her life, but it was worth a try. Maybe Zelda would have a book on the subject. She scavenged each drawer for anything pointed that she could shove into the lock, coming up empty-handed when Isha began to squawk at her.

"I'm sorry, Isha. I know I haven't been the best friend these last few weeks. Let me get you some food and fresh water."

Isha flapped her wings and made an even louder squawk. It was like she was trying to tell Wrenna something. Wrenna scanned Isha, looking for any signs of injury or looking for anything out of the norm. Isha flapped her wings even harder, acting as if she wanted out of her cage. Wrenna opened the cage door, and Isha quickly flew out. She circled around the bunk room and landed on the floor next to Wrenna's bed. Isha dove under the bed. Only the tips of her tail feathers were now visible. Moments later, she wiggled backwards, out from under the bed with a long piece of metal in her beak.

"What is that, Isha? Let me see."

Wrenna got down on one knee as Isha walked closer to Wrenna and dropped the long, slender piece into Wrenna's palm.

"Where did this come from?" Wrenna shook her head in disbelief. How did Isha know what she was looking for? "Isha, how did you know?"

The onyx raven looked up at Wrenna and made a soft chirp, nuzzling Wrenna's hand with her beak and head. Wrenna sat back on the floor, shocked and astonished at all the events that had just transpired. First, the fire opal showed up out of nowhere, calling Wrenna, whispering to her as she slept. Then, witnessing Stiles murder those humans, tossing them into the pit, realizing what kind of Fae he was and the lies she had been told for so long. Not only from Stiles, but also from her father. The lies that surreptitiously surrounded the city she had grown up in. The city she felt safe in. She had lived her entire life here, so naive to all this evil.

Next, discovering humans. She was still comprehending that there were others out there. Others that were different from her, not Fae but something totally different. She wondered if her father had always known about humans. She wondered if Zelda was aware of this other species. And now Isha was reading her mind? There was no way that could be possible, but how else did you explain the piece of metal? She hadn't spoken a word to anyone about her rescue mission and what she was looking for. Isha seemed to know exactly what was going on. Wrenna closed her eyes, took in a deep breath, and exhaled out of her mouth, making a loud sigh. She sat on her floor next to her bed for a few moments just breathing, thinking about everything. Isha perched on Wrenna's leg, chirping softly, reminding Wrenna that she was still there. Wrenna reached into her pocket and pulled the opal out, opening the palm of her hand, allowing Isha a view of it. Wrenna wanted to see how she reacted to the opal. Maybe the raven knew something about it; it was worth a try. Isha bent down. Placing her beak on the opal, she closed her eyes.

Wrenna shook her head. "What the heck?"

Isha stood up and leapt into the air, landing on Wrenna's shoulder.

"Okay, this is weird."

When Wrenna was born, Isha was already a part of her family. Her father told her that the onyx raven was her mother's bird, a gift he had given her before Wrenna was born. The raven always sat on her mother's shoulder and went everywhere with her. Once Wrenna was old enough to be responsible, she became the bird's full-time caretaker. She tried and tried to get the bird to come out of her cage, tried to pet the bird, and for all these years, Isha's only interaction with Wrenna was from within her cage. Now, all of a sudden, Isha had a change of heart. This added to Wrenna's overwhelming confusion. She got up slowly, fearful the bird would fall off her shoulder, but Isha just stood tall and strong. She grabbed her backpack off the floor and slid the large piece of sharp, pointed metal inside, slinging the backpack over one shoulder, avoiding the shoulder that Isha currently sat on. Wrenna put the opal back into her pants pocket and reached for her bunk room door. She turned down the hallway towards the stairs.

"Please don't fly away, Isha, please," Wrenna said to the bird.

Wrenna quickly exited the municipal compound unnoticed by any staff. It felt odd walking outside with a large raven sitting upon her shoulder. Other Fae stared at her in shock. Birds in the wild were completely extinct; she had been told they had died off centuries ago.

The Fae citizens had known that the chief, Wrenna's mother, and now Wrenna owned a bird, but they never really ever believed it to be true. Well, now Wrenna was confirming the story. Soon Wrenna reached The House of Books, pulled the door open, and found Zelda standing behind the counter as if she was waiting for Wrenna's arrival.

"Well, well, well, looks like that old bird finally came to its senses, huh?" Zelda said, smiling.

"Yeah, I don't really know what has gotten into her today. It's been a strange couple of days for sure. Let's just say Isha's newfound friendliness is the most normal thing that has happened to me lately. I have so many things I need to talk to you about. You got a minute?"

Wrenna headed straight through the curtain of beads back towards Zelda's living space, away from any prying ears, not giving Zelda time to answer. Zelda simply turned and followed.

Wrenna told Zelda everything. All the crazy things that had happened: the humans, the pit, the prisoners, the way the opal whispered to her, called to her. Zelda listened. Didn't say a word; she only listened. Finally, Wrenna finished speaking. It felt like hours had passed, but it had only been minutes. Zelda stood up, placing her hands on her hips, and walked around the room, looking towards the floor. She seemed to be pondering on the correct words to say.

Finally, she turned to Wrenna and said, "This has been going on for many, many years." She released a long breath and continued, "I have wanted to tell you the truth for a very long time. The guilt of it all has killed me for so long. There is so much you need to know, so much you do not know. I think it's time the truth comes out."

Chapter Six

They sat down; both had coffee cups in their hands. It was going to be a long story. Zelda brought some of her famous coffee cakes in on a large, bright yellow platter after she locked the front door. She decided to close early so they would not be disturbed. Wrenna began to pick at her fingernails; she was so nervous to hear what Zelda had to say. She felt betrayed by her father. Stiles and now Zelda having secrets only compounded Wrenna's thoughts. Zelda was the closest thing she ever had to a mother, and this betrayal felt like a deep cut to Wrenna's heart. They sat across from each other, Wrenna sinking into an old comfy couch, pulling one of Zelda's homemade crocheted blankets over her lap. Isha was perched on the back of the couch, watching Zelda as if she was waiting to hear what she had to say as well.

"First off, let me just say I am sorry. I wanted to tell you the truth about your past so many times. I wanted to tell you the truth about what was going on behind everyone's back, but I have been forbidden to," Zelda said.

"Who forbade you to tell me and why? If I am to be the leader of this city one day, you would think I would be the first to know," Wrenna replied, sitting up more, straightening her back.

Zelda exhaled for a long moment, pinching the top of her nose. "Your father forbid me to."

Wrenna wasn't surprised anymore. She was fast realizing that her father wasn't who he had pretended to be her entire life. "So tell me everything, please. I deserve to know the truth. I don't have much time to try to make this right, to try to fix this."

Zelda looked at her with fear in her eyes. "Wrenna, you cannot do what you plan on doing. It is far too dangerous. There are things of this realm and others that you have no idea about!"

"Well, tell me then!" Wrenna yelled back.

Zelda's eyes widened. "They have been capturing the humans for centuries. They use them as a type of sacrifice to one of the Gods, they call him Yama. He is the God of the underworld, the God of death. He is said to live deep below us, lower than the lava. Only a few Fae have ever seen him. The legends say he has four massive arms, large, serrated teeth, and skin the color of darkness. Yama is everything you fear, everything you feel that is evil. He waits for humans to be sacrificed. He uses the vice grip of his arms to hold them down while he sucks their life force from their bodies. Yama is said to control an army of beings, and these beings are sent above to retrieve more souls. Souls that he has deemed impure, unworthy of this living. Your father and all of the chiefs before him have continued this practice. They believe it will keep the city and the Fae that live here safe. When you saw your friend pushing those humans into that pit, that is what they were doing. Appeasing the god of the underworld, doing what they believe is right. By getting these sacrificial offerings themselves, Yama's beast would stay away. They would not come to our city, within the walls."

After Zelda's words slowly sunk in, Wrenna's body felt as if it were hovering. She seemed as if she were watching herself from above.

"This cannot be real, this cannot be real! What about *The Book of the Sacred Code*? What about all the beliefs of Brockman, Sanub, and Liabe? The words that have been preached to me since I was a child. How the Fae are to treat others the way they wish to be treated. How we're supposed to uplift those who have fallen, becoming a force for the fallen to lean on. You're telling me that my father willingly goes against everything he speaks about, everything written?" Wrenna wept.

"Dear, I wish I were lying to you. I wish this wasn't reality, but it is," Zelda said, reaching for Wrenna's hand. "As for the humans, they do not live beyond the wall. They do not even live in this realm."

"What do you mean, this realm?" Wrenna asked.

"The humans are taken from another place. A place far from here, one that we can reach if we try," Zelda said.

"They live beyond the wall?" Wrenna asked.

"Somewhere else. A place I myself do not fully understand." Zelda paused, giving Wrenna time to speak, and then continued, "Sadly, the humans were chosen to be the dedicated offering to Yama. The elders believe they are the most impure of souls. As I have gotten older, I have tried to forget about all this, act like it's not happening. I knew one day you would find out. I knew this was coming eventually. But I do not know how the officers have been able to travel to where these humans are. I don't know all of the details, but I do know it is all true. I have a book here somewhere about Yama if you would like to read the legends."

Wrenna placed her head in her hands and rested her elbows on her knees. She needed to think. "If the humans are not from here, then how do I help them? I don't know how to get them back to where they are from. And I thought all our Gods were of a transcended form. Are you telling me that there is an actual living God?" Wrenna took a quick exhale and ran her hands down her face. Wrenna continued before Zelda had a chance to respond. "Okay, I need a place to hide them until I can figure this all out, but I can't leave them there. That room in the basement looked like a place where they cut things up to look inside. I heard Stiles say that's what Arban planned to do to them. I can't leave them there. I can't let that happen." Wrenna's words began to shake.

Wrenna started to feel her body begin to tingle. She felt a warmth start swirling around inside her chest and stomach. She thought maybe she was starting to have a panic attack. Isha squawked loudly and jumped from the couch to Wrenna's shoulder like she noticed the change in Wrenna as well.

Zelda moved to sit next to Wrenna, placing her hand on her back. "You must be aware. Stress can cause a storm to brew inside you. It can be dangerous if you are not careful. These unbridled emotions can bring forth your powers more rapidly than most would like. One thing you need to know about your powers, Wrenna, is the truth that you have been kept from for so long. It has been said that your powers are unlike any Fae's. We have no idea what to expect when they do become fully awakened. I do know your father has been praying to the Gods for your powers to be what has been prophesied. Arban has said that your powers will be stronger and more charged than any we have seen. Your father anticipates these prophecies to be fully true. He holds a great expectation for you to be the weapon the Fae need to take full control and no longer be servants to Yama. I fear for you, Wrenna, I really do."

Zelda looked at Wrenna with tears flowing down her wrinkled face. Wrenna had never seen Zelda this way, so vulnerable, so unguarded. She could see true fear in her eyes, but she could also see love, a protective, motherly love clouded in worry.

Zelda continued, "I want to help you. It's the least I can do for you, my dear. I can't continue to pretend like this isn't happening. I can't stand by and let you face this on your own. There is so much more you need to know, but we have little time. I do agree those humans will not last another night in that cell. There is something Arban wants from them. I am not sure what that is, but there's a reason they have been kept there as prisoners. Go back there, get them out, and bring them back here. I will hide them in the basement until we figure out what to do next."

Wrenna stood up quickly, causing Isha to sway on her shoulder. It was time to go; the rest of this story could wait. She had to act now before this surge of bravery mixed with adrenaline wore off.

She headed towards the door when Zelda yelled out to her, "Wrenna, do you have that opal on you?"

Wrenna reached into her pocket. "Yes, I do, why?"

"Give it to me. I will fasten it into a necklace. It could bring you great protection and help you harness your power when it decides to fully present itself."

Wrenna stepped forward and placed the fire opal into Zelda's hand. Isha sung loudly as if she was agreeing to what Zelda was saying. Zelda took the opal, then headed quickly to her desk in the back corner of the room. She moved with such an expertise, wrapping the fire opal in a green, thick plant like twine, making a braided little cradle for the opal to fit perfectly into. Then she attached the opal to more twine that was braided several times to create a sturdy necklace. Zelda walked to stand behind Wrenna's back. She swung the necklace around her neck and tied it securely in place. Wrenna spun around and swallowed Zelda into her arms, embracing her tightly. The hug relayed a sense of forgiveness Wrenna felt for Zelda. She didn't blame her for not telling her the truth all these years. She would be devastated if something happened to Zelda, and she was glad she didn't put herself at risk by divulging the truth. But now they both were embarking on very dangerous territory, and the Gods only knew what would happen.

Wrenna pulled away from Zelda, looking into her eyes. "Thank you, Zelda, for always being such a bright light in my life, for always being there when I needed someone, and just for everything. Thank you."

With that, Wrenna walked through the beaded curtain towards the front door, spun the lock open, and walked out. It was time to fix all of this, all the bad that her father had done, all the bad her ancestors had been doing all these years. Standing there, Wrenna looked up into the nothingness above and closed her eyes.

My destiny is my own to create, not my father's, not anyone else's. Today I am choosing my path, and I am taking it without hesitation, without fear, without regret. I have to do this. This is who I am supposed to be, this is what I am here for. I will be the leader this city needs by making this right and doing the right thing.

Isha rested her beak on Wrenna's head, chirping quietly, giving her blessing to Wrenna's thoughts. It was as if Isha heard them. Wrenna headed towards the municipal compound, determined to make this right, and nothing was going to stop her. She got to the front entrance of the building, pulled her passkey from her pocket, and the door swung open to Ralf sitting behind the desk.

"Well, hello, Wrenna," he said. "How are you today?" His eyes grew wide as he noticed Isha sitting on Wrenna's shoulder. "How did you get that raven to finally leave your room?"

Wrenna didn't respond and just kept walking towards the basement stairs that led to the barracks.

Ralf swiftly stood and bolted towards Wrenna. "Where are you going, Wrenna? You know your father doesn't want you down there with all those Fae males."

He reached out and grabbed her arm, pulling her towards him. Wrenna flung his arm off of her and spun around, facing him.

"Have you known this bargain all this time too? You have been around long enough to have seen or heard something, surely. I bet you are just like everyone else. Keeping secrets seems to be the theme around here," Wrenna said.

Ralf gasped and took a step back, shock filling his gaze. "Um, I am not sure exactly what you're talking about. Could you please enlighten me?" Ralf said.

"No, I don't have time to talk. I am done talking!" Wrenna yelled.

"Wait, please, Wrenna. Let me just explain. There is a lot that I know, things I can't discuss right here. Please, let's talk more in private," Ralf pleaded.

Wrenna decided to give Ralf the benefit of the doubt. It couldn't hurt to listen to what he had to say. Ralf led Wrenna back towards the large front desk and walked behind it to a door. Ralf pulled his passkey out and placed it in front of the locking mechanism. The door opened, and they both went inside. The small space was covered floor to ceiling with books, notebooks, scrolls, maps—you name it. Ralf reached for the small lamp on a paper-covered desk, flipping the light on. He sat down in the chair behind the desk and gestured for Wrenna to have a seat in the other small chair just across from him.

"Listen, Wrenna, and listen to me carefully. This is not something you want to get yourself into and definitely not something you want to be screaming about. Please tell me what you know. What is going on?"

"Why should I trust you, Ralf? You have known about all this, and you were too cowardly to do a damn thing about it," Wrenna said, Isha squawking in agreement.

Ralf grunted, shifting in his chair. "Wrenna, you have no idea what I have done and what I have not done. If you would like to know the truth, I have been fighting to fix this for many, many years. I was almost killed for digging my nose into your father's business. Why do you think I am now a desk jockey? Do you think I chose to hang up my boots and sit behind a desk? This is my punishment for meddling where I was not supposed to. I was told to never mention one word of it to anyone or I would be next in line for that pit they have out there."

Wrenna sat back in her chair and waited for Ralf to continue.

"Wrenna, please tell me what is going on. What are you planning on doing? I can help you. I want to help you," Ralf said.

"There are five humans being held captive downstairs in the barrack cells, and I am going to free them. Zelda said I can hide them in her basement until I figure out how to get them home to wherever it is they are from," Wrenna replied.

Ralf laughed under his breath. "You will never get them back to where they are from, Wrenna. That's impossible, unless you know how to fly one of those geothermal crafts they have. That is the only way in and out. That is the only way to get there." Ralf paused and pointed his finger to the ceiling of the small office. "Up!" Ralf finished.

"Crafts? The humans mentioned that. What are they?" Wrenna asked, still trying to comprehend what he meant by "up."

"Arban has found a way to make a craft that can transport itself and its occupants from our land to other places, places above and below us. I haven't been able to figure out exactly how they work, but I have seen them. They do exist," Ralf said while digging through the many papers on his desk and pulling out a sketch.

He shifted in his seat, leaning forward, handing a sketch to Wrenna.

"This is what I put together based on just a brief glimpse I've seen of these crafts. I can't figure out how they are creating the power to make them fly, but I think I have an idea as to how they are moving from our land to these other places. I just haven't found actual proof."

So this was why Ralf always had his head in books, why he was always scribbling on paper or doodling.

"I think for now we take this one step at a time. I have to save those humans first, and then I'll figure out the rest," Wrenna said, standing up out of her chair.

She headed towards the office door when Ralf spoke. "Wrenna, you are about to take steps into something that you can never return from. Once you do this, there will be no going back. And if your father finds out you know about this, there is no telling what he will do. Please be smart about this. Let me help you. I won't be able to live with myself if something happens to you."

Wrenna reached for the doorknob and responded with, "Okay, you can help. Follow my lead. Let's go."

Ralf walked out from behind the desk and exited the office just behind Wrenna. They turned towards the doorway that led downstairs to the barracks.

"If we get down there, Ralf, and there are officers, let me do all the talking, okay?" Wrenna ordered.

"Wrenna, the officers are off on patrol right now. I have their schedule memorized. I do see people entering and leaving this place repeatedly. It's my job, after all," Ralf said.

"Oh, good, one less thing to worry about. What do you know about these humans? Are they dangerous?" Wrenna asked.

"I have never encountered one myself, so I honestly have no idea," Ralf said.

"Great. Well, let's just hope for the best, I guess," Wrenna said.

Descending down into the dark barracks, Wrenna could feel her heart beating faster. Once they reached the landing, the entire bunk area came into view, and no officers were in sight. Wrenna led Ralf back towards the cells, praying to the Gods that the humans were still in their cells. Wrenna abruptly stopped. Isha flew from her shoulder and landed on a nearby bunk. Wrenna remembered the hidden door under the stairs. She spun around, looking back to see if the outline of the door was once again visible.

"What is it?" Ralf asked.

"Under those stairs, there is a hidden door that leads to what looks to me like a surgical lab or something. There is also a box filled with tubes that have an orange glowing substance in them," Wrenna said, with her eyes still looking in the direction of the hidden doorway.

"Show me," Ralf said.

Wrenna took a quick glance back towards the cells, then back towards the hidden doorway. "Okay, but we have to make it quick. I don't want to get caught down here."

They both walked underneath the stairs, the glowing light clearly visible. Wrenna looked at Ralf, gesturing with her head towards the glow. His eyes open wider, understanding her gesture. Wrenna placed her hands onto the door and pushed in. The door swung open with no problem. The orange glow spilled out in the bunk room. Ralf pushed past Wrenna, entering the room first. Ralf poked his head in, then stepped all the way into the room. Wrenna began to follow when she heard Ralf gasp. He backed up, tripping over Wrenna, his body weight forcing her to step back into the bunk room.

"Oh Gods, oh Gods, oh Gods!" Ralf whispered. He bent over, placing his hands on his knees, looking as if he was about to be sick.

Wrenna placed her hand on his shoulder. "What is it, Ralf? What's in there?"

"Wrenna, don't go in there. Please, just don't go in there," he said, looking up at her, tears fully forming in his eyes.

"What is it? Tell me, or I will go in and find out for myself," Wrenna said.

"There's a body, a very mutilated body. I couldn't tell who it was, but it's horrible, Wrenna. Please, just close the door. Let's leave. This is too dangerous!" Ralf stood now, bracing his hands on Wrenna's shoulders. She saw in his eyes that what he had seen was something awful.

"Okay, Ralf, I won't go in there. Do you think it was one of the humans? I overheard Arban, my father, and Stiles talking about studying these humans. Do you think Arban cut one up to look inside?" Wrenna could barely speak the words, bile rising into her mouth.

"Wrenna, I don't know who did this, but I wouldn't put it past Arban. He is a vicious person. He definitely is capable of doing these sorts of things."

Ralf closed the door behind him. They both turned back towards the cells on the other side of the bunk room.

"Let's go release the others before Arban decides to come back and finish what he started in there," Ralf said.

They both headed quickly to the cells, spotting the rest of the human prisoners. The one she had spoken to early, Abel, the male human, was standing, leaning his head on the long rock columns. The other three were sitting together on the floor. They had their arms wrapped around each other. Wrenna thought she heard what sounded like crying.

Chapter Seven

The feeling in the room was an overwhelming sense of sadness and despair. Wrenna felt it at the core of her being. Ralf stood behind her, most likely taking in the appearance of the humans, this being his first time seeing them. Wrenna walked closer to the cell when Abel looked up in her direction.

"I thought you were going to help us. Instead, you left us to that thing. He took Ashley. We could hear her screaming," he said, tears streaming down his face.

His skin was a warm, golden color, nothing like the Fae here in Shambhala. He had dark, almost black hair that was cut short, almost buzzed to his scalp. Wrenna took in a breath, looking at his face, her heart aching for his loss.

"I am so sorry. I came back as soon as I could," Wrenna said, softly knowing that that was a lie.

She could have been there sooner. She had wasted too much time talking with Zelda and Ralf. She took her backpack off and dropped it to the floor. Pulling the zipper open, she then reached in and grabbed the massive piece of metal. Isha jumped from the bunk and flew to a nearby table. She looked on as Wrenna rammed the metal into the door of the cell. The other humans in the cell began to stand up, still holding on to each other tightly. Ralf walked closer and crouched down next to Wrenna as she jimmied the metal into the lock.

"Here, Wrenna, let me. I know a thing or two about lock picking," Ralf whispered.

Wrenna stood up and took a step back, allowing Ralf to work on the door.

"They tortured Ashley. How do we know these two won't do the same thing, Abel?" one of the female humans said.

"We have no other options at this point. I just want to get out of this cell and away from that room." Abel looked in the direction of the hidden room under the stairs.

Wrenna walked closer to the cell. "I am so sorry. I promise we are going to help you. We're not gonna hurt you," Wrenna pleaded with the female human. "I have already met Abel. What are your names?" Wrenna said to the other humans.

Abel turned and looked at the others. He widened his eyes as if gesturing for them to respond to Wrenna's question.

"No, maybe she has her own hidden agenda. Maybe she is going to take us and sell us off to someone else. I'm not making friends with these things," one of the female humans said.

The other male human pushed his way towards the rock columns that separated them from Wrenna. He stuck his hand through, reaching towards Wrenna. "Hello, I'm Felix. It's nice to meet you."

Wrenna reached out and clasped his hand, shaking it. "It's nice to meet you, Felix," Wrenna said.

Felix turned towards the two female humans. "And this is Gemma and Willow," he said, pointing to each.

Wrenna took a moment to look at them, noticing their beauty and uniqueness. They looked nothing like the Fae she had grown up with. Felix had fair skin, kind of like the Fae, except he had little freckles speckled all over his face and arms. She couldn't see his hair due to the hat he had pulled down over his head, covering his ears and some of his forehead. His eyes were a bright blue color, so blue they almost looked like the purest of water. Willow had beautifully creamy brown skin, like nothing Wrenna had ever seen before. Her eyes were deep brown, and her hair was pulled into large, twisted braids on each side of her head.

Wrenna was struck by her beauty. Gemma had similar skin as Abel, golden brown, her eyes also a brown color. She had long blonde, curly hair tucked under a hooded sweater. As Wrenna stood there, staring at the humans, taking in their rarities, a loud bang abruptly pulled her from her trance. Everyone looked down at Ralf as the cell door swung open.

Ralf quickly stood up, looking at Wrenna. "Told you I could do it," he said. Wrenna smiled and placed her hand on his shoulder as a thank you.

"Okay, we have to be super quiet, and we have little time to get you guys out of here before the patrol officers get back. I have a safe place for you to stay until we figure out what to do next," Wrenna said.

"What about my sister? I can't just leave her there," Abel said, looking towards the hidden room under the stairs. Ralf looked at Wrenna and shook his head. She remembered how he looked when he went into that room earlier.

"I don't think you want to remember her like that. I know this must be incredibly difficult for you, but we have to leave now if you and the others want to have any chance at making it out of here alive," Wrenna pleaded, looking directly into Abel's eyes.

She could see the sadness in his eyes, the gold flecks shining brighter under the light. Abel dropped his head, his chin touching his chest. He closed his eyes, tears streaming out of each corner. He then nodded his head, understanding Wrenna's concerns. They all turned towards the stairs and began ascending.

Ralf was the first to the door. "Stay here for one second. Let me go check and see if it's clear."

Ralf exited the stairwell and closed the door behind him. The rest waited in the quiet darkness; the only sound was Wrenna's heart pounding in her chest. Isha flew in and landed on Wrenna's shoulder once again. The humans took notice but showed no signs of shock to see a large raven. Moments later, Ralf was back. He opened the door and motioned for them to follow him out into the hall. Wrenna let the four humans exit first, and she followed behind. Ralf led them to the large double doors that opened up to the outside of the municipal compound. They all slowly walked outside. Wrenna turned and looked up at the place she called home for so long. She now felt only an emptiness for the great building. With the secrets hidden inside, it would never feel like home there again. Thankfully, the walkway was empty, everyone home eating dinner with their families at this time. Wrenna felt like she was going to pass out. Fear of getting caught swirled around in her chest. They soon reached the front door to The House of Books. Ralf reached for the door and pulled it open, peeking inside, giving the all clear.

"Why are we here?" Willow said, looking towards Wrenna.

"I know it's hard to trust me, but this is a safe place for you all while we figure things out. My friend owns this store. She is very kind and wants to help hide you all for a time," Wrenna said.

Once they had all safely entered the store, Zelda walked from behind the beaded curtain.

"Follow me, my friends. Come, come, hurry," Zelda said, gesturing with her hand.

Ralf led the way. The humans followed, Wrenna bringing up the rear. She gave Zelda a quick hug, squeezing her shoulders as a sign of thanks. Ralf continued towards the back of the store, looking back towards Zelda, asking where to go next with his eyes. Zelda pointed to a bookshelf in the far back corner.

"Where's the door to the basement, Zelda?" Ralf asked.

"Hold on to your pants. I'll show you," Zelda declared sternly.

She shuffled quickly to the bookshelf, gripped the top corner of a large golden book, and pulled it downward. The bookshelf then swung open, revealing a secret entrance to the basement. Ralf was the first to head down the stairs. Candles had already been lit. Zelda had prepared for their arrival. Everyone moved down the stairs, and Zelda swiftly closed the secret door behind them. Once down in the basement, they were surrounded by shelves of old books, canned food, and jars of herbs and seeds. In the center of the room were two large couches with blankets spread out over them. Between the couches, there sat a table lined with food, water, and the moka pot steaming with fresh coffee.

"Have a seat, my friends. Eat, drink. If anyone would like to wash up, I can bring you back upstairs to the washroom," Zelda said.

They all sat on the couches, seeming to be too nervous to reach for food at the moment. Wrenna grabbed the moka pot and poured herself a massive cup of coffee, dumping in all her favorite additives. In the center of the table sat several bowls filled with a variety of items Zelda believed to be the best flavor enhancer for any coffee. Wrenna agreed. One bowl was filled with sweet cubes, another with a lovely ground herb that always gave Wrenna's coffee a little spice. Wrenna reached for a tall glass pitcher that contained Zelda's famous sweet cream, adding it to her coffee as well. She felt exhausted, mentally and physically, but being down in this hidden basement gave Wrenna a brief moment of pause, helping her to feel a little less worried.

"What now?" Gemma said, looking towards Abel.

"We have to figure out how to get you back to where you're from. Ralf knows a little bit about the geothermal crafts they transported you here on. My first priority was to get you guys out of the barracks and out of Arban's reach," Wrenna said, looking around the room.

"Yeah, you did a really great job at that. Ashley's dead!" Gemma said.

Her words were like a knife to Wrenna's heart. She looked at Abel, noticing a wince in his face.

"I am so sorry for what happened to your friend and your sister," Wrenna said, placing her hand on Abel's knee.

Abel quickly pulled away, looking down at the floor.

Wrenna continued on. "I have nothing to do with those things that go on in that room in the barracks. Honestly, I just found out that place even existed just a day ago. All of this is new to me, and I'm in complete shock. If I had known earlier about all of this, I would have done something sooner," Wrenna said, looking around at each human and Fae in the room.

She felt a bit of anger resurfacing in her gut towards Zelda and Ralf for not telling her these things sooner. But what good would that do now if she brought it up? It would only cause more strife.

"There isn't much that can be done today. I suggest everyone get some food in their bellies and rest. Wrenna, dear, you better get home soon before someone notices you missing. Ralf, you too," Zelda said with her motherly authority.

Wrenna guzzled down the rest of her coffee, stood up, with Isha still perched on her shoulder, and headed towards the stairs. Ralf's footsteps followed close behind.

Wrenna, Isha, and Ralf walked back to the municipal compound together without speaking. Wrenna was so exhausted. Once they reached the compound, Ralf pulled out his passkey to unlock the door. They had been gone maybe an hour. As they entered through the large double doors, Wrenna abruptly stopped and took in a nervous breath. Stiles stood waiting at the front desk with a couple other patrol officers.

"Where the hell have you been, Ralf? Anyone could have come in here. You have but one job. It's super simple: guard the front door," Stiles yelled towards Ralf.

Wrenna stepped between the two. "He was helping me!" she said without fully thinking through her excuse.

"Helping you do what, Wrenna? What could this worthless old geezer possibly be helping you with?" Stiles asked.

"I, I... needed help with Isha. She was lost, and he helped me find her," Wrenna said, reaching up to give Isha a pat on the head.

Isha squawked, clearly annoyed.

"I don't understand. How the hell did that damn bird get outside? I've never seen that bird even come out of its cage, let alone go outside," Stiles said.

"Well, it doesn't really matter what Isha was doing. I told you why Ralf was gone; he was helping me. So let's drop it and move on," Wrenna said with a newfound authority.

Stiles's eyes grew wide with shock. She had never spoken to him like that. As a matter of fact, no one had ever spoken to Stiles Mahon like that and gotten away with it.

Wrenna began to walk towards the stairs. She turned and said, "See you later, Ralf. Thanks again for your help."

Ralf waved briefly towards Wrenna, giving her a small smile. Then he turned to Stiles and said, "I do apologize, sir, but when the boss's daughter asks for help, you help. I will be sure to notify someone next time." And he headed towards his office and closed the door behind him.

Wrenna began climbing the stairs when Stiles yelled out to her, "Wrenna, wait, I need to talk to you." Stiles ran to her side, leaving the other officers by the front doors to wait. "Look, Wrenna, I'm sorry, but Ralf has a job to do, and so do I. My job is to make sure you and your father are safe. When he leaves his post unmanned like that, that puts you both at risk. I can't let him get away with that without consequences."

Wrenna looked deeply into Stiles's eyes. "He works for me, and so do you. I don't have to answer to you, so I said let it go, and I meant it. Do you understand, officer?" Wrenna yelled.

She had so much hate and disgust inside her towards Stiles after all the things she had recently discovered he had done. Killing the humans, abusing them, treating them like lawbreaking criminals. Sleeping with Myra. All of it was too much, and she didn't care if he got upset. She wanted him out of her life.

"Yes ma'am," Stiles said, squinting his eyes.

Wrenna felt the anger radiating off Stiles, but she knew he could do nothing to her. Her father would kill him. Wrenna turned and bound up the stairs. She could feel Stiles's eyes watching her, piercing through her. Wrenna sprinted down the hall, and Isha flew up ahead. They both reached her bunk room. Wrenna, with Isha perched on her shoulder, dashed inside. Wrenna locked the door behind them.

Maybe that will keep Stiles off my back and out of the way for a while. Isha had flown in and went straight to her cage. Wrenna fell onto her bed, reaching for the opal necklace, closing her eyes.

Wrenna spoke aloud. "Well, my first mission is complete. Now I just gotta figure out how to get them out of here and back to wherever it is they are from. Then I have to try and stop any more humans from being kidnapped." Wrenna ran her hands down her face and continued speaking to herself aloud. "I can't believe just a few days ago I was lying here peacefully, reading a book without a care in the world. Now it seems like the fate of so many rests on my shoulders." She expelled a loud exhale from her mouth. Her mind continued to race, but she felt her body begin to relax. Her body succumbed to the overtaking of exhaustion. Within just moments, Wrenna was pulled into sleep.

The screaming was so loud, it pierced her ears. She had trouble seeing. There was so much smoke surrounding her. She stumbled, tripping over something, her hands landing on what felt like wet clothing.

She got to her knees, lifting her hands closer to her eyes so she could see them more clearly. Blood coated her hands. It ran down her wrist on to her forearms. She looked down on the ground, looking for the source of the blood. In front of her, lying on the ground, was Zelda, unrecognizable. She was dead, her eyes open, staring into nothingness. Wrenna screamed in horror. She reached for Zelda's dress, pulling on it, trying to lift her up off the ground. She needed to get her help; she needed to save her.

Wrenna began calling out, "Someone help me, please. I need help over here!"

All she got back in return was other screams, other calls for help. Wrenna began looking around. Sprinkled all over the ground were dead and injured Fae. The smoke burned her eyes, and tears poured down her face.

What happened? What is going on?

Wrenna slowly stood back up, leaving Zelda's lifeless body on the ground below her feet. She spun around in a wide circle, taking in the whole scene. Then the ground beneath her began to rumble and shake. She braced herself as the ground continued to vibrate in what seemed like a rhythmic pattern. Over and over again, something was growing closer, something big. Wrenna's heart was pounding in her chest. She had to run and hide, but she couldn't see where to go. The *boom, boom, boom, boom* kept coming closer and closer. The pit of Wrenna's stomach began to burn, and she felt a swirling of power stirring within her. She reached for the opal around her neck. She closed her eyes just seconds before a bright orange light hit her. The light was coming from above. She peered upward, searching for the source, but the light was too bright. Wrenna began to feel a strange sensation well up deep inside her; it felt like a pull. Her hair began to lift off her head, and her shirt was pulled upward. It was as if some invisible force surrounded her. Everything looked as if it were being siphoned from the ground and pulled upward. Wrenna looked all around at the bodies floating in the air. They were frozen, suspended in time. She spun around in the air, looking all around her when from the darkness and smoke, she saw something. An incredibly large beast. It had a Fae-like form but towered over her like something only her imagination could conjure. She could just barely make out an outline of the gigantic monster, seeing clearly its piercing red eyes. The eyes were floating in the darkness. She could feel a gust of warm air engulfing her; it smelled sour. Wrenna was stuck hanging in the air as this giant came closer to her.

Then out of the darkness, a deep voice spoke. "Well, if it isn't Queen Rayna. She has graced us with her presence."

Wrenna woke up, opening her eyes to her darkened bunk room. Isha sat curled up in her cage, still sleeping. Wrenna sat up, feeling like she was in some sort of alternate reality. A thick fogginess clouded her mind as she slowly batted her eyes open. Her head felt groggy, coupled with a massive headache. Wrenna stood up from her bed, wobbling on her feet. She made her way to the washroom. She turned on the sink and splashed cold water onto her face. Lifting her head to the mirror, she looked at herself, giving her face a few quick pats. She tried to wake herself up, tried to pull herself from the fog she now felt. Her mind began to wander back into the dream she had just had. It felt so real, like she had lived it, as if she had a flashback to a past life, maybe. Wrenna squeezed her eyes shut, blinking them open wide a few times. She felt sadness, seeing her dear friend Zelda dead in her dream. It caused a trickle of cold shivers to run down her spine. The images of all the slain, dead Fae, blood everywhere, the screams. They flashed through Wrenna's mind. Then there was the giant thing that spoke to her, calling her someone else's name. The dream felt incredibly real, but she knew giants were not real, and her friend was not dead. This is the second time she'd had a dream of this same battlefield.

Who is Queen Rayna? Maybe Zelda would know, or maybe it was just a name from a dream and it had no meaning whatsoever. Wrenna grabbed a towel from the rack and dried her face. She sat on the edge of her bed and looked to Isha, who was now gulping down water from within her cage.

"I think it's time I speak with my loving father about all of this," Wrenna said, speaking aloud.

Isha squawked and bound from her cage to Wrenna's shoulder.

"Well, I guess I won't be doing it alone then, huh, Isha?" Wrenna said as she nudged Isha's beak with her knuckles. She stood up slowly, still feeling wobbly, and headed to her father's room.

Chapter Eight

Wrenna knocked on her father's bunk room door. It was after midnight, and she wasn't sure if he'd still be awake.

"Come in," her father said.

"Father, are you up?" Wrenna said as she peeked her head around the door.

"Yes, Wrenna, what is it at this hour?" Chief Thain said from his bunk room desk. He seemed to be always working.

"Father, I need to speak to you about something," Wrenna said as her father looked down at some papers on his desk.

"What is it, Wrenna? It is late, and I have an early morning," Chief Thain said, still looking down.

"I took the maintenance path the other day during my run. I came across a circular rock structure several miles out. It had a door, but I couldn't get it to open, and I couldn't see inside. What's it for?"

Chief Thain looked up from his papers, his eyes wide. "What were you doing that far out? You know it's not a safe place."

"Yes, I realize that, Father. You have told me a million times. I didn't get killed or maimed, I'm fine, so just answer my question," Wrenna responded. She wasn't going to back down from her questions. She was committed to getting answers.

"Oh, that is just maintenance access to the geothermal pipes for the city. It's a storage house for the main shutoff values for the city's water."

Well-scripted answer. She knew what it really was, and she was just testing her father. Wrenna wondered how many lies he would tell.

"Why do we have a wall around the city? I want the truth about what's out there that it's supposed to be protecting us from. Or is it to keep the citizens in?" Wrenna continued.

"Where are all these questions coming from, Wrenna?" Chief Thain asked.

"I have just been thinking. There isn't much I actually know about the city and if I am to be the future leader, I think I need to know these things." It was a perfect response, Wrenna thought.

"I do agree, Wrenna. You do need to take a more active role in this city. It won't be long before you are sitting where I am, doing my job, and it isn't an easy one," Chief Thain said.

"Okay, then. Tell me. What's outside the wall?" Wrenna asked sternly.

She wasn't going to leave until she got some sort of answer, either a lie or the truth. Something to cut a clear picture of who her father actually was. Did he care about this city and the people in it, or was he a deceitful leader like the rebels said? Chief Thain stood up from his chair, resting his hands on his desk, leaning forward.

"You know why the wall is there, Wrenna. To help the people of Shambhala feel safe and to keep any unwanted Fae criminals out. You can't understand what is out there beyond those walls, Wrenna. You have never been there; I have kept you safe from it." Chief Thain walked around the desk and placed his hands on Wrenna's shoulders, continuing, "I guess it's time for you to hear the truth." He paused, then took in a long inhale. "There are other species of beings, nasty, vile things beyond the wall. They live in filth out in the surrounding land. These beings will do whatever it takes to scavenge and steal to survive. They are uncivilized and will kill even their own if that's what it takes to persevere. We built the wall to keep things like that out," Chief Thain admitted.

"So how many other species are out there?" Wrenna said as she turned her back towards her father, looking out through the window into the dark city.

"There are many other things out there. It is a big world we live in, but most things stay away. We have the blessings of many Gods on our side that help keep our city safe. The things out there, they have a sort of understanding with us, and we with them. But there are many other species that we do not congregate with. Our ancestors, the ones who founded Shambhala, wanted only the purest of Fae living here. We are an elite species, and in order to keep it that way, we have to keep the others out."

Wrenna spun around and looked into her father's eyes. "What gives us the right to say we are an elite species compared to anyone else? Who decided that we deserve protection more than anyone else?" Wrenna didn't wait for her father to answer. She continued her questioning. "So when the patrol officers head out for supplies, where do they go?" Wrenna asked.

"Well, Wrenna, my child, we make trades with other species beyond the wall. They have things we need, and we have things they need. Like I said, we have a mutual relationship that has been intact for a very long time. Things have always been this way," Chief Thain said.

He was walking towards his door, ushering Wrenna towards the exit.

"The time is getting closer for me to receive my venerated dismissal of duties. It's only a matter of months away, and you will have to step in as leader. For now, I am proud you have taken an interest in something other than those books you get from Zelda. How is that old cuck, by the way?" Chief Thain asked as he placed his hand on Wrenna's lower back, pushing her out the door.

"Zelda is great. Same old crazy Zelda." Wrenna looked at her father and plastered a fake smile on.

"It is late, Wrenna. Now head off to bed. We can discuss all of this later. I will see you tomorrow maybe."

"Thanks for the chat, Father."

Chief Thain shut the door, and Wrenna turned and headed down the hall towards her bunk room door. He barely gave her any new information; she already knew most of it. Wrenna knew the other species her father talked about was in fact the humans he had been abducting and sacrificing. Watching him weave his way around the truth made Wrenna cringe. Her conversation had confirmed her father was quite the deceiver, moving her to realize that her entire life had been nothing but a lie.

Wrenna headed back to her darkened bunk room. She felt like this had become a ritual of sorts. Learning new information, mostly hard facts, then sitting in her desolate bunk room, dissecting everything she had learned. Wrenna rested her head on her pillow, but sleep was nowhere in sight. She lay wide awake, her mind racing.

What am I going to do?

She knew her father had to be hiding more from her and the people of Shambhala. She couldn't believe that she had never seen one of these geothermal crafts in her life. No one had ever once mentioned them or any of these newfound facts. The city wasn't very big, and she had explored most of the businesses and buildings. As a kid, she would wander off and look around the city, spying into Fae homes, curious as to what a normal Fae family unit lived like. Over the last several years, the city had built multiple greenhouses, and she hadn't fully inspected all of them. Maybe that was where they kept their secrets hidden? Wrenna also knew she had to get a closer look into that pit. She wondered what was down there. Isha stirred in her cage, fluffing her feathers. Wrenna, now lying in her bed, rolled over, looking towards Isha.

"You wouldn't know where they are hiding those crafts, would you, Isha? Of course you don't. You have been stuck in this room your whole life, just like me." Wrenna asked and answered her own question.

Isha chirped several times, like she was responding to Wrenna's question.

"I don't speak raven." Wrenna laughed.

She sat up and moved closer to Isha, opening the cage door. She reached in and stroked the raven's head.

"How come all these years you have been so quiet and all of a sudden, you have decided to show your true personality?"

As Wrenna looked to Isha, she noticed a manifestation of light shining back at her from within the reflection of Isha's eyes. Looking down, searching out where the light originated, she found the fire opal glowing. The connection to the glowing light seemed to awaken a feeling in Wrenna's body. A warmth bubbled from Wrenna's chest. It poured out, flowing from her center and moving to the rest of her body, making her skin tingle along the way.

What is the deal with this thing? Wrenna clasped her hand around the opal and returned her gaze to Isha.

The raven was in what looked like a trance. Her eyes locked on Wrenna's necklace. Wrenna quickly released the opal and allowed it to dangle, giving Isha full view. Isha continued staring, her eyes widening as the opal grew brighter. Wrenna was a bit shocked as the light illuminated her entire bunk room. Isha kept her stare locked on the fire opal. Then out of nowhere, the glow birthed a powerful gust of air, blowing Wrenna's hair up and back. The energy in the room began swirling around, the light growing brighter and brighter. Isha held her trancelike stare. Then a huge flash exploded from the opal. Wrenna squeezed her eyes closed in response. Only seconds later, Wrenna blinked her eyes back open. She shook her head and blinked her eyes several more times, trying to pull herself from what felt like a hallucination.

She was no longer in her bunk room. Wrenna looked around, not recognizing where she now sat. The ground under her was a beautiful green. She reached down, pressing her fingers into the thick, plant-covered ground. The green was damp but soft and had the texture of Zelda's crocheted throw blanket. It was definitely some sort of plant but not one Wrenna had ever seen before. This green thick sponge plant covered the entire ground for as far as she could see. In the distance were large rock masses. They reached upward, their peaks out of Wrenna's view. The rock masses were covered with large plants, making it hard to see what lay on the foundation of each. Wrenna swiveled around, looking to find what waited behind her. She gasped, seeing what looked like more plants, similar to the ones that crawled up each rock mass. They grew from the ground beneath her, big pieces of each plant spreading across the ground like long fingers. These massive plants were covered in a brown, rough-looking material at the base and at the very top, green leaves. There were dozens upon dozens of these massive plants covering most of the ground behind her. Wrenna kept looking around, taking in her newfound reality. This place was different. The landscape was nothing like Shambhala.

"Where am I?" Wrenna asked herself. "Maybe I am dreaming again," Wrenna said aloud. She didn't see any buildings or homes; she didn't see the massive wall that surrounded the city. All she saw was a vast, empty space covered in beautiful green. Wrenna took a deep breath in when suddenly from above her, she saw a beam of light pouring from the sky. She looked up towards the light. It was so bright she had to squint her eyes. It felt warm on her skin. She couldn't see where the light was coming from, but she knew it was somewhere high above her. Wrenna began lifting herself up, pressing her hands into the green plants that were beneath her.

"What is this place?" Wrenna said, standing up, getting a better view of her surroundings.

As Wrenna stood there, taking in the sights of her surroundings, she started to feel air blowing on her skin. The air was coming from nowhere once again. It swirled around her body, blowing through her curly hair. It felt as if it were coming from the giant rocks. There were many things that made this new place feel so different then Shambhala. The climate was completely different from what she was used to, much colder.

"I am so confused," Wrenna said aloud.

She reached up and clasped her hand around the fire opal. *I wonder if the opal did this.*

A soft voice came from just behind her. The voice replied to Wrenna's question. "Yes, the fire opal and your fire power within you. They both brought you here."

Wrenna spun around to find a woman standing before her. She must have come from within a cluster of the large plants to her back. Wrenna peered towards the woman, her heart sinking to her feet. The woman before her looked almost identical to Wrenna. Long red, curly, flowing hair; big olive-green eyes. She was dressed in a long white sleep gown. It moved as the air breezed past her.

"Who are you?" Wrenna said.

The woman walked closer, reaching her hand out towards Wrenna's face. "I am your mother, Wrenna," the woman said.

"Uh, my mother is dead. She died giving birth to me," Wrenna replied.

The woman placed her warm hand on Wrenna's cheek. "I did die when you were born, but not while I was having you. I got to hold you, look into your beautiful eyes. I got to feed you and cuddle with you, but only for a few moments," the woman said.

Wrenna shook her head. "No, my father said my mother died during birth."

"Well, I am sorry, my child. He lied to you. My death was not from you or your birth in any way," the woman said.

Wrenna took in a deep breath. "If you are my mother, what happened to you? How am I seeing you right now?"

"My life was taken from me by someone I thought I trusted. I was given an elixir for pain, but it was not for pain at all. It was made to cause me to fall asleep. Eventually, I would wake to endure the last hours of my life, suffering through torment and agonizing pain. A pain that would not compare to losing you, my child," the woman said.

Wrenna reached her hand up, placing it on the woman's hand, grasping her fingers. "Who did this to you?" Wrenna asked.

Their hands fell towards the ground, fingers intertwining.

"If you are dead, then where are we? Am I also dead?" Wrenna asked.

Wrenna's mother shook her head. "No, my dear, you are not dead. My friend Isha has sent you to me, giving me this opportunity to speak to you. She feels it is time for you to know who you really are. To know what it is you are destined to do for the Fae of Shambhala, for the humans on the surface, and for yourself," Wrenna's mother said.

"Isha brought me to you?" Wrenna said.

"Yes, she is, or was, one of my only friends. Many years ago, after your father gave her to me, a new soul reincarnated itself within her. Isha is a changeling. She has been bound to that raven's body for many years. Your father had the Great Oracle cast her magic upon Isha, preventing her from ever changing back. This new soul that now inhabits her body is connected to mine by the vow of devotion. We are forever linked, even in death. I don't even truly know if this new soul is male or female or what her true form is, but she has devoted her life to me and now you."

Wrenna was trying to take in all of the words this woman, who looked exactly like her, was saying.

The woman who claimed to be Wrenna's mother continued talking. "You are in a place some call the surface. It is where I am from. I am what is called a human, Wrenna. You are a part of me; you are part human. This place that I lived in is in severe danger. Isha sent you back to a time when I was alive, when the surface was vibrant and flourishing. The humans were all free, and they inhabited the surface in peace. This is but a visual representation of what things used to be."

"I don't understand. I thought in order to get to where the humans live, I would have to be taken by craft. How did I get here in a blink of an eye? So you are saying we are in the past?" Wrenna asked, shaking her head, confusion crossing her face.

"Yes, Isha is a very rare and powerful changeling, Wrenna. There is none like her. With the help of that opal on your chest, Isha's soul was awakened, and she was able to send you here to me. Before, she was not strong enough to access her powers. They lay dormant for so long. That fire opal on your chest is used to help Fae and other species tap into the powers gifted to them by the Gods, opening up newfound capabilities. We are meeting in a time when I was still alive. That is the only way for us to meet. So yes, we are in the past," Wrenna's mother said.

"You look so much like me, but you do not have the ancient markings like the Fae," Wrenna said.

"I am human, Wrenna. I was from the surface. I was taken from my home and brought to Shambhala unwillingly."

Wrenna's eyes widened. "So how did you meet my father? How did you get to Shambhala?"

Wrenna's mother looked at her, taking time to think over how she wanted to respond to that question. "Wrenna, sweet child, this will be a story that will change everything you know to something completely different, something very dark. But it is time for the truth to be told to you, because your destiny is much greater than anything we will ever know."

And she began...

Chapter Nine

I grew up in a small town with very few people, and when new people showed up, everyone would hear about it. I had awoken early that day to go help mother with the goats. We had to milk them every morning. After my chores, she sent me out to drop off milk and collect empty jars from fellow townsmen to refill with milk and sell. After fighting with our two billy goats, Sam and Jasper, I finally got the cart ready and led the two stubborn goats down the rock path. As I neared our closest neighbor, I saw several men dressed in hooded jackets, men I did not recognize. They seemed to be looking for something. The neighbor, Bjorn, was there amongst the men, and when I got closer, that's when I noticed Bjorn was on his knees with his hands tied behind his back. Bjorn was shaking his head, and I heard him say, "I don't know what you are talking about, I swear." Once I realized what I saw, I took a step back, tripping over Sam as he stood there chewing on grass. I fell backwards, hitting my head on a rock. I felt dazed, and the world was spinning around me. As my vision slowly came back to me, I looked up, and standing over me was one of the hooded men.

He looked down at me and asked, "Are you okay, miss?"

He slowly reached out his gloved hand toward me, preparing to help me up. I hesitated but eventually reached for his hand and allowed him to lift me up off the ground. The man helped steady me on my feet, as my balance was still a bit off from the fall. I took a quick look under the hood, only seeing a shadowed face.

"I am so clumsy sometimes! I'm so sorry to bother you and your comrades," I said to what looked like a younger man, based on his outward build and stance. He continued to hold my hand. "I will be on my way. Thank you for the help," I said, pulling my hand free of his.

Remembering Bjorn, my neighbor, and the state he was in before my fall, I quickly looked around. But the other men, including Bjorn, were gone. It didn't seem like a friendly encounter. As I turned to the two goats who were still munching on grass, the young man tapped on my shoulder, getting my attention.

"Wait, miss, are you sure you're okay?" he said.

I hesitated, but there was something about him that seemed familiar. He didn't feel like a danger.

"Yes, I'll be fine. No worries, thank you," I said.

I turned once again back to my cart and goats. I grabbed the lead to my cart and started to pull the two stubborn billies forward.

The young man called out to me once more. "My name is Azazel, by the way. You can call me Az. It's nice to meet you. I hope to see you around, maybe buy some of that milk."

I looked back at him, feeling embarrassed of my poor manners. "Oh yes, um, I am Mary. Nice to meet you. You're new in town? Where do you live? I'll drop some off at your home tomorrow."

I finally got the courage to take a full head to toe look at Azazel. He was dressed very differently than I had ever seen. Shiny boots, what looked like military pants, and on his belt, several large knives. He had a heavy cloak on with the hood pulled over his head. I still couldn't get a good look at his face and didn't see any visible hair from his head, only a small tuft of hair on his chin.

"I am sure we will run into each other again. I'll find you, if that's okay?" Az said.

We were in a small town. Only one small dirt road ran through it, so he couldn't miss me on my daily rounds.

"Sounds good. Oh, what happened to Bjorn? Is he okay?" I asked. I knew I shouldn't pry into other people's business, but curiosity got the best of me.

"Oh yes, everything is just fine. Nothing to worry about," he replied.

Oddly, I felt like I could trust his words, so I let go of any further questioning on the subject. I continued on down the road.

I didn't mention my run-in with Azazel and the others to my parents and definitely didn't mention Bjorn. The last thing I wanted to do was cause a scene over something I wasn't even sure about. I barely slept. I spent most of my night thinking about Azazel; it was like he had some sort of spell over me. My mind seemed to drift towards thinking about him more often than not. I kept wondering what he looked like under that cloak. He seemed so mysterious.

The next day, Azazel was waiting for me just a short distance from my house. As his dark figure came into view, I felt a smile creep across my face. He helped me pull my cart and went with me to each delivery, making conversation along the way. I told him about my parents and the farm and what life was like in our small town. He mostly asked me questions and didn't talk much about himself. I could only imagine where he was from and wanted to ask so badly what he was doing here, but I couldn't find the courage.

After finishing my route, we steadily made our way back towards my house.

"Well, Mary, I have had a lovely time getting to know you better. I enjoyed our conversation."

"Me too," I replied. For some reason, I could barely speak. I couldn't come up with words.

Az and I became good friends over the next couple weeks. I would always run into him on my route. I finally got the nerve to ask him questions. He told me his family was not from here and they were just here on business. His father was working on some sort of roadway system to help make traveling in and out of the town easier. Az always wore his hood pulled down over his face and his hands covered with gloves. He was charming and seemed very smart, but deeper down somewhere, there was this familiarity to him. He came back every day, same time, same place. Weeks went by, and we began to develop this friendship, one like we had been friends for years. We would laugh and joke and even flirt. I definitely had a crush on him. I thought about him all the time.

My mother even noticed a change in me, but I still kept Az a secret from her, too embarrassed and scared of what she would say.

One day, after making all my pickups and deliveries, Az reached out and grabbed both of my hands as words poured from his lips. "Mary, I will be leaving here tomorrow. I know we just met, but I really like you and enjoy our time together. I don't know if you feel the same about me, but I feel this deep connection to you. I feel like I have known you my whole life. I just don't know what I'll do without seeing you every day. I feel like you deserve more than this place, doing this same thing every day. You deserve more than this, and I can give that to you. My family, we are quite wealthy and powerful. My father is the leader of our city, and one day I will take his place there. I know we just met each other, but I was wondering if you would come back with me. Come back home with me?"

I stepped back, trying to pause long enough to digest the abundance of words he just sent my way. I soon started to realize what he was actually asking me, and it all began to sink in. I couldn't just leave my family and everything I knew to go live somewhere else with this man I had just met.

"Az, I have only just met you. I don't even know what you look like," I said. "My parents would never allow me to go with you. Truthfully, they don't even know you exist."

With that, Az stepped back and dropped his hold on my hands. He slowly began to reach up to his hood. "Before I go further and show you my face and what I look like, I want you to know there is no need to be scared. I am just like you. I just appear different."

I raised both of my eyebrows. I wasn't sure what he meant. I thought maybe he had something wrong with his face. I didn't know what to say. Confusion was all that rattled through my head.

"Mary, promise me you will not be frightened. Promise me you will give me a chance to explain," Az said.

I paused once more, imagining the things that could be under that hood. I was curious enough to want to find out, so I replied, "I promise."

Az dropped his hands from his hood, looked around, then grabbed my hands again and pulled me into the wooded area that stood just behind us. He scanned the area once again, seeming to feel more hidden now. He reached up and slowly lowered the hood of his cloak. First, I saw black hair, wavy and messy from being under the hood. Then his forehead came into view. His skin was extremely pale, almost blue. Finally, his full face became visible. I took a step back, dumbfounded. I thought it had to be a joke.

"Please don't freak out, please," Az said as he took a step closer, reaching for my hand.

I quickly pulled it away. "What is this, some kind of a sick joke?" I said.

"No, Mary, please just let me explain."

I couldn't take my eyes off him. He was absolutely beautiful. I began scanning every inch of his face, his ears, his neck. "What is going on then, Az? I am so confused. I feel like I have lost my mind."

Az turned away from me and kicked some rocks on the ground. "I told you, I am not from here and that's what I meant. I truly am not from here, like from the surface," he said as he stomped on the ground. "But this doesn't change the way I feel about you. We have this deep connection, one that I have never felt before with anyone where I am from. I don't want to lose what we have."

Az turned back and looked at me directly in the eyes. My whole body went still and calm. I was no longer confused or anxious. Az walked toward me, grabbed my hands, and pulled me closer, pressing me into his chest. I looked up into his eyes, taking in his face. The warmth from his body felt so good; it was like home.

"Please, Mary, I don't want this to end. I need you. I want to be with you, but I can't stay here. Come back with me, and I promise I will bring you here to visit your parents after we get you settled in. Don't you want more for yourself than milking goats and living in a small town with nothing, no future? I can give you the world. I can give you adventure. I know it's scary, but don't you think it's time to take a risk for once in your life?"

I stared up into his eyes, the sun shining down, reflecting off his skin. It shimmered in the sun like nothing I had ever seen before. I knew deep down I couldn't go with him, this man I just met, this man from another place. But for some reason, my soul was pulled to him and was telling me to go. I began nodding my head. No words, only my head gesturing yes.

I woke up from the best sleep of my life, thinking it all had to have been a dream. After slowly blinking my eyes open, things began to come into focus. I wasn't in my bed. I wasn't in my room or even in my house. I quickly sat up, panicked, not knowing where I was or how I had gotten there. I was lying in a massive four poster bed. The room was dark, the only light coming from a stone fireplace. The door cracked open, and Az stepped in.

"Oh, you are awake. Good," Az said as he stepped into the room with a tray of food in his hands. "You have been sleeping so peacefully, I didn't want to wake you. Are you hungry?" Az sat the tray of food down on the table next to the bed.

"Where am I? What's going on?" I said.

"You said yes, Mary. You said you would come with me. So we are here now. This is my room, my home," Az said, acting like I didn't just wake up in a completely different place, like this was at all normal.

"How did I get here? One minute we are standing by the road, talking, and the next I am here." I held out my hands, using them to express my confusion. "I didn't even get to tell my parents goodbye or get my things. This all happened so fast, and you still haven't explained how I got here."

I quickly jumped from the bed, noticing I was no longer in my own clothes, now wearing a white sleeping gown. My mind ran rampant with emotions. Anger, fear, sadness. I felt so confused.

Az walked up to me and placed his ungloved hands on each side of my face. "Look at me, Mary. Breathe. Try to calm down, and I'll explain everything."

I felt my body calm as I peered into his eyes. It felt like he had some sort of power over me. I could feel it in my chest. Unfamiliar fingers reached into the corners of my mind. My body began to relax. My knees buckled, and I found myself sitting on the edge of the bed. Az sat down next to me, pulling me in closer.

"I am sorry it had to be this way. I am sorry you didn't get to say goodbye to your parents. I had to do it this way, for your safety and to protect your parents. The way we travel to and from the surface is very tricky. The details are something we do not want those on the surface discovering. That is why I had to bring you here quickly, to avoid further questioning. I also feared they wouldn't let you leave. I feared what they would think if they knew the truth."

I turned to Az. "And what is the truth, the full, complete truth, Az? I need to know. You can't just take me from my home and not tell me everything. If you want me to even begin to calm down, I need to understand what the hell is happening!"

My frustration was rising again. I could feel my body begin to tense.

"Okay, Mary, I'll tell you everything from the beginning."

Az told me everything. I sat back and listened, took every word in. I was in shock from all of it. I had been kidnapped from my home, the surface, and brought to another. This place, The In Between, as Az called it, was deep within the earth. Az's family was very powerful. They were the official leaders to the city I now sat in. The humans, like myself, had no idea of this city's existence. They had no idea of the things going on miles below their feet. Az told me that they traveled to the surface often, bargaining with the humans, trading goods. He said they had a peaceful relationship with the humans for the most part. Az, his father, and a few others went to my town on the surface to scout out locations for future entries or portal shafts, as Az called them. He explained how they used these portal shafts to travel to and from the surface. Apparently, they were secretly hidden all over. Most humans had no idea they even existed. Az continued on, explaining the city he lived in, how it was a place free of crime and everyone was happy there. He told me that the city itself was surrounded by a massive wall, put there to help keep the citizens safe. This wall had been there for centuries, doing its job very well.

"I am next in line to lead this city. My father is now the chief. He runs the city and takes care of the Fae people. You, Mary, are human. I am a species called Fae. Fae people are good people. We live with the best intentions, to use less, to live without excess. We believe in giving when we can, and the Gods will give us blessings and good karma in return."

"As I am not feeling well, I need to lie down." I rested my head on the bed and closed my eyes. My body and mind were worn out by the overload of information.

"Yes, rest if you need to. I will be here for you when you are ready to talk more. I understand you are probably so confused. Rest now, my sweet Mary."

With that, Az got up from the bed and went to the door, leaving me alone in this foreign room once again.

I couldn't sleep. My mind was too busy racing. I had so many thoughts, so many worries. I wondered if my parents were beside themselves with worry looking for me. The realization that I was now in the ground, deep below the surface, miles away from my parents, made me feel incredibly alone and frightened.

Soon, hours turned to days, days turned to weeks, and before I knew it, a year had passed. I had accepted my new place here, my new duties as Az's wife. He had a way with words, his energy drawing me in, making me feel safe to agree with his every wish. I met his father and his many friends. All the Fae people looked the same. Each had pale blue skin, strange, tattoo-like markings, and pointed ears. Then there was me, the human amongst them. There were a few people who were brave enough to speak to me—those who worked in the compound we lived in. Those who did speak to me would ask me countless questions about the surface and my people's culture and way of life. Az was busy most days, leaving me to sit in our room, wondering. I wondered if my mother still thought of me. I worried about the farm and who was taking care of the goats. I thought of my poor father.

One night, late in the evening, Az returned to our room. He peeked his head around the edge of the door. "Mary, close your eyes. I have a surprise for you."

I put down the book he brought me home last time he was out and closed my eyes. It was a weird relationship we had. When he was away, I resented him for stealing me away the way he had. I felt such bitterness in my heart towards him. Then as soon as he came around, the energy in the room would change. My heart would change. I swear, he had a spell on me.

"Do you have your eyes closed, Mary?"

"Yes, Az, I do."

He walked into the room. I heard his steps getting closer. He sat down next to me on the bed.

"Okay, you can open them."

I opened my eyes to a massive black bird perched in his hand.

"Where did you get that?" I asked, scooting back for fear of the creature he had brought into our room.

"It's for you, to keep you company when I am away. I know it can be very dull here, and you get lonely. This is a raven from the surface. I found it for you on my last trip up. Do you like her?" Az looked at me with a smile as he pushed the bird in my direction.

"I've never been around a crow before. I mean, I've seen them flying around the farm, but—"

He stopped me before I could continue. "It's not a crow, Mary. It's a raven. They are different."

I didn't see much difference.

"I was told by a human that ravens are very smart and loyal. I figured it would be the perfect pet for you. You can even teach it to talk," Az said with excitement in his voice.

I had no idea how to teach a bird to talk, but I nodded and gave Az a smile in return.

"Thank you. I love it," I said, even though I was thoroughly frightened of it. Az leaned in and placed the bird on my shoulder, then gave me a kiss on the cheek.

"I am so happy you love it, Mary. I love you and want you to be happy here. I will do whatever it takes."

I smiled a half smile and replied, "I love you too, Az, thank you."

He stood and left the room.

Chapter Ten

I sha had become my only friend, since I barely left our room and was alone so often. Az was always so busy performing his duties for the city. It just felt so different there. The land was so barren and empty. The ground was covered in sand, no animals, no plants, just deserted nothingness. I would sometimes go to one of the greenhouses, surrounding myself with a small resemblance of home.

At night, when I was alone with Az, I'd feel so safe, so warm, so loved. It was like when Az was around, there was some sort of switch in me that flipped. Az's company seemed to always make me believe I was where I wanted to be, but the minute he left me, my skin crawled with an urge so great to get out of there.

As time went on, I felt only despair and sadness being in that place. Az took me around the city, showing me what would soon be ours. The huge wall that surrounded the city was quite ominous. It didn't make me feel safe. It made me feel like the prisoner I was. I'd soon come to the conclusion that I was never going to return to the surface, never going to see my parents again, no matter how many times I asked. I went about my days putting on a fake smile and pretending to be someone I was not. Isha was always with me, my support, my friend, even though she could not speak. Until one day, something felt different. I noticed a change in me, in my body. I could feel a deep warmth inside me. Pure love was growing. Something I knew would end my loneliness, would fill the space within me that had been ripped apart coming here. A child.

As my belly grew, I grew to despise Az. It was like the spell he had over me no longer worked. My eyes began to open to his true ways, his coldness, his arrogance. I had one focus, one endless hope: to leave that place and take my baby with me. I secretly devised a plan, Isha being the recipient of my thoughts. I was going to find a way back to the surface, taking Isha and the baby that was quickly growing inside me. Az didn't notice the change in my feelings toward him. All he cared about those days was the baby. He hoped it would inherit mostly Fae traits, magic, iridescent skin, making me feel once again inferior in so many ways. He would talk endlessly about how our baby was going to one day be the leader of our city and it was going to be the greatest change this city has ever witnessed. He told me that he went to see the Great Oracle, someone who bestowed and saw visions of the future. Az told me that the Great Oracle had told him that our baby would be like no other, bringing forth powers never seen before. Our child was to be exactly what Az and his family had been looking and waiting for for centuries. A half-human, half-Fae, the conqueror of all, he would say. *The Book of the Sacred Code* had no writings about the Fae ever being half bred with another species, which destined our child to rewrite the future of the Fae people. I, on the other hand, didn't want my child to be brought into this place, a place surrounded by walls, surrounded by lies. I knew that my child's life would not be used as a pawn in this web of evil that I could feel cast over the entire city, over its people. I was determined to raise my child in a place of freedom and peace, and Shambhala was not that place.

The longer I was in Shambhala, the more injustice I saw. Az and the patrol units would head to the surface once or twice a week to bargain with the humans. Many of our resources came from the surface, from my people. I began to realize that it wasn't a mutual business deal, but more of the Fae stealing what they wanted and leaving the humans with nothing in return. I had no idea the true nature and devastation that was being forced upon my people. I didn't know anything about their enslavement and how they were chosen as the official sacrifice to the Death God. It was only later on that I was given the full details of that truth. The Fae people of Shambhala did not know that human beings even existed, let alone the relationship the Fae had with them.

I would often ask Az about the way the Fae treated the humans, and his response would always be, "It is the way. There is no other."

It was like a script he had practiced, accepting the awful things he and his father would partake in on a daily basis.

The Fae were simple people, easily satisfied. They didn't need much to live, and they all seemed pretty content with the way of life. I would sometimes hear the conversations of the staff, those who worked within the walls of the compound.

"Oh, thank the Gods for our many blessings. If it wasn't for the great leaders of our city, where would we be?" Their whispers of my ever-growing belly seemed fouler. Many would turn their heads as I'd pass, shaming me for carrying a half-breed child or being an outsider, a human.

Eventually, Az became more distant, more sour towards me. Once he became the new official leader of the city, I rarely saw him. Our conversations were focused on only one thing when we did see each other: the child growing quickly inside me. My life had become what he was so adamant about helping me get away from. The same thing every day, no adventure, no life. I was stuck in a small city, hidden behind walls, repeating the same things every day, with no foreseeable future of change. Until finally, my life would forever change due to the birth of my baby.

I was awakened one night by severe pains in my lower abdomen and back. Pain like I had never experienced before. I knew immediately that the baby was coming, and fast. I yelled out the door of my room, hoping one of the staff would hear me, praying they would get here fast. Before I knew it, Az had barreled through the door with the midwife. They both still had sleep in their eyes, coupled with anxiety. It all happened so quickly, the pain being so intense I couldn't think of anything else. I only did what my midwife told me to do. Breathe, push, breathe, push. Az paced the room, his coldness ever-present. Not long after the first pains woke me, I was hearing the cries of my beautiful baby, a little girl. She was the most perfect thing I had ever seen in my life. She had red hair like me. Her eyes were dark, still being too early to tell what color they would be. Her skin was pale blue like her father's, and she had pointed ears like all the Fae people. She was here. She was everything I had imagined and more. The midwife placed her in my arms, and immediately, my heart swelled with an undeniable, unbreakable love. I knew at that moment I had to protect her from this awful place.

My wish to save my child from the trap of Shambhala was quickly squashed. I had fallen asleep with the baby in my arms only to wake empty-handed. I quickly tried to get up from the bed, panicked, but I soon came to realize I was restrained around the wrists and ankles. I was strapped to the bed. My heart began to pound from adrenaline and fear, and I began to scream for someone to come and explain to me what was going on and where my baby was. The door cracked open, and Az poked his head in like he had so many times before. Only this time, his face was shadowed by evil. I knew this was his doing.

"Where is Rayna? Why do you have me tied to the bed?" I screamed.

"Calm down, Mary. Screaming won't do you any good. This is my house, after all. The baby is fine. She is with the midwife, getting a full medical evaluation. Can't be too careful. She is the future of this city, after all." Az's voice was solemn and dark. "This has to happen, Mary. You had to have known this was coming," Az said as he walked closer to the bed.

"What has to happen?" I said, feeling my heartbeat in my throat.

"You were simply a means to an end, that is all. An end that this city will need to flourish and succeed like it has never before. You were our ticket to a brighter future of more control, more power, and acceleration into the future. You were simply a pawn in this game of chess, and now we no longer need you."

I began shaking my head. "What do you mean you no longer need me? Where is my baby? I want to see her now!"

Az only laughed, now towering over me in the bed. "Your baby? She is not your baby. She is my child. Like I said, you were just a mere tool to maneuver my way to getting what it is I want. "

A knock on the door pulled Az's attention away. "Come in," he said.

The door opened, and an older gentleman was standing there, one I had never seen before.

"Come in, Arban, and shut the door behind you."

The man walked in, closing the door quickly.

"This is Arban, my seer. He will be helping you out of this situation," Az said, gesturing towards Arban. "Oh, and Mary, I do want to thank you for giving me this gift. I know it hasn't been easy, but with a little help from my powers, manipulation made things a bit easier for you. Definitely helped to get you into my bed. Humans are so easily manipulated. Their emotions are so fragile, so weak. All it took was my presence to transform you into a very impressionable, weak servant." Az smiled with pride.

Everything was making sense now. During the last year, so many times I had felt like butter around Az, my actions not mine, as if I were a puppet and he were pulling the strings. Within moments of him leaving my side, my body filled with hate and anger towards him. But it was him controlling my emotions, using his dark, twisted powers on me. It was him that tricked me into coming here, tricked me into thinking I was in love with him.

"This is the way it has to be. It's better for everyone. And since you have given me this gift, I will spare you as much pain as I possibly can. Am I understood, Arban?" Az said, turning towards the man still standing near the door.

Arban only nodded. Az walked closer, bending over and placing one last sour kiss on top of my head. Then he swiftly turned and walked out the door. I never saw him again.

I began to scream as loudly as I could. "Help me! Someone, please help!" To my dismay, no one came to my aid. Arban reached into his shirt pocket and pulled out a vial filled with a bright orange substance. He walked closer to me as I thrashed about in the bed, screaming. Arban bent over closer to me, reaching his hand towards my nose. He squeezed it shut, squeezed it so tight. His eyes peered back at me, empty and calm. I kept resisting, but there was no hope. The restraints were too tight, and no one was coming to help me. Eventually, I couldn't keep my mouth closed any longer. The moment my lips parted, Arban was pouring the liquid into my mouth. I choked and tried to spit it out, but he covered my mouth with his other hand. The liquid felt warm as it ran down the back of my throat, some going into my nose, making my eyes burn. Within seconds, my whole body felt warm, and a great sense of relaxation overcame me. I no longer had feeling in my body. All went still. My eyes closed to blackness.

I soon awoke somewhere else, somewhere dark and cold. I could feel my body resting on a cold slab. It felt like rock. There were small bits of orange light surrounding me. I could not move. My body was still being controlled by the liquid. I lay there for what felt like hours when the door finally opened, Arban stepping inside.

"Well, I told the chief I'd make this as painless as possible."

He walked closer, leaning over a small table next to me. I couldn't make out what was on the table. It was too low for me to see. Arban stepped more into the orange light and smiled.

"I lied," he said, laughing.

He reached for something on the table, and I heard a clanking metal sound. I could feel my heart pounding in my chest, my pulse rapid in my throat. I had no one; I was alone. My baby had been taken from me just like everything else. Now my life would be taken, taken slowly in this cold place. Arban stepped closer. He had a sharp tool in his hand. It looked like a cattle prod we used on the farm. I could see a fiery hot point at the end. Slowly, he brought the prod to my stomach, the place where I created life, and he stuck the hot steel into my body. My heart began pounding harder. My body began to convulse, and then once again, there was blackness.

I was there in that room for days and days of torture and pain. He would whisper in my ear as he carved his knives into my body. "I do enjoy hearing you scream. Oh, sweet Mary, watching your life slowly slip away brings me pleasure like no other."

Arban used several different tools to aid in his unholy tactics to destroy my body. I tried to keep my mind on the face of my daughter, on her beauty. Praying she was okay and safe. I would sometimes think of the farm, of my goats and my parents, wishing more than anything I could go back there to my simple life before all this. Arban would leave me to bleed, leave me to suffer alone. The only sign of life was the orange glow coming from a box on the floor. No one else ever came in the room; no one came to save me. He never gave me food, only giving me little bits of water. The joy Arban got from prolonging my life just a bit longer to satiate a dark satisfaction he craved was maddening in itself. As

I lay in my own filth, my body covered in cuts from his abuse, I began to pray for death. I prayed my body would soon give up and set me free of this place, from this pain. The darkness would come only after passing out from the pain, and in that darkness, I would dream. Dream of seeing my daughter grow. She was everything I had ever imagined she would be. She was happy and free, away from this horrible place, away from this prison. At long last, my body no longer had the strength to keep going. My heart gave me permission. It set me free from the endless torment and suffering.

Rayna will be okay, I thought. *I am ready to leave her now.*

I died there with the belief that maybe one day we would meet again in another place, a place better than this one.

Chapter Eleven

Wrenna was thankful for the truth that her mother shared. She finally understood why she was so different, why she felt out of place in Shambhala. There were so many questions Wrenna wanted to ask her mother, but she couldn't find the words. Coming to terms with the fact that her father was an evil, conniving man wasn't hard for Wrenna. All her life, she had never really been that close to him. There was always a sort of disconnect there. As she had gotten older, she had figured he was just a cold man who had trouble expressing his emotions, and she accepted that much to be true.

"I am so glad you are okay and safe," Wrenna's mother, Mary, said after finishing her story. "I only got to hold you for a brief moment but for that moment, I knew I loved you more than anything in this world. I couldn't be there with you to protect you and help you grow up, but I knew you had great strength and you would be okay." Mary grabbed on to Wrenna's hands.

Wrenna began to feel a slight pressure build in her chest. She had noticed this change in her body happening more often now. She wasn't sure if it was the new stress causing it or if it was just a sly coincidence that her powers had decided to reveal themselves at this particular time in her life.

Wrenna stepped back, looking around. "Is this the surface where you are from?" she asked as she pointed towards the spongy ground beneath her.

"Yes, in a time before you were born, before I met your father, this is where I lived. It was a beautiful, peaceful place before the Fae and those beasts took hold of it. It was so full of life. Green plants covered the ground, animals roamed freely, and my people flourished. In its current time, it is a dark place where humans live in fear. So much has changed since I left the surface, and it has all been your father's doing. His power is one that is very secretive. Not many know what he is capable of. He can manipulate and twist one's emotions to suit what he wants. He did it to me for many years. I'm sure he has done it to you as well," Mary said. "I hate to bring you all this bad news the first time we meet, Rayna, but we don't have much time together, and I need to tell you everything."

"Wait, wait," Wrenna said, shaking her head. "Who is Rayna?"

A big smile crossed Mary's face. "When you were born, that is the name I gave you. I had a dream one night while pregnant with you. In that dream, there was a great light, and from that light came a voice. One that I did not recognize, but I found myself trusting the words it spoke. The voice told me that you would be a great blessing to this world. It told me that I should name you Rayna, meaning queen, pure, and holy. So I took that dream as a sign and did what it said. I hoped it was more than a dream. I hoped it was my own prophecy, given to me by the unknown," Mary said.

"I have heard that name before in my own dream. My dream was not as peaceful as yours though. The voice that spoke to me acted as if it knew me already. As if I had used this name my whole life. No one else has ever called me that, not even my father," Wrenna proclaimed.

All this information all at one time was beginning to give her a headache, and that pressure in her chest was beginning to turn to fire.

"Listen to me, Rayna. We don't have much more time here together. You have to know that my dream did come true. You are special; you are a blessing. Your father chose to bring me to the In Between where Shambhala is. He chose to get me pregnant for a reason. To create a half-Fae, half-human. This is something that has never been seen before amongst the Fae people. Your father was privileged by his position in leadership, giving him access to the humans on the surface. No other Fae has ever been in your father's position before. A position so powerful and so corrupt that it sent him on a path searching for whatever he could do to take full control. He knew the possibilities of who you would become, and he was correct. The reason I am meeting you here and now is to guide you on a better path, the right path. The powers that lurk within you are your ticket to helping all. If your father has his way, he will use you to take complete control over the surface and even conquer the great darkness deep below the In Between. He wants to use you as a weapon, Rayna, and I came here to try to stop that from happening. As you know, the humans are being sacrificed to appease a dark God. They have been living in squander and filth, with little to no resources to survive. They live every single day in fear, hiding from capture. The surface is a war zone. Humans are facing genocide, Rayna."

Wrenna's chest was now burning horribly. She felt like she might pass out.

"Stay with me just for a few more moments, Rayna, my dear," Mary said, walking closer to Wrenna, pulling her in, wrapping her arms around her. "You can do this. You have the strength and the power within you. You will face tremendous obstacles, things you can never imagine, but I know you can do this. I want you to allow your powers to awaken. Give in to them." Her mother kept going. "You are the key to everything. You are the savior. It is you who can make Shambhala free and free the humans that live on the surface. No more living behind walls; no more living in fear. You are the key, Rayna!"

Wrenna couldn't take it anymore—too many questions and too little time to get answers.

"I don't understand what I gotta do. I don't know the first thing about any of this," Wrenna yelled, pulling away from her mother. "I can barely take care of myself, let alone save everyone else." Wrenna began walking towards the patch of thick, tall plants. "Did my father know you named me Rayna? In my dream I was called Queen Rayna, a dream that felt so real I can still smell the fire and rubble." Wrenna put her hands on her face and took in a deep breath. She continued to speak. "I feel like my life has been a complete and utter lie."

Mary stepped closer, keeping the space between them minimal. "Listen, things may seem bleak right now, like you are so lost and confused, but you have the strength within you to overcome all of this." Mary paused. "I think your father changed your name to spite me, to cut me deep once more even after death. You were Rayna to me. I trusted the voice in my dream. When I told your father about my dream and what I wanted to name you, he hated it immediately. After I was gone, he must have changed it."

The burning in Wrenna's chest was progressively intensifying, making it hard for her to focus. Wrenna's mind was spinning out of control, causing her to drop her hands to her knees. She pulled in long breaths, hoping it would help soothe the nauseousness she was now feeling.

"It's okay, Rayna, just breathe. Try to calm the storm within by focusing on your breath." Mary placed a hand on Wrenna's back. Wrenna found herself closing her eyes.

Minutes later, the noise in Wrenna's head subsided and the nauseousness in her gut lessened. Wrenna opened her eyes to her mother smiling down at her.

"I don't know how I am supposed to help. I don't even have fully awakened powers yet. I don't know how I am going to get to the surface in the first place."

"You will figure it out. I know you will. As for your powers, they will come. Be patient, Rayna."

Wrenna pressed her lips together, sending a loud breath out of her nose. "Do you know about the crafts, the ones they use to travel to the surface?" Wrenna asked.

"I know only a little. I have traveled aboard one once but unfortunately, I do not remember. Your father once told me where Shambhala was, how it is deep within the earth. He told me those crafts are used to travel to and from the surface. They are powered by a substance that only Arban and your father know of. I was never privy to know what the substance was. I assumed it was something they were taking from the humans on the surface. Your father forced the humans to do and give him many things, including the blueprints to build those crafts."

Wrenna reached for her necklace, where the fire opal lay against her chest.

Mary continued, "Those opals, like that one on your neck, were discovered by the humans as well. Humans were slaves, forced to dig tunnels from the In Between to the surface. Along the way, they found those opals. The Fae then used them to boost their own powers. Your father told me about a story written in *The Book of the Fae Powers*. It talked about how the mystical fire opal could be used to amplify Fae powers. They scoured the tunnels, using humans to dig further. Once again, many human lives were lost during this time. Tunnels collapsed. Some starved to death, and others were lost in the darkness, never to be seen again. The humans have been held captive, abused, exploited, and murdered by the Fae for many years."

Wrenna had definitely heard enough. All of her suspicions had been true. After all of the things she had learned over the past few weeks—seeing the fire pit and the humans being thrown in, finding the opal, her dreams, everything—all lined up with what her mother was telling her now. She just didn't know where to start, how to even begin making things right.

"You have to find where they store the crafts. They hide them in Shambhala out in the Badlands. In a substation they built on the outskirts of the city. But Wrenna, it is very dangerous there. Once you get out into that desolate land, there are things out there that can cause you great harm. Creatures that live within the ground. They scavenge and consume any waste that is left behind. They are servants of a dark God, Yama. They are his trash collectors. Your father told me they called them Death Worms. They burrow underground, only surfacing when they hear the vibrations of something moving above them. They purposely put that substation out there, knowing it would be guarded by these awful things. That is why he created the endless negative rhetoric he so freely shared with the Fae people. Pounding the true stories of crazy warrior rebels and how they roamed the outskirts of the city. He hoped the stories would be good enough to keep the Fae from growing curious and stumbling upon the hidden truths. He wanted to keep the Fae citizens obedient and docile, along with keeping his secrets buried. Your father made a deal with Yama. The Death Worms would stay away from Shambhala, and in return he would provide plenty of human souls for Yama's consumption. As long as your father held up his end of the bargain, the people of Shambhala would be safe, but many human lives would be lost in doing so. Before you head into the Badlands, you must start the awakening of your power. It will be very useful going forward. Go back, find Zelda. She will know how to help you. She has been around for many, many years. She is one Fae who knows who I am, who knows the truth about me. You are my daughter, and I know the strength that is within you. It is time now for you to go back and take on this task. Fulfill your destiny and fix what your father and his father before have done."

Wrenna was filled with a great apprehension, worried she could not do what was being asked of her. She had never faced any sort of challenges in her life, nothing like this. And now the weight of the world was placed on her shoulders. She was the best hope for the future of all.

"I will do my best, Mother, to make you proud, to fix it. I wish we had more time together. Will I ever see you again?" Wrenna couldn't hold back the tears any longer. All of the emotions had become too much. "What if I fail? What if I can't do it?"

"Rayna, you can do it and will do it. I will be there with you in spirit, but I am afraid this is a one-time thing, you and me. I wish I could spend more time with you on better terms. I wish I never had to leave you. There is so much I wish. But that is not how things were meant to be. This was the plan. This is the way our lives have been written. This is what made you who you are, and from that you will become something even greater. Someone that will change history, that will change the fate of humankind. You must have faith in yourself, for with that faith you will grow and evolve and conquer."

She grabbed Wrenna in a tight hug, squeezing her, both now crying together. A bright light shone into Wrenna's eyes, and wind swirled around them. Before she could pull away to see what was happening, she felt a snap.

She was back in her room, kneeling on the floor. The fire opal was still in her hand, and Isha was there, still in the trance. She had returned to her reality. Taking a big, deep breath, she shook her head, coming out of a sort of haze. Her skin was covered in sweat, her chest warm with fire. Isha squawked as if to say *you're back*, awakening from her trance-like state. Wrenna fell back onto the floor. Exhaustion consumed her.

Her eyes began to feel so heavy, she wanted to sleep. She rolled over onto her side and allowed her eyes to fully close as she drifted off to sleep. She did not dream, as if her mind was too full to dream. She only slept. She would give herself one more good night's sleep before all hell broke loose.

Chapter Twelve

Wrenna found herself heading straight to The House of Books the next morning. No one was up yet at the compound, not even the servants. She couldn't wait. She had to learn how to use her powers, and fast. With all the new information and the completely unbelievable experience she'd had last night, she was so energized with urgency. The front door was locked, so she began pounding on the door with her fist. She heard Zelda moving about inside, finally coming into view, eventually meandering over to unlock the door.

"I need you to help me awaken my powers," Wrenna blurted out before the front door even had a chance to close behind them.

"First, coffee," Zelda responded with a raspy, dry voice. She had clearly just woken up.

Wrenna huffed. "We don't have time!"

Zelda began walking towards the back room. "There is always time for coffee, my dear."

Zelda seemed to move slower than normal this morning, but finally, she had two hot cups of coffee poured, and she sat down in her oversized chair.

"I have so much I need to tell you about. I met my mother last night!" Wrenna spoke so fast she wasn't sure Zelda heard her.

"Excuse me?" Zelda replied, rubbing the sleep out of her squinty, droopy eyes. "My dear, your mother has been gone for twenty-five years. How could you have possibly met her?"

Wrenna adjusted herself in her seat on the couch. "I don't know how it really happened. One minute I was sitting in my room, and then the next minute, I was gone. Somewhere else."

Zelda pursed her lips with worry. "Was this a dream?"

"No, it wasn't a dream, it was real. It was like some sort of paradigm shift. My opal started glowing, and then *poof*, I was transported to the past. To a time when my mother was still alive and on the surface. She told me so much, everything. I know how she died, the horrible things my father has done, and what Arban has done! Zelda, my mother told me that I need to ask you for help, that you would know how to help me awaken my powers."

Before she could continue, Wrenna remembered the four humans in the basement.

"The humans downstairs, are they okay? How did things go last night? Oh my gosh, I completely forgot that they were here with you."

With everything that had happened since leaving The House of Books the night before, Wrenna had completely forgotten that four humans were waiting in the basement, waiting to be brought back to their home. Zelda stood up and moved to a seat next to Wrenna on the couch. She placed her hand on Wrenna's knee.

"Wrenna, my child, breathe. Try to slow down. Just take a moment to breathe. They are fine, probably still asleep. They finally ate some after you left, and I brought them some clean clothes I had, ones from the lost and found. I didn't have much, but they made do. They have been through a lot, so I just let them be, let them know they were safe here. I gave them space and haven't checked on them this morning."

Wrenna began to feel a little calmer, but she still felt a sense of impending doom. With that, Wrenna spontaneously began to cry, tears streaming down her face. It was as if a wall, one Wrenna had built so long ago, had reached a breaking point. Zelda pulled her into her chest, giving Wrenna time to release.

"Now, now, my dear. It's going to be okay. Let it out. It's okay to cry, it's okay to feel." Zelda placed her warm, wrinkled fingers on Wrenna's chin, pulling her face up, peering into her eyes. "We will figure this out, me and you. We will get through this."

It was a promise, one that Wrenna knew Zelda would keep.

"My mother, she was so beautiful. She was everything I had imagined her to be. I wish I had more time with her. I wish things were different. We spent most of our time talking about the giant sham of a life I live. She spoke of you, how you knew about her," Wrenna said, wiping the tears from her face.

"Yes, my dear, I do remember your mother. Only a few of the Fae were shown the truth of who she really was. Your father placed strict control over the city. He didn't want to have to answer the potential questions her presence here would stir. He blinded the citizens with his power, except for me, Ralf, and maybe a few others. He tried to manipulate me into helping him when he took you from your mother. When I refused, he threatened me, told me if I ever spoke of the things I knew, he would kill me with his own two hands. I was so frightened, so I swore to him I would keep quiet. I never told anyone what I knew. For a time, I stayed away from you. I watched from a distance. I watched you grow, and I always made sure you were well taken care of and safe. It wasn't till that day many years ago, when you came into the bookstore for the first time, that I actually spoke to you. After you left my store, your father forced Ralf to speak with me. He begrudgingly reminded me of what would happen if I ever spoke of the truth. I didn't want to cause any trouble for myself, so I kept quiet." Zelda stood up and walked to place her cup in the sink.

She stood there with her hands upon the lip of the sink. "I prayed to the Gods you would always be able to live a life free from all this dark history. I keep with the story that your mother died during childbirth only to protect you. I know how disappointed you must be, but I did it because I love you, and I can't stand to see you hurt."

Wrenna quickly stood up and walked over to Zelda. "I am not mad at you, Zelda, never. You did what you thought was best for all of us. You did the right thing." Wrenna wrapped Zelda in a big hug, feeling the woman's fragile, thin body against hers. Wrenna pulled away, looking into Zelda's deep eyes. "Now it's time. You have to help me awaken my powers and learn how to wield them. I have to put a stop to all this, all these lies. I have to do what's best for all. For the Fae and the humans on the surface. I have to do this for my mother and all those who have lost their lives in this twisted bargain my father has made. Will you help me, please?"

Zelda shook her head up and down, responding with no words.

Before the lessons began, Wrenna wanted to check on the humans downstairs. She wanted to ask them what they knew about the craft that transported them to Shambhala. After pulling back the hidden book-shelf, Wrenna walked down the stairs and found all four of the humans sitting upright on the couch. Felix had his arm around Gemma. She rested her head on his shoulder. Abel sat with his head in his hands, his elbows resting on his knees. Willow lay back on the couch, her knees pulled into her chest. They all took their gaze in Wrenna's direction.

Abel quickly stood up. "Did you find a way to get us out of here?"

"I am working on it, I promise. There is so much I have learned through the night. I have a plan, but I am going to need your help," Wrenna said, looking around the room at all four of them. "What can you tell me about the craft they brought you here on?" Wrenna continued.

Abel shook his head. "Nothing. We didn't see it. it was like one moment we were running from one of those giant creatures, the next a bright orange light, and then we were in that cell, here."

Wrenna paused for a moment. "Giant creatures? What do you mean?"

Abel raised his eyebrows. "You really don't know what's going on, do you?"

Wrenna shook her head no.

"For some reason, once those giants showed up, everything went black. It was like our sun burnt out. We have been living in complete darkness. Then the giants started invading and destroying everything in their path. They roam the land, searching for people. We had to find safety in caves, abandoned buildings, or makeshift bunkers. We only come out when we need more supplies. Some of us have been separated from our families. We have no idea if any of them are dead or alive. It's been this way there for years, maybe longer." Abel looked up to the ceiling, taking a deep breath.

"What is a sun?" Wrenna asked.

"It's a source of light. It provides warmth and helps things grow. It's hard to explain."

Wrenna didn't ask more. She felt it wasn't the time for a full lesson on the things on the surface.

"I am going to find a way to get you back there to your family," Wrenna said.

Abel laughed under his breath. "My family is here. They are all I have left." He looked at his fellow humans and continued, "At this point, I don't know if I even wanna go back there. Here we face much less frightening things than back there."

Gemma began to speak. "Are you kidding me, Abel? You heard what they did to your sister. I don't know which is worse, those things back home or the torment Ashley slowly endured in that room."

Tears began to fill Abel's eyes. "Ashley was the only true family I had left. She was my blood. Our parents were on a trip when all this began. We never saw them again. Ashley and I survived for months in our basement until we decided to leave to find more supplies and maybe more people."

Felix began to speak. "We ran into Ashley and Abel in an abandoned warehouse, an old packaging plant. I guess we all had the same idea, that maybe it hadn't been completely picked over. We were wrong."

Wrenna walked further into the basement. "You all are safe here for now. No one knows you are here, but soon they will realize you are no longer in that cell, and they will begin searching for you. I'll do my best to keep you hidden for as long as possible. Zelda is going to help me. We will figure something out. I promise."

Gemma laughed. "I'm still confused why we should trust anything you say. Sorry, but you are one of them."

Abel returned to sitting next to Willow on the couch. "I am having a very hard time being able to trust anyone, but what do we have to lose?" he said to Gemma. He turned back to Wrenna and said, "We are just tired of hiding in basements, tired of living in fear."

Wrenna couldn't imagine the pain and fear they had been dealing with for so long. She vowed to herself right then, she would fix this and help the humans, but first she had to learn her powers. Her mother insisted her powers were the key to resolve all of this devastation and corruption. Wrenna prayed to the Gods her mother was right.

Thirty minutes later, Wrenna was back upstairs, waiting for Zelda to get dressed. She had returned the hidden bookshelf to its place, hiding the humans downstairs. She had gotten them fresh water and some food from Zelda's pantry. They would be fine there for now, but it was only a matter of time before the patrol officers, including Stiles, began looking for them.

Zelda walked out of the wash room, dressed in her usual garb. She was fastening her necklace when she said, "Are you ready?"

Wrenna quickly followed her, leaving Zelda's living quarters and heading back to the very back of the store. She watched Zelda reach for a book on a shelf. Zelda quickly found the book she was searching for. She slammed a massive dusty book down onto the counter: *The Book of the Fae Powers.*

"This book has been around since the dawn of creation, alongside *The Book of the Sacred Code.* Both being a guideline to the life and traditions of the Fae people," Zelda stated.

She began to gently open the front cover of the book. She flipped through the pages, searching for something that Wrenna wasn't sure of. She finally discovered what it was she was looking for.

"There will not be anything in this book about half-Fae, half-human powers, because that has never been, at least not until you. But in this book, it talks about the awakening of powers, how to control them, and how to use the fire opal, or how Fae of the past used the opal to amplify their own powers. I want to read through this and see if there is something in here I don't know about before we begin."

Wrenna pulled the counter stool up and sat down, allowing Zelda time to read. They were quiet for what felt like hours.

Finally, Zelda looked up, saying under her breath, "Okay, that's what I thought." She closed the book and turned her gaze to Wrenna. "Okay, everything I thought I knew was correct. The process of awakening can be a challenging one, especially if the powers were not quite ready to show themselves naturally. This process can be tiresome and even painful. Are you sure you want to do this?" Zelda reached across the counter, placing her hands on Wrenna's.

Wrenna had never been more certain about something than this. This wasn't just some random goal, like reading ten books in one month or running further than she had the day before. This was saving the world, saving the Fae people, maybe even saving the human race. This was a big endeavor, but Wrenna was willing to take the chance. She was definitely scared and nervous. Failure wasn't an option at this point. So many people relied on her to succeed in this.

She looked into Zelda's eyes. "I want to do this. I can do this." Wrenna stood up from the stool, and wild energy began moving within her body. "Knowing what my mother suffered, what Abel's sister suffered, and the horrible things the humans on the surface have endured, I have to do this for them. Tell me what to do. We don't have much time, so whatever you tell me to do, I will."

Zelda walked around the counter and placed her hands on Wrenna's shoulders. "Okay, let's get started."

Chapter Thirteen

Zelda and Wrenna left the store, locking the door quickly behind them. Zelda flipped the sign on the door she often used that said Be Back in 15. They wouldn't be back in fifteen, but it was their best bet to keep a low profile, to keep people from wondering why the store was closed, at least for a little bit. They both walked down the walkway towards the city wall, the opposite direction Wrenna had run that day she stumbled upon the rock circle and the pit of fire. They took a turn that led them toward a cluster of giant boulders, ones that were large enough to block anyone in the city from seeing.

Once behind the rocks, Zelda dusted off her long robe and turned and spoke to Wrenna. "We should be safe here for a little bit, but there is no telling if someone saw us walk out here, so we have to work quickly."

Wrenna began to feel nauseous. Her stomach was in knots.

"Okay, tell me where to start first. I have been living my life for the longest time praying to the Gods my powers would stay away forever. In the academy, I blocked out most of the lectures the professors taught on Fae powers and the process of awakening. So you will have to start with the basics," Wrenna said, squeezing her hands into fists, feeling somewhat embarrassed to admit this.

The younger Fae in the city, those coming into adulthood, took the awakening of their powers very seriously. The anticipation of what their powers would blossom into was a kind of coming of age amongst them. Their parents even threw parties to celebrate. It was considered a rite of passage that they all looked forward to. Wrenna, on the other hand, never cared much about those sorts of things, unlike her father, who talked about it endlessly to other Fae city officials. "I'm sure Wrenna's awakening will begin any day now. It's going to be something for the history books. The Great Oracle has prophesied it." Wrenna would cringe when she heard him talk about it.

"Let's begin with working on your breathing techniques. If everything your father believes is true about you, we have to be prepared, and breathing is the first step to master it." Zelda had worry in her eyes, something Wrenna had never seen from her before. "First, start with taking an inhale through your nose. Try to fill up your lungs all the way, and then slowly exhale out of your mouth. You have to find a rhythm to your breath, one that can help you stay anchored to your body, keeping your mind calm. Once your powers begin to emerge, your breathing will be crucial. It will be easy to allow your powers to completely take over, letting yourself slip away. You will have to stay grounded and connected no matter how much you want to let go," Zelda said.

Wrenna already had studied and practiced much of this at the Moksha Academy. One of her many professors there insisted that they would need this type of breath control practice one day. Another thing Wrenna now wished she had paid more attention to from her academy days.

Wrenna closed her eyes, slowly drawing her breath in through her nose. Once she had filled her lungs, she slowly began releasing the air from her body. She quickly found the sense of calm engulfing her body after just a few breaths. Her unreluctant mind was still wondering. She always had trouble getting control of her thoughts, now more than ever.

She heard Zelda speak. "Now, my dear, you must think of an intention in your soul. The one we now search for, but it must be the purest of intentions. Bring your complete focus to what it is that you seek."

Wrenna began to picture her mother standing there in that evergreen space, the place where she had gone to visit her—the surface. She imagined her beauty and the words she spoke, trying to do her best to remember as many details as she could. It wasn't just the Gods who had given her the powers that now lay dormant within her. Her father was also a piece of it.

He had used his powers for only bad, for his manipulations, and Wrenna was so scared she would turn out just like that.

She felt her mind begin to doubt her intentions, her thoughts only whispering, *You can't do this. You are too much of your father's daughter. Your destiny is one you cannot control. It is already written; you are to be just like him.*

Her mind began to spin out of control. Only negative thoughts occupied her awareness. She felt like an imposter within her own body.

From the darkness of her mind, she began to hear Zelda calling her name. "Wrenna, Wrenna, can you hear me? You have to stay in control, control of your breath and your thoughts. Do not let them control you. Do not let them twist the energy of your mind."

Flashes of Isha, her nightmares, the dead bodies on the ground, her mother's face—they all shuffled through her conscious mind. These thoughts jumbled so fast she started to lose herself amongst them.

Zelda's voice pierced through all the noise once again. "Wrenna, you can do this. What is it that brings you joy? What is it that you wish to see for your future, for the future of this place you live in? You have the control. Nothing else does. You are your mind. You control your thoughts; they do not control you."

Zelda kept using words to redirect Wrenna's endless negative thoughts, pushing her in the direction of reclaiming her mind. Wrenna pushed back at the endless chaos by imagining her mother's face, seeing her smile. She had found a memory that brought her the joy she was looking for. And just like that, her thoughts snapped into place. Now she only heard her breath flowing from her nose, and she only felt her heart beating in her chest. She had found a way to take control and find that place Zelda kept pushing her towards.

"Listen to my voice, my dear. Once you find that place of solitude, stay there and keep control of your breath."

Wrenna heard Zelda in the foreground of her mind, her voice only a whisper.

"When you seek out your powers, this is the place you will go first, no matter what. If you rush, if your mind and thoughts are not steadied, your powers can overcome you, especially with that opal around your neck."

As soon as Zelda mentioned the fire opal around Wrenna's neck, she began to feel a warm sensation on her chest. The sensation wasn't painful or scary, it was welcoming. It felt like her mother's arms, like a sanctuary of protection, like a place she could call home. At that moment, Wrenna's mind, breath, and body became completely in sync with one another. Deep down within her core, she felt energy, a steady, tranquil flow. The energy spiraled up her spine, into her chest, filling her up. It steadily continued, moving up and down her body. She started to feel light-headed. Her mind softly glazed over now with this new intoxicating energy. She wasn't afraid; she welcomed it. Her eyes had been closed and now through her thin eyelids, she began to see a brightness. An orange light seemed to be surrounding her. She kept her eyes closed, totally embracing the moment of pure bliss. It was like nothing she had ever felt before. Nothing compared to it. No runner's high, no toss in the sheets with Stiles, nothing was this amazing.

Finally, Zelda began to speak. "Wrenna, it has awakened. Just stay focused, keep breathing. You have to allow the energy of your power to fill you up. Allow it to take over your body. Keeping hold of that pure intention in your heart and mind. Allow the energy to fill up all the spaces within you, and allow it to flow without any doubt, without any fear. Now slowly open your eyes."

Wrenna listened to the words Zelda spoke, allowing her to be her guide. As Wrenna peeled back each eyelid, she discovered the light was coming from her. It was cascading from the space just above her eyes. Once she opened her eyes enough to allow the light in, she felt an unnatural change in her body. Something moved from within the corners of each eye. Startled by the odd new feeling, Wrenna felt her breath quicken. Her energy shifted just briefly. Wrenna blinked her eyes, trying to clear her vision. Something, without Wrenna's control, moved over each eye. Blinking several more times, Wrenna could now barely see through whatever it was. Her vision was hazy for a few more moments until it began to finally clear.

"What the hell was that?" Wrenna asked, rubbing her fist in each eye. She could feel something had settled over both eyes, like an internal shield of some kind. Wrenna looked around, taking in her new line of vision. She found Zelda standing in front of her, her eyes pressed together tightly.

"Did you open your eyes?" Zelda asked.

"Yes, I can see. The light isn't bright for me. I have, I don't know how to explain it, but I can see." Wrenna didn't have the words.

"Good, my dear. I am not sure what your powers entail, so we have to take this slowly, one step at a time. What do you feel? What is going on in your body?" Zelda asked, her eyes still closed tightly.

"I feel amazing. It's like nothing I have ever experienced. I don't feel afraid or scared. It feels like something is in my body, moving around. It doesn't feel foreign though. It's like a source that has been within me my whole life has finally been freed," Wrenna answered.

"Okay, so your power cannot just be a bright light. There's got to be something else to it. It might take a little bit to figure it all out. Now, in *The Book of the Fae Powers*, I read that Fae must access a deep core memory. By doing this, you will begin to evoke your powers. Now listen carefully, Wrenna. You must be careful of the memory you choose as your access point to your powers. Depending on the nature of the memory, the energy inspiring this memory will reflect the action of your powers. Do you understand what I am saying?" Zelda asked, stepping closer to Wrenna. Still her eyes were glued shut, and she reached out to grab her hand.

"So I need to think of something that brought happiness to my life, something that created a positive impression to my mind and heart?" Wrenna asked, squeezing Zelda's hand.

"Yes, my dear, it must be something good. If it is a bad memory, one filled with negativity, your powers will manifest in that nature. Only allow this one memory in. Keep everything else as is in that place of balance," Zelda said.

The energy flowing through Wrenna's body moved like a snake, traveling within every crevice, in every cell. It moved so fluidly, creating solidarity within Wrenna's soul. She started to envision the same memory as before, the one that brought so much love and peace to her soul. The moment her mother embraced her for the first and last time.

Wrenna allowed her mind to travel there, feeling the air on her skin, the smell of the ground. The sight of her mother's face, her hair, her skin. Every second of the blip in time, Wrenna welcomed into her mind. The feelings it created within her, love like she had never seen or felt before. That would be her chosen memory. She would keep it stored away in her heart, always there when she needed it. It was one last gift her mother had given her, one that would be the key to her powers.

Once Wrenna settled into the memory with her complete being, she felt yet another shift in her body. It was like a crack had opened deep inside her. Warmth now flowed like the snake, transversing her entire body. The orange light exploding from the space between her eyes began to dim, and the shields on her eyes receded back into their hidden places. She saw Zelda open her eyes. Their hands were still clasped together.

"Well, I think you did something. How do you feel?"

Wrenna furrowed her brow. "I feel different, like I am a new me, but there has got to be more to it, right? Don't most Fae have special abilities? Things that manifest from their powers?"

Zelda smiled. "This will take time, my dear. It will come in stages, slowly progressing on its own. We have completed the first steps in the process. It sometimes takes young Fae years before they can awaken, control, and wield their powers. You must be patient with yourself. It will come with time."

"That is one thing I don't have right now, Zelda. I don't have time to wait," Wrenna said with frustration.

"Come, let's head back, give you a break. I think it would be best if you and the humans discussed what you plan to do next. You are right, you do not have much time. The patrol officers will soon be searching the city for the escaped prisoners," Zelda said.

"Will you come with me? I don't think I can awaken my powers again without you. Your voice and words helped calm and guide me. I need you to help me, please, Zelda."

"Wrenna, you must do this on your own. I can't always be with you," Zelda said while looking down at her bracelet-covered arms. "My time is swiftly nearing its end. I am old, Wrenna. I am definitely too old to continue on this journey with you, but I will be here when you return. That I promise."

Wrenna embraced Zelda, squeezing her tightly. She had always been such a light in Wrenna's life, one of her best friends.

"Thank you, Zelda, for everything. You don't know how thankful I am to have you in my life." They both turned back towards the city, walking out from behind the pile of giant rocks.

Someone called out to them from afar. It was Stiles and the other patrol officers. Wrenna glanced over at Zelda. Their hands were still clenched tightly. "Let me do the talking," Wrenna said.

Stiles ran up to them, out of breath. "What are you two doing out this far? It isn't safe out here."

"I can take care of myself, thank you very much!" Wrenna replied back to Stiles, with her usual stubborn attitude.

She knew she had to stop him from asking too many questions. Wrenna quickly stepped closer to Stiles, dropping Zelda's hand and reaching to grab Stiles's hand instead.

"I'm only kidding. Thank you, Stiles, for always keeping our city safe. We couldn't ask for a better, more handsome head officer," she said with a smile. She knew she had to stroke his ego a little, helping him to lose his complete chain of thought. He loved when people told him how amazing he was.

"Let's get you young ladies back to the city," Stiles replied, putting his arms around both Wrenna and Zelda.

They began walking back down the walkway towards the city.

"I will take you back to The House of Books, Miss Zelda. And Wrenna, I think your father was looking for you this morning. Maybe you should head back to the compound and see what it is he wanted."

Wrenna and Zelda took a quick glance at each other. There was no time for all this. They had to get the four humans back to the surface. It was time to get the ball rolling and take some serious action.

"Oh, thank you, but I left my things at The House of Books. I'll go back there with Zelda and grab my stuff, and then I'll head to see my father. Maybe I will see you later," Wrenna said with a wink.

She had to hold back the vomit that was now rising in her throat. Just being around Stiles, truly knowing what kind of person he was, made her physically sick. All those years she let him put his hands wherever he wanted. Just thinking now of what those hands were capable of made her entire body tremble.

"What's wrong, Wrenna? Are you cold? Maybe you are feeling sick again?" Stiles asked, completely oblivious.

"No, no, I'm fine," Wrenna replied.

All three walked towards The House of Books until the walkway forked, Stiles heading one direction, Wrenna and Zelda heading the other. With a wave of his hand, Stiles was off, heading towards the municipal compound. Wrenna turned to Zelda and rolled her eyes.

"Didn't you two have a thing going on at one time?" Zelda asked.

"Yes, that was before I knew he was a disgusting murderer. To add to his disgustingness, he is also sleeping with Myra Elsher on the side. Not that that even comes close to the murder thing. Oh Gods, I am so ashamed of myself for even being with him at all," Wrenna said with another shiver.

They reached the front door to The House of Books, spotting Ralf sitting cross-legged on the ground outside with his nose in a bundle of papers.

"Ralf, what can I help you with? I probably won't be opening today," Zelda said.

Ralf swiftly stood from the ground, dusting off his pant legs. "I was actually looking for you, Wrenna. I have some information for you on what we talked about the other day. You know, about those things you were interested in learning more about." Ralf said all of this trying to be as inconspicuous as possible.

"Ralf, Zelda knows everything, and I mean everything," Wrenna said with a smile.

Zelda shook her head and placed the key in the door. All three entered the store. Zelda locked the door behind them and flipped the closed sign.

"You have to work on a plan," Zelda said as she headed back towards the back room, Ralf and Wrenna following.

"A plan for what? What are you guys planning?" Ralf said with serious concern in his voice.

After they had reached the back room, Ralf looked in the direction of the hidden staircase. "Are they still down there?"

"Of course they are, you damn fool. Where would they have gone?" Zelda said.

Wrenna sat down into Zelda's oversized chair. "I've decided I am going to head out towards the Badlands. I will be taking the humans with me, of course. I have to get them home before they find them and kill them or do worse. My mother told me they house those crafts out there in a substation. Well, I'm gonna find one," Wrenna said, looking at Ralf.

Ralf looked confused, and then he spoke. "Okay, I'm not really sure about the whole speaking to your mother and all... but I do know that once you find one, you have to know how to operate it, right? That's what I am here for. I found the manual to one of the older models of the crafts in the basement storage. It took me all night to find it, but here it is," Ralf said as he extended a worn, dirty wad of papers towards Wrenna. "I don't know if this will help any, but it's worth a read. I haven't been involved in the doings of your father for quite some time, so I don't know the advancements they have made," Ralf said, looking towards the floor.

"This is so helpful, Ralf. It's more than I had before, so I will take what I can get. I appreciate you putting yourself at risk for me. And I am sure Zelda can fill you in on everything later. Thank you so much."

"Well, I'm doing it for everyone. It's the least I can do," Ralf said.

"Oh, one more thing, Ralf. What do you know about the Death Worms, the things that live in the ground out in the Badlands?" Wrenna asked.

Ralf's eyes widened as he took a few moments to answer. "Those things are terrible. We didn't have to worry too much about them bothering us. They mostly stayed away from the patrol units. It was like they avoided us as if they were told to. But I did hear stories of them, awful stories. One officer witnessed one eating a dead human carcass once. I was told it was a human that had died during transport. After hearing only stories of the creatures, I guess the officers were curious to actually see one. They brought the body out into the desert, not far from the substation, and left it. Several of them climbed to the top of the substation and waited. Eventually, a Death Worm burrowed its way from beneath the sand and snatched the body. The officers only briefly caught a glimpse of it but the stories they told of it are very frightening. They said the thing was massive. They described it having long, tentacle-like appendages on its body. Its skin was a rough gray texture, almost dead looking. The body of the creature was long, like twelve feet long, and it was cylindrical in shape. There were no limbs on the creature, so the officers just assumed they use the tentacles to move through the ground. One thing that really creeped me out was they said it didn't have eyes," Ralf said.

"How do they see then?" Wrenna asked.

"Well, I guess since they live underground, it's dark most of the time, so they really don't need eyes to see. They use the vibrations in the ground to find their prey. I'm assuming they have excellent hearing," Ralf said.

"Good to know. Thank you once again," Wrenna said.

"No problem, Miss Wrenna. Please be careful out there. It's very dangerous," Ralf said. He continued telling Wrenna a few details of what the terrain would be like and the direction towards the substation.

Zelda sighed. "I am going to make more coffee. I say we spend the next few hours devising a plan. Once everyone goes to sleep, you guys can head out. It will be more dangerous after hours, but that's your best chance at not getting caught." She walked towards the front of the store to start the moka pot.

"I will go and collect any supplies I can, things you might need on your journey. It is very dangerous out there, Wrenna. I don't know if you understand what you might face," Ralf stated.

Wrenna had no idea what she was about to face, but there was no turning back now. Once she decided to go into those barracks to speak to the imprisoned humans, she had lost all right to turn back.

Chapter Fourteen

They waited until the Fae in the city were all asleep. Wrenna's father was locked away in his office, and the staff of the municipal compound were all off duty. Wrenna hoped Stiles hadn't taken her invitation from earlier seriously, but it was only a matter of time before someone noticed she was gone. She wanted a big head start, aiming to give her and the humans ample time to get out of the city. Stiles finding an empty bunk room would certainly spring the search into action much faster then she would like.

Wrenna headed out towards the Badlands, and the four humans followed. She knew that her father had patrol officers who monitored the area, but Ralf was going to try his best to distract them for a little bit. Wrenna now had Isha perched on her shoulder and her loaded backpack slung across her back. She couldn't just leave Isha behind, not knowing when or if she would be back. Abel, Felix, Gemma, and Willow now had large packs on their backs loaded with all the supplies they were able to gather, stuff Ralf brought back to them, and some other things they found around The House of Books. Wrenna had a roughly drawn map that Ralf had given her, one he made from memory.

"So what is the plan?" Abel asked Wrenna, following closely behind her.

"I found out where they store the crafts they use to travel from here to the surface, but it is going to be a very dangerous trek to get there. There is a chance we might encounter some obstacles along the way," Wrenna said, looking back towards the four humans, quickly moving off the walkway onto the sandy ground.

"Please, enlighten us. What kind of obstacles?" Gemma asked with concern.

"Yeah, I hate surprises," Felix said.

Wrenna shrugged her shoulders. "Well, I was told of things out here. Creatures."

"Like the giants?" Willow asked.

"No, different creatures. Ones in the ground. Look, there's a chance we won't even encounter one, so let's just keep moving and not worry about it right now," Wrenna said.

"Well, I'm gonna worry. There's no stopping that now," Felix said.

Wrenna peered down at a rusty old compass Ralf had given her. He told her that he thought the substation was west, so that was the direction she kept towards.

"So once we find this place, what if we run into those guys that hurt Ashley? You know, more officers?" Willow said.

"There is a strong possibility we will. I will deal with that when it happens. Those Fae males work for my father, so they work for me. When we see them... I don't know, I'll come up with something," Wrenna said.

"Well, that's reassuring," Willow said.

"I have some pilot experience. I used to fly planes for the air force, a branch of our military on the surface. I might be able to help with the craft once we locate it," Abel said.

"Oh wow, that's amazing. I have a manual for the craft, well, an old one, so I will let you check it out once we have stopped to camp," Wrenna said.

"Stop and camp! How long will it take to get there?" Gemma asked, seeming frustrated.

Wrenna knew they'd had a long journey already. They had to be so exhausted.

"Do you know how far this place is?" Abel asked.

"I only have a guess. Ralf did what he could and tried really hard to remember, but it has been so long since he has seen one. He used to be a patrol officer many years ago. He said he was there during the initial build. He was in charge of the security watch for the substation during that time. I am sure a lot has changed, so everything right now is an educated guess," Wrenna said.

"*What*? So we are going out here to God knows where, putting our trust in you, all on a *guess*?" Gemma said.

Wrenna understood their worries. She was extremely nervous, but she had to go with what she had.

"I don't understand why you haven't been here before. Aren't you the boss's daughter?" Felix said.

"Yes, I am, but I have been very sheltered from all of this my entire life. I told you before, I had no idea any of this stuff was going on," Wrenna said. "I have been living in total oblivion. Honestly, I can't believe I have been so selfishly blind to all the deceit. I should have believed all the gossip about the Fae warrior rebels. They always said my father was a fraud and a liar," Wrenna continued. They all fell quiet after that, walking on, deep within their own heads.

The group all continued, following the map and compass. Soon the city was so small, Wrenna could barely see it. Up ahead, a massive rock formation began to appear. Ralf told Wrenna that they needed to go through some large rocks. Once on the other side, they would enter the true Badlands. That was where things would get dicey, where they could encounter the Death Worms. Wrenna had once read a book about something similar, but they were only a few inches long. Wrenna's mother didn't give her many details of what to expect, so she could only imagine what they looked like. Wrenna tried to push the thought of them out of her head, praying to the Gods that they wouldn't come upon any. As they got closer to the rock formations, Wrenna stopped and dropped her pack onto the sand. Isha flew off into the rocks.

Maybe scoping things out.

"Look before we go any further, I want to be honest with you about what it is we could possibly stumble upon as we move forward. I asked Ralf for more details about the creatures out beyond these rock structures. He told me that they hunt from deep below the ground. They burrow underground, only surfacing when they hear the vibrations of something moving above them," she said.

The four humans looked back at Wrenna, waiting for her to continue on.

"These things sense vibrations. They can hear what's above them moving around. They have long, tentacle-like appendages on their bodies. That's how they move about under the ground. They are in the Badlands, so we will be safe here while we are in these rocks. But once we reach the other side, we will no longer be safe from them. These rocks should absorb any sound we make, therefore keeping us housed in a safe bubble for the time being," Wrenna said.

"Do these creatures have a name?" Abel asked.

"They call them Death Worms," Wrenna said.

"Oh shit, sounds about right," Felix said, placing his hands on his face, taking a long exhale.

"Nothing surprises me anymore," Willow said, shaking her head.

"Okay, so what do we do to get past these things on the other side of the rocks?" Gemma asked.

"Honestly, I'm not sure. I hadn't thought that far ahead yet," Wrenna said with guilt.

"You mean to tell me you have no idea how we are going to get past these Death Worm things? What kind of rescue mission is this? It sounds more like a death trap," Gemma said.

"I'm sorry. I am just as lost as you are. All I know is I want to help you all find your way back up to the surface. I'm doing the best I can," Wrenna said.

Wrenna picked up her pack and began walking forward towards the rock structure that lay ahead. The others followed without further comment.

Wrenna headed between two large rocks, rocks that resembled an entrance gate. They looked to have been perfectly placed there to give those passing through a path to enter. Isha came flying back, landing on Wrenna's shoulder.

Wrenna looked up at her and said, "Anything to worry about in there?" Asking Isha as if she would respond.

Isha shook her entire body, puffing up her feathers and chirping softly.

"Well, that's not helpful," Wrenna said to the bird.

Once inside the rock formations, the atmosphere slowly began to change. No longer sandy, dry, or dull in color, but transforming into a warmer atmosphere. Wrenna immediately felt the change, her skin reacting the moment she entered. She looked down at her bare arms. Her once barely there markings began to darken. Her skin, with the dewiness in the air, looked as if it was changing colors. Wrenna looked up. All four of the humans glared at her.

"What's up with you? Is this normal?" Felix asked, suggesting the strange, sudden changes in Wrenna's appearance.

"Yeah, as soon as we got within these rocks, I noticed your skin starting to look different. It almost looks golden!" Gemma said.

"I'm not sure what's going on. This has never happened to me before. Ralf didn't mention that anything like this would happen here," Wrenna replied, lifting her arms in front of her face. Isha squawked loudly, flapping her wings, seemingly noticing the change in the atmosphere as well. Wrenna felt a warmth stir in her chest and looked down to see the opal around her neck glowing bright orange.

"Okay, now your necklace is glowing. What is going on?" Gemma asked.

"I don't know, but this place just feels different. The atmosphere is strange to me. Well, let's keep moving and see what's up ahead," Wrenna said as she continued walking deeper into the rocks.

They continued on further into the rocks. All were quiet, as if on edge. The rocks were all perfectly placed, creating a path, one that allowed them to walk single file deeper into this newfound world. The ground was less sandy, more solid. The humans didn't seem to notice the change in the ground below them like Wrenna did. The air pressed down on them, bringing in more warmth, leaving a wet dew on their skin. Wrenna's eyes scanned the surroundings, taking in the newness of it all. Eventually, the ground began to turn green, covered in the same plant that Wrenna had seen when she had visited her mother. The green spread from the ground onto the rocks, even growing up the sides of some of the rocks. It was so beautiful to Wrenna. As they weaved through the rocks, everyone moved without speaking. It was as if they each were taking in the beauty and calm of the hidden world they had all discovered.

The rock structure began to open up. They walked into a clearing that was circular in shape. In the middle of the circle, the ground was covered with more thick green plants. Wrenna bent down, grazing her fingertips through the plants. Abel beside her bent down as well and plucked a single, tiny plant.

He brought the plant up to eye level. "A clover, a four-leaf clover at that," Abel said.

"They are all four-leaf clovers," Gemma said, picking several.

"Wow, I have never seen anything like this!" Wrenna said, looking around, eyes wide. "What's the significance of it?" she asked.

"Uh, well, it's a plant that is usually pretty hard to find. There's a lore that if you find one, it will bring you luck," Felix said.

"Well, this is the luckiest place ever, I guess," Gemma said, bending down and picking several more clovers.

Wrenna looked at the tiny little plant pinched between her thumb and her index finger. She slowly spun it around, taking in the small color variants and the lines that swirled on the leaves.

"We have some plants in Shambhala but nothing like these," Wrenna said, still staring at the tiny plant.

Isha squawked loudly and flew off Wrenna's shoulder, heading off into the distance, quickly vanishing amongst several large boulders.

"Well, maybe she has some personal business to attend to," Abel said as he watched Isha fly off.

"Let's just make camp here. I am sure she is just checking things out. She hasn't left the city or even my room for as long as I can remember. She is probably excited to be out and about," Wrenna said, smiling back at Abel.

The four humans dropped their packs into the clover bed. Willow, Gemma, and Felix plopped down next to their packs, sprawling out onto the ground. Abel squatted down, shifting through the clovers, still in astonishment. The others allowed their exhaustion to quickly take over, closing their eyes. Wrenna was still standing, taking in the full beauty of her surroundings. Just minutes later, out of the corner of her eye, she caught a glimpse of what looked like movement. Wrenna's curiosity got the best of her. She turned and started walking towards where she had seen said movement.

Abel stood up and yelled to her, "Where you going?" as he ran after her.

"Oh, I just want to check things out a little bit, try to see if I can find Isha," Wrenna said.

"Here, wait, I'll go with you. I don't think it's a good idea if you go by yourself," Abel said.

"Uh, okay," Wrenna said as she turned back towards where the movement had occurred moments before.

She walked slowly, her eyes scanning every inch of the area, taking it all in. Wrenna and Abel stepped over several rocks and ducked their heads under one that had fallen into another.

"I don't think we need to go real far. It might not be safe," Abel said.

"I'm just checking things out. I'd like to find my bird, but if you're scared, you can go back," Wrenna said, looking back at Abel with a smile and a wink.

"I'm not scared, I'm just smart," Abel replied with a smug grin crossing his face.

Several small rocks began falling from above them, bouncing down the larger rocks they were standing amongst. They both looked up to see something small scurry off.

"What was that?" Wrenna asked.

"I don't know, an animal? Maybe it was Isha," Abel replied.

"Like I said before, we don't have animals here. Well, at least we don't have animals in Shambhala. Those things are only in books and tales. They're not real. And I don't think Isha would be hiding from us like that," Wrenna said.

"Okay, well, Isha is an animal, by the way. She's an animal, so you must have others. Maybe you just have never seen them before. I mean, you didn't know about those Death Worms until recently," Abel said, scanning the surrounding rocks.

"My bird was a gift from my mother. It came from..." Wrenna paused. "It came from the surface."

"Well, yeah, your bird is a raven. We had those on the surface, at least, before everything," Abel said.

Wrenna felt guilty. She knew Abel's true meaning to his vagueness. He was talking about before the Fae invaded the surface, making it an unsafe place for anything to live.

"Ralf didn't say that we would encounter anything within the rocks. He said beyond the rocks, but nothing here," Wrenna said.

A shuffling sound happened just in front of them, pulling their attention forward. Wrenna immediately went towards it.

"Wait, at least let me go first, just in case," Abel said as he stepped in front of Wrenna. They continued forward, walking further and further away from where the others were camped. The rocks got closer and closer to one another. Soon they came upon a rock with a large cutout hole in it. It looked like an entrance to some sort of dwelling.

"It looks like a cave," Abel said, wiping his dirty hands on his already dirty pants.

"A cave?" Wrenna asked.

"Oh yeah, I forgot," Abel said, shaking his head. "Um, it's like a naturally formed room inside a large rock. This looks like a small cave, but it could go back further then we realize. It looks like this rock goes pretty far in that direction," Abel said, pointing ahead of where they stood. They couldn't see very far due to the abundance of rocks wedged and stacked all around them.

"I don't think we can go any further," Abel said.

"Well, I guess we have to go in," Wrenna said.

"I don't think that's a good idea. It's incredibly dark in there, and we have no idea what we might find. Maybe we should just go back to the others and wait there for Isha to return," Abel said as he turned to head back.

Wrenna kept peering into the dark void beyond the small hole in the rock. She closed her eyes and began taking deep breaths in her nose and out of her mouth. She needed light, and she knew exactly where to get it. She started using all the steps Zelda had taught her, drawing on the memory of her mother. Abel turned back, finding Wrenna in a sort of catatonic state.

"What's going on? Hello," Abel said, snapping his fingers in front of Wrenna's face, trying to pull her out of it.

"If I were you, I'd close your eyes," Wrenna said without changing her expression, still staring into the darkness.

"What? Why?" Abel said.

The feeling of calm and solidarity filled Wrenna, allowing her to pull from within, finding the coil of her powers lying in wait. She noticed the experience seemed a lot easier this time. Wrenna was able to quickly move the dormant powers up her spine, unlocking the light that came with it. She felt an automatic shift, and her third eyelids moved into place, ready for what was to come next. The same bright light from before came spilling from between Wrenna's eyes, but the light was much brighter this time. She saw Abel squeeze his eyes tight, even turning his head away.

"What the hell is happening?" Abel asked.

"I forgot to mention, this is just a little something I have been working on. Something I can do. I'll have to explain later. Just keep your eyes closed. Here, give me your hand." Wrenna reached out, grabbing Abel's hand.

With Abel's hand in hers, she began to walk into the small entry of the cave.

"Watch your head," Wrenna said, helping Abel bend down low enough, avoiding hitting his head on the rock above.

"I really hate this idea," Abel said with his eyes completely closed, relying on Wrenna to guide him.

The cave instantaneously filled with light. As they walked further in, the space opened up.

"You can stand up now," Wrenna told Abel as she looked around the cave.

Wrenna scanned the space. It appeared to be a tiny home or what looked like living quarters for a small Fae. There was a small table, a little bed in the corner with blankets disheveled on top of it. Wrenna furrowed her brow, confused.

"What do you see?" asked Abel.

As Wrenna's eyes searched the room, she quickly found the being that most likely inhabited the cave dwelling. Hiding behind a small rock wall, little eyes peered back at them. Wrenna could only make out what looked like a tiny creature. It almost looked like a Fae. It had pointed ears, big eyes, but it was smaller in stature. The light didn't bother it at all. It was like it was in a trance, staring at Wrenna.

"Hello," Wrenna said.

"What is it?" asked Abel.

"It's a little, um... I'm not sure. A tiny Fae creature, maybe," Wrenna said to Abel. She continued, "It's okay, you can come out. We won't hurt you."

"What do you mean, a tiny Fae creature?" Abel asked nervously.

Wrenna stepped a bit closer to where the tiny creature was hiding.

"It's okay, we mean you no harm. Don't be frightened," Wrenna said, dropping Abel's hand and lowering down to her knee.

Wrenna reached a hand out, waving her fingers, gesturing to the little creature to come forward. Slowly, the creature came out from behind the small rock wall. It had some Fae features, like the pointed ears of course, but it was vastly different. Wrenna had never seen a creature like this before, not even in the many books she had read. It was about three feet tall, maybe shorter. It had stringy gray hair falling down its back. It wore a tiny vest with a white collarless shirt underneath. It had on loose pants that were cut just above the ankle and no shoes. The clothes were not what Wrenna's eyes focused on. It was the opal tied around its neck. Wrenna was shocked to see the opal around her neck was the same as the one around the creature's neck. The little creature walked closer, giving Wrenna a better view. Its face was white, wrinkled, and had several scars. It looked like the face of someone who had lived a long, brutal life. One of the many scars went across his right cheek and over his lips, ending just at his chin. Wrenna didn't feel fear or like he was a threat to her and Abel. She stayed kneeling down, her eyes at his level.

Then the little creature began to bow his head and spoke. "Hello, Queen Rayna."

Chapter Fifteen

Wrenna's eyes widened in shock. Firstly, the creature spoke, and secondly, he called her Queen Rayna.

"No, my name is Wrenna. It is nice to meet you," she said, offering a quick bow in return. Wrenna was pulled away from the encounter when she heard Abel shuffle behind her and clear his throat.

"Ah, Wrenna, can you please tell me what is going on?"

Quickly, the creature scurried off behind the rock wall, no longer visible.

Wrenna turned towards Abel. "Abel, you scared it off."

Before she could turn back towards the hiding spot of the little creature, he was back with a lantern light, understanding that Abel couldn't open his eyes. Wrenna allowed the flow of her powers to recede back, causing her light to dim and eventually vanish. The creature put the lantern down onto the small table. He then set about moving around the cave dwelling, tapping the various lanterns scattered throughout the space. He placed just one of his short fingers upon the lanterns. They then lit up spontaneously.

"Wow, that's handy," Wrenna said. She turned back to where Abel stood waiting.

"Abel, you can open your eyes now," Wrenna said. He slowly began peeling his eyelids back, blinking a few times and allowing his pupils to adjust to the light.

Once he saw the little creature standing before them, he stumbled back, saying, "What the hell is that?"

Wrenna turned her head towards Abel and said, "Don't be rude. We are in his home. Try to show some respect, please."

"I'm sorry," Abel said to Wrenna. He then looked towards the small male creature and said, "I apologize. Please forgive me for being rude."

The creature bowed his head once more, suggesting his forgiveness.

Wrenna turned back towards the creature. "We were not expecting to find someone here in the rocks. Do you live here alone?" Wrenna was still thinking about how he had called her Queen Rayna before, just like that thing in her dream. How did he know Rayna was her real name, one that her mother had given her, and what was the deal with the queen part?

The male creature walked forward, extending his hand to Wrenna, and said, "Hello, good lady, my name is Marrick. This is, or was, my home at one time. I lived here once a long time ago with my family."

"Oh, your family? Are they still around?" Wrenna asked.

Marrick shook his head. "No, good lady, my family is no longer with us." Marrick's eyes saddened as he looked down to the rock floor.

"I am so sorry for your loss," Wrenna said. She continued, "We have come from the city of Shambhala, just east of here. Do you know where that is?"

Marrick answered, "Yes, I have been there before."

"Oh," Wrenna said, confused. "No one has ever mentioned seeing someone of your kind in the city."

"Well, yes, they wouldn't have. I have been imprisoned for some time, only recently finding my way back here, back home," Marrick said, his eyes lingering on the necklace around Wrenna's neck. She reached up, grabbing the opal in her hand, wrapping her fingers around it.

"You have a fire opal as well."

"Yes, I had forgotten I had one hidden here until my return."

"Oh, I see," Wrenna said. She continued, "I found mine on the walkway just outside The House of Books in Shambhala."

Marrick smiled. "Yes, The House of Books, one of my favorite places in the city. I used to like to go there and see what kind of books I could find to bring back with me. I so enjoyed exploring the many stories in books," he said.

Wrenna smiled. Wrenna wondered why Zelda had never mentioned anything about Marrick. Then again, there was much Zelda hadn't told her.

"What do you know about the Death Worms beyond these rocks?" Abel blurted out.

Marrick's eyes widened. "They are vile, vicious creatures. We are lucky they do not come within the rocks. It has been many, many years since I have encountered one of those beasts," he said.

"We are headed out into the Badlands. We are looking for a substation out there, possibly one manned by Fae patrol officers. Do you know anything about that?" Wrenna asked.

"Even more vile than the Death Worms, those Fae. Please, good lady, I mean no disrespect to you. Those officers, they are brutal killers. They lack even an inch of kindness in their bones. They took my family, tortured them and killed them. I'd rather deal with the Death Worms than those Fae patrol officers."

Wrenna dropped her head, looking back at the rock floor. She shook her head, disgusted. She spoke but only a whisper came out. "I'm so sorry."

Marrick walked right up to Wrenna, placing his hand on her bent knee. "No, do not be sorry. It is not your doing. You are not like them. You are our savior," Marrick said.

Wrenna lifted her head and looked into the small creature's eyes. They were the color of the sand, a soft yellow. His eyes looked sad, and downturned wrinkles surrounded them.

Marrick continued, "Your story has been written. It has been told to those seeking a savior. You will be the one to free us from the evil that now holds us. You are the brightness that has come to pull us from all the darkness we have been overtaken with for far too long."

Wrenna felt a tear begin to fall from her eye. She wondered where Marrick had gotten these predictions about her. Her thoughts began to express puzzlement as to how he knew that her story was already written. In what or where? Before she could think on it much more, she felt

Abel place his hand on her shoulder, stepping closer. The three stood there in silence for a moment, connected. Marrick's hand on Wrenna's knee, Abel's hand on Wrenna's shoulder.

Wrenna closed her eyes, trying to ward off any more tears. When she opened them, she was no longer kneeling in the dim cave dwelling. All three of them had instantaneously traveled to another place. Wrenna, still kneeling, looked around at their new surroundings. They were perched upon a massive rock ledge. The rock protruded from an even bigger mountainous rock, one covered by a plethora of green plants. Wrenna stood. She stepped closer to the edge, looking down. There was a colorful, bustling city below. She squinted her eyes, trying to get a better view as puffy clouds moved past. She couldn't tell if the beings below were Fae or human because of how high up they were.

She turned to Marrick. "Where are we?"

Abel stepped up next to Wrenna, glancing down at the city.

Marrick smiled and answered, "This is your land. This is your realm. You will rule over all that your eyes can see."

Wrenna looked out into the distance, only seeing green.

"This looks like where I am from, the surface, before the Fae attacked us," Abel said. He looked out into the vast beauty. "I haven't seen trees like this in a long time," he continued.

"It's beautiful," Wrenna said.

She hadn't seen anything like it, ever. In Shambhala, there was only sand. The colors there were so dull and bleak, but here there was nothing but beauty and color.

Marrick spoke. "I wanted to show you what has been foreseen, show you the future. This is where we can all live one day in peace. To get there you will face so much. It will be a journey like no other. There will be times when you want to give up, run, or maybe even die, but it will be worth it. The future is not for certain, but this is what has been foretold. This is my hope for you and all those who dwell below. The ones who now live in hiding and in fear, this is my hope for them too. Wrenna, you are the key to change what is going on. You can change the path the Fae people are on."

Wrenna felt a pressure begin to stir in her chest. It was like something was taking the breath from her lungs. "How do you know all these things, Marrick? Just a few weeks ago, I was living my very predictable life. Lying around all day, sleeping in, reading. I only had a little bit of idea of what my future would look like. A future I wasn't very interested in, honestly. And now with all the things happening around me, all the things that have changed over the last few days, I don't know what's gonna happen to me next. But right now, at this moment, I couldn't be more ready to take this step towards this future you talk about, Marrick." Wrenna pointed out into the boundless stretch of trees and beauty.

Marrick looked up at Wrenna, and a smile crossed his face. It was like life surged into his being. His eyes sparkled with excitement. "I would like to go with you if you will have me. I would like to be of service in any way I can. My life is now yours, my queen. I can fill you in along the way of how I came to learn of your future and the path you will take ahead," Marrick said, bowing low, so low his head nearly reached the ground.

Wrenna turned to Abel. She raised her eyebrows and lifted her shoulders. She turned back to where Marrick waited. "I don't see why you couldn't come along," Wrenna replied.

Marrick returned to standing. They stood there for just a few more minutes, taking in the view, when Marrick spoke once again. "It is time we head back now, good lady. We must all be connected in some way to travel back together. Take my hand, and take his hand in the other."

Wrenna placed one hand in Marrick's and one in Abel's. Within seconds, with just one blink of her eye, they were back at the cave. "Wow, that's something I don't think I will ever get used to. Well, what now?" asked Abel.

"I think we should head back to the others. We need to prepare for tomorrow," Wrenna said, looking at Abel.

"My queen, you plan on traveling into the Badlands, am I correct?" Marrick asked.

"Yes, I have to find a way to get to the substation there. We plan on finding a way to the surface. Then from there, figure out what will be the next step in stopping all of this."

Marrick looked up at Wrenna. "I must go with you. My people spent centuries mapping the Badlands to make it safe for travel. It is a place that if entered into without knowledge of its illusions, you could be lost forever. I can provide my knowledge as we travel through the treacherous terrain." Marrick looked around and continued, "There is nothing here for me anymore. I have been gone from here for so long now, this no longer feels like my home."

"You said you have been imprisoned. Was it my father's doing?" Wrenna asked Marrick.

"I am afraid so, but do not fret. It was time well spent. My imprisonment turned into something that I will be forever grateful for. Now that I am free, it is time I fulfill a promise I made to a dear friend so long ago. I will continue on alongside you. I will be your devoted servant, giving what I can to help you fulfill your destiny," Marrick said.

Wrenna gave Marrick a small smile. She found herself pondering the mysterious creature's past. She hoped she would have time to learn more about him as they traveled forward.

The three of them left the cave after Marrick had collected a few of his precious items. Items he had left there before Wrenna's father had taken him prisoner. He hurried about, easily finding things as if he had never left. A poem his wife had written him, a small doll that belonged to his daughter, and a knife, one he had given to his son as a gift. He piled other items into his pack, pulled his thin hair back, and covered his head with a small hat. It was very worn and ragged, knitted from a pale green yarn.

"My lucky hat, still right where I left it," Marrick said with a smile.

With his pack on his back, they headed back towards the large circular area where the others were waiting. Marrick walked faster, getting further ahead.

Abel turned back to Wrenna and said, "He grabbed a hat. You would think he would have gotten a pair of shoes as well."

Wrenna just shrugged, trying to stifle a laugh.

Once they had reached the clearing, Felix came running towards them. "Oh, thank God, we thought you guys were dead," he said.

"Thanks a lot for leaving and not telling us where you were going, making us sit here thinking only the worst," Gemma said, still sitting on the ground.

"Well, it doesn't look like Willow was worried," Wrenna said.

Willow was fast asleep, her head covered with a small blanket. Wrenna looked around, not seeing Isha. "Did Isha return?" she asked.

"No, we haven't seen her," Gemma said.

Wrenna spun around, looking for Marrick, assuming he had reached the circle before she and Abel had. "Have you all seen anything else while we were gone?"

"What do you mean, anything else? Like what?" Gemma asked, her voice sounding nervous.

Abel spoke. "It's okay, Gemma, it's nothing to worry about. We found a small cave and when we went inside, we found..." He paused. "Someone."

Wrenna spun around, looking into the rocks that surrounded them.

"He is probably nervous. He will come out on his own time, I am sure," Wrenna said. Just then, Wrenna heard a whistle behind her. She spun around once again, and standing on top of the rock stood Marrick. Gemma gasped, Felix stared blankly, and Willow continued sleeping.

Abel spoke. "What a way to make a grand entrance, Marrick."

Then Marrick jumped down from the rock, landing on the bed of clovers. Gemma stepped back, stumbling over her pack and falling back onto the ground. Felix ran to her side, laughing, and said, "Are you okay?"

He reached down to try to help her up. Gemma only pushed him away. "Stop it, it's not funny, Felix."

Wrenna thought it was funny, but her eyes shifted back to Marrick.

With all the commotion, Willow sat up, rubbing her eyes. "What the hell is going on? Can't you guys see I am trying to get some sleep?"

Willow's eyes fell on Marrick, who was standing only a few feet from her. Willow just closed her eyes and lay back down.

"Well, guys, this is Marrick. He used to live here among the rocks. He will be traveling with us, helping us along the way. He knows the safest path through Badlands and can help us get to the substation," Wrenna said.

"What is he?" Gemma asked. "Not trying to be rude, but—"

Felix cut her off. "Well, you are being rude, Gemma, you are," he said.

"I am of elfish descent. We are an ancient sect. My people used to be great in numbers. Over the years, the collective has died out. Mostly from battles and lack of supplies. Fae, the ones that are now taking over the surface, they are the ones who killed off most of my people," Marrick said, looking up at Gemma. He continued, "I am here to serve my queen in any way I can, so I only wish to help you all on this journey." He bowed once again.

"Why did he call you queen?" Gemma said, looking towards Wrenna.

"I'm not really sure about that yet." Wrenna shrugged her shoulders.

"Let's all get settled in. We should probably try to get some sleep. We have a big day tomorrow. We need to be well rested," Abel said.

"I don't know about you guys, but I think I'd rather stay here and face Death Worms instead of those giant things," Gemma said.

"So you have met our friendly Nephilim. You can thank the Death God for those guys. The Nephilim are said to be a kind of hybrid. Some say the displaced Death God bred with a female human on the surface many centuries ago. From that encounter came a siege of Nephilim upon the earth. We can also thank Yama for the Death Worms as well. He is the cause for all of this. He is to blame. If it wasn't for that foolish treaty the Fae made with him centuries ago, this place, the In Between, and the surface wouldn't be in the chaos they are today. Wrenna's ancestors were the ones that decided to go into business with Yama the Death God. What an idiotic idea." Marrick continued speaking as he pulled his sleeping mat from his pack.

Everyone else had found a space on their own mats, Wrenna lying in between Marrick and Abel.

He continued, "You see, the Fae were a peaceful group at one time. The city didn't have that wall around it, and Fae were allowed to come and go. The elves were free to travel amongst the Fae to trade goods and services. We all had a lovely, copasetic relationship. Eventually, the In Between, where we are now, started to have shortages of crucial supplies. Our food supply ran dangerously low, and we could not get anything to grow. It was like the sand was cursed. The plants would blossom, only for them to turn black and rot away. The elves retreated to this part of the land amongst the rocks. We stored up all the supplies we had and did our best to survive. When the Fae learned of our little stockpile, that is when they came and took it all, and along with the food, they took many lives. We didn't have the numbers to defend ourselves, so we had to retreat, hiding in what caves we could find. Eventually the Fae, after pillaging our little settlement here, left. Only a few of us survived. My entire family was lost in the battle. The Fae leaders become very selfish and greedy, only caring for their city. So they began to build the wall, keeping everyone out. But that didn't help them with food and growing things to eat. Wrenna's grandfather and that evil seer that works for her family found a way to summon the Death God. They made a bargain with him to help them with the sand and with growing crops. In return, they would provide him with the impure souls he viscously craved."

Everyone lay quietly, listening to the story, even Wrenna, this being as new to her as it was to the humans.

Marrick continued, "The Fae tried sacrificing some of their own people, but it wasn't good enough for the Death God. The souls of the gentle people of Shambhala were not impure enough for Yama's liking. He told the Fae about the people on the surface, how their souls were damned. How the humans were the most corrupt of all the beings in and on this earth. So the leaders of Shambhala forced those beyond the walls of the city to become their slaves. And when that wasn't enough, they began taking the humans from the surface and enslaving them as well. They all were made to dig up through the rock, up into the blackness above us. Creating tunnels to the surface. Many died from being worked to death. Others encountered the Nephilim within discovered subterranean caves. The Nephilim live and transverse within the caves that are located in the dirt that is above us but below the surface. With this deal the Fae made with Yama, it kept most of the Fae safe from the Nephilim's wrath. Everyone else was fair game."

Marrick rolled over onto his stomach, placing his chin on his hands. He yawned and continued, "There is much that goes on that the Fae leaders keep hidden from the citizens of Shambhala, including you, Wrenna."

"Yes, there is a lot. I feel so naive to have never seen any of this. How selfish of me to be so absorbed in myself. I should be ashamed," Wrenna said.

"Don't be ashamed, my queen. Your father kept a lot of these things hidden by using his manipulation power. It is not your fault," Marrick said.

The others sat quietly, possibly as shocked as Wrenna was after hearing Marrick's story. Wrenna felt so many things—disappointed, shocked, sad, but most of all, she felt guilt. She had been living without a care in the world, all while so many were suffering.

Marrick yawned again, rolling back to his back. "That's enough for tonight. We will talk more in the morning."

Chapter Sixteen

Wrenna couldn't sleep. The guilt was keeping her awake, and she was worried about Isha. She was so angry at her father. How could he do all of these things and still smile and pretend? How could Stiles be a part of all of this and never mention a word? How could he walk around acting like everything was okay? Wrenna lay staring up at the blackness above them. *There is a whole other world up there.* They had been there all along, and the majority of the Fae had no idea.

Wrenna was deep in thought when Abel spoke. "It's not your fault, Wrenna. You didn't know. I don't blame you. I want you to know that. You are the first ray of light we have seen. For years now, things have just gotten worse. We have lost all hope. Especially when we were caught, we thought we would die that day. But for some reason they kept us alive and brought us down here, and then you showed up. I think everything happens for a reason, Wrenna."

Wrenna turned her head. Abel was looking at her. Their eyes met. He had the most amazing eyes she'd ever seen. She quickly stopped her mind from wandering to a lustful path. "Well, thank you, that means a lot to me. I promise you now, I will make things right. I will help your people. I will right the wrongs of my father and his father."

"I believe you," Abel said.

"You know, just a few weeks ago, I was complaining that I had to do service work, cleaning and working in the greenhouse. And you and your friends were fighting for your life," Wrenna said, shaking her head. She continued, "Now I am here, in this place. My whole boring existence flipped upside down. My entire life has been a lie."

Wrenna felt tears coming. She pulled her hands to her face, crying quietly.

"Wrenna, you have to allow the past to be the past. You have to try to look forward to tomorrow. Yeah, this shit is bad. It's awful. You didn't know about it then, but you do now, so now you can take the steps towards making it better."

Abel reached out and placed his hand on Wrenna's wrist.

He kept talking. "Honestly though, I don't understand why the weight of all of this mess is placed on your shoulders. Why you? Is there someone else that can help us?" Abel asked.

"I'm not one hundred percent sure why I have been chosen to take on this seemingly unrealistic task. I've had many tell me that it has been prophesied that I will be the one to change the future of many. My mother is human, and my father is Fae. I am the first half-human, half-Fae to ever be born. My father was told by an oracle that in order for him to be in full power of all, he needed to sire a hybrid. Well, I guess that's me. Now that I have learned all of this new information about what's really happening, I feel it is my obligation to do something to fix it," Wrenna said, pulling her hands off of her face. "I have been told so many times these last few days that this is all my destiny. My entire purpose of being born is to help attain the freedom for those in need. My father's plans for me were more in line with his own beliefs. Control and conquer. Now that I am on my own, I now control the choice. I control my destiny," she said as she yawned.

"I don't know what is to come tomorrow, but I think it's worth a shot. We really have nothing to lose, at least those on the surface don't. Things can't get any worse there. I know you have plenty to lose, and I do appreciate what you have done for us so far. Thank you," Abel said, squeezing Wrenna's wrist, emphasizing his thanks. "I am sure you are very tired. Let's get some rest," Abel said as he turned his gaze back upward. "And to be honest with you, today has been one of the coolest days in a long time. I've been living in hiding for so long, and then I went to thinking I was going to be tortured to death. Now I am here with you in a bed of four-leaf clovers. I mean, that's gotta mean my luck is changing for the better, right?"

Wrenna laughed. "I mean, if you say these little plants bring you luck, and we are lying in thousands of them, then I believe you are right."

They got quiet for a few moments.

"I am sorry about your sister," Wrenna said.

"Yeah, me too," Abel said.

"Do you have any other family up there?" Wrenna asked.

"No, I mean, I haven't seen my parents in years. I don't know if they are alive or dead. Ashley was my only sibling. I came from a very small family. These guys are my only family now," Abel said.

"Where did you meet them?" Wrenna asked.

"Well, I stumbled across Felix when I was scavenging for food in an abandoned warehouse. A place where humans store food and other random things. He was lying in the back, hurt pretty badly. I guess he had a run-in with someone else. They took all his supplies and beat him up pretty bad. They stabbed him in the thigh with a knife. He almost bled to death. I got him patched up the best I could, and we have been together ever since. I think that was probably a year ago. Then we found Gemma in the middle of the forest. It's a place with tons of trees, like the place we somehow went to with Marrick. She was wandering, lost, dehydrated, and close to hypothermia. And Willow, she actually saved us. We were running from a couple of those giants when Willow lit a massive fire, one so big it lit up the sky. We have learned that those things do not like fire very much. She was staying in an old bunker. She brought us there, where we stayed for a couple weeks. But once we ran out of food and water, we had to leave, and we have been together since," Abel said.

"I can't imagine what you guys have been through," Wrenna said.

"What about you? Do you have any siblings? Any family? Besides your father," Abel said with sarcasm in his voice.

"No, just me and him. There is Zelda, the lady that owns the bookstore. She's probably the only other Fae I would even consider family.

My mother..." Wrenna paused. "She was actually murdered by my father, but that's a whole other thing." Wrenna yawned again. She rolled towards Abel. He rolled over, returning the gesture. They just lay there, both quiet until Wrenna's eyelids became too heavy for her to hold open any longer.

Wrenna woke up to Marrick standing over her. "Wake up, good lady. We best be getting a move on."

Wrenna sat up. Everyone else was already up, their packs on their backs. Wrenna rolled her sleeping mat up and said, "So today, we follow Marrick's lead. His people were the ones to map out safe passage through this place."

"Yes, my people have been gifted with the sight. The Badlands are not what they seem to be. There has been a shadow of illusions placed upon the land we shall soon travel. If one does not have the sight, they will be lost to the Badlands forever or eaten. Please, I ask each of you to follow my precise instructions and trust in me to get us to the other side."

Wrenna looked around at everyone; they all seemed to be in agreement.

"Ralf told me that the Death Worms have excellent hearing and the vibrations from our feet or our voice can attract them. So we need to walk lightly and stay very quiet," Wrenna said.

"If I may, good lady?" Marrick said, wanting to add something. "The Death Worms are big and very fast. Once they begin to hunt their prey, they like to torment their victims by eliciting fear. They can sense the vibration of one's heart in their chest. The faster the heartbeat, the more they hunger for their victim. They can induce fear, they can smell it. They feed off of fear, they like to bathe in it, and then they attack. So if one does show up, we need to stand very still. Try to keep our heart rate as low as we can and wait them out. Allow me to lead, walking a little bit ahead of everyone. Stay vigilant and follow my exact steps. This place is full of illusions that will entice you, but you must keep moving forward," Marrick said.

"This doesn't sound sketchy at all," Willow said, raising her eyebrows.

Wrenna shook her head, taking in a deep breath. She looked down at the open compass in her hand and headed west.

The five of them followed Marrick. He led the way, being the one most familiar with the area. He led them around the rock formations, the one that held his cave dwelling. They followed a narrow path, one that looked to have been walked many times. It led them to a rock with what seemed to be a natural stairway built into it. Marrick walked up the stairs, having to jump from one stair to the next. Abel followed Marrick, taking the stairs easily. Felix followed, then Gemma and Willow. Wrenna was the last to climb the stairs. Soon they were all standing on top of a large, flat rock with nothing but open desert ahead of them.

It looked endless. There were very few random rocks scattered throughout but nothing else.

"This is going to be so much fun," Willow said.

"Many Fae have wandered out into this place. If the Death Worms don't get them, then dehydration, insomnia, and delirium eventually does. By looking at it now, it may look endless. That's an illusion. Some Fae have the capability to camouflage things. By binding their power to this place, it will stay camouflaged forever. There is a very strategic pattern of walkways, hidden of course, that will help us navigate this place. The elves have placed markings, some on rocks, some in the ground, to help make navigation of this place easier. When you look out there with an unknowing eye, you can't see the labyrinth zigzagging across the barren land. If you do not follow and solve the maze, you will never get out of here," Marrick said, pointing out into the vastness. "This substation you are looking for is hidden by this illusion. The wards that have been put up around this place are very powerful. There has to be a reason for it. They have to be hiding something very important to them."

"Well, let's find out," Wrenna said.

Wrenna took one final look back, sending a quick prayer to the Gods that Isha would find her again or find her way back home. She hated leaving her behind, but there was no time to wait.

They walked down the embankment on the other side of the large rock. They each stepped gently onto the sand. Marrick turned around and placed his finger on his lips, telling them all to be quiet. He began walking ahead of them all, keeping his gaze on the sandy ground below. They all walked in a single file line. When Marrick zigged, they zigged, and when he took a sharp right, they also took a sharp right. They all walked as lightly as possible, trying to keep from making any noise. Wrenna felt like the terrain around them kept changing, the illusion shifting the further they went. Marrick kept his head to the ground, reading markings hidden on rocks. When Wrenna looked down, she didn't see anything but yellowish sand and random scattered obsidian rocks. She felt at complete ease with Marrick's lead. It was odd. She felt so much trust in him after only knowing him for a short time, but he was easy to trust. He felt like someone she had known her whole life.

Wrenna walked lost in thought, following closely behind Abel. She noticed he kept looking back at her. Always checking in on her and the others, making sure everyone was safe. She appreciated that about him. A characteristic Stiles never exhibited, to say the least. Wrenna didn't have a whole lot of interaction with males except the brief crossing of paths with patrol officers back at the compound. The only males she spent much time around were her father and Stiles, and both failed in any way of being decent Fae. Abel was different. It could have been the situation, maybe because he was human, from a different culture. He just seemed more genuine, actually caring, something Wrenna wasn't used to. She even noticed the care Felix gave to Gemma. Her well-being was important to him. They would bicker and argue sometimes, but she could see in his eyes the care he had for her.

Not paying attention, lost in thought, Wrenna tripped over a rock, a marker for the path. She landed hard on the ground, face first. Abel turned quickly, dropping to his knee to help her. Everyone else turned to see.

"Are you okay, Wrenna?" Abel whispered. Wrenna placed her hands down into the sand, pushing herself up off the ground. She had sand in her mouth, up her nose, and even in her eyes.

"Dang, you really ate it," Felix said, laughing.

"Be quiet!" Marrick said angrily.

Then the ground began to rumble. Everyone froze.

Gemma whispered, "Is it one of those worm things?"

Wrenna got to her feet. Abel helped dust her off, and she noticed his hand innocently coming extremely close to her chest.

Marrick whispered back, "Stay still. Do not move, no matter what."

The ground beneath them shook, causing Wrenna to fall forward into Abel's arms. They all stood as still as they possibly could. Marrick reached into his vest and pulled out a small knife. It looked huge in his hands. Wrenna began to feel her heart pound in her chest.

"Look!" Willow pointed, trying to speak low.

She pointed off to the right of where they were standing. Wrenna saw a mound of sand that looked to be moving towards them. Wrenna could clearly tell something was moving under the sand, something large. She wanted to run. The urge was so strong to just take off.

Marrick whispered again, "Stay put. Do not move."

Wrenna looked around at everyone, realizing she was still in Abel's arms. She quickly pulled away, keeping her feet planted. Felix and Gemma had reached for each other, arms outstretched, holding hands. Willow stood next to Marrick. Her eyes grew big as she looked off towards the massive sand mound moving closer and closer to where they stood. As it got closer, Wrenna could feel the tension and fear radiating off of the others. The natural instinct to get away from something that could be a threat stirred in everyone. She looked back at Abel. His eyes were glued to the large mound of sand. They watched as it stopped about ten feet away from where they all stood. She looked towards Marrick. He gestured with his hands, holding them up, pleading for everyone to stay still. She looked towards Willow, Felix, and Gemma. Gemma was crying now, making small audible sounds. You could cut the fear that surrounded them with a knife. It was like a pressure so grand, pushing down on her chest. She could barely take it. It finally became too much for Gemma. Without warning, she dropped Felix's hand and took off. She began running across the desert in the opposite direction from the massive mound of sand, where the beast was waiting beneath.

Wrenna pulled in a fast breath. Felix yelled, "Gemma, stop!"

The massive mound of sand began moving again, not towards Wrenna and the others, but towards Gemma's pounding footfalls.

"Son of a bitch," said Marrick under his breath.

"We have to go get her," Felix pleaded.

"That isn't the only Death Worm out here. There are others. They are probably waiting just over there, waiting for us to move." Marrick turned towards the direction the first worm came from. "These things are smart. Stay put if you want to live," Marrick said.

"We can't just leave her out there," Wrenna said, looking towards Marrick.

"If we leave this path, we will not find it again. We will be lost in this place. Even if we try, we will not find her. This place is ever changing, the illusion twisting and evolving. You may think it all looks the same, that all we have to do is chase after her. If we don't get taken by the worms, we would be lost in the changes this place makes."

Willow began to cry. Felix dropped to his knees, putting his head in his hands. Abel just stared off towards Gemma, her silhouette just a small blur now.

"But she's right there," Willow said, pointing towards the tiny profile of Gemma in the distance.

"She may look to be there. The illusions created by this place, by Fae powers, are meant to fool you. They do not want you to find what they have hidden out here. They want you to be lost in this place," Marrick said, pleading.

They all stood there, quiet for some time until they could no longer see Gemma, no longer see the massive, moving mound of sand that went after her. Felix was sobbing into his hands. Abel walked softly to stand next to him, placing a hand on his back for some comfort. Willow just stood, staring off.

Soon Marrick spoke. "I am sorry for your loss, my friends, but we must move forward. As long as we stay on this path, follow the markings, we will be safe from those beasts. We must move forward. Our fear has already begun to penetrate the sand. It won't be long before the Death Worms sense where we stand." Marrick turned and began following the markings only he could see.

Willow turned and followed him. Wrenna and Abel both helped lift Felix off the ground. "We have to go find her. We can't just leave her out there," Felix cried.

"I know, man. Maybe she will find her way to the substation. Maybe she will meet us there," Abel said, trying to instill a bit of hope for his hurting friend.

"I think we should keep moving. We need to listen to Marrick. He knows what this place is like," Wrenna said.

"But she's out there. She's all alone. We gotta get to her before that thing does," Felix said as he fell back down to his knees, crying.

Abel just looked at Wrenna. Both of their hearts broke for Felix. Wrenna felt helpless in the situation, her heart telling her to chase after Gemma but her mind telling her to listen to Marrick. Abel pulled Felix back up off the ground and flung Felix's arm over his shoulder. They began moving forward. Wrenna followed just behind the two males. Felix began to sob, and Abel carried him forward. Wrenna looked out into the distance. Gemma was nowhere in sight. Wrenna exhaled, wiped her face, and walked on.

Chapter Seventeen

They spent hours following Marrick's directions, his many twists and turns through an unseen maze. No one spoke, and Felix cried the whole way.

Willow was the first to speak. "Do you think we can stop and rest sometime? My feet are killing me."

"I could use a little break too, if possible?" Wrenna said.

"We are about halfway. There is a spot hidden up ahead. It's a large rock, with a hollowed out open space where most stop to camp. We should be there soon. Let's get there, and we will stop and rest for a while. We should be safe there," Marrick said as he continued moving along the invisible path. "No one knows how it got there, but invisibility shields have been placed around it. Most travelers say that this place was a gift from the God of Death to those who travel into the Badlands. Kind of a little reprieve to rebuild their strength. They say he would much rather indulge in one that is at full strength rather than someone who is weak and on the verge of death. He leaves the weak ones for his scavengers," Marrick continued.

"By scavengers, you mean the worms?" Willow asked.

"Yes, the Death Worms and the Nephilim."

"Oh, I hate those things too," Willow said.

"They aren't seen much here in the In Between. They travel through the cave systems, going from the place where Yama resides to the surface. The In Between is the Death Worms' domain mostly," Marrick continued.

"So is there anything else that we need to worry about down here?" Abel asked. He kept his arm around Felix's waist, allowing his friend to rest into him.

"The Fae. Well, some of them," Marrick said, looking towards Wrenna with apologetic eyes. "And the lingering powers and wards left behind by those Fae. The wards and illusions are meant to manipulate you into seeing what you want to see, not the truth. The illusion surrounding the desert is only the beginning. There are many wards placed upon this place. We must always be on our toes. Remember, if you see something that seems too good to be true, it probably is. No matter how much you think you know that it is real, it isn't. Just like when we lost your friend to the desert. The illusion could've shown her running, only disappearing when she reached a great distance. But in all actuality, she could have been eaten within seconds of leaving the marked path. The Fae, commanded by the God of Death, have cast great illusions upon this place. Illusions that are put here with the purpose of destroying those who enter the Badlands," Marrick said unapologetically.

Felix began audibly crying once again.

"That's pretty cold, little dude," Willow said, looking at Marrick.

"I do apologize for my brash words. You have lost a dear friend, and I should have been more kind with my words. Please forgive me," Marrick said, looking back towards Willow. She nodded, gesturing an acceptance for his apology.

What seemed like hours later, they finally reached a massive, flat rock, hollowed out like a giant bowl. They all crawled into the bowl-shaped rock, dropping all their heavy packs down. Felix immediately rolled over to his side and curled up, only small sounds coming from him now. Willow crawled up next to him, leaning onto her pack. She began rubbing his back, trying to show comfort.

"How do you know we will be safe here and those things out there can't get us?" Abel asked Marrick as he dropped his pack, falling down to his knees.

"Because this place is off-limits. There are wards up to keep anything out."

"But how do you know that for sure?" Abel asked.

"I know because the story of this place has been passed down from generation to generation in the elvish community. Some of the elders were here when this place was spell cast, when these tricks and illusions were placed. They were slaves to the Fae, forced to help create and even possibly help place this rock here, so they say," Marrick said, placing his hands behind his head, leaning back more.

"I don't trust stories," Abel said.

Wrenna sat down on the other side of Felix, crossed her legs, and slouched forward.

"What other option do we have?" Wrenna said.

Abel kicked at the dust. "Well, I guess you're right."

"Let's try to rest up the best we can. We won't make it through this place with a lack of sleep. We have to keep our wits about us," Marrick said, closing his eyes.

Abel leaned back into his own pack. "I don't think I am going to be able to sleep in this place," he said, looking at Wrenna.

"Me either," Wrenna said.

Within minutes, Marrick was snoring, and Willow was lying on Felix's shoulder. They both had their eyes closed. Abel and Wrenna were the only two left awake.

"This place is scary quiet. I have not been somewhere this quiet I don't think ever," Abel said.

Wrenna turned to her side so she could get a better view of Abel, who was lying on his back, looking up into the darkness overhead.

"I feel like I have lived in this kind of quiet my entire life," Wrenna said.

"What do you mean?" Abel asked.

"The compound I live in is so quiet. My father is always gone or locked up in his room doing only the Gods know what. The servants and groundskeepers stay to themselves. Their job is to be invisible. I am pretty much alone most the time, Isha being the only company I have, or had, I guess. Well, besides Stiles."

As soon as Wrenna mentioned Stiles's name, she immediately regretted it.

"I thought you didn't have any siblings?" Abel said, rolling to his side now, facing Wrenna.

"I don't," Wrenna said. She paused. "Stiles is the asshole patrol officer that brought you here."

Abel raised his eyebrows. "Oh," he said.

"We were kind of, barely, sort of together. Before I knew about all this, before I learned the truth," Wrenna said, defending herself.

"So you guys were dating?" Abel asked.

"I wouldn't say we were dating. It was kind of a convenience thing for me, something to do. If that makes sense," Wrenna said, watching Abel's face.

"Something to *do* in more ways than one," Abel said, laughing quietly.

Wrenna rolled her eyes. "Yeah. I guess. I grew up with him. His father worked for my father, and he was just always around. Naturally, we had to interact with one another. We both just kind of became curious and one thing led to another and..." Wrenna said.

"And you guys were like friends with benefits, or did you care about him?" Abel asked. He continued, "I'm sorry, it's none of my business."

"No, it's okay, I don't have anything to hide. I thought I did have feelings for him at one time. He spent most of our time together talking about himself. He is incredibly self-absorbed. After I grew up a little, I realized we could never have something long-term. I will admit, sometimes he can be sweet. At least at the time, I thought he was. When I was lonely and feeling down, he would try to cheer me up. Now I realize it was all fake. He never really cared about me," Wrenna said.

"I see," Abel said. He rolled back to his back, placing his arms behind his head.

"I had no idea the kind of Fae he truly was. I never saw that side of him. I knew he was an asshole, but I never imagined how sick he truly was," Wrenna said.

She felt guilt swell up in her chest.

"Some guys are really good at disguising themselves," Abel said.

"Truthfully, we had nothing in common. He wasn't someone I saw myself married to, even though he thought differently," Wrenna said.

"He wanted to marry you?" Abel asked.

"Yeah, but not because he actually cared about or even loved me. He wanted to be married to the leader of our city, another stepping stone for himself to be closer to the top," Wrenna said.

Abel stayed quiet for a moment, and then he finally spoke. "I'm sorry, that guy is a creep. You deserve better," Abel said, seeming to immediately regret being so straightforward.

Wrenna smiled. "I'm not really sure what I deserve, but I never let it bother me. I knew what he wanted, and I wasn't going to let him have it. I was using him, honestly," Wrenna said.

"So you never knew about the things he was doing or what your father was doing?" Abel asked.

"No, I swear, I was always in my own little world. I hated my reality, so I buried my face in books. Spent a lot of my time at The House of Books with Zelda. I avoided any type of responsibility when I could. I put blinders on to anything that didn't fit into my little world," Wrenna said.

"So how did you find out what was really going on?" Abel asked.

"I was out for a run one day. I had run out past my normal route. I needed to burn off some energy, so I just kept going. Let's just say I stumbled upon Stiles and some other patrol officers. I saw them doing unspeakable things to humans. I was so shocked and confused. I immediately began to investigate. Once I opened that door, there was no looking back. The truth was always right in front of my face. I mean, I was living in the same place they were torturing people."

Right when Wrenna said it, she stopped.

"I'm sorry," she said, reaching out, placing her hand on Abel's arm.

"It's not your fault. I have lost so much, so many people in my life. My heart has become dead to the pain of loss at this point, but my sister, that was a hard one. Her loss is like a knife buried in my heart. I still haven't truly mourned her. It's like she isn't really dead. It's like she went someplace else, and one day I will find her again," Abel said.

"Well, in some ways that is true," Wrenna said. They both lay there on that cold rock, quiet. Until Wrenna couldn't keep her eyes open any longer, eventually falling asleep.

Wrenna found herself in a dream once again, a dream so real she could feel it in her body. She was with Abel, Felix, Willow, and Marrick, and they were running across the desert. They were following Isha as she flew in the sky above them. It was as if she was leading them somewhere. The ground beneath them was shaking, shaking so much they could barely stay on their feet. Wrenna feared looking back, feared seeing what was behind them, so she kept her eyes forward.

Marrick yelled ahead, "Keep going. Do not stop, do not look back."

His face was distorted, almost unrecognizable. In the dream, Wrenna tried rubbing her eyes, trying to get a better, clearer view of Marrick's face, but it stayed twisted and warped. The ground began to move so violently, knocking Wrenna off her feet. She fell to her knees. Beneath her the sand began to rise, growing into a large mound. There were several more large mounds that grew around her. She could no longer see the others. A Death Worm emerged from the sand. Its massive body arched into the air, standing tall above her. Its bare face and long tentacles peered down at her, its gaping mouth wide in Wrenna's face. Within the mouth were rows and rows of sharp, bloody teeth. Wrenna squinted her eyes, looking past the staggered, razor-sharp teeth. Deep within the Death Worm's throat, Wrenna was shocked to see Gemma screaming back at her. It was as if she was trapped, waiting to be fully swallowed whole. Gemma screamed back at Wrenna, making eye contact. Wrenna just stared back, frozen with fear. Then the Death Worm swooped down, swallowing Wrenna. There was only blackness.

Wrenna jolted up, awakening herself from her nightmare. She looked around. Everyone else was still asleep. She was covered in sweat, her heart pounding out of her chest. The dream felt so real. Wrenna noticed the fire opal tied around her neck was now vibrating and glowing orange. She felt pressure push on her chest from the inside. Wrenna gripped her knees, pulling them into her chest, trying to create a barrier, keeping the pressure from exploding outward. She took a long exhale out of her mouth, hoping to calm the turbulent storm within. She knew she wasn't going back to sleep for fear of returning to that nightmare.

Wrenna sat alone with herself until the others began to stir awake. She knew she would feel her lack of sleep later, but for now she was thankful to no longer be in that nightmare. In reality, she was living a nightmare and those creatures were out there now, waiting. That thought kept Wrenna on edge.

Abel pulled himself up off the ground, rubbing his eyes. "Did you get any sleep?" he asked, looking at Wrenna.

"Yeah," Wrenna lied.

Marrick pulled on his pack. "Let's get moving. The longer we are here, the longer the illusions have to try to work their way into our minds. We must stay vigilant."

Willow pushed Felix, waking him. Everyone looked exhausted, like the brief time they spent trying to sleep actually did more harm than good.

"Another day of wandering out in this desert, following around an elf, praying we don't get eaten by a giant worm," Willow said as she stood, patting the dust from her pants.

Felix's eyes were swollen, his face red. He didn't say a word.

They returned to the path. Marrick led the way. Wrenna started calculating the last time she had heard Felix speak. Her heart broke for him. Felix and Gemma clearly had some feelings for one another. Maybe they hadn't taken the steps fully into a relationship, but there had been something there. Wrenna could tell Felix cared deeply for Gemma, the way he took care of her, helped her, and even looked at her. Wrenna could see the desperation and hopelessness in Felix's eyes when he peered out into the desert, searching for her. As if he hoped that Gemma would find her way back to them, like she had never been lost in the first place. Wrenna tried to stay hopeful, mostly for Felix, that it was still a possibility that Gemma would come back. It was hard to keep that hope alive, especially after her vivid nightmare. Seeing Gemma buried deep inside the Death Worm, screaming for help. That was an image Wrenna would never free herself from. Wrenna scanned the desert, looking out in the distance, finding no signs of Gemma.

Marrick continued on with his head down, focusing on the markings. "I need everyone to be aware of what is to come up ahead. You cannot see it right now, but once we get a little further ahead, we will reach two statues that symbolize the Great Oracle. Many have traveled these deserts seeking the truths told by the Great Oracle. I myself have never encountered her, but many of my ancestors have. She will only present herself to someone she deems worthy. Like everything else in this vast, dark land, she is held under the illusion. We will pass through the two statues thinking nothing happened or changed, but there is a chance one of us could be chosen. If you are chosen, she will then become visible to only your eyes. The ancestors say that once the Great Oracle presents herself to you, all time stands still."

"This place just keeps getting better and better," Willow said.

"So if we are chosen to see her, what then?" Abel asked.

"If you are chosen to witness the Great Oracle, she will speak the truth to you, bad or good. She could tell you your future, your past. All the stories say that each being has a different experience, but it is up to the Great Oracle to decide. You cannot ask her questions, for she will only tell you what she believes you need to hear," Marrick said.

"And when should we be near the place where this Great Oracle is?" asked Willow. Felix was still staring down at the ground in a haze of sadness. Wrenna listened with great intrigue. She didn't think she was worthy enough to be chosen but if anyone here was, she selfishly thought it should be her. Wrenna found herself praying to the Gods that the Great Oracle would call to her because she had so much she needed to know. The future of the Fae and the humans on the surface rested in Wrenna's hands, and any truth of what was to come could be tremendously helpful. Wrenna hoped that if she were chosen, the Great Oracle could give her more insight about her now blossoming powers. There was so much Wrenna needed to know. As she walked on, her list of reasons for needing to speak with the Great Oracle only grew.

Chapter Eighteen

They continued on, following Marrick. If someone were watching them, they would have thought they were crazy. Marrick walked in random patterns, taking sharp, invisible corners that only existed in some alternate reality. But they all followed blindly with anticipation of the possibility of stumbling upon the Great Oracle. As they walked, Wrenna thought of those who traveled this land in the past, marking the path, and those who might have gotten lost to the illusion along the way.

Wrenna felt like they had been walking for hours, her thoughts racing with wonder and worry. Soon Wrenna began to feel a tingle originate from the spot upon her chest. It was glowing, the flecks of colors spiraling out of control. She looked up at the others. They didn't seem to notice. It felt as if the tingle in her chest started to spread to her head, her arms, and her legs. Soon her entire body was vibrating so violently, she felt as if she was going to throw up. As she looked around at the others, they all seemed to now be stuck in their place, frozen. Wrenna tried to speak out, but no words were able to escape her lips. Wrenna's mind was lost in a state of confusion, quickly shifting through potential causes of her disarray. The vibration continued on, causing her vision to pulse in and out. She felt as if there were a large drum in her head and every time someone would pound the drum, all her senses heightened. It was like something was pulling her from this place to another, beat by beat of the drum. Then Wrenna heard a loud snapping sound permeate her eardrums. The sound was so loud it caused her to close her eyes and draw in her body, tucking her hands and arms into her chest, rounding her back. When she opened her eyes, she was no longer standing in the desert with the others. She had once again traveled somewhere else.

Wrenna was now standing in a place that looked similar to the clover bed they had slept in a few nights before. The ground below her feet was covered in green plants. Some plants were viny in nature, spreading out like long fingers, tangling upon anything they touched. As Wrenna looked around, she noticed a smoky fog floating in the air around her. It was so thick her eyes had trouble seeing through it. Once again, several large rocks were stacked about the area. There were a few that looked to be built into the shape of what looked like a chair. The chair had a tall back covered in more viny plants. The bench of the chair was wider than what a normal chair would have been, as if it was made big enough for several Fae to sit. After taking in more detail, Wrenna decided the chair resembled more of a throne than a chair. The back crept upward in three points, like it was purposely made that way. Wrenna stepped closer, trying to peer behind the tall back of the throne, finding nothing but thick fog.

Wrenna said, "Hello."

She thought back to what Marrick had told them about the Great Oracle. She wondered if this was her doing. Or was it another vision gifted to her by the fire opal around her neck?

"Hello," an old, raspy female voice said from behind Wrenna. She quickly spun around, finding no one was there.

Wrenna turned back towards the plant-covered throne. "Who is there?" she asked.

The voice replied, "I believe you know whom you are speaking with."

"My name is Wrenna. I guess you called me here," Wrenna said.

"Yes, I did call you here, but you did not answer my question. Who are you?"

Wrenna raised her eyebrows. "I did answer your question. My name is Wrenna Thain. I am from the city of Shambhala," Wrenna said.

"I did not ask where you are from. I asked who you are. I believe you have recently discovered who you truly are," the voice said.

Wrenna spun around, searching the space, finally deciding the voice was coming from the thick fog that surrounded them.

"I assume you mean what my name really is. Is that what you're asking?" Wrenna said.

"You cannot know the truth without first accepting who you truly are. You must remove the veil you have worn for so long. You must peel back the many layers of what it is you and others have built to protect you from the truth before your eyes can truly see."

The voice was now coming from the space near the throne.

"Layers, what layers?" Wrenna asked.

Then the space of the throne began to change, and something started to appear. Wrenna blinked and shook her head, trying to bring whatever it was into focus. A circle of vines and clover, sitting atop a being's head, was the first to come into view. Slowly, hair became visible, white, thin hair, puffed up around the vine clover ringlet. Wrenna then realized it was a crown. Slowly, the entire body revealed itself. It was a woman, a very old woman. She wore a thick, very worn, and ragged gray cloak. Her hands were interlaced, resting on her lap. She had long nails upon her boney fingers. Wrenna wasn't able to see her feet due to the long cloak reaching to the ground. Her face was the last to become visible. Wrenna noticed her eyes immediately. They were solid, milky white, having no color at all. The lack of pupils made the female look frightening, along with her sunken cheeks and wrinkled face.

She spoke again. "Tell me who you truly are."

"I don't know what answer you want from me," Wrenna said.

"I am the Great Oracle. You have been given the gift of sight; do not waste it. You must look deep within and seek the truth for yourself. You must find out who you truly are before you will be given the answers you seek," the Great Oracle said.

Wrenna was unsure what to tell her. Over the last few days, Wrenna had discovered her life was an elaborate maze of lies.

"I think I am going to need more time to find out that answer. I am going to need a lot more time," Wrenna said, dropping her gaze to the clovers she now stood in. Wrenna looked back up at the Oracle, waiting for her to respond.

"Time is something I do not have to spare. My time is precious, and I do not wish to waste it on waiting for you to find yourself." Slowly, the Great Oracle began to fade out of existence.

Wrenna stepped forward. "Wait, wait, don't go. I'm not trying to waste your time. Please, forgive me. I was told I am a queen. Of what and where, I don't know, but please, can you help me understand?" Wrenna blurted out.

The Great Oracle stood frozen, halfway invisible, as if waiting for more.

Wrenna continued, "I feel something stirring inside of me. It's like a force that dwells within me, one I have just recently unlocked. I can feel it pushing its way out. It feels like there is something very powerful waiting beyond the precipice of my soul to be given permission to come into this world. Please, can you help me understand what it is? I have this yearning to know more about who this queen is and how I am to become her. How I can help the Fae, how I can help the humans. I want to make things right, but there are mountains of fear that are stopping me. It is what is holding me back from fully allowing myself to embrace what lingers within me. I can feel it. Please, can you help me to not be afraid?" Wrenna said, placing her hand on her chest.

The Great Oracle had apparently approved of Wrenna's speech, her body fully visible once again. "You can overcome any fear by facing it. Once you realize there is nothing to fear, fear itself becomes an illusion," she said.

Wrenna paused and thought. "There is so much I fear. I will never get my old life back. Things will never be the same. What if I am a failure? What if I can't become this Fae I am expected to be?" Wrenna asked.

"Your father came to me once, many years ago. Before you were even born, I had seen what your future would hold. I cannot say that all the things I saw for you back then will still be, but I can say that many of the things in my visions have come to fruition. Like you being here with me now. I knew that one day I would speak with you, but I wasn't sure what path you would be on. I can now see you have chosen the path of change, a path led by good. Wrenna, you will be queen one day, but for now, you will be the Savior. You will be the Bringer of Light," the Great Oracle said.

Wrenna paused, taking in the words that left the Great Oracle's lips. The Bringer of Light. She thought of the orange light that she had recently discovered within herself.

"Can you help me understand my powers? I am able to bring forth a light, a light so bright it blinds those around me. But that is the extent of what has manifested from the awakening of my powers so far," Wrenna said.

"You cannot rush the awakening process, but you must know that there is so much more to come for you. I have seen what it is you will be capable of. You, my dear child, will have the power to save those who are lost. You will be able to see what one's true desire is. Your power will allow you to determine if one is worth saving or if one is forever lost to the darkness that consumes so many. You will be the Bringer of Light to all of the earth. Above us and even deep below us," the Great Oracle said.

"How will I know when I am ready?" Wrenna asked.

"When the time comes, it will be a moment of pure clarity, of pure oneness with all that is you. Right now you might feel lost and confused, but the goodness within you will bring you the willpower to move forward and take on the responsibilities that have been bestowed upon you," the Great Oracle said.

"Why now? I mean, I have been living all this time unknowing of any of this and now all of a sudden, this knowledge and burden is mine to bear," Wrenna said.

"This burden has been given to you by your father. He is the one who has entrusted you with liberating those in need," the Great Oracle said.

"It is his fault they are all in need of rescue in the first place. So now it is up to me to fix this mess he has created?" Wrenna said with anger.

The Great Oracle smiled and said, "There is still much you do not know, but with time you will become more enlightened to what your destiny truly is. Until then, you must stop holding back what it is that lies in wait within you. Embrace it. As long as you stay on the path of choosing good and light over darkness, everything else will fall into place."

"Okay, so I just need to trust my gut instinct and go with that? That's what you are saying. I need to stop second guessing myself," Wrenna said.

The Great Oracle's wrinkled mouth began to turn upward like a small grin. "Wrenna Thain, you are on the right path to becoming who you truly are meant to be. Soon a great and mighty metamorphosis will take place, one so great, all the realms will drop to their knees and bow to you."

Wrenna recalled her vision of her mother there in the vast green space up on the surface. The words her mother had spoken to her. She recalled all the times Zelda had told her about her greatness. Even her father knew what Wrenna had buried within.

The Great Oracle stood and took slow steps down off the rocks where the throne sat. She walked towards Wrenna, coming to stand close enough, making Wrenna have to turn her gaze upward. The Great Oracle was just that: great. She was tall, and her energy was powerful. Wrenna could feel it as she got closer. Slowly, the Great Oracle reached out and grasped the fire opal that was hanging around Wrenna's neck. The moment her boney fingers wrapped around the opal, Wrenna felt her feet begin to lift off the ground. Her entire body became paralyzed. Some unseen force was lifting her upward. She could no longer see the Great Oracle but could feel her hand on the fire opal necklace around her neck.

The raspy voice came once again. "Your future is not written in stone; you will choose which path you follow. From there your destiny will unfold. You will not go at this alone, and you may even face a great heartache along the way. Your power is one of a kind, something no Fae past or present has ever seen before. It is a power that can save the souls of the lost. It can mold them into kind and just beings. Your power can change the trajectory of many who are lost. You cannot save anyone without first cutting the head off of the serpent or else the body will still move."

Wrenna was still held there in place, hovering, frozen, and could only listen.

The Great Oracle continued, "Wrenna, you will reach the darkest corners of the earth, bringing light where it is needed. In the future, many will turn to you for guidance. I foresee those lost, considered impure, who roam this earth, will be the first to seek your healing. You must go now and move forward with the faith that you have greatness within, along with the capabilities to alter the future of the earth."

Wrenna started to feel her body come back to life. She moved her head to look down at the Great Oracle. She still had her hands around the fire opal. Her milky white eyes looked up at her. Wrenna could see the many lines in her face much clearer, being so close. Wrenna found her voice once again and said, "I am ready."

Another loud zap, and Wrenna was sent back with the others. They were all still standing in the same place she had left them. They were no longer frozen in time; they were walking forward. No one had even noticed or felt the blip of stolen time, having no idea that Wrenna was gone and had returned.

"So what does this Great Oracle look like?" Willow asked Marrick.

"There are many stories of what she looks like, but they say she looks different for every chosen one. She never looks the same," Marrick said.

"Are you okay, Wrenna? You look pale," Abel asked, pulling Wrenna out of her trancelike stillness.

"Oh yeah, I am fine. Just tired," Wrenna said.

Wrenna wondered if she should tell them that she had met the Great Oracle or if she should keep it to herself. Not having the energy to talk, she just kept quiet and continued on the path with the others.

"We should be getting close now to the substation. Only a little bit further," Marrick said.

They all had been pretty quiet for the last few hours, exhaustion and hunger weighing on them all. Wrenna was curious if anyone else was taken away to meet the Great Oracle and they were just keeping it to themselves like she was. The thought of asking was quickly lost when Marrick stopped and pointed in front of them. In the distance stood a large building. Wrenna turned around to look back at the distance they had traveled, only seeing vast, barren desert, everything hidden behind the illusion.

"Do you think we should come up with a plan before we get to the substation?" Abel asked.

"Yes, definitely," Wrenna said.

"I may be of some help, if you don't mind, my queen. I can go and scout out the area first, take a look around. I am very good at not being seen. It's kind of my thing," Marrick said.

"Okay, if you think you will be okay, you can go on ahead of us and check things out. Once you come back, we can decide what we want to do from there. We can stay back here out of sight and wait," Wrenna said.

"Yes, I think that is a good first step. You all stay right here; you are far enough away and still hidden by the illusion. I will be back within an hour. If I am not, then you guys can decide what to do from there," Marrick said.

"Okay, sounds like a plan. But if you don't come back, we will come looking for you. I wouldn't ever leave you there," Wrenna said.

They both gave each other a brief smile. Marrick turned and took off towards the substation. Wrenna, Abe, Felix, and Willow all dropped their packs in a neat circle. Felix dropped down to his knees and fell to the ground. He hadn't spoken since Gemma ran off into the desert. Willow sat down next to him, exhaustion clearly taking hold of her.

Willow looked over at Wrenna and shook her head. "I don't know if he will be able to continue on," Willow said.

"Well, he can't stay here and just die. He has to keep moving with us," Abel said.

"He is having a really hard time. Can you give the guy a break?" Willow asked, raising her voice.

"I understand he's having a hard time; we all are. But if he gives up, he will be lost just like Gemma, just like Ashley," Abel said.

Willow huffed a breath and fell quiet.

"Let's all try to get him where we need to go so you guys can get back to the surface. We have to try," Wrenna said.

"I don't want to go back to the surface," Felix said. The first words he had spoken in a day. "I am done, done with all of this. I am tired of the pain, all of this pain. Every person I have ever loved in my life is dead. Things aren't going to get any better. We are all going to die. I might as well stop trying to avoid the inevitable," he cried.

"I can't imagine the pain you all have been through; I am so sorry," Wrenna said.

Felix lifted his head, wide-eyed, and looked directly at Wrenna. "It's your people that have done this to us. Your father. Your people are horrible, evil things. They are the reason for all of this!" Felix said with so much hate in his eyes. Tears ran down his face.

Felix stepped closer to Wrenna. His anger pushed into her, forcing her to step back. Abel quickly stepped in between Felix and Wrenna. He put his hands on Felix's shoulders.

"Stop, Felix! I know you are hurting; I know you are in pain, but this was not Wrenna's fault. She is not like those other Fae who have hurt us. She is different," Abel said.

"They are all the same. If you are too blind to see that, then I don't know what to tell you," Felix said as he got up and walked towards the substation.

Willow looked at Abel and gave him a brief, small smile and went after Felix. Abel just stood there, watching his friends.

Wrenna spoke. "Thank you, but he does have a valid reason to not trust me. You all have lived in such fear and destruction for so long, my people being the ones to cause it. I am not like them. Hopefully, soon I will be able to prove that to him."

"You have proved it. Look what you have done so far for us. Rescuing us from that cell, getting us to a safe place, and now risking your own life to get us home. I think you have shown that you are not like your father," Abel said.

He stepped in closer to Wrenna and wrapped his arms around her. Shocked, Wrenna resisted at first, but the warmth of Abel's body, his energy, made her feel at peace. Wrenna returned his embrace. They stood there for a brief moment, and then Abel let her go and turned and walked towards Felix and Gemma. They stood together about a hundred feet away. Wrenna sat down next to their packs, allowing them some time alone, just the three of them. Wrenna's heart continued to break as she watched them hug each other, Felix now sobbing. She could feel their suffering. She wanted to make it better for them and so many others.

Chapter Nineteen

After some time, the three humans returned to where Wrenna sat amongst their packs. They waited there for Marrick to return from his reconnaissance. Things were quiet. Felix had fallen asleep, and Willow pulled a book from her pack and began to read. Abel was lying on his back, looking up into the nothingness. Wrenna stayed quiet, lost in her thoughts. Today had been a lot for Wrenna. Her meeting with the Great Oracle replayed in her mind. She thought more about how she had held back, avoiding her responsibilities for so long. The words the Great Oracle said to her echoed in Wrenna's head over and over again. "Those lost... will be the first to seek your healing." Wrenna couldn't imagine how she would be able to heal the lost but hoped that the mystery of it all would unravel sooner rather than later.

Wrenna already felt a change happening. Since speaking with the Great Oracle, she felt as if a door had unlocked inside of her, releasing some of pressure that had been bearing down on her. Wrenna never had a choice in her life. Everything had always been decided for her. She was to become the leader of the city and be like her father. She was to be an example to the Fae people, do her duties, follow the rules. Now she was determined to make her own rules, to make her own path.

"You cannot save anyone without first cutting the head off of the serpent or else the body will still move." Wrenna recalled the Great Oracle's words. That bit didn't make complete sense to Wrenna. She thought maybe the Great Oracle was talking about her father, removing him from leadership and the other Fae following. Or maybe the Great Oracle was talking about Yama, the God of Death. Maybe she meant that the only way to end all of this pain and suffering and injustice was to cut his head literally off. Either way, Wrenna was motivated more than ever to end it and bring peace back to the In Between and the surface above. Wrenna was ready to reunite all.

After what seemed like forever, Wrenna started to think the worst had happened to Marrick. Just before Wrenna opened her mouth to speak, to devise their next steps without Marrick, he appeared in the distance. Abel lifted himself off the sandy ground and looked towards Marrick, as if he had sensed his approaching arrival.

"Finally," Abel said.

He stood up and reached his hand down towards Wrenna, who was still sitting. Wrenna put her hand in his, and he helped her up. Felix and Willow stayed in place. A few minutes later, Marrick was standing there amongst the group once again.

"So what did you find out?" Abel asked him.

"It's heavily guarded. There are a lot of patrol officers there. And Wrenna's father. They are looking for you," Marrick said, looking at Wrenna. He continued, "I heard them talking that the humans were missing and that they think they kidnapped Wrenna."

"Oh, great," Wrenna said.

"I did find a large bunker, one big enough to house a craft. I wasn't able to get inside due to the excess of patrol officers. I think if we return there, possibly when they are sleeping, we could get inside. It should be lights out soon," Marrick said.

"Okay, let's go," Wrenna said.

Abel bent down, pulling Felix up off the ground. Willow stood up as well. They all put their packs back on and began to follow Marrick.

Before she knew it, they had reached the substation. The landscape around the substance was much like Shambhala. It was surrounded by large boulders, giving them plenty of cover to hide behind. Wrenna couldn't see any Fae from where they hid. It all seemed quiet. Marrick motioned to follow him forward. They bent down, trying to make themselves smaller, less visible. The substation looked dark. Only a few lights were still on. Wrenna assumed her father would be back at the municipal compound by now, sitting at his desk, looking over endless paperwork. She wondered if he actually cared that she was gone, wondered if he was truly worried. Most likely, Chief Thain had other motives causing his concern. If the humans had actually kidnapped her, he would have been worried about the many questions it would bring once Wrenna had returned.

Once they reached the building, they pressed their bodies against the outside wall of the station, looking to Marrick, waiting for his next command. Marrick slowly sidestepped, keeping his back to the wall. He led them towards the back side of the substation. Soon the entrance into a large, fenced area became visible. Once they reached the open gate, they quietly ran in. There were no patrol officers keeping guard at the gate, which seemed off to Wrenna. Marrick led them to a large, circular rock pile, similar to the pit Wrenna had discovered days prior. They all hide behind it, pausing there for a brief moment to prevent detection. Wrenna looked between the rocks and just as she had thought, another fire pit.

Willow whispered, "What the hell is that?" as she also looked in between the rocks.

"You don't want to know," Wrenna whispered back.

Marrick peered out from behind the rock circle to check to see if it was clear to run to the large bunker in the center of the fenced-in station yard.

"Okay, we have to move fast," Marrick said as he took off running.

The others quickly followed him, heading to the only doorway into the bunker. Once they reached the door, Marrick placed his hand on the doorknob and twisted. It wasn't locked.

"This all seems too easy. Something isn't right. Stop! Wait a second. Something isn't right. No guards, no locks. I think this is a trap or something," Wrenna said.

Marrick dropped his hand from the door handle. They all froze.

Wrenna walked to the front of the line. "I want to go in first, just in case. If it is a trap, you all run. They won't hurt me," Wrenna whispered.

The others nodded, agreeing with Wrenna's idea. Wrenna turned to the door, reached for the handle, and pulled it open. She walked inside. The big space was mostly dark, and Wrenna couldn't see much. Her eyes went right to the center of the building where the only light shone. There stood Stiles with a grin on his face. "I have been waiting for you, Wrenna."

Wrenna slowly pulled the door shut behind her, hoping the others hadn't been seen.

"Stiles, I am so glad I found you," she said.

Wrenna quickly devised a plan to act as the victim, acting as if she had been running from her captors.

"You were looking for me? I thought we were the ones looking for you and those heathens you are with," Stiles said.

Wrenna knew at that moment she couldn't continue with her ruse. Stiles stepped closer to Wrenna, standing tall, dressed perfectly in his neat patrol officer uniform and shiny boots.

"Wrenna, did you actually think your father wouldn't find out what you have been up to? Did you think I wouldn't find out?" Stiles said.

Wrenna took a long inhale, trying to think what to do next.

"I know they are out there, those mutts that you have kindly befriended. Thinking you will be their savior and help them escape. There is no escape, Wrenna. There is nowhere to go," Stiles said as he got close enough to Wrenna that she could feel his breath on her face.

He lifted his hand to her chin, pulling upward with his cold fingers.

"I thought you and I had something between us. A future, possibly together. I thought we had the same values and goals for our city. The same goals as your father. But it looks like I am wrong." Stiles dropped his hands and turned his back to her, stepping back into the light.

"Same values and goals, are you serious? You and I are nothing alike. Anything we ever shared was a mistake, something I wish I could take back. You disgust me, Stiles. Your values and mine are on very different spectrums. You wish to destroy, hurt, and kill. I don't want to do any of those things. You and my father have been hiding these horrible lies from me for who knows how long. I am nothing like you or my father," Wrenna said.

As Stiles turned back to face Wrenna, an ominous smile crossed his face. Pressure started building in Wrenna's chest. She could feel her emotions begin to awaken something within her. She felt something lingering just below the surface, as if it was there lying in wait.

"You're right, you are nothing like me. You are a coward and weak. You must get that from your mother," Stiles said.

Wrenna felt a pang of anger press against her heart. She wanted to rip his head off, but she refrained. Stiles began to walk further away towards what looked like a desk. He pressed a button, flipping on more lights. With each switch, a different bay of lights clicked on. The large bunker was circular in shape. Each switch clicked a light on around the circular building, leaving the center dark. Wrenna looked around the large space, squinting her eyes, trying to make out what stood at the center of the building. Stiles finally pressed the switch to light up the massive center space, and there stood what Wrenna could only assume was the craft they had come all this way for. It was cylindrical, lying on its side. Wrenna could clearly make out the hatch that gave one access to the inside of the craft. It was maybe thirty feet long, big enough to transport things like prisoners.

"Is this what you are looking for, Wrenna?" Stiles asked.

Wrenna pulled her stare from the craft and looked back towards Stiles, who now stood just feet from her. She stepped back, bringing her defenses back up.

"What do you think you're gonna do, Wrenna? You wouldn't even know how to control this thing if you tried. Do you really think saving a couple worthless humans is going to do anything? Their kind is being slaughtered as we speak up on the surface. They are worthless. Their souls are lost. They are known to be the most impure of any. Is it really worth it for you to throw away everything you have, your future?" Stiles asked, trying to soften his approach.

Wrenna had seen this act before—the many times he came to her room late at night, looking for one thing.

"You do not know what my future is. I make my future, no one else. Not you, not my father, no one," Wrenna said.

The fire opal around her neck, now buried beneath her shirt, started to vibrate. Wrenna remembered what Zelda told her back when she helped her initiate the awakening of her powers. Zelda had said to breathe slowly, slow down her mind, and control her thoughts.

Wrenna began to focus. She needed more time. She took slow, steady breaths in and out of her nose, calming the powers that stirred within.

Stiles laughed. "You think your father did all he has done, breeding with one of those things, manipulating you, and grooming you all these years, just to allow you to throw it all away? Your father is a smart man. He has a plan for you, and there is no escaping it. Wrenna, don't make this hard on yourself. Those things out there, they aren't worth it."

Wrenna realized Stiles knew that the others were waiting outside the bunker. She continued on, trying to give them time to run.

"What is it that you bring to the table, Stiles? Your powers haven't even presented themselves. What do you provide to my father other than being his obedient slave that jumps at his every whim? You do realize that my father doesn't even like you. He just manipulates you to do his dirty work. What makes you think my father will even keep you around much longer? I mean, you are a dime a dozen to him," she said. Wrenna tried to put a sour taste in Stiles's mouth towards her father.

"You're a liar," Stiles said.

Wrenna continued, "I know you have this delusional thought that you and I will one day marry and lead the city, that you will lead the city. That's never gonna happen!" Wrenna said.

Wrenna saw out of the corner of her eye, behind Stiles where the craft stood, shadows of bodies shuffled by. It was Abel, Felix, Willow, and Marrick. Marrick twisted the hatch door, and Wrenna watched as they quickly slipped inside. Stiles was too engulfed in his rage to even notice, his eyes only on Wrenna.

She continued, "I myself have been using you all these years. You only helped cure my boredom, nothing else," Wrenna said, looking down at her hands, allowing Stiles to simmer in his anger.

"You lying bitch. I used you. You're my ticket to becoming the leader, and it will stay that way. Nothing will change that, not you, not your father," Stiles said.

"Myra might think differently," Wrenna said with a smirk.

Stiles's eyes grew big. Wrenna continued, "You think you're the only one who knows secrets here, Stiles? I know all your little secrets."

She saw lights begin to flicker on in the craft. They needed just a little more time. Wrenna had to keep Stiles's eyes on her, giving the others more time to get the mechanics of the craft figured out. Wrenna had hoped Abel had some idea of what to do to get that thing going. With his past military experience, possibly he would.

"I don't really know how you live with yourself, Stiles," Wrenna said.

"I live with myself just fine, Wrenna," Stiles said as he walked closer to her once again. He reached out and grabbed both of her arms and began pulling her towards the door. "Let's go. I am taking you back to your father. I'll deal with the mess you have made later. Those humans won't get too far from here. If we don't find them, then a Death Worm surely will."

Wrenna tried to pull away from Stiles. They began to struggle. Wrenna's fight or flight response kicked in, causing her heart rate to accelerate. Within moments, she felt a welcome pressure build in her chest. By now, Wrenna had started to recognize the powers that dwelled in her. She knew this was the first step of their awakening. She felt a burning intensify in her chest, but this time things seemed different. There was a strange buzz inside her. It traveled throughout her skeleton, reverberating outward. Goosebumps covered Wrenna's body from head to toe. Stiles noticed the change and abruptly dropped his hold. Soon, the orange light once again appeared from the space between her two eyes. Stiles immediately stumbled back, falling to the ground, covering his own eyes. Wrenna felt the familiar membranes slide into place, protecting her eyes from her own bright light. She didn't waste any time. She took off running towards the craft, spun the door hatch, and jumped inside. Just as she landed on the floor, she took a moment to pull her light back in, promptly shutting down her powers. This process was much easier to Wrenna now, no longer citing apprehension. A small smile crossed Wrenna's lips at this private realization.

Inside sat Willow and Felix. Wrenna reached back up to the craft door and flipped what was seemingly an obvious inner chamber locking mechanism. Within seconds, she heard Stiles outside the door, banging and yelling for Wrenna to open.

She could hear his muffled voice. "You can't stay in there forever. Where are you going to go from here, Wrenna?" Stiles said.

He had no idea that the others were inside with her. Moments later, the craft began making a light humming sound, as if it was powering up.

Stiles yelled, "What the hell, Wrenna? Get out of there before you hurt yourself and the rest of us."

Wrenna stood up, looking around.

"Abel and Marrick are doing this?" she asked Willow.

Willow pointed to a closed door. "They are in there. Abel thinks he can get this thing going."

Wrenna turned towards the door and pushed, going inside. She saw Abel sitting behind a massive panel with a million lights and switches. Marrick sat on the other side of the panel. He could barely reach.

Abel turned to look towards Wrenna. "This isn't far off from the control panel on some of the planes I have flown during my military days," he said.

Wrenna stepped closer.

"They definitely stole this technology from us because it is very similar," Abel said.

Marrick stood on his two feet in the chair to get a better look. "I have no idea what any of this is, but just tell me what to do, Abel," Marrick said.

In the moment, a loud bang came from the outside of the craft.

"I take it he isn't too happy out there. Does he know we are here with you?" Abel asked.

"He'll have to get over it. I think he thinks you all are waiting outside somewhere for me. Do you think you can get this thing up?" Wrenna asked Abel.

"I think so. I had a look through that old manual Ralf gave you, so I might be able to figure something out. If not I guess we will die trying." Abel smiled.

Wrenna looked outside, looking for Stiles, but she couldn't see him. The craft was pretty low to the ground, so it would have been impossible to see Stiles from where she was standing. Wrenna thought that maybe he was at the back of the craft, trying to find another way inside.

"I am gonna go make sure this thing is locked up and secure so that asshole can't get in." Wrenna turned and walked back through the door. Willow was sitting on the floor still next to Felix.

"Did you guys see any other way in this thing?" Wrenna asked as she looked around. There seemed to be only one way in and one way out. Right when Willow went to answer Wrenna, they heard yelling coming from the front of the craft. Wrenna ran back through the door, and Willow and Felix followed. They all couldn't fit inside, so Willow and Felix peeked their heads in.

"What is it?" Wrenna asked.

"Your good buddy must have gone for help," Abel said.

Wrenna looked out the front window and saw what looked like twenty or more patrol officers. Stiles stood with them.

"Wrenna, you spoiled little bitch, come out now. I am losing my patience."

Stiles obviously couldn't see inside. There must have been some sort of tint or shield on the front window.

"I am going to gut that Fae if he talks about you like that again, good lady," Marrick said, placing his hand on his small knife.

The group of patrol officers walked closer to the craft, forming a big circle around it.

"You aren't going anywhere, so stop messing with our craft. Your father worked very hard to acquire that, but I am sure you don't care. You know, Wrenna, you are a spoiled, lazy little brat. Don't you think it's time you grow up and act like an adult for once? Just because you don't get your way, doesn't mean you can act out and mess everything up that your father has worked so hard for," Stiles yelled.

Wrenna leaned in over Abel's shoulder and yelled back, "Kiss my ass, Stiles."

Abel laughed as he flipped a few more switches.

"Bad news, Wrenna. I don't think this thing has enough power to actually fly," Abel said.

"Well, that isn't an option right now. If we don't get this thing going, Stiles and all those Fae out there will kill you all. And the Gods only know what he will do to me," Wrenna said.

The patrol officers started pounding on the outside of the craft, thinking that the sound would push Wrenna out.

"Good lady, my queen, I feel you have the strength in you to power this craft. Seek what it is we need at this time to help us, and I believe you have the capabilities to manifest it," Marrick said.

Wrenna just looked back at Marrick, taking a moment to try to comprehend his words. "I am still learning. My abilities are only emitting a light. That's all I have been able to conjure," she said.

"There is more. You just have to open yourself up and allow it to surface. What do you think that light is made up of? It is energy from within you, my queen," Marrick said.

"How do you know that?" Wrenna asked.

"Everything is made up of energy. Very few have the abilities to manipulate that energy. You must try. Take what you have learned about yourself so far and use that to focus on what you seek. Find the light like you have before, but this time choose where you want that light or energy to flow. Remember, with that opal upon your neck, it can be very dangerous when invoking one's powers. You must choose positive energy and use your powers for good. The fire opal is known to amplify one's powers, so you must aim for a manifestation moving you towards right-thinking," Marrick said.

Wrenna placed her hands on the front panel of the craft, wanting to make a connection with the mechanics she would be trying to reach. She then closed her eyes. Wrenna began to slow her breath, breathing in and out of her nose. Finding her inner space, the place she had stored her most joyful memory. She quickly set her intention, pointing her thoughts to only good.

She recalled the words Zelda had spoken to her. "If your mind and thoughts are not steadied, your powers can overcome you."

It was hard to keep her focus with all of the patrol officers banging outside. Wrenna slowed down her mind, blocking out any noise the best she could. Soon the loud banging sounds became muffled and eventually stopped. Wrenna felt like she was the only one there. She sensed a calmness flooding her, her body and mind at peace. She found the memory of her mother holding her tight and used that once again to generate her powers. She began to reach down deep inside of her chest, seeking the light, pulling it up. Within moments, the light moved down her arms and out of her fingertips. Wrenna saw the brightness of her light and felt her built-in protection, her hidden eyelids, slide into place. Abel and Marrick covered their eyes, and Willow and Felix began to back out of the tiny space.

Wrenna noticed an energy moving throughout her entire body, flowing from her fingertips into the places of the craft that she was touching. Several more lights flickered on, and sounds began to emanate from the front control panel. Whatever she was doing was working. She had no idea how but knew it was working.

"Wrenna, I can't see, so you're gonna have to flip the engine switch," Abel said, assuming Wrenna had achieved their goal.

"Where is that?" Wrenna asked.

"Look for a large red button, most likely towards the center of the control panel. It will have a clear cover over it. You will have to lift the cover off and flip the switch," Abel said.

Wrenna looked around the panel towards the bottom. She found what she was looking for perfectly placed between Abel's two knees. Wrenna leaned forward, reaching over Abel's shoulder. She had to press her body into him in order to reach the covered engine switch. She opened the cover and flipped the switch. The craft's engine rumbled, and the entire thing jolted with the power of the engine. Wrenna was caught off guard and fell forward, headfirst, into Abel's lap. As she landed, she quickly pulled her power back in, dimming the bright orange light that was engulfing the craft.

"Holy shit, I am so sorry," Wrenna said.

Her head was down, and her bottom half was up, her legs kicked in the air. She felt Abel's hands go to her waist and start to pull her upward.

"Are you okay?" Abel said with a laugh as Wrenna found her feet on the floor once again.

Wrenna felt her face go red. She looked down at Abel, her hair a mess and her shirt disheveled.

"Dang, this thing has some power," Wrenna said.

Soon the loud bangs and yelling from outside the craft pulled Wrenna from trying to think of something to say.

"Are you two done? We gotta get out of here," Marrick yelled over the loud engine.

Abel reached for one last switch and flipped it. Wrenna felt the craft's front end begin to lift up.

"You better get back there with Willow and Felix. Find a seat and strap in," Abel said, still holding a smile on his face.

Wrenna quickly turned and went back to the others, hearing Abel and Marrick buckling themselves into their chairs.

Willow and Felix had pulled down two chairs that were folded up against the wall and started buckling in. Wrenna could hear the patrol officers outside still screaming and pounding on the craft's metal walls. Wrenna pulled her seat down and jumped in, quickly pulling the straps around her shoulders. As the craft lifted up, the front end maneuvered to point upward.

"Where is this thing going to go? Are we going to blast through the building?" Wrenna asked.

"Well, we gotta go up. So I hope they have a way to retract the ceiling of this place or else we are about to blast through it," Willow said.

The power from the engine grew, and the entire craft began to vibrate rapidly. Wrenna closed her eyes and held on to her straps. The craft was now standing on end. Wrenna's body pressed back into her chair.

"God, I hope Abel knows what he is doing," Willow said.

"We are gonna die anyway. Why not in a fiery explosion?" Felix said.

Wrenna heard Abel yell from the front of the craft, "Hang on, guys, we are about to take off."

Chapter Twenty

Wrenna felt like she was going to be sick. The craft thrust upward, pressing Wrenna even harder into her chair. She couldn't move her head to look over at either Willow or Felix, and she couldn't hear anything but the loud engine. Wrenna wondered if Stiles and the others scattered when the engine turned on, still believing it was Wrenna controlling the craft. Wrenna's heart pounded in her chest; her mind began to race.

What if we don't make it and we all die?

She couldn't believe where she was at and what she was experiencing at this very moment. Her life had changed so drastically from the boring days of lying around in her tiny bunk room, reading books.

The craft moved upward. Wrenna wished she could see out the front window. Her imagination ran wild, picturing the view to the outside as the craft thrust upward. She assumed they were traveling through one of the many tunnels dug by the Fae and human slaves of the past. She could feel in her body the change in pressure. It was like a two-ton weight was pressing down on her. Then out of nowhere, the engine began to level out, and the cabin became calm and smooth. Wrenna was now able to look over at the others.

"How are you guys doing?" she asked.

"I feel like I am going to barf, but other than that, good," Willow said.

Felix sat with his eyes closed and didn't respond.

"Abel said he thought there was a tunnel directly above us and the craft was docked at a launch station. I guess he was right," Willow said.

Wrenna turned her head back, facing the doorway to where Abel and Marrick manned the controls. There was no way she could get up from her seat and get to that door. She would just fall down towards the back of the craft. She stayed strapped in and waited.

The craft traveled, smooth and steady, making its way up the tunnel. What felt like a day later, Wrenna noticed a shift in the engine, going from smooth to a rumble once again.

She heard Willow yell from where she was sitting. "I think we are there," Willow said. Wrenna felt her heart begin to beat harder in her chest. She could only imagine what to expect once Abel had docked the craft on the surface, who would be there waiting for them. Since they had stolen a craft from her father's patrol officers, she could only assume more patrol officers would be waiting for them upon landing.

Wrenna felt the craft stop, feeling the sensation of it just hovering in place. Wrenna held her breath and waited. Soon the craft began to move backwards. Only moments later, there was a loud boom, and the craft rocked violently side to side.

Wrenna closed her eyes. *This is it; we are going to die.*

She felt a jolt, and the craft stopped. The front end, where Abel and Marrick sat, began to lower down, the entire body of the craft slowly leveling out. Wrenna, Felix, and Willow no longer were pressed into their seats but were now sitting upright. Wrenna didn't feel the pressure on her chest anymore and was able to place her feet on the floor and move her body more freely.

"I think you are right. We have landed. Remind me to give Abel a kiss for getting us through that. I don't know what I would have done without him," Wrenna said to Willow and Felix, no longer having to yell over the engine.

"I'm sure he would appreciate that," Willow said with a laugh.

Wrenna peered over at the two humans who were now unbuckling the straps to their seats. Felix's face didn't change much, but Willow was smiling. Wrenna got out of her seat and stood up, curious to see what the outside looked like. She went to the door and pulled it open. Inside, Abel and Marrick were unbuckling their straps as well.

"We have arrived," Abel said with a smile.

"Wow, thank you so much. I am so glad that it is over with," Wrenna said, looking at Abel.

"I'm just thankful that it went as smoothly as it did. There were so many things that could have gone wrong. Luckily this thing has an internal programming already uploaded into the control panel. It follows the same route over and over again. So once you find how to activate that, you are good to go. Plus I did have a little experience. I once got to train on a few prototypes, planes that had some of the more advanced technology. The technology was extremely similar to this," Abel said.

"Well, I am so thankful for you both. I don't know what we would have done to get here. If I had to operate this thing, I would have killed us all," Wrenna said.

Marrick hopped down from where he sat and looked up to Wrenna. "Are you ready to face whoever waits for us outside? We have docked at a landing station, one that I can only assume will be manned with some of your father's patrol officers. How do you want to go about handling this? It is only a matter of time before the others from below will surface somewhere else and inform who is here. Abel and I believe that there is only room for one craft per tunnel. So the officers below will have to find another craft in another tunnel in order to travel to the surface. That will buy us some time. Maybe you can go out first since you are Fae. They will most likely recognize you, which is to our advantage now. You can tell them you came here with your father's permission to scope out things. Devise some kind of diversion so we can get off the craft without being seen," Marrick said.

Willow and Felix poked their heads into the small control room.

"Okay, I'll go out first. I'll let them think I came here alone. I don't think they will believe that, but we can try. I'll lure them to the front of the craft so you all can see me, and then that will be your chance to sneak out," Wrenna said.

"Sounds like as good of a plan as any," Abel said.

Wrenna turned and headed back towards the exit door. The others went into the control room and shut the door behind them. Wrenna turned the hatch lock and pushed the door open. Standing outside the door was a tall, skinny Fae male dressed in a patrol officer uniform.

"What the hell is going on? We aren't expecting passage at this hour!" proclaimed the officer.

Wrenna recognized him immediately. "Yeah, sorry about that, this was an unexpected launch," Wrenna said.

The young officer looked at her and furrowed his brow. "Aren't you Chief Thain's daughter?" he asked.

"Yes, Wrenna, nice to meet you. Think we might have met once. Aren't you dating Myra Elsher? Issan, right?" Wrenna asked.

"Yeah, that's right. We went to the academy together. Honestly, I knew who you were the moment I saw you. The hair," Issan said, pointing to Wrenna's head. "I didn't receive any word that you would be traveling here. Are you alone?" he said as he peeked in the craft, looking for anyone else.

Wrenna walked forward, backing him out of the craft, taking steps to get out as well.

"Yeah, I have been training to learn how to operate one of these crafts, you know. I wanted to know how things work since I will soon become chief and all. So I decided to test my training out. Please don't tell my father," Wrenna said, peering up at him with her best pouty face. Wrenna reached out and placed her hand on his arm. "Can we please keep this to ourselves? I just got so bored back home. I needed some adventure, you know?"

Wrenna decided she would pretend she knew it was wrong but was feeling rebellious, hoping the officer would understand and maybe give her forgiveness.

"Well, I am just here to keep guard of the station. The other officers have left for the evening. Why don't you follow me to the officer barracks, and you can wait until the others arrive in the morning. I mean, I wouldn't feel comfortable letting you leave this substation. It's pretty dangerous outside," Issan said.

He turned and began walking towards a door, one Wrenna assumed would lead them to the barracks.

"Okay, that sounds good." Wrenna followed him. She looked back towards the craft, hoping the others were watching and would know when to exit.

Issan led the way. "I can't believe you just took a craft without anyone knowing. That seems crazy. Well, Stiles will be here in the morning. I'll let you talk to him about it. I am sure he is pretty pissed," Issan said with a laugh.

"Stiles already knows I took the craft, and yes, pissed is an understatement," Wrenna said.

Issan looked back at her with wide eyes and laughed. "Hey, better you than me, I guess."

They soon reached a doorway to a large room, one that looked like the barracks back at the municipal compound. It was lined with bunk beds, dark, and smelled awful.

"Why don't you wait here? Make yourself comfortable," Issan said.

"Look, you seem like an understanding Fae. So I am going to level with you. I am here for a reason. I can't really tell you the reason because you will think I am crazy, but if you could just act like you never saw me or something, that would be so helpful," Wrenna said.

"How do you expect me to act like I never saw you? You literally docked the craft in the station I am guarding. There is no other reasonable explanation," Issan said.

Then, out of nowhere, a loud bang came from the landing station behind them. Issan quickly turned and ran towards the sound to investigate. Wrenna went after him, hoping that the others were just simply making a diversion of some kind. Issan busted through the door, only to find nothing.

"You did come up here by yourself, correct?" he asked Wrenna.

"Yes, of course," Wrenna answered.

"Maybe you picked something up in the tunnel on the way here. That is a definite possibility," Issan said.

"Pick up something? Like what?" Wrenna asked.

Issan raised his eyebrows. "Maybe you need to wait back at the barracks. Let me look around and make sure it's safe," he said.

The officer turned and went towards the craft, and Wrenna

followed. He walked around the outside of the craft, slowly taking in anything that could be out of the ordinary.

"The hull looks good. No damage or signs of something attaching itself to it," he said out loud to himself.

"What could attach to it?" Wrenna asked.

"I told you to stay back." He shook his head, annoyed. "Look, there are things that live in those tunnels, things you don't want to encounter. We call them Tearer Hogs. They will eat you alive in only a few bites if you don't watch it," Issan said.

"Oh, wow. Have you seen one before?" Wrenna asked.

"Yes, they are about the size of you or me. They don't have eyes but can smell meat from a mile away. They have massive paws attached to their heads that they use to dig around in the dirt and sand. They are not something you want to mess with. We have lost a few officers to one. We captured it and disposed of it in one of the fire pits," Issan said, still walking around the craft, looking under it to make sure nothing was hiding.

Wrenna figured the others had left the craft, but she wanted to be sure. The last thing she wanted was for the others to stumble upon one of those Tearer Hogs.

"Well, it looks to be clear to me, but we can't be too sure. It could have run off and is hiding somewhere, waiting," Issan said, looking at Wrenna with a concerned look on his face.

Suddenly, another loud bang blasted out, coming from the back corner of the station. The corner was covered in darkness, making it impossible to see if anything was hidden there.

"Okay, there is definitely something over there. Please get back. I don't want you to get hurt. I'll be the next thing they throw into the fire pit if I let that happen," Issan said. He moved towards the darkened corner, his body on high alert. "If it's a Tearer Hog, please run to the barracks and shut the door behind you."

Wrenna didn't move. She wasn't sure if it was an actual Tearer Hog back in the corner making the noise or just Abel, Felix, Willow, and Marrick tricking the officer.

A loud howl radiated from the corner, along with a shuffle of movement.

"What the hell was that?" Wrenna asked.

"Tearer Hog for sure," Issan said as he stepped into the darkness.

Wrenna stood back and watched as the officer vanished.

Instantly, there came a rustle of clothes, a few grunts, and then a loud thud. Wrenna took off running towards the dark corner, pausing just before. She took a few deep breaths and awakened her light, shining it into the darkness. She found Issan lying face down, his body limp, his eyes closed. Standing over his body stood Abel and Marrick. Willow and Felix pressed themselves against the far wall, all with their eyes shut.

"Oh, thank the Gods. I thought you were a Tearer Hog eating him alive," Wrenna said as she quickly dimmed her light.

"We overheard you both talking about Tearer Hogs, and then I had an idea," Marrick said, opening his eyes.

"What, to pretend to be one?" Wrenna asked.

"Exactly," Marrick said with a smile.

"Then I used a takedown tactic I learned in the military: put him fast asleep," Abel said with a light laugh, eyes opening.

"He is still alive, right?" Wrenna asked.

"Yeah, I just knocked him out for a little bit. He'll wake up with a headache, that's all," Abel said.

Wrenna looked towards Willow and Felix. "What about you two?" she asked them.

"We did absolutely nothing," Willow said, looking at Felix.

"Makes sense," Wrenna said, laughing.

"Can we get the hell out of here, please? I think I'd rather face those giant things out there than stay here with the Fae scum for one more minute," Felix said.

Abel quickly turned to look towards Felix. "Hey, let's not be disrespectful towards the two that have saved us and risked their lives to bring us back here," Abel said.

"Well, if it wasn't for their kind, we wouldn't be going through all this shit in the first place," Felix said.

Abel turned to look towards Wrenna, his gaze apologetic. Wrenna agreed with Felix. It was the Fae that had done this to them.

"He's right," Wrenna said as she turned and headed towards the doorway that led to the barracks.

Marrick ran to catch up with her. "This is the surface. It is a much different place than Shambhala. I want you to prepare yourself," Marrick said.

"The Nephilim?" Wrenna asked.

"Yes. We mustn't storm out of here unprepared for what's out there," Marrick said.

They all continued on, walking to the other side of the barracks where a large door stood; it had two great windows. Through the windows, they could only see darkness. Abel ran up, stopping just in front of the door.

"We can't just barrel out there. It's not safe. It is dark out there, so we won't be able to see much. Those giants, the Nephilim, hunt by smell. It's our fear that they can smell from miles away. So no matter what, we have to try to stay as calm as possible. Much like the Badlands, you can't panic."

Before Abel could finish, Felix pushed past the rest of them and walked through the door. Willow took off after him, both vanishing into the darkness.

Abel stood in the open doorway, yelling after them, "Guys, wait!"

They didn't respond. Wrenna watched as their silhouettes vanished into the darkness.

Marrick looked up to Wrenna. "I guess we follow them, but stay close and stay calm," Marrick said.

Abel walked out the door first. Marrick followed, and Wrenna was last to leave the building.

"Should I use my light to help us see better?" Wrenna whispered.

"No, they will see it. Here, take my hand so we can stay together. Our eyes will begin to adjust some, which should help us see better," Abel said.

Wrenna placed her hand in Abel's. All three of them walked out into the darkness, not knowing where they were or what would appear before them. Until they heard a scream up ahead.

"Willow," Abel whispered.

Chapter Twenty-One

The screams grew louder, more visceral and full of utter fear. Wrenna couldn't see anything and was completely trusting Abel to lead her.

"I need to awaken my light; it can help us see where she is," Wrenna said.

"No, don't. They will see us. We will find her, just follow me," Abel said.

Wrenna hoped they would find her in time. Whatever was happening to Willow, it did not sound like she would last much longer. From the darkness ahead, Wrenna heard a gurgling sound. She was close. Abel began to speed up his walk, Wrenna being pulled close behind.

"Be careful, my friends," Marrick called out as he fumbled his way closer to them.

On Wrenna's next step, her toes hit something lying on the ground, causing her to thrust forward and slam to the ground, palms first. She couldn't see anything, only feeling a wet warmth under her palms. She erupted into an automated frenzy, feeling around beneath her, searching. Wrenna's hands soon landed on what could only be body.

"Wrenna, are you okay?" Abel asked.

Wrenna looked up towards the sound of Abel's voice but could only see an outline of him. She saw a small shadow standing next to him, recognizing it was Marrick.

"I fell on something; it feels like a body," Wrenna said.

"Let me help you up," Abel said. Wrenna felt a hand land on her shoulder, and he began lifting her up off the ground.

"Do you think it's Willow or Felix?" Wrenna asked.

"I don't know, I can't see well enough to make out who it is," Abel said.

"Willow, can you hear me? Felix, where are you?" Marrick whispered.

No one responded. Wrenna tried to wipe the wetness off her hands onto her already wet pants. "I am covered in something. I think it's blood," Wrenna said.

"Here, let's go over here," Abel said, pulling her towards a large shadow of what looked like a structure of some kind. "Let's get inside here, where it's safe."

"Wait, let's go back. I can feel the face and try to make out who it is," Wrenna said.

She wished she had thought of that while kneeling on the ground next to the lifeless body, but it all had happened too fast for her to think.

"Let's get into a safe spot. Whoever it is out there, we don't want to end up like that," Marrick said.

"Duck down, Wrenna, so you don't hit your head," Abel said as he led her into the structure.

Marrick easily followed. Wrenna sat down, leaning her back into what felt like a rock wall. She slowly took deep breaths. Wrenna needed to verify if what she was currently covered in was truly what she had thought it was. Concentrating and pinpointing her focus to just a small sliver of her powers, she began to draw it out to the tip of a single finger, praying to the Gods that the structure would obscure the light as it illuminated the small space. She really focused on keeping her powers funneled into one spot the best she could. The light gave off just enough brightness, allowing Wrenna to see Abel bent down, with his hands on his knees, his head avoiding the slab above them. Marrick stood upright as if this makeshift shelter was made perfectly for him. As the light radiated from her finger, Wrenna was more able to see her hands, arms, and the rest of her own body. She gasped softly, now knowing without a doubt she was in fact covered in blood. Abel and Marrick's eyes were wide as they also took in the sight of the blood that covered Wrenna's body.

"That was a body I tripped over out there; this is their blood," Wrenna said, her voice trembling with fear.

Abel crawled closer to Wrenna, wrapping his arm around her shoulder. "You have to try to stay as calm as possible. We can only pray that body out there isn't Felix or Willow. Hopefully they are somewhere safe out here in the darkness. They have experience with all of this; they know what to do. But if you begin to panic, those things will find us," Abel said sternly.

"The Nephilim!" Marrick said, looking around the small space.

"Yeah, I bet that's what happened to whoever that is out there." Abel took a long exhale and continued talking. "Every encounter I have had with a giant has been different. I guess it depends on their mood. I'm not really sure. Some will toy with their victim, maybe maim them and watch as they suffer. Letting them slowly die and leaving their body there to rot. Others are quick to scoop up their victims and straight away eat them in one bite. And then there is the worst of all. I have only seen, one time, a Nephilim actually devour only the soul of its victim. I will tell you, witnessing someone die that way was the scariest thing I have ever seen," Abel said.

"They take the souls to the Death God. He feeds upon them," Marrick said.

"Seeing that, it changed me. Watching someone's soul being ripped from their body is something you can never forget," Abel said.

"Sounds awful," Wrenna said.

"If they aren't killing, they are destroying whatever comes into their path. All of our cities and homes lay in ruin due to the destructive ways of those things. Now it is as if hell is on earth," Abel said.

Wrenna continued to allow the small light to pour from a single finger. Marrick sat down, then dropped his pack and leaned back on it, closing his eyes.

Wrenna looked over to Abel and asked, "What were things like here before... all of this?"

"It was wonderful. It felt like the world was boundless, an open book to do whatever I wanted. After leaving the military, I was honorably discharged. I decided to travel and see the land. I left the small city I had grown up in with just a bag full of clothes and a map. I saw so many beautiful places. Places I will never forget. About around the time my impromptu adventure ended was when out of nowhere, there were these people, or I guess, Fae, that showed up, demanding things from our leaders. They went around meeting with many of our city officials, making these ridiculous demands. They were hoping to make a deal with our leaders. This deal was, they get to take some of the humans, and we get to continue to live freely. Well, our leaders didn't agree. They refused to allow them to take our people. So in return, the Fae released one of the Nephilim giants upon one of our largest cities. It demolished the city and took hundreds of people by force. After that, our leaders panicked and brought in the military, thinking they had the capability to take down one of those things. They soon found out that they could not kill it. No amount of ammunition could take one down. We tried tanks, bombs, even nuclear missiles, but nothing worked. In the process of trying to kill the Nephilim, we killed off and poisoned much of our land. Leaving our food supply decimated, many of our people dead, and the city leaders and government desperate. So they made the deal. We would allow the Fae and these beasts of theirs to come here, take who they wanted. In return, most of the elite and important people would be safe. Meanwhile, the rest of us had to hide and scrounge for food and live like rats amongst the destruction. After the nuclear weapons were used, our sun no longer came up. The earth was covered in complete darkness. The ground was poisoned, our livestock all died, and the people have been living like this ever since," Abel said.

"How are the elite able to survive if crops no longer are able to grow?" Wrenna asked.

"We heard from a group of people we met who were traveling together that they found the place where the elites were hiding. It's a great mountain. Within the mountain, they have built a massive bunker, the size of the entire mountain. All of the most important people on earth were brought there. In this bunker, they have plants of all kinds being able to grow by using an artificial light system. They said this mountain was guarded by many of the Nephilim, so getting inside was pretty much a death sentence," Abel said.

"This is the bargain that your father is bound to with the Death God," Marrick said, his eyes still closed. "The Nephilim are also servants of the Death God," Marrick continued.

Abel looked at Wrenna, raising his eyebrows.

"So the Fae people made a deal with the Death God to capture humans from the surface and sacrifice them—for what reason though?" Wrenna asked.

"I'd say for the same reasons as the humans gave in and made their deal. Fear. The Fae, your father and his father before, and many more before them had one ultimate goal: to take control of the surface. They want full and total power of as much of this planet as they can get their hands on. In order to do that, they must appease the Death God. He is the only one that can stop them from what they want. They have to keep him happy and in return, he will leave them alone while they devise a plan to defeat him," Marrick said, keeping his eyes closed with his arms now behind his head.

Wrenna huffed out a loud breath, anger filling her chest. "This is the shit I was born into. This is what my life would have been if I stayed there and obeyed my father?" Wrenna said.

The other two didn't respond, but Wrenna knew what their answer was.

"What should we do now? My whole plan was to help you guys get back to the surface, but there is nothing here for you all to come back to," Wrenna said.

Wrenna's heart broke for all of the humans who had been suffering here on the surface all this time. She was disgusted in her people, the Fae.

"What can we do to stop this, to fix this?" Wrenna asked.

"I don't really know, honestly. I think the elites that are held up in that mountain are too afraid to do anything. They are afraid of the Nephilim, and they are too selfish to risk their own lives to try to help the rest of us," Abel said.

The moment Abel spoke his last words, the ground rumbled beneath them. Wrenna pulled her light back in and gripped Abel's arm.

"Is that one of them?" Wrenna whispered.

"Shhhh," Abel said.

The ground shook beneath them, slowly growing more violent. Wrenna knew what it was: a Nephilim coming towards them. Her heart began pounding. Her body felt clammy and sweaty.

"I can smell you from here, Queen!" A loud, raspy voice sounded from outside the rock structure. The darkness seemed to have gotten darker, and the ground now stood still. Wrenna could hear her heart beating in her ears. It was pounding out of her chest. She put her hand over her mouth to try to keep from making any noise. The rumble of the giant's movement shuddered through Wrenna's body. She could feel it getting closer. Wrenna felt Abel pull her closer to him, squeezing her tight.

"You reek of your father!" the Nephilim said. They began to hear things move outside the rock structure. It sounded as if the giant was moving things around, searching for them.

Wrenna sensed an odd change in her body. A buzz of energy, not from herself but from another source, grazed her skin. She paused, trying to collect herself and attempting to understand this new awareness being presented to her.

"The smell of your fear is like a field of wildflowers," the Nephilim said.

Wrenna's skin was covered in goose pimples, the hair on her arms now standing on end.

Marrick whispered, "Stay here, dear lady. I will lead him away. Then you two run."

"NO! Wait, Marrick, don't go!" Before she could finish her sentence, he was gone. "Marrick," Abel whispered.

Moments later, Wrenna noticed a blip of light from a crack in the rock wall. The ground stirred beneath them once again, but this time it was moving in the opposite direction. Wrenna and Abel crawled to the opening they had entered through, their eyes looking in the direction of the light. It looked like a small fire. It would appear and then disappear, moving further and further away. The buzz of energy that once enveloped Wrenna's body was now fading away.

Abel leaned into her and whispered, "Did you know Marrick could create fire?"

"No. Well, maybe," Wrenna said.

They watched a massive dark shadow, darker than the darkness around them, follow Marrick's fire. Wrenna remembered seeing Marrick tap several lanterns back at his cave home, and they became lit with just his touch. Now she watched him light up a path, helping her and Abel to get away.

"Come on, let's go," Abel said.

"We can't just leave him," Wrenna said as she felt tears begin to slide down her cheeks.

"We can't let what he is doing be for nothing. Let's go. He has given us a chance to run away," Abel said.

She felt Abel pull on her arm, leading her in the opposite direction, away from the Nephilim.

"No, stop, I'm not leaving him. I'm not doing this again. Aren't you sick of running? Aren't you sick of watching your friends die?" Wrenna said, her voice louder than a whisper.

Wrenna pulled away from Abel and looked to where Marrick was still lighting small fires and the dark shadow was still following.

"Hey, you! I'm over here!" Wrenna yelled.

All went still around her for a brief moment. The buzz of energy that once touched her skin immediately returned. A sickness moved in the pit of her stomach. The Nephilim changed its direction, now heading straight for where Wrenna and Abel stood. Wrenna squinted her eyes, trying to get a better image of the beast to no avail.

"Wrenna, we have to go. It's coming this way. Let's go," Abel said, trying to pull Wrenna the other direction.

Wrenna's feet stayed planted to ground. She was frozen. As the Nephilim moved closer, Abel pulled harder on her arm. Wrenna stood firm, her thoughts imagining her impending death.

"There you are, Queen," the giant said.

As if it was natural, Wrenna did the only thing she could think to do: awakening the light from within and shining it upon the incoming giant. The internal membranes of her eyes moved into place, preparing for the blinding brightness of her light. The pressure pushed outward in her chest once again. And like a dam breaking loose, the orange light spilled from her. The ground and all the things around her came into view. She could see Abel; he had turned his back to her and was shielding his own eyes with his hands.

"Abel, go, hide! It's not safe for you here!" Wrenna yelled to him.

Wrenna turned back towards where she thought the Nephilim had been standing. Her light filled the sky, and the giant came into view.

Wrenna peered into the massive black eyes of the Nephilim that stood before her. It had two great horns spiraling from its head, gigantic sharp teeth, and it stood so incredibly tall. Wrenna had to lift her chin towards the sky to take in the full enormity of the beast. Wrenna's light didn't seem to affect the giant. It didn't turn away or cover its eyes.

"You are a measly little thing, aren't you?" the Nephilim said.

Its voice rumbled in Wrenna's chest.

"Queen Rayna, in the flesh. I have only heard stories of you, and now here you are before me," the Nephilim said.

Wrenna waited for it to scoop her up and eat her whole, but it only stood there, studying her. She waited for the giant's next move, her light billowing outward.

"Well, I am waiting," the Nephilim said.

Wrenna quickly turned and took off running in the opposite direction, leading the beast away from Marrick and Abel.

The giant ran after her. Each step it took shook the ground, causing Wrenna to trip and fall. She got back up each time and continued on. She could see ahead in the distance what looked like the remains of several large buildings. She forced her legs to keep moving, thankful she had taken up running in her past life. Soon she came to a half demolished multiple story building. She ran inside. She immediately pulled her light back in, trying to hide her exact location within the building. Wrenna ran up several levels of stairs, stumbling as the building shook. Rubble and dirt fell down around Wrenna, and debris hit her and knocked her over.

"Good idea, Wrenna, now what?" she said to herself, second guessing her choice to hide in the building.

"You can only hide from me for so long, little queen!" the Nephilim yelled from outside.

The buzz of energy moved through her now, the closeness of the beast causing a sinking feeling in her stomach. Fear emanated from her being. With that fear also came the agitation of something inside her. Wrenna had felt this feeling before. It was as if something else resided in her. It was stirring, moving around now. A heat like she had never felt started to spin and move, coming from her center and traveling to each limb. Wrenna lay there, sprawled out over several stairs, looking up through a hole in the roof. It was like she couldn't move. Her body no longer her own, this thing inside her slowly possessed her an inch at a time. Every cell in her body was changing ever so slightly. She could feel herself transforming from the inside out.

This is it; I'm dying. This is what dying feels like.

She had lost all connection with her body. The once dormant energy was now controlling her. A loud ringing vibrated in her ears, a sound that was not coming from the outside world but from within. It was so loud, it felt as if it were piercing her brain. Just before she lost herself completely, she heard a loud snap. It was as though the sound resonated from deep down in the core of her being. It was as if something had been unleashed. Something that had been buried down was now free. This something didn't feel foreign; it was a welcoming feeling. Wrenna's chest lurched upward, like some unforeseen force was lifting her. Her entire body was pulled from the stairs where she lay. Her feet had now found the floor. Her sense of control had returned, but there was something else still there residing within her. The breath was pulled from her body when she noticed something was different. She lifted her hands toward her face, taking in the shocking outward transformation. Through the darkness, her skin was barely visible, but she was able to see. She blinked a few times, unsure if her mind was playing tricks. It appeared that her skin looked different. Wrenna dropped her hands, wiping them on her pants, making sure it wasn't grime she was actually seeing. She lifted them back up towards her eyes, taking in once again this change. Her skin was no longer the traditional pale, iridescent Fae skin. It had become golden. Wrenna's eyes widened in shock. She flipped her hands over and then back again. She moved her gaze up each arm, noticing that her ancestral markings were no longer there. Wrenna continued examining her body, full of astonishment.

Before she could dwell on the changes for too long, the giant spoke again. "You still in there, Queen? Come out and let's finish this. I am tired of your games." His voice shook the building.

Wrenna slid the protective membranes back over her eyes as if she had been doing it her entire life. Confidence now flooded her. Fear seemed to have left, along with her pale skin. She felt the new, bold energy stir within her once more, encouraging her to let go of anything else that might be holding her back. And so she did.

Like it was as natural as breathing, Wrenna called upon her powers. This time, flashes of colors moved behind her eyes. They swirled and spun about. She pushed more, freeing her light from the space between her eyes. The light poured out, not the orange color as before, but now a bright angelic white. It swiftly filled the stairwell and poured into every crack and crevice of the broken building. Wrenna's spine began to tingle with a coolness, like nothing she had felt before. The coolness ascended up her body, filling her neck and shoulders, soon reaching her head. Her mind became calm, her thoughts no longer a jumble. She now had full and complete clarity of her now reborn self.

Then a whisper: "You can defeat them. You just have to manifest what it is you want, and it will be yours."

Wrenna spun around, searching for the voice, finding no one near. She paused, taking in the message and the feeling she now felt come over her body.

"I will defeat them," Wrenna said aloud.

With that intention set, she headed up the crumbling stairwell, moving to the next floor.

"I can smash this building with just one fist and crush you, Queen. But I would rather taste your sweet soul upon my lips," the Nephilim said.

The fragile building began to shake as Wrenna climbed further up the stairwell, her light illuminating the way. She finally reached the roof, finding the door still intact. Wrenna pulled it open and stepped out into the darkness, locking eyes with the waiting giant. Wrenna's heart faltered for only a second before she bore down and pulled from the spiraling flow of energy moving within her.

"Well, beast. Here I am. Kill me if you must, but I will not go down without a fight," Wrenna said.

The Nephilim bent down and laughed, baring his yellowed teeth. "How is it that you expect to fight me? You are just a weak little creature," the Nephilim said.

Wrenna planted her feet into the rubble-covered rooftop and looked up towards the giant. He smiled back at her, lifting his hand and moving to reach for her. Wrenna closed her eyes and focused her mind, connecting completely with the force that now resided in her. She directed this very powerful surge of energy towards the Nephilim, making it pierce the giant's skull and flow into its brain. The giant, feeling her presence now, stumbled backward in shock. Wrenna bored into its mind, pushing deeper. She used the energy as an extension of her own mind, allowing it to bleed into the giant's consciousness. Soon flashes of memories echoed Wrenna's mind. Images of the Nephilim torturing and killing helpless humans flicked by. Wrenna saw and felt what the giant felt. How each and every time it took a life, amusement and enjoyment filled the Nephilim's mind. It never once had a second thought about what it was doing. It never once felt sadness or remorse.

"Get out of my head, little bitch!" the giant yelled.

The Nephilim's words pulled Wrenna from the cacophony of screams bellowing from its thoughts. Realigning her focus, she moved her energy, manipulating it into finger-like tendrils. She used the tendrils to encase and grip the beast mind. The Nephilim froze, held in place, unanimated.

"I can see you like the things you have done to these people. Slaughtering the innocent and taking their souls. It only brings you joy. And for that, I must end you," Wrenna yelled to the paralyzed Nephilim.

Wrenna moved the tendrils, allowing them to weave through the Nephilim's mind. She knew that without a mind, nothing could survive. Its existence would no longer be. So she squeezed tighter. As her powers pressed more into what was essentially the giant's life force, she could feel its consciousness slipping away. Wrenna pulled more energy from herself, adding to the force within the Nephilim's skull. And just like that, its body went limp, and it fell back, plummeting to the earth. The building shook, the ground rumbled, but Wrenna kept her feet firmly planted, standing strong. She ran to the edge of the building and looked down at the now lifeless body of the great Nephilim. A big smile crossed her face. She knew she had just defeated what was thought to be indestructible. At that moment, Wrenna knew she was ready. Ready for whatever it was her future would be. She looked towards the sky and took in a deep breath, embracing the feeling of her new body, the power and the energy. It felt as if she had been lost her entire life, and now she was home. She was reborn.

Chapter Twenty-Two

Wrenna walked back down the stairs of the decrepit building, her feet shuffling through the remains of someone's past. She looked around, finding the broken hole in the wall she had entered through. Wrenna peeked out, allowing her light to illuminate beyond the building, casting upon the ground. Abel and Marrick both emerged from hiding, their eyes pressed shut. Wrenna quickly dimmed down her light just enough to allow the two to open their eyes, showing her newfound control. Abel's eyes widened as he took in her new appearance.

Marrick dropped to one knee and lowered his head. "My Queen."

"How? You killed it! How did you kill it?" Abel said as his eyes continued to wander over Wrenna's golden skin.

Marrick continued to rest on one knee, his head bowed.

"Marrick, you can get up," Wrenna said. She looked at Abel. "My powers." Wrenna held her arms out in front of her, taking in the changes to her skin, having a loss for words. "I feel so much energy moving around inside me," she said, looking down to the now standing elf.

"Seems that your powers have completed their awakening. The metamorphosis is complete," Marrick said, looking up at Wrenna.

"I have never seen anything like this. No other Fae in our city had their skin completely change colors once their powers awakened," Wrenna said.

"You are different, my queen. There is no one on this earth that is like you," Marrick said.

"How do you know so much about me, Marrick?" Wrenna said.

Before Marrick could answer, Abel yelled out to them, "Holy shit, you made his brains mush. Look, they are oozing out of his ears." He had moved closer to the dead giant.

Wrenna and Marrick moved to stand next to Abel. They all took in the size of the beast.

"If you can kill one, you can probably kill them all. Don't ya think?" Abel asked.

"We mustn't forget about Yama. I don't think he will just sit idly by and allow that. He controls them. He probably already knows about what happened here. We have to be careful," Marrick said.

"If Yama controls them, he'll probably be sending more here soon," Wrenna said.

"I have never seen two of them together. I think they are very territorial. So I would say we have some time. I don't know how they communicate with one another, so we should stay aware and try to be as quiet as we can. We still need to try and find Willow and Felix," Abel said.

"They can't be far," Wrenna said.

Wrenna took one last look at the dead Nephilim. She turned and began heading back towards the substation. Abel and Marrick followed. Wrenna kept her light dim to help with the search, and they tried their best to retrace the path they had taken earlier. The massive piles of rubble and debris loomed over them, Wrenna's light making things easier to see. Buildings were pulverized, and their scraps littered the ground. It was hard to tell where one started and another ended. Wrenna looked around, taking in the devastation. She took in a sharp breath once she noticed scattered amongst the debris were bodies. Most were buried beneath the rubble, with only bits of the body sprouting out, the rest barely visible. Then Wrenna remembered the body, the one covered in blood that she had tripped over earlier. She began to scan the scene, looking further down the trail. Up ahead, lying across the path,

Wrenna saw the body tangled up, still there. She turned and looked back at Abel and Marrick.

"There are so many bodies," she said.

"Yeah" was all Abel was able to say.

They kept moving forward towards the fresh body on the path. They all seemed to have the same thought.

Abel broke the tension. "I have seen them toy with a person for hours, like it's a game," he said.

"I went into that thing's mind before I killed it. I saw the horrors your people have been facing. I saw the evils that now walk upon the surface." Wrenna shook her head. "It's gut-wrenching," she continued.

Wrenna scanned the area as they continued walking. She allowed her light to reach a great distance. The carnage continued for miles, beyond where her eyes could see.

"The entire surface looks like this?" she asked.

"As far as I know. Every time we come across others out here, they all have the same stories," Abel said.

"This is part of the bargain your ancestors made with Yama. They help him get here on the surface to feed, and in return, they are safe from him and all the beasts he has unleashed to do his bidding," Marrick said.

Wrenna shook her head in disgust. They walked further, getting closer to the broken body. Then they all stopped. The body came into full view, and the realization of who it was hit them all at once. Abel took off running towards it. Once he reached it, he dropped to his knees. Wrenna and Marrick walked closer, both affirming the identification of the dead body. It was Felix, or what was left of him. His body was badly mangled, all twisted and disfigured. He was the one Wrenna had tripped over. It was his blood that now covered her shirt and pants. Abel buried his head in his hands and wept. Wrenna moved closer to Abel's side, placing her hand on his shoulder, offering her condolences the only way she knew how. Marrick stood looking off into the distance, allowing Abel and Wrenna a moment. It was silent around them. The only noise heard was the cries of Abel, his heart broken once again.

After some time, Abel stood up without a word and grabbed Felix's arms and pulled his body off the path. Wrenna watched, allowing him space. Abel then began piling broken boards on top of Felix's body, covering him up.

"I can't bury him like he deserves. So this is the least I can do," Abel said, looking at Wrenna, tears covering his face. He said it as if he was asking but also making a statement.

Wrenna answered, "I am sure he would appreciate anything."

Marrick and Wrenna helped. Once they finished, Wrenna and Marrick stood quietly to give Abel a few moments alone with his friend.

After some time, Abel finally spoke. "I am so tired of losing people." He shook his head.

"I'm sorry, Abel," Wrenna said.

He looked down at the ground, rubbing his eyes with his hands. "Well, what now?" he asked.

"I'm not sure. I haven't quite thought that far," Wrenna said.

All three sat there silent, as if in contemplation.

Wrenna finally spoke. "Where can we find this mountain, the one where your leaders are hiding?"

Both Abel and Marrick shot quick glances at Wrenna.

"I came here originally to bring you all home. I've done that. I wouldn't say successfully, but we got you back here. You lost two, possibly three of your friends in the process, and for that I am sorry, Abel. But I can't just go back, knowing all of this shit is happening. And now that I know I can do something about it, I'm gonna. Not only for your people, but for the Fae living below in complete and utter oblivion. For the elvish people too, for Marrick's family. I could go back home, go back to pretending that none of this ever happened. I could go back to hiding in my bunk room, buried in books. But I don't want to go back to that, back to being someone who lacks any self-respect. I can't allow my mother to have gone through what she did for nothing. I feel like now I have a purpose, and I am going to fulfill that purpose even if I die trying," Wrenna said.

The two males continued to look at her as she continued.

"I think the only thing we can do is start here on the surface with your leaders. They have hidden long enough. It's time they take responsibility for what they have done to their own people," she said.

"I will follow you, my queen. I believe in this purpose. I believe in you," Marrick said.

"I have come this far, I might as well finish this. I am tired of living on the run, in hiding. I want my life back," Abel said.

Wrenna smiled back at the two males. "Thank you both."

Those were the only words Wrenna could muster. She felt a kinship to her newfound friends. Something she rarely felt in her lifetime, and she was happy about it.

"I wonder if Willow made it somewhere safe," Abel said.

"I hope so too," Wrenna said.

Her mind flashed to the memory she saw while possessing the Nephilim. The images of it eating a powerless human trapped in its mighty hands. She hoped that hadn't happened to Willow.

"Abel, do you have any idea which direction we should go to find this mountain?" Wrenna asked.

"Now that I am able to see better, I do sorta recognize where we are. This is close to where Felix and I stayed a few nights in an old wine factory. There were other people staying there as well, nice people. They told us they had come close to the base of that mountain but were too afraid to even attempt climbing it. They told us it wasn't far from here actually. They said maybe thirty miles or so," Abel said.

"How long would it take us to walk there?" Wrenna asked.

"Oh, probably two or three days. Maybe more depending on what we encounter along the way," Abel said.

Wrenna turned and looked back towards the substation. She wondered if Issan was still passed out or if he had awakened and called for the other patrol officers to return.

"Do you think we could take that craft? Would you be able to fly it long distance?" she asked Abel.

"I might, but I can't promise anything. I think that would get us there much quicker and help us to avoid any more Nephilim. The time we got picked up, the craft seemed to be working alongside the Nephilim. So I think if we can get it to fly, we should go for it," Abel said.

"Did they land the craft and then take you into custody, or what happened?" Wrenna asked. Marrick listened.

"No, the craft stayed hovering over us. I'm not sure how it works, but there was this glowing orange light that surrounded us. The next thing I knew, we were all being lifted from the ground. It was like some sort of force pulling us upward. Next thing we know, we are inside with Fae officers all surrounding us," Abel said.

Wrenna looked down towards Marrick. "You know, when I was back in the municipal building, in the room where Ashley..." Wrenna paused. "Well, you know, in that room, there was a cabinet. It was filled with tubes. Each tube was filled with an orange glowing substance. Do you think the two are connected somehow?" Wrenna asked, looking back to Abel and returning her gaze to Marrick.

"Well, I think that seer, Arban, does some terrible things. There are stories that he experiments on Fae. He was trying to find a way to extract powers from them," Marrick said.

"So that's where the missing Fae have gone. It was Arban taking them and using them for his little experiments. Another sinister thing that I am sure was orchestrated by my father," Wrenna said.

"These are just stories. If he was to take a Fae's powers, especially a Fae who had a fire opal, they could amplify that power even more," Marrick said, reaching for his fire opal necklace.

"Maybe they took as much technology as they could from the humans but needed more. So they started killing their own," Abel said.

"I think they are still doing it. They have to be. Why would they have tubes full of a strange orange substance? Plus, that would explain where this opal I found came from. Arban probably dropped it by accident. That Fae is wicked," Wrenna said. Wrenna paused in thought. She looked to Marrick and asked, "Why does Yama want impure souls? I don't think I have ever asked that."

"They say he is creating an army," Marrick said.

"An army for what?" Wrenna asked.

"To take back the place he came from. The stories say Yama was exiled from a place beyond this earth. A place he called home. Where that is, no one truly knows. So when he was sent here to the deepest part of the earth, he began building his army. An army he plans to use to take back his home."

Wrenna took a deep breath, exhaling completely.

"This is so messed up," she said.

"Yeah, that's for damn sure," Abel said.

They stood there once again, all three taking a moment to grasp the enormity of their situation.

"Well, I think we should go back into the substation and see what we can do. I don't know who will be there waiting for us, but I guess we'll see. If it all works out and we get that craft in the air, we can head towards that mountain. Then we can see if we can sway your leaders to help us. If we tell them I can take down a Nephilim, I don't know, maybe they will be more willing to join us," Wrenna said.

She started walking towards the building. The two males followed.

Chapter Twenty-Three

Wrenna reached for the two large glass doors, pulling them open. She abruptly stopped before entering.

"Let me go in first. Alone. If there are officers there, I'll talk to them, but I don't want to risk anything happening to you guys," Wrenna said.

"I'm going with you," Abel said, shaking his head.

"Me too, to the ends of the earth," Marrick said with a reassuring smile.

Wrenna knew that she couldn't talk them out of it. They had already gone too far together.

They walked through the barracks, slowly entering the large room where the craft currently sat. Standing, waiting for her once again, was Stiles.

"Well, did you enjoy your little excursion? Did you see what you needed to see? I love the new look, by the way," Stiles said.

There were at least twenty other patrol officers standing behind him, one being Issan.

Stiles stepped forward more. "Who are these mutts you have with you?" he asked smugly, lifting his chin to point towards Marrick and Abel.

Wrenna saw Abel and Marrick each stepping up and standing at her side.

"I don't know, you might remember slaughtering some of his people," Wrenna said, looking towards Marrick. "Or you might remember dragging him to a cell, holding him hostage there until Arban was ready to do whatever it is he does during his little experiments," Wrenna said, looking towards Abel.

"No, I don't seem to recall. Of course I am very busy these days, you know, getting rid of trash. It all starts to look the same after a while," Stiles said.

"You should be ashamed of yourself, honestly. What is in it for you, Stiles? What is my father giving you for doing all of this?" Wrenna asked.

"You," Stiles said.

Wrenna paused. She had been making it so easy for Stiles, allowing him to lie in her bed, giving him access to her life. After all, it wouldn't be her decision anyway. She fell right into their game. Wrenna's skin flushed red with shame under her new golden hue.

"Well, I am glad my father doesn't make those decisions for me anymore. I'm choosing my future now. He no longer has any say in what I want or who I'll be with," Wrenna said.

She took in a full breath and straight off, her light emerged, falling on Stiles and the other patrol officers. She held back, keeping her powers reigned in, only wanting to give just a glimpse of her newfound transformation.

"Pretty impressive. Looks like you are becoming exactly what we need to finish this," Stiles said with a smug smirk.

"You want to know what I have become, Stiles? Something you will never be. I have become someone who wants the best for everyone, no matter the species. I believe in goodness and freedom. I am not selfish and greedy like you and my father. I am the change that will fall over those lost and struggling. The things my father wants, what you want, I will never accept, I will never be okay with," Wrenna yelled.

Stiles laughed, not taking any of Wrenna's words to heart. "So is this slimebag your new late-night roll in the sheets?" Stiles asked as he looked towards Abel but talked to Wrenna. "She's not the best in bed, but she is coming along. I did teach her as much as I could," Stiles said to Abel.

Abel rushed forward, Wrenna quickly grabbed his shirt, pulling him back.

"Don't fall for it. He's just trying to push your buttons," Wrenna said.

Stiles continued, "Or maybe you're sleeping with the elf. That would make more sense." Stiles laughed, looking around the room at the other patrol officers, who then quickly joined in.

Marrick pulled his small knife from his belt loop.

"Oh, looks like this little guy wants to fight," Stiles said.

Wrenna moved forward, standing in between Stiles and Marrick.

"I'm going to give you all the opportunity to walk away. Let us take the craft, and no harm will come to you. But if you choose to try to stop us, I can't promise what will happen next," Wrenna said, trying to intimidate the officers with her words.

Stiles laughed. "Wrenna, what makes you think you are capable of killing? You just said you believe in goodness. I mean, come on. You have lived such a sheltered, privileged life and now you think you are some sort of vigilante, willing to kill if necessary. I don't think you've got it in you," Stiles said.

He began walking closer, getting only a few steps away from Wrenna.

"A lot has changed. I have learned that I am willing to do whatever I have to to make things right for the good of the Fae and the humans. I don't want to kill anyone but if it comes to that, well, that's what has to happen," Wrenna said.

"You think she lacks the ability to kill? Why don't you go ask that dead Nephilim out there?" Abel said.

Stiles paused, looked towards the ground, sniffed, and rubbed at his nose with his hand. The patrol officers all froze, holding their breath.

"You had a run-in with a Nephilim, you say. The one that roams around here?" Stiles said, pointing towards the doors that led to the exit. "You know, your father did say you would be powerful one day. I don't know if I ever really believed him," Stiles said.

"I don't want to have to puree your brains like I did to that giant out there, but I will if you try to stop us," Wrenna said.

With those words, Stiles bolted forward, grabbing Wrenna's shoulders. He flipped her around and pulled her into his chest. Stiles drew a knife and pressed it firmly into her neck. Wrenna, now facing where she had been standing moments ago, looked back at Abel and Marrick. She saw fear in their eyes.

Stiles pressed a kiss to her cheek. "I knew you weren't as strong as you were putting on," Stiles said.

The other patrol officers began to form a large circle around them all, moving between Abel, Marrick, and the exit.

"You guys are surrounded. Why don't you tell your little friends to give up and make this easier on us? I promise I won't hurt them," Stiles said into Wrenna's ear.

Wrenna looked at her two friends. They stood frozen, waiting for her next move. Stiles slid his free hand down Wrenna's body, cupping her breast.

"For old time's sake," he said, whispering into Wrenna's ear.

Wrenna sensed energy begin to stir beneath her skin. The same energy she felt before she faced the giant. A calm fell over her. Her body began to relax in Stiles's grip. He shifted as if noticing. The fire opal around Wrenna's neck glowed brightly, seeming to be in sync with her powers. Wrenna looked back at Stiles.

"Wrenna, is this all worth it to you? Losing everything that has been given to you for some worthless lowlifes?" Stiles said with the knife still pressed into her neck.

Wrenna kept her mind clear, not giving Stiles's words any footing to disrupt her blissful state. She continued allowing the force within her to emerge once again, feeling again a cool, moving spiral of energy travel up her spine. Her head and neck filled with a crisp awareness. Wrenna could feel the abundance of power linger, waiting to be freed. She took in another deep breath, twisting her powers into small tendrils of moving energy. Each tendril coiled and crawled from Wrenna and snaked their way into Stiles's mind. He froze, clearly noticing something but unsure just yet as to what. Wrenna worked her fingers of energy throughout Stiles's mind. Reading his thoughts, evoking his consciousness. Wrenna began to feel Stiles's emotions, his senses, his every thought. The activity of his mind began to pour into Wrenna's. She was overcome with arrogance, pride, deceit, anger. All these things filled

Wrenna's consciousness like they were her own. She felt everything he was feeling at that moment and in all the moments before. A thick sludge of pure evil overwhelmed her senses. Wrenna felt herself take in more deep, calming breaths. She was trying to pull herself out of the sludge and find her way back to her own mind. It was as if time around her stood still, Abel and Marrick still standing there, waiting. Wrenna, now able to distinguish her own mind from Stiles, decided to make her presence known. The tendrils of energy compressed and constricted Stiles's mind. He let out a loud gasp.

"What the hell are you doing, Wrenna? Get out of my head, you bitch!" Stiles yelled, pushing Wrenna away.

Stiles stumbled back, falling to his butt. He pulled his knees into his chest and put his hands on his head.

"I told you, Stiles, I will do whatever is necessary. I don't want to hurt you. Please don't make me do this," Wrenna said.

Stiles yelled to the other officers, "Get them!" He was still sitting on the ground, now shaking back and forth.

Wrenna quickly moved, reaching for more of her powers, allowing multiple strands to spring forth and slither their way out and into each one of the officer's minds. Every one of them shut down, their feet planted in place. Within seconds, the officers fell to the ground. Some were screaming and some were still lost in the pain of their mind, blankness in their eyes.

"Stiles, I will do what I have to to fix this, the mess you, my father, my family has made. I don't want to have to kill you and everyone else along the way. How would I be any different than you?" Wrenna said.

No one spoke. Abel stepped forward and placed his hand on Wrenna's shoulder. "You are right, you don't want to be like them. There has to be another way."

Wrenna looked into his eyes, tears streaming down her face. In her mind, the memory of Stiles laughing and tossing those innocent humans into the fire pit played over in her mind.

"Stiles is a murderer. He doesn't care about me or your people. He only cares about himself. I saw into his thoughts; he is a bad Fae. I don't think he will ever change," Wrenna said.

"Do you want their deaths to haunt you for the rest of your life? Trust me, there is always another way," Abel said.

Wrenna turned back to the room of Fae flailing about on the floor. Her anger pushed her to bear down a little harder. Stiles and the officers writhed in pain, causing them to shake uncontrollably. Wrenna knew what they deserved, and she wanted them to get what they deserved. Marrick stepped forward, standing between Wrenna and the Fae.

"My queen, you are not a murderer, you are a savior. You must remember that. You can change this cycle of never-ending death. You have an opportunity to make things different. Spare them," Marrick pleaded.

Wrenna contemplated Marrick's words.

Marrick continued, "You can see what truly drives each of these Fae. Look within each of them. You will see what it is that is motivating them in their actions. You can see whether their soul is lost to darkness or if they still have a chance to make themselves better. Use the gift of your powers. Use it to cast your own judgment upon them, see if they can be redeemed or if they're destined to continue with evil," Marrick said.

Wrenna turned back to Stiles, who now was lying still on the ground, blankness in his eyes. Wrenna returned to his mind, searching for the truth of Stiles and what drove him. What motivated him? Was he entirely bad or was there a morsel of goodness hidden within him? She looked into the other officers' minds, one at a time. Each one's mind was littered with evil, impure motivations, these motivations being what led them to be who they were and to do the things they had done.

"Save them. Help them see the good and become better," Marrick said again.

Wrenna pulled from deep inside. She closed her eyes again and breathed deeper.

How can I help them? How can I change them and make them better Fae males? Wrenna prayed to the Gods some sort of answer would soon come to her.

"I can share with them a part of me that is pure. A part of me that is good and giving. I can fill them up with love and kindness, giving them a new sense of motivation, a new sense of being better," Wrenna proclaimed.

She felt her heart flutter, feeling like it was going to jump from her chest. The fire opal glowed brighter, and the air around her began to move. Wrenna pulled from her own heart strands, allowing positive energy to flow up through her tendrils of power. She felt them loop around the life force of each officer. She felt her energy flow freely into them, replacing the bad with good. The darkness that once lurked within their minds, the darkness that controlled them, was now filled with her light. Wrenna's light. It was like peeling back many layers of darkness, filling the empty spaces with light. She could feel a shift in their minds, a change, like a veil had been lifted. Each officer opened their eyes, blinking away what was there before and being born again to a newness, a place of purity and kindness. Wrenna looked around to each officer, and she could see the change. It radiated from them like a glowing light. She had reached them, changed them, saved them.

Wrenna brought her attention back to Stiles's mind, choosing to save him for last. The darkness inside of his mind was so thick Wrenna could barely weave her way through it.

She spoke to him from within his thoughts. *Stiles, it's not too late for you to change.*

Only Stiles could hear Wrenna's question. The others around her just stood, frozen in time, unknowing of Wrenna's actions.

Stiles, I don't think this is who you really are. I don't think you want to live like this. I think you are just too wrapped up in what my father wants you to do. You have been too busy trying to please, trying to be someone you are not, Wrenna said in his thoughts, speaking directly to Stiles.

Stiles spoke out. "You are such a disappointment to your ancestors, to your father. You let this worthless human sway you with his dick, and now you think you can change the world. Well, you can't. There is no hope. This darkness is who I am. It is who I want to be!" He laughed.

Wrenna squeezed a bit more, pressing into him. She allowed her words to penetrate his thoughts again. *Then I have no choice. I must get rid of you and what it is you represent.*

Stiles spoke outwardly once again, the others only hearing Stiles's side of the conversation. "You are weak. You don't have it in you to be rid of me. Or do you have a little darkness in you after all?" Stiles said.

Wrenna paused, realizing he was speaking the truth. If she were to kill him like she had the Nephilim, she would be no different than him. Wrenna looked at all the newly changed officers, their eyes clear. They looked back at her, waiting.

"I need you all to restrain him and take him to the cells. Lock him there until I get back," Wrenna said.

Issan, the officer from before, stepped forward. His face looked softer, younger. He reached down, lifting Stiles up off the ground. He was still paralyzed by Wrenna's powers.

Wrenna looked into his eyes. "Thank you, officer," she said.

Another officer stepped up to help, wrapping a locking tie around Stiles's wrist. Issan didn't speak. None of the officers did, they just obeyed Wrenna's request. Issan and a few others dragged Stiles off.

"You are a worthless whore, just like your mother! You're a traitor! Just wait until your father finds out what you have done! You will pay for this!" Stiles yelled as Issan took him away.

The other officers all turned, fell into a single file line, and headed towards the barracks. Wrenna was able to relax her shoulders a bit now. She turned and looked at Abel.

"I'm sorry he spoke about you and your people like that. He is—"

Abel lifted his hands, stopping Wrenna from continuing her thoughts. "You do not have to apologize for him or anyone. I know you are not like him or your father," Abel said with a small smile.

"Thank you," Wrenna said. Not ready to discuss what just happened, Wrenna looked to her male friends and spoke. "Let's see if we can fly this thing," Wrenna said as she moved towards the awaiting craft.

"I think flying straight up and landing is probably the easy part. It was all programmed into the software. This craft is really only used for going back and forth from the In Between to the surface. Now, switching it over to manual pilot and actually flying it may be a whole other challenge," Abel said as he followed Wrenna and Marrick to the craft.

"All we can do is try," Marrick said.

Once inside, Abel scanned the control panel. He looked for a way to deprogram the installed flight patterns. Wrenna had no clue about any of the lingo he was using as he pressed different buttons and turned different dials. She stood between the two males lost in all the buttons. Abel flipped a switch that was encased in a clear box, causing an alarm to sound. Wrenna covered her ears.

"I don't know how to override this. I'm not sure if this is going to work," he said.

"What if we get an officer to help us?" Marrick said.

Wrenna took in a big breath, trying to think, trying to figure out what they should do. There was no time to walk thirty miles on foot, risking getting caught or worse, facing another Nephilim. She could go ask one of the freed patrol officers, like Marrick's suggestion, but there was something driving her to figure this out herself. Marrick's voice pulled her from her thoughts.

"You were able to make your way into the minds of those officers and the giant, right?" Marrick asked.

Wrenna just looked at Marrick. They both knew the answer.

Marrick continued, "Well, what if you were able to weave your way into the mechanical system of this craft? Maybe you could access the engines and driving mechanisms?" he said.

Abel looked up to Wrenna. "It could work," he said.

"I can try," Wrenna said, lifting her eyebrows.

She placed her hands on the controls and closed her eyes. She pulled from her powers, coaxing a few small tendrils outward. She moved tendrils to the ends of each finger, allowing them to flow directly into the control panel. Now being more familiar with her powers, she was able to keep her light dimmed, finding her complete focus on the flow of energy. The lights on the control panel lit up all at once.

"Well, you are doing something," Abel said.

Wrenna continued to focus as she pulled more power, more energy from her body, willing it to fire up the mechanics within the craft's engine. She was now able to see inside the engine, taking in its varied complexities. She took in the massive size of the engine, noticing it was surrounded by long tubes, similar to something she had seen before. Tubes like the ones that were stored in the cabinet back in the room under the stairs at the municipal compound. Within the tubes was the same orange substance. Only these tubes had a soft glow, barely visible to the naked eye. Wrenna plunged her energy into the gas-like substance. Right away, memories started to flash into Wrenna's mind. Memories that were not her own. Painful, terror-filled memories from someone who had suffered greatly. Wrenna's knees buckled. Her hands went to the back of Abel's and Marrick's chairs. She was transplanted into someone else's body. In her bones she could feel excruciating pain. Her skin felt like it was being peeled from her body. She heard screams, ones that were not her own. In another flash, she was on that table in that room under the stairs. She blinked her eyes a few times, and above her stood Arban. In one hand he held a large blade and a set of toothed forceps in the other. Wrenna was reliving someone else's memory of what they had gone through on that table. She felt Arban reach into her chest, clamping the forceps down on something inside. He dropped the blade down on the small silver table and grabbed a syringe with a long, thick needle. He plunged the needle into a place deep in Wrenna's chest. She knew she wasn't really there; it was only a memory. Fire grew inside her chest, and more screams billowed out around her. Through the tears in her eyes, Wrenna saw Arban lift the syringe filled with the orange glow. She squeezed her eyes closed tight, feeling an emptiness engulf her body. She blinked once more and was back in the craft. Abel and Marrick now stood with their hands around her, keeping her from falling to the floor.

"These ships are powered by the stolen energy from Fae people. That's what he had in those tubes in that room under the stairs."

She looked at Abel, knowing he would know this room.

She continued, "They have been taking the power from the Fae, draining them of it and using it to power these crafts. The Gods only know what else they have been doing with it," Wrenna said as a stream of tears poured down her face.

They took a few moments. No one spoke.

Wrenna was the first to break that silence. "My father is evil. How could he do this to the Fae he says he is trying to protect? They trust him."

Wrenna stepped forward, placing her hands back on the panel. She sent the tendrils of power thrusting into the engine, heading straight for the tubes. She pressed her energy, allowing it to mix with the stolen powers. She took in a few deep breaths, and then the engine powered up. The rumble of the engine shook the floorboards. Wrenna pulled in another breath, allowing her energy to flood each wire, every valve and switch. She became the engine; she became the craft. The force that once rested in her now gave life to the craft, making the two one. Wrenna imagined the craft slowly rising from the landing pad. The craft then emulated those thoughts. She kept her eyes closed, keeping a steady hold on her powers. She heard Abel flip several switches.

"This switch is supposed to open the overhead roof panel, but it's not working," he said.

Wrenna sensed panic in his voice.

"Wait, look, that officer! I think he is opening the roof for us!" Abel yelled.

Wrenna allowed her gaze to turn out the front window, just in time to see Issan standing there, his hand pressed down onto a button.

Wrenna smiled. *He is way too good for Myra Elsher.*

Wrenna closed her eyes once again, returning to maneuvering the craft. She was able to spread her scoop of vision to the front of the craft, giving her a clear view of the outside. She could see all the way around them, detecting every angle and edge of the long, cylindrical craft. Pulling more energy, she was able to lift the craft higher, slowly moving it up and out past the building's frame. Momentarily, they were outside, engulfed in darkness. Wrenna heard more switches flipping as Abel turned on the outside lights.

"Thanks," Wrenna said to Abel.

One less thing she would have to worry about.

"I'll do what I can to help from here," Abel said.

Wrenna's eyes took in the space around the craft as it floated above the building.

"Do you know which direction to go from here?" Wrenna asked Abel.

"If we stay west, we should head right into it. Our nose is currently pointing north, so can you rotate the craft to the left a bit? I'll tell you when to stop. I'll use this compass here," Abel said as he peered down at the control panels. Wrenna slowly rotated the craft with her mind.

"There, stop there. Now if you move straight forward, that should take us west. I'll help keep you on course," Abel said.

"Okay, thanks," Wrenna said.

They traveled forwards, with very few words spoken. Wrenna stayed focused on keeping her mind linked with the craft. Abel helped navigate, and Marrick stayed quiet, not wanting to interrupt their work. The light from the craft cast its wide net upon the ground. Wrenna took in the devastation, the wreckage caused by the Nephilim, the consequence of their vicious hunger.

It took less than thirty minutes for the great mountain they had been looking for to appear through the front window of the craft.

"There it is. That's the mountain," Abel said.

"With us being in a Fae craft, they will probably welcome us without question," Marrick said.

"Do you see anywhere to dock the craft or a way to get in the mountain?" Wrenna asked.

She continued to move the craft closer when she noticed a rock structure built into the side of the mountain. The rock momentarily began sliding open. From the opening, an intense light, so white it was almost blue, gleamed upward, brightening the sky.

"I guess they saw us coming and automatically opened the entrance door," Abel said.

"It's the craft. It's our entrance key," Marrick said.

Wrenna used her powers and directed the craft towards the illuminated opening.

"Okay, what's the plan?" Abel said. He looked over at Wrenna and waited for the answer.

"Let's take this head on. No more fear, no more hiding," she said.

Marrick nodded his head in agreement.

"Sounds like a plan," Abel said.

Chapter Twenty-Four

The inside of the mountain had been hollowed out, creating a multi-layered chamber. The space was well lit by incandescent lighting placed in uniform patterns spanning the immensity of the chamber.

"It looks like they have completely hollowed out this mountain. Their access goes down below the ground," Abel said, looking down, taking in the enormity of it.

Wrenna could clearly see how the humans had created several entry points that looked to offer access further down below the base of the mountain. There was a landing pad elevated above what looked like a cargo hold. The cargo hold was lying in the middle, stacked full of large boxes. Beyond the cargo hold were several outcroppings, where numerous humans stood. They were wearing what looked like an olive-green shade uniform. As Wrenna slowly lowered the craft closer to the landing pad, she was able to take in the details of each human. They all had utility belts wrapped around their waist. Each belt was loaded down with a variety of hardware. These humans all wore matching helmets with straps across their chins.

"The army," Abel said.

"These men, are they your military forces, the ones you fought with?" Marrick asked.

"No, I was with a different branch, but yes, they are just one part of the human military," Abel said.

Wrenna lowered the craft perfectly, lining it up with each corner of the landing pad. The moment the craft touched down, she released her powers, causing the engine to lose power.

They heard the doors beginning to unlatch from the outside.

"Okay, are you ready?" Wrenna asked.

"Yeah, as ready as I'll ever be. Wrenna, just know they have weapons, so be careful," Abel said.

Wrenna nodded.

The door swung open, and a large male human dressed in full army uniform stepped into the craft. He looked at them, shocked.

"You are not patrol officers! I need some sort of explanation before you may depart this craft. Who authorized your use of this craft?" the male human said.

Wrenna stepped forward to speak first. "Hello, officer—"

Before she could even continue, the officer cut her off. "General!" he said authoritatively.

"Oh, I am sorry, sir. General," Wrenna continued, sending a backward glance to Abel and Marrick, who were now standing just behind her. "My father is Chief Thain, leader of Shambhala."

"Yes, I know Chief Thain. He didn't mention he had authorized this unplanned arrival," the general said.

"No, he wouldn't have. He doesn't know about us coming here, sir. My friends and I have traveled here to possibly discuss with your leaders a way of defeating the Nephilim," she said.

"Defeating the Nephilim, really?" the general asked. The general's eyes widened. His mouth pursed. "Come with me," he said as he abruptly turned to leave the entrance of the craft.

Wrenna turned towards Abel and Marrick. They both held blank faces, unsure of what was coming. As Wrenna exited the craft, the vast space of the mountain quickly became clearer. She looked up, taking in the height of the ceiling above her. Draped all over the inner side of the mountain walls was a labyrinth. Wrenna clasped the railing that ran along the outer edge of the landing pad and looked down. Platforms and walkways crisscrossed from one side of the mountain to the other.

These walkways gave humans a way to navigate each level. As Wrenna continued to look down, she could see many humans moving about. Some dressed in full army uniform, some wearing white coats, and a few dressed in plain clothes. They followed the general as he led them down the first stairway coming to the loading dock. They swiftly turned and headed down the second stairway. At the bottom of the second stairway, they came to a wide walkway that branched out to several rooms. Wrenna could see into each room through the large glass panel window chiseled into each door. Inside each room, there were men and women sitting at desks, some shuffling through papers, others looking to be plotting locations on large maps pinned to the wall. The general led the three of them to the end of a hallway where they found a large door.

He turned to them. "Wait here. Do not move, do not touch anything," he said.

The general entered the room, leaving them standing outside to wait. After several minutes, the general finally returned.

"He has agreed to see you," he said.

"Who?" Wrenna asked.

Without answering, the general pulled and held the door open, allowing Wrenna, Abel, and Marrick entry. Wrenna took in a quick breath as her eyes fell upon who awaited them in the room. Behind a long stone desk stood her father, Chief Thain.

"Hello there, daughter of mine. Well, look at you. Looks like your powers have finally fully awakened. A day I have been waiting for for twenty-five years. But looks like I missed it, didn't I?" Chief Thain said, his face stoic.

Wrenna, shocked, spoke with a trembling voice. "Father." She didn't know what to say.

"We have been looking for you everywhere. You know, we thought some of our captures had kidnapped you and used you as a way to escape, but things seem to be the other way around," Chief Thain said.

"I don't understand. One minute I am learning of you capturing the humans, and now you're here working with them. Which side are you on?" Wrenna asked her father.

Chief Thain spoke, avoiding her question. "Who are your friends, Wrenna? I believe I might recognize the elf."

Wrenna looked towards Marrick, noticing Marrick's face change as he looked back at Chief Thain. Marrick only stood quiet.

"Well, it seems you have found your way back to us, old friend," Chief Thain said to Marrick.

Wrenna looked from her father to Marrick, waiting for their dialogue to continue. Marrick didn't respond.

Wrenna stepped closer to her father. "You have been a busy man all these years, keeping me locked up behind the walls of the city while you murdered and enslaved so many humans. You are the reason our own people have been going missing. All this time you have been lying to me and everyone else in Shambhala," Wrenna said.

While she waited for her father to come up with another lie, she wondered what the story was between her father and Marrick. Marrick had never told her the full story.

Her curiosity pushed her to speak. "You are the reason Marrick's family was killed. Then, if that wasn't punishment enough, you threw him away, locked him up. Do you not have any remorse for the things you have done?" Wrenna said, directing her words with anger towards her father.

"Well, I guess your little friend Marrick didn't tell you the full truth, now did he?" Chief Thain said.

"He has told me plenty, dear father," Wrenna said.

Chief Thain laughed. "Would you like to tell my lovely daughter the truth, or would you like me to?" Chief Thain asked Marrick.

Abel stood close behind Wrenna, listening quietly.

"I don't want to hear anything from you, Father. Every word that you have ever said to me has been a lie. Why would I believe another word out of your mouth?"

The chief paused, giving Marrick the chance to speak first. Not needing much time to think it over, Marrick moved forward and took Wrenna's hand into his. He pulled her downward, bringing her closer. Wrenna soon had to drop to one knee.

"Yes, your father made me a prisoner, but it was for a crime of redemption. Many, many years ago I worked for your father. My family was suffering dearly. We didn't have much food, and resources were becoming very scarce. It seemed that times were so bad that I had to make a deal that would unfortunately bind me to your father. I did it for my family," Marrick said, and sadness filled his eyes.

"You worked for my father. Doing what?" Wrenna asked.

Chief Thain chuckled.

"This was before you were born, my queen. I had to do whatever I could to help my family," Marrick said.

"Well, what did you do?" Wrenna asked.

"I was well known for my stealthy capabilities, my ability to go unseen. Your father sent me to the surface to do some reconnaissance for him," Marrick said.

"Oh, come out with it, you weakling," Chief Thain yelled.

"Just tell me the truth, Marrick. I am tired of being lied to," Wrenna said, still holding Marrick's hand.

"I was the one who picked your mother." Marrick blurted it out.

Wrenna looked to her father, then back to Marrick. Abel stepped up and placed his hand on Wrenna's shoulder.

Marrick continued, "My job was to find the best candidate for your father to breed with. I was looking for a human girl who I thought would have the most potential. He wanted someone he could easily manipulate and control," Marrick said as a tear rolled down his face.

Wrenna was shocked. She dropped Marrick's hand and stood up. "Why would you not tell me?" Wrenna asked, looking down at Marrick, feeling her heart break a little.

"I did not think of the hurt that would come from what I was doing. All I thought about was saving my family. I did it for them. But if I would have known the future of your mother and what he had planned for her, I would have never done it," Marrick said.

Wrenna paused, looking at her father as he sat back in his chair, his big arms crossed over his chest. Wrenna took a brief moment to think this over, then spoke again.

"Why did you pick my mother? What made you choose her?" Wrenna asked.

"She was lonely. I watched her for weeks, Wrenna. Her life seemed bleak and monotonous. I thought maybe, whatever happened with your father, that maybe it would be a better life than she was living. But now, after my time spent locked away, I have come to realize her life before wasn't bleak. It was peaceful. It was her life, and I didn't have the right to choose for her. What I did was unforgivable, and I wish I could change things. I wish I could go back." Marrick was sad as he wept.

"Why did my father put you in prison then?" she asked Marrick.

"When I learned the truth of what your father planned to do to your mother after your birth, I was devastated. I wanted to help her, to save her," Marrick said.

Chief Thain stood from his chair, slamming his hands on the desk. "That's enough reminiscing about the past," he said.

The chief circled the desk and walked towards Wrenna. He grabbed her shoulder and pulled her closer to him.

"Wrenna, there is much you do not know. Much I have kept from you, but it has all been for good reason. I did this all for our people, for you. Now look at what you have become. See, Wrenna, everything I have done has been to lead you right here, right where you are now," Chief Thain said, squeezing her shoulders.

"Yes, Father, but I am here for a different reason. Not for the reasons you want. I am here because I choose to be, to make things right," Wrenna said.

"Wrenna, you are just confused right now. The company you have been with has brainwashed you into thinking your people are the bad guys in this, that I am the bad guy. How do you think the Fae people have been able to live in peace for so long? They have everything they need to survive. Shambhala is the safest place on this earth. I did that," Chief Thain said.

Wrenna felt like believing him. He was right after all; the Fae of Shambhala were mostly safe and lived pretty good lives. She felt a tug of war in her mind as her thoughts raced back and forth between what she had thought she believed and leaning towards what her father was now saying.

"But what about the Fae? You and Arban are responsible for those gone missing. Those Fae weren't safe. They thought they were, until one night an officer burst into their homes and dragged them off to that room under the stairs. Yes, Father, I have seen your and Arban's room you use to torture and kill those you take hostage. The room you let my mother be murdered in," Wrenna said, raising her voice.

As she spoke, she could feel something tugging at her mind. An outside dark force trying to penetrate her thoughts.

"Yes, but once again, all of these actions are for the greater good, dear daughter. Did you just want me to let the city you lived in, where our people lived, be taken over? I had to do what I had to do to keep Shambhala safe," Chief Thain said.

A sharp pain electrified her brain, causing her to pause. It was as if a knife had been rammed into her skull. She felt her knees become weak. Through the haze of pain, Wrenna realized it was her father. He was trying to probe her thoughts with his manipulation powers.

"So tell me, Father, what is it protecting Shambhala from?" she asked. Wrenna knew the answer, but she wanted to hear the words come from her father's mouth.

"Our family, our ancestors, have had a bargain in place. A bargain that protects the Fae people and allows us to live in peace. Even I have to answer to someone, Wrenna, someone more powerful than any Fae or human combined," he said.

"How did this bargain happen?" Wrenna asked.

Chief Thain leaned his forearms onto the desk and continued, "Years ago, our people were enslaved, tortured, battered, and beaten. Many lives were lost. Our people were being forced to work, building the tunnels you came here through. A very powerful God called Yama was the one condemning our people to a life of slavery. He is the ruler of the underworld. He is the God of Death, Wrenna. So in order to save our people and free them from his enslavement, our ancestors made the decision to accept the bargain he laid before us," Chief Thain said.

"Why is he doing this to us, to the humans? What is his end game?" Wrenna asked.

"The stories say that centuries ago, he returned from a battle that took place somewhere beyond our earth. A place no Fae has ever been. A place, I am told, humans return to when they die," Chief Thain said.

"Abel, do you know of this place?" Wrenna said, turning towards Abel.

"When humans die, some believe we go to a place called Heaven. We like to think it is high above the earth, beyond everything in the sky. It is a place of peace, where our souls can finally rest," Abel said.

"Svarga Loka, the place of rebirth," Marrick said.

Wrenna turned back to her father. "And?" Wrenna said.

"Yama lost this battle. His punishment was that he would be sent to the center of our earth for all of eternity. He would live there surrounded by darkness, having no sense of time. He would wander the darkness, forever searching. No one knows truly who sent him there. Stories say other Gods chose that place as his prison. What the other Gods didn't foresee was Yama would eventually find his way. He was more powerful than they had given him credit for. He found a way to unleash his power on the earth, in it and on it. So the beings of earth were left to deal with Yama. The Fae were his first victims," Chief Thain said.

"And will this bargain ever be fulfilled? When will he be satisfied?" Wrenna asked.

"I don't believe he will ever free us from this bargain. We helped free his beast. We have gotten them to the surface. He has been getting the impure souls that he wants, but still he is not satisfied. Unfortunately, when we made this bargain, we only wanted our freedoms. We didn't realize the more impure souls he got, the more powerful he became. His grip around us only tightened. You see, we have no choice. We do the things we do to save our people," Chief Thain said.

"This bargain might have saved the Fae from slavery, but it damned all of mankind. I don't see that being for the greater good, Father," Wrenna said.

Wrenna felt a singe of electricity zap her brain. This time it was much smaller, much less painful. She knew her father was losing the battle, that his manipulation wasn't strong enough to sway her anymore. Wrenna moved to the desk, placing her palms down on the smooth surface. She bent over, bringing her eyes parallel with her father's.

"So I am part of this bargain? I am bound to be Yama's devoted servant, since I am your daughter?" Wrenna asked.

"Yes," Chief Thain said.

"Well, unfortunately for you, dear father, that doesn't fall into my plans. That is not who I am, and I won't do it."

Chief Thain pushed himself from the chair he was sitting in, standing upright. "Wrenna, you are bound to this family. Do you wish to condemn Shambhala?" Chief Thain said.

"No, I do not wish to condemn Shambhala. But I also do not wish to kill innocents in order to protect our city. There is another way," Wrenna said. Wrenna lifted her palms from the desk and stood tall, mirroring her father's move. "Why did you do what you did to my mother and then lie to me about it my entire life? I will never forgive you for that," Wrenna continued.

Chief Thain only stood there, waiting for Wrenna to continue.

"I have gone twenty-five years not knowing anything about my mother. I thought she died while having me, and now I find out you murdered her! What do you have to say about that?" Wrenna asked.

She felt a jolt of uneasiness in her mind. Her father pressed his powers one last time. She could feel him trying to make her more submissive, more docile. Wrenna allowed him to think his tactics were working, giving him an ounce of control. She saw his eyes darken and smolder, and one brow lifted slightly.

"Wrenna, please stop with this absurd story that the elf has told you. It is clearly a lie. Why would I murder your mother? I loved her dearly. She died holding you in her arms. It was a great pain to me, and that is why we never talked about her. I am sorry I couldn't talk about her with you. I was selfish," Chief Thain said, still driving his manipulation into her mind. "Now please, I would like to have some privacy with my daughter. You two, you can wait outside," Chief Thain said, gesturing for Marrick and Abel to leave the room. "Wrenna, please ask your friends to wait for you outside. I only need a moment of your time. I'd prefer to talk about these private matters with just you."

Wrenna didn't fear her father. Unbeknownst to him, she easily blocked his powers. So she agreed to ask Marrick and Abel to leave the room.

"Guys, please wait outside so I can have a moment with my father alone," Wrenna said, looking back at Abel and Marrick.

"Are you sure, my queen? I do not wish to leave you alone with him," Marrick said.

"I will be fine. Don't worry, Marrick," Wrenna said.

"Okay, we will be just outside if you need us," Abel said, trusting in Wrenna's choice to be alone with her father.

Marrick and Abel left the room, closing the door behind them.

"Now, Wrenna, let's put the past aside for now. There are pressing matters in regards to your powers we must discuss," Chief Thain said.

Wrenna could still feel her father's manipulation trying still to find control. She wondered how often in her life he had bewitched her with his powers. She was thankful her newly awakened powers were able to now give her the capabilities to detect his presence.

"Okay, let's hear it," Wrenna said.

Chief Thain walked to the back of the office. Wrenna watched as he opened a small hidden door in the wall with just one press of his hand. A bright orange glow poured from the room as Chief Thain walked inside, disappearing. Wrenna waited. Soon Chief Thain returned, carrying a black box in his hands. He walked to the desk and set the box down. Chief Thain slowly lifted the lid of the box and pulled out a clear orb. It was like nothing Wrenna had ever seen before. She felt the opal on her chest, hidden under her shirt, begin to vibrate and radiate warmth like so many times before. The chief, with the orb in his hand, walked closer to Wrenna and held it out before her. He pulled his hands away as if he was going to drop it but to Wrenna's surprise, it only hovered midair. The crystal orb floated in place. Wrenna looked into it, seeing a swirl of colors moving about. The colors spun and moved about much like the fire opal had. Chief Thain walked back to the black box on the desk. He reached in and pulled out a small knife.

"This is the Eye of Hereafter. It was gifted to us from the Great Oracle of the Badlands. Our family has used it for generations to see what is to be," Chief Thain said.

Wrenna, curious, let her father continue.

"We need to see if you will be capable of doing what needs to be done. To protect the future of our people," Chief Thain said.

He reached for her hand, lifting the blade's edge to her palm. Wrenna held her breath.

"This will hurt, but it must be done," Chief Thain said.

Then he slid the knife into Wrenna's palm. Wrenna winched with the pain.

"Now place your hand around the Eye," Chief Thain said.

Wrenna allowed her curiosity to drive her actions forward. So she placed her hand on the Eye, doing as her father told her to.

As soon as Wrenna's hand encircled the Eye, she felt a shock of energy enter into her body. Her eyes rolled back; she no longer could feel her physical body. Her father and the office were no longer there. It had all fallen away. Wrenna was floating, with her hand still gripping the Eye. Floating in a void of light. The light was all around her; she could see nothing else. A blissfulness surrounded her, one that she had never experienced before. She felt lightweight, almost like all of the burdens of life had been lifted. From the nothingness that surrounded her came a voice. "Queen Rayna the savior has returned."

Chapter Twenty-Five

Wrenna gave herself a moment to allow her eyes to adjust to her new surroundings, taking in the stellar place. She looked around, only seeing a white emptiness. The ground below her was blanketed with a cradle of softness. Wrenna spun all around, her eyes searching for any semblance of life. There was nothing, only white open space.

"Hello?" Wrenna said.

She felt her body begin to relax, and her body and mind were swallowed up with calm. Seconds after the words had left her lips, a space just before her seemed to crack open. It looked like a hidden doorway. One moment everything was white, the next, an orange glow spilled before her. The light pooled on to the ground and all around Wrenna.

A voice came from nowhere once again. "Welcome home," it said.

The voice seemed to reverberate through the endless emptiness of the place Wrenna now stood. It was a man's voice, one that was bold and echoed in Wrenna's chest.

"Who's there?" Wrenna asked.

The orange glow of light appeared to darken as if something was blocking its reach. A shadow moved into view. Wrenna had to squint her eyes, trying to make out what the shadow was. Her body was overcome with a woozy feeling as if she were intoxicated by something.

Wrenna slid the membrane into place, using it to help see better. The shadow moved beyond the bright light, coming into better focus. Wrenna could now see standing before her was a man. The man, who looked to be hovering, floated closer to Wrenna. She took in the beauty of the man's appearance. The man had golden skin, much the same as Wrenna's new skin. His hair was metallic strands of gold. It floated and swayed as the man proceeded forward. As he got closer, Wrenna noticed his eyes were solid white, no irises or pupils, much the same as the Great Oracle. Across his nose were speckles of golden flecks, similar to Wrenna's freckles. He moved to a stop just a few feet in front of Wrenna.

"You are beautiful like your mother," the man said.

"Who are you? How do you know my mother?" Wrenna asked.

The man smiled; he had big white, sparkling teeth.

"The Eye of Hereafter sent you here to me. Seems it is time for you to learn some truths, truths that will catapult you into your destiny. My name is Lord Surya. This is the place that I dwell, here amongst the heavens," Lord Surya said, opening his arms wide.

"The heavens?" Wrenna asked, remembering her father mentioning this place before. "Am I dead?" she continued.

"No, child, you are not dead. That is a state you will not know for a very long time," Lord Surya said.

"How do you know my mother?" Wrenna asked again.

"I know your mother, but your mother did not know me," Lord Surya replied.

Wrenna raised her eyebrows, confused. "What do you mean?" Wrenna asked.

"Your mother was a very intricate part of my divine plan. A plan that would change the course of history. You see, when she was brought to the In Between by Chief Thain, it was I who led her to be chosen," Lord Surya said.

"Wait, what? I thought Marrick chose my mother, and then my father took her," Wrenna said.

"I have been given the blessing to see the future for all beings upon the earth. I saw your mother's future, and so I took the opportunity needed to redirect her purpose and derail the plans of your father. The Battle of the Greats had just ended, and I felt I needed another form of protection to keep things in balance. That something is you," Lord Surya said.

Wrenna shook her head. "How did you redirect my mother's purpose, as you said?" Wrenna asked.

Lord Surya looked at her, reached his hand out, and placed it on her shoulder.

"Twenty-five years ago, a piece of my soul was given. I sent it to be reborn into another body. It was reborn into you, Rayna. When your mother got pregnant, she and Chief Thain believed it to be both their child. They believed each had given a piece of themselves to create you. I knew the future opportunity the child of the chief of Shambhala would have one day, so I decided to intervene. Your mother had no idea, nor Chief Thain. The reincarnation took place, and a part of me was born. You, Rayna, you are a descendant of mine," Lord Surya said.

"Who are you?" Wrenna asked, her mind feeling like a maze of discombobulated information.

"I am Lord Surya, the God of the Sun. I am the ruler of this realm, the place where souls return home to stay or are once again reincarnated and sent back to earth. That is how I was able to send a part of me to create you," Lord Surya said.

"But why would you do that?" Wrenna asked.

"I knew that one day, Yama would seek his vengeance. That day I banished him to the depths of the earth, I knew that I was not rid of him. He was once my greatest ally but when he began consuming the souls of the heavens and refused to stop, I knew I had to force him to leave this realm. This realm was created to be a sanctuary for the souls who have completed their life cycle on earth, and I had to protect them. But he refused to leave the heavens. He insisted this was his realm to rule over. So he began to twist his evil into beings, creating flesh-eating demons, using them to aid in his advances to take over this realm. Many celestial beings of this realm fell to earth as they were also consumed by Yama's evil. His hunger surged through anyone he touched, taking control. They followed Yama, bowing down to him, devoting them-selves to his cause. Eventually, I was able to cast him and his devilish henchmen out, but I knew Yama's hunger had not yet been satiated. I knew he would one day return," Lord Surya said.

"So you sent a part of your soul down to create me?" Wrenna asked.

"Yes. You see, your father believes you are a very powerful half-human, half-Fae. He was told by the Great Oracle when he was much younger that one day his child would become the tool he needed to succeed and become the greatest Fae in all of history. She instructed him to seek out a female human to birth his child. The Great Oracle informed him that this child would have a power like no other Fae ever known. She proclaimed to him that his child would be a great and mighty conqueror of all of earth. Chief Thain thought the Great Oracle was implying that this child would help him achieve his wish, that he could use the child as a weapon. So he did as the Great Oracle told him. Unknowing that I was the one who had orchestrated my own plan. What your father does not know is the Great Oracle is an ally of mine, and she too wants to stop Yama. Your father cannot beat Yama on his own, and his hope is that you will be what the Great Oracle has predicted. You will be the one to defeat Yama. I also believe this, but my vision for you is much different than that of your father.

"You see, Rayna, your father and I have different end goals and different motivations, but we both want to use the same tool to get what we want. He is led by selfishness, aspiring to be the grand conqueror of all. He wants to rule those on the surface and those who live within the earth, and he is willing to reach his goals through whatever means necessary. I, on the other hand, hope that you will be the one to cleanse the souls of the earth and help them find their way back to the good. Yama has weaved his evil darkness into so many, and it is you that can purge this contamination, making the souls pure once again. You see, by poisoning the souls of the humans on the surface, Yama wants to turn those souls into an army. With this army, he plans to conquer the earth. Once he is strong enough, with a great enough army behind him, he will then come for the heavens. Rayna, you are the heir to this realm; you are the heir to all that is good and pure. You, Rayna, are the savior of all of mankind, those who dwell on the surface and to those who reside within. You can even save the lost to the underworld. It will be you that will change the future of all," Lord Surya said.

Wrenna was frozen, her head shuffling through all of the new information that had been given to her.

"All of this is just..." She took a deep breath, exhaling. "I don't believe in the things my father does. I do not want to help him. The things he is doing and has done are unforgivable. I want to be better. I want to make things better. I can feel within my soul goodness and love. With that force inside of me, so far, I have been able to see the thoughts and what motivates someone to be the way they are. Can I use that to help make things better?" Wrenna asked. She worried about her return, knowing Chief Thain would be there waiting for her. "What does he think the Eye is showing me right now?" Wrenna asked.

"He believes it is showing you how to use your powers to defeat Yama but only to benefit what he seeks. I am telling you that you can defeat Yama. I believe you want to change what is going on. I believe you want to save and help those lost," Lord Surya said.

"I do," Wrenna replied.

"If your father does not agree to fix what is going on and change, then you have to stop him. But it is you who will decide his punishment. It is you who will decide the punishment of those who have chosen evil and darkness," Lord Surya said.

Wrenna stood still for a few moments, her mind racing, shuffling through all of the life-changing information Lord Surya had just divulged to her.

Lord Surya stepped even closer. "It is time now, Rayna, for you to take your rightful place. It is time for you to do what it is you are destined to do," he said.

"Why can't you do it? I mean, no disrespect, but haven't you already battled Yama and dealt with this sort of thing before? The weight of all of this is heavy on my shoulders. I am not sure if I can handle it," Wrenna said.

"My time is coming to an end. I no longer have the strength to fight, for I have reached my final stage of enlightenment. My soul will soon dissolve into nothingness and be blown away with the great wind. That is why you, as my child, must take my place. I don't have much time left. Rayna, can you do what it is that is asked of you? Can you be the savior the earth is so desperately looking for?" Lord Surya said.

Wrenna took in a long inhale, closed her eyes, and thought of the faces of her people, the Fae. Their innocent lives being torn apart like the humans that lived on the surface. She thought about Abel and his family and friends. The pain the humans had suffered, their freedom lost, their peace shattered. She thought about Marrick, how his entire family had been ripped from him, all in the name of Yama. She thought of her mother. Wrenna had to do this for them, for all of them.

She shuddered, then spoke. "Yes, I can. I will. I'm new to my powers. Will I be strong enough to face these things, to do what it is you speak about?" Wrenna asked Lord Surya.

"Rayna, you will find your way as you go. You have my gifts in your blood. You are as much of me as you are your mother. She gave you your will, your beauty, and most of all, your heart. From me, you have inherited the power to see someone's true self and what it is they are on the inside. You have the ability to feel what they feel, to know what their true intentions are. With that ability, you can help them choose to change and be better. With your light, the light of the sun, you can fill them up with the energy they need to be better. With this power, you can save the souls of many who have been condemned to a life of darkness and transgressions. You can change the outcome of this world to be a better place," Lord Surya said.

Wrenna felt her heart overflow with love, a love she had only experienced one time before. The time her mother came to her in a vision. She peered into her newly discovered father's eyes and knew he was spreading that love to her. The warmth filled the expansion of her chest, and with that love came trust in Lord Surya's words.

"My trust is with you," Wrenna blurted.

The need to bow her head pushed into her mind, and so she did.

"After you change the world, you will become the true queen, serving the people and Fae with zero expectations of anything in return. You will be looked to for guidance, and you will be respected to no end. This I see, my daughter, Queen Rayna," Lord Surya finished.

He stepped closer, placing both hands on Wrenna's shoulders. He leaned in and pressed a gentle kiss to Wrenna's forehead. His closeness gave Wrenna a better view of him, his pure golden skin. It shined like the sun. He wore a long robe that went all the way to his feet. He looked so very young, but Wrenna could feel his wisdom and purity as his lips met her forehead. Lord Surya stepped back and smiled. His body began to shift into dust, starting from his feet. His body gradually disappeared into nothingness.

"Goodbye, my daughter," he said in a whisper.

She blinked her eyes, and she was back in the office. Her father, Chief Thain, stood in front of her, and her hand was still clasped around the Eye.

"What did you see, Wrenna? Tell me at once!"

Chapter Twenty-Six

W renna had returned to Chief Thain standing wide-eyed and impatient before her. He waited for her to respond, but Wrenna's mind was still trying to comprehend the details she had just experienced.

"Wrenna, you should have received a vision, one that will reveal to you your true powers and what they can be used for. The Great Oracle prophesied that you would be gifted the powers to help our family gain the control we need and propel us one step closer to ruling the entire earth and finally defeating Yama. Please tell me what the Eye of Hereafter has presented to you in your vision."

Wrenna took a moment to articulate the right words to express her answer to her father's question. She knew all along he was expecting something great from her, but what he wanted was not what Wrenna wanted. Wrenna's beliefs fell in line with Lord Surya. She wanted a better future. One free of death and destruction. She wanted a future where all beings could be free to dwell on the earth without fear.

"Father, we both want the same things. For the Death God Yama to be stopped. We both want the bargain your ancestors agreed to to no longer be binding. We both know this symbiotic relationship between Yama and the Fae cannot be sustained forever. That is why you need me to stop him. But what you want is to control the earth, the In Between, and the surface. You want this change only for your own selfish reasoning. I don't think you care about the humans and helping free them from what's going on. I think you will do whatever you think is necessary to take full control. I won't help you do that, Chief, I just won't," Wrenna said looking into her father's eyes, or who she once thought was her father.

Chief Thain's eyes widened. Wrenna hoped that calling him Chief instead of Father would help him feel the disconnect she was already having towards him.

"If we end Yama, who will have control of the humans? We could use the humans to help advance Shambhala. We ourselves have achieved some advancements in creating easier growing methods. You've seen it yourself in the greenhouse. Imagine if we had the abundant space available on the surface. We could use our methods to grow more food. Instead of taking the supplies by force like in the past, it will just be ours for the taking. Once we defeat Yama, we must maintain that control. You have to understand this, Wrenna. The potential future for the Fae people would be glorious. These humans have so many things that would benefit and help propel the Fae people forward. We could eventually live on the surface, take over and grow our population. We do have the purest blood of all the species on earth. It is only right that we rule," Chief Thain said.

"No, I will not stand by while you continue killing off the entire human race and while you take over their lands. There is a better way. One where all beings can thrive and live prosperously, without force, without more death. You are led by your ego, Father. You can lead with your heart. Things can be different, but it's up to you to make that decision. What do you want to do? You know where I stand in this. What path are you choosing?" Wrenna gave Chief Thain an opportunity to respond, hoping his choice was for a better path.

Chief Thain stood there, his face even paler than it was naturally. He looked back at Wrenna, pausing before speaking.

"Well, Father, are you willing to go about this differently?" Wrenna asked one last time.

"It won't work. Humans cannot be trusted. They will not work with us without force. Trust me, Wrenna, why do you think I am here now? We have the control we need to keep it. We need to keep their leaders under our thumb," Chief Thain said.

Wrenna found herself blocking out her father's relentless continued preaching of his case as she welcomed the force within her to rise to the surface. She pulled a sliver of power, freeing it, just as before with the officers and the Nephilim. She let the tendril of power cascade into her father's mind. She went searching to see if there was any hope for him to change, if he was capable of choosing a better path. He continued talking, not noticing Wrenna's presence pillaging its way through the maze of his mind, weaving round his thoughts. His motivations, easily found, were nothing but pride, greed, anger, and selfishness. Wrenna tried to sway his thoughts, tried to change them to purer, good intentions, but his mind stood firm. A giant wall of darkness blocked Wrenna. Much like the wall that now stood around her city, Shambhala. The walls of his mind were thick with years and years of living in these patterns. Chief Thain's consciousness had been permanently changed many years ago to believe that this way was the one true and only way. He had been killing relentlessly for so many years, it was now second nature to him. Life, human or Fae, meant nothing to him when it came to getting what he wanted. He was willing to do whatever he had to to get what it was he so desired. Life was merely a means to an end in the chief's eyes and nothing else. Wrenna saw that now within this man that she had lived with for twenty-five years, a man she called father.

"Wrenna, are you listening to me? I need you to help me do this," Chief Thain yelled. Wrenna accepted that there was nothing she could do to persuade him to give up his way of thinking. There would be no way to change him. It was too late. The darkness had already penetrated his soul too deeply.

"I want you to know that I have lived my entire life wishing you saw me. My entire life, all you cared about was the powers that I might have one day. Powers that would help you kill more innocents and find what it was you wanted: full control. You never cared about me or my mother. We were just pawns in this game you have been playing. My whole life, I knew I was different then you and that I wanted to be nothing like you. Today, I know why. Over the last few weeks, I have learned nothing but horrific things you do without a second thought just to get what you want. Things that disgust me, things I could never imagine doing to another soul. I am ashamed to be known as your daughter. Well, after today, that ends. I have been awakened with the truth, dear father, a truth that can and will end you."

Wrenna paused, stepping closer to Chief Thain, standing taller now. She felt her shoulders broaden and all her self-doubt fall away.

"My whole life, I knew I didn't belong, and I was right," Wrenna said.

"Wrenna, you are my daughter, my blood. You have some of the most powerful ancestors. You have been born into a line of the purest blood. Our family has battled for years to get to where we are today. You are the next step in that. Everything I have done is for you," Chief Thain said.

"Just stop with this illusion. You keep spilling lies. You didn't do this for me, you did it for yourself," Wrenna said. She wanted him to know the truth, that he was not her real father. She continued on. "You want to know what the Eye of the Hereafter showed me? It showed me my real father, the man who gave me my soul. We don't have the same blood running through our veins, Chief Thain. You have only been tricked into believing so."

Wrenna felt the power within her chest begin to spiral and move up and down her spine. She found the light that resided within, allowing it to course from her body. This time, instead of only coming from the space between her eyes, her light emitted from every inch of her body. It caused Chief Thain to cower and squint his eyes. Sweat now lined his brow. Wrenna felt the pureness of the energy surging throughout her body, now more than ever before. Wrenna could now distinctly detect the essence of Lord Surya flowing within her every cell. Wrenna smiled with bliss.

"I am not your daughter. I am the daughter of the Sun God, Lord Surya. I am him reincarnated. You, Chief Thain, have the option to cease your evil ways, stop the destruction and your selfish motives. If you do not agree to do as I ask, I will have no choice but to take action. This is no longer about what you want. It is for the greater good of this earth and all the beings that live upon it," Wrenna said.

Chief Thain stood up quickly, trying to seem less scared, and laughed. "What is this, some kind of joke? I will not bow to you; it should be the other way around. You are lucky, daughter, to even be here now. I should have known what would come of breeding with one of those mutts. That Oracle speaks lies. You are an abomination to my family. After everything I have given to you, a home, food, you do this to me," Chief Thain said.

Wrenna could feel the anger and hate rush from Chief Thain's mind, her powers now mingling amongst his thoughts. She could feel the darkness growing, the uncontrollable evil perforating the room.

"There is no hope for you. I can see that you will never change. From all the things you have done in the past, you have no remorse for them. Not even an ounce of regret," Wrenna said.

She released her restraint, clamping down around Chief Thain's mind. This caused him to collapse, falling to his knees before her.

"I thought you said you would not bow, Chief," Wrenna said.

The chief's eyes grew bigger, now realizing what Wrenna was doing.

"Yes, that is me. You are witnessing the powers you prayed to the Gods to see from the day of my birth. With a flick of my wrist, I can end you. Isn't it ironic how things have played out, Chief?" Wrenna paused, giving him time to think over her words.

"I will give you one last chance to make the choice to change, to become better."

Wrenna shifted through his thoughts and waited to see if there was even one sprinkle of hope. But nothing came.

"You cannot change me, Wrenna," Chief Thain whispered. "I am who I am, and I am proud of that. Everything I have done to bring our family, our city to this moment has been my choice. And I do not have any remorse for killing your mother or anyone else. I should have killed you the day you were born. I was such a fool to trust the Great Oracle. Even more a fool to have put my trust in that elf, allowing him to pick your mother. This is his fault. It is his fault that you are a weak-minded inbred. I should have killed him instead of giving him even a hint of life when I banished him to be imprisoned in that stupid bird. That was but a gift compared to what I should have done to him."

Banished him in that bird? Wrenna thought as Chief Thain continued his tirade.

"I gave too much. I was too kind. I should have forced you to awaken your powers sooner. I gave you too much free will. Maybe it is somewhat my fault as well, that things have turned out so." The chief paused.

Wrenna knew what she had to do, that there was no other choice. She never felt love from the chief, not like the love she felt for those brief moments she was in the presence of her true father, Lord Surya. That was how a true father was supposed to make you feel. Wrenna never had that with the chief, not once in her life.

"I am done being but a mere tool in this plot you have to control and rule this earth. I have given you the opportunity to repent and begin to change, but you have chosen to give into the darkness once more. It is over. You are done," Wrenna said.

Wrenna allowed her powers to expand to fill up the space of Chief Thain's entire skull Her light illuminated so bright, the entire room was now filled with her light. She closed her eyes, and in that moment, Chief Thain's life came to an end.

When Wrenna opened her eyes, allowing her powers to recede, her light dimmed once again. She looked around the room. Chief Thain was gone. Wrenna had ended his physical existence but chose to send his consciousness away to a place where he would be lost forever. To the Badlands, a place Chief Thain had used for so many years to punish those who tried to leave Shambhala. A place he would now roam endlessly, looking but never finding what it was he was looking for. A gift she had inherited from her true father, the ability to move from one dimension to another or from one place to another. She used this gift to send the chief away to endure endless suffering.

Wrenna was startled from her thoughts when the door to the office swung open. Abel and Marrick walked in.

"Are you okay, Wrenna?" Marrick asked.

Wrenna, still having a bit of sourness towards Marrick for what he had done, fell to her knees before him. "Marrick, tell me where my father sent you away to prison."

Marrick paused, slowly reaching for each of Wrenna's hands. "Just knowing the truth may be hard to believe. Your father banished my soul to be trapped inside Isha's body. You see, Isha has the power to change,

her body becoming a vessel to house any soul that might need a tempo-
rary home. Well, your father took advantage of that fact." Wrenna
dropped her eyes to the floor, tears falling down her cheeks.

"You were there all along?" Wrenna quickly realized Marrick would
have been there for all of Wrenna's private moments, her times there
with Stiles, and her cheeks flushed.

"Yes, my queen. Please let me explain. Your father banished me to
Isha's body when your mother was still alive. He wanted me to watch
her suffer. He wanted me to be there when her life ended. I tried to help
her the best I could, but there was only so much I could do as a raven.
The day you were born, I was blessed with seeing how proud she was of
you. I watched as she laid you across her chest and kissed your tiny head.
There is nothing like a mother's love for their child. And when they
took you away, I had to watch your mother's heart shatter. Then when
they stabbed her with that needle and dragged her off, my heart black-
ened. I knew I would never see her again. I knew what I had done, that it
was my fault she was condemned to her horrible death. After that, I let
my anger, my remorse, and all of my sadness bury me further into darkness. I completely shut down. Before long, I lost any control of Isha. I
was just there surrounded by darkness. I couldn't see through her eyes
or hear through her ears. So I was there, but I didn't see you, Wrenna. I
never even knew I was with you all that time. Until one day, the opal I
had began to vibrate and glow. The next thing I knew, I was there in
your bunk room with you. You had your fire opal, staring into it. I think
that's what freed me. That's what pulled me from the darkness."

Marrick paused. He peered up into Wrenna's eyes. They both had
tears streaming down their faces.

"I want you to know, I did try to help her before I was banished.
When I was still me, I went to the municipal compound, and I was
gonna take her away from that place. An officer caught me shortly after
and took me to your father. He sensed my betrayal. He manipulated the
words of guilt out of me," Marrick said.

"I wish I would have known. I would have tried to free you. I am so
sorry, Marrick," Wrenna said, pulling the elf closer.

"I am sorry for what I have done to you, to your mother," Marrick
said.

"I know, I forgive you," Wrenna said. They embraced one another, tears now falling freely down their faces.

"How did you finally return to your body?" Wrenna asked.

"That day we all went into those rocks, I remembered that was my home once. Something was pulling me in. So that's when I flew off. I was my lifeless body, buried in the dirt that called to my soul. And just like that, the powers that held me to Isha's body broke free and my soul returned to my body. Luckily, whoever buried me years ago did a terrible job, and I was able to dig my way out. Shortly after that, you and Abel found me in my home," Marrick said.

"Well, I am glad you are now free. I am glad to have you in my life. What about Isha?" Wrenna said.

"Isha is a changeling. She will travel on, looking for other drifting souls that she can help," Marrick said.

Wrenna wiped the tears from her face as she turned and looked to Abel, remembering he was still there. Abel smiled back.

"Where is your father, Wrenna?" Abel finally asked.

Wrenna let go of Marrick's small hands and spoke.

"He's gone. Not dead, but somewhere else," Wrenna said.

She gave the two males an opportunity to ask more questions, but they did not. They only stood there, stunned by what Wrenna had done, their imagination being the only form of answers. So with that, Wrenna turned towards the door. She walked past the two males and left the room.

Wrenna felt the power of Lord Surya surging through her veins. Her skin gleamed golden. The color had become more vibrant, bolder. She could feel an energy like no other pulsing through her body, swirling along her spine. Her powers lay awake just at the surface. It quaked as if it would erupt from her body at any moment. Her steps no longer felt like steps. It was as if she moved more smoothly, as if she were gliding along the ground. A lightness in her body made her feel new, reborn. The layers of her past now fell away, and the truth of who she truly was emerged. She felt free. All the questions she had, she now had the answers. Everything she sought in life, pondered, feared, it was all lifted from her shoulders. As she walked back down the hallway, heading back towards the many offices occupied by the humans, she no longer felt any constraints about what it was she had to do. Wrenna's path was clearer now than ever before.

"Wrenna, I am sorry, but I gotta know what happened in there. You seem different. You even look different," Abel said, running to catch up with her. Wrenna turned to her friends. Abel and Marrick, they looked at her as if seeing her for the first time.

"She is reborn," Marrick said. Marrick dropped to the floor, lowering his forehead to the ground. Abel stood there, uncertain as of what to do, confusion crossing his face.

"What does that mean, she is reborn?" Abel asked.

"Bow down before Queen Rayna, the Savior of All," Marrick said from the floor.

Abel looked at Marrick, then back at Wrenna as if he was asking her what he should do.

"You don't have to bow. Marrick, please get up," Wrenna said.

Marrick got to his feet quickly.

Abel spoke again. "What happened in that office, Wrenna?" he asked.

"There are no longer questions as to what my path is to be. I know. I ask you both to walk alongside me on this journey. I ask that I can trust you both to help me," Wrenna said.

"Till the day I die. I have known all along what you would be, Rayna. I dreamt about you in the darkness. I took the vow of devotion with your mother, and now I shall carry that vow on with you, my queen. You are a light that will bring forth freedom for all. I am forever your follower; my heart is yours," Marrick said.

Wrenna looked to Abel. "What about you, Abel, can I rely on you? I need your help to gain the trust of the humans once again. I need your voice and your knowledge about the surface," Wrenna said.

"Yeah, I have followed you this far. At first, it was hard for me to trust you. I just thought you were like the others, but you have proven that you want only to help. You can rely on me..." Abel stuttered and then continued. "Queen Rayna," he said with a smile.

"Good!"

Wrenna stepped towards Abel, grabbing his arm, and pulling him into her body. She placed a gentle kiss upon his lips and pulled away with a smile. Abel stared back, his eyes wide with shock. Wrenna didn't really know what came over her, but she didn't regret the kiss. Abel was a genuinely good man, something Wrenna had rarely seen in her life. She quickly pulled herself from thinking too much into it and continued speaking.

"It's time to correct my father's wrongs," Wrenna said as she turned and continued down the hallway.

The general came out of one of the offices, watching as Wrenna and her two male friends walked towards him.

"General, I want to talk to your leaders. Where are they?" Wrenna said.

The general turned and started walking in the opposite direction. "Follow me," he called back.

The general led them down a long corridor. They passed several other officers. The officers all seemed in a daze, as if they had just awoken from a deep sleep. The general abruptly turned into a small entryway, a holding space just before a large doorway.

"On the other side of this door are the men you are looking for. But before I take you in this room, I need you to explain to me what's going on. It feels as if I have lost a block of time. Last thing I remember, I was finalizing orders to send soldiers down into the tunnels. I had received orders from my superiors to initiate an attack on the Fae. That's the last I remember until just moments ago. After speaking to several other soldiers, they all seem to have the same occurrences. One minute preparing to depart, the next as if waking up from some sort of spell with blocks of time missing. Can you help me understand that? I know that the Fae had come in and began to take control of our military. They had somehow persuaded the leaders to agree to it. My men and I had decided on our own that we would not stand for it. We could no longer allow our people to be taken." The general, wide-eyed, looked at Wrenna.

He continued, "You came here, and something changed. It is as if a veil has been lifted and this fog has gone away from our minds." He looked to Abel and spoke again. "Can you tell me what is happening here, soldier?" he asked Abel.

Wrenna had no idea how the general could tell of Abel's past military background, but she allowed him to answer the general.

"Wrenna came here to help you all take back what is ours and free our people. We can trust her; she is not like the others. She freed me and other humans from prison cells down below." Abel gestured to the ground.

"I believe my father, Chief Thain, had you all under his powers. He has, or had, the ability to manipulate the thoughts and actions of others. He has been controlling you all for some time now. I think that's where the blocks of missing time went. Once I sent him away, his grip on you and your men was lifted. You now have a clear mind once again," Wrenna said to the general. She turned to Marrick and Abel. "Let's just keep it Wrenna for now. I am not quite ready for the whole queen thing."

Abel shook his head, and Marrick nodded with a bit of apprehension.

"How can my men and I help?" the general asked.

"First things first, I think we need to take care of the people on the surface. Getting rid of those things, those Nephilim," Wrenna said.

"Nothing we have could take them down; we have tried everything," the general said.

"She killed one," Abel blurted once again, looking from the general to Wrenna.

"How many do you estimate are out there?" Wrenna asked.

"We truly have no idea. More than thirty that we have counted so far. They come up through the tunnels. We believe they live in cave systems within the earth. There is no telling how many more are down there. They have been the biggest threat to us so far. We still are not sure why they are here and what it is they want from us. The Fae have also been a huge enemy to civilians. They don't harm the military due to the agreement they have with the men on the other side of this door," the general said.

"Now that my father is no longer in the picture, technically I am the new leader of Shambhala, of the Fae. The deal they had with my father, well, it is now with me. I need to talk with them," Wrenna said.

"Yes, I will go meet with them now. I will come back to get you shortly," the general said, turning and leaving the hallway, entering the large door.

Wrenna, Abel, and Marrick stood in the corridor quietly. They all seemed lost in their thoughts.

"I am a bit nervous about these men, my queen. I mean, Wrenna," Marrick said.

"We have been dodging giants and death worms. I think we can handle old ordinary men," Abel.

"I just don't think these humans will see eye to eye with you as easily as we are hoping they will. We must be careful and stay vigilant while negotiating with them," Marrick said.

"Yes, he is right, Wrenna. I have a great deal of experience with these people. They are definitely untrustworthy. They are a lot like your father. They have only their best interest in mind. I saw it many times when I was enlisted. Many times we had to do things that were just morally not right. That's one reason I got out when I did," Abel said.

"What do you suggest?" Wrenna asked both males.

"I think you can handle yourself, but there's one thing you should know. These men do not treat females with high regard. So don't expect them to show much respect," Abel said.

"I will make them respect me if I have to," Wrenna said. She turned her stone face towards the large doors and went quiet. They waited.

Several minutes later, the general finally returned, peering from the cracked door.

"They will see you now. Follow me," the general said as he turned to enter the room.

Wrenna looked towards Abel and Marrick, and they all three followed the general. The general led them into a great big room. It looked like a theater. There were rows of chairs lined up, leading up to a second floor. In the front of the room was a large stage with a long table. There were bright lights shining down on the men lined up behind the table. Wrenna looked up to the humans, surprised. Each man looked to be very old, their skin pale and thin. A few had patches of hair, but most were completely bald. These men looked like at any moment, they could keel over and die.

These are the leaders I need to worry about, these feeble, frail men.

The general spoke. "Sirs, these are the folks I mentioned. They would like to speak to you about the situation."

The general turned and gestured towards Wrenna, motioning for her to step forward and speak.

"Namaste, gentlemen. I am Wrenna Thain, daughter of Chief Thain. I have recently inherited my position as the leader of my city, Shambhala. My first creed as leader is to hopefully work with you to take back the surface and free your people. I was hoping we could come together and devise a plan to defeat the Nephilim, freeing the people of earth from the ongoing genocide being afflicted upon them." Wrenna paused, waiting for one of them to acknowledge her by speaking.

They sat frozen, staring blankly back at Wrenna and the others. She walked forward, getting closer to the men. This time, she raised her voice. She freed a soft glow of light from within. She could see the reflection shining back at her from the dull, opaque eyes of the men. If they wouldn't listen to her words, maybe a brief demonstration of what she could do would rouse them. Wrenna projected small tendrils of her power into each man's mind, wanting to get a better picture of who they truly were and what they stood for. As she pierced into their consciousness, she was immediately overcome with darkness. It was hard for her to keep control of her powers. The darkness that filled the men's mind was so thick and concentrated, it was hard for Wrenna to even breathe. She saw things they had done, disgusting things. She felt their every motive, each one being more sick and twisted then her father could have ever imagined. She found nothing other than pure emptiness, fully encompassed with blackness and evil. Wrenna hadn't encountered anything like this yet. Not even the Nephilim's mind was this wicked. The men sat still as if they welcomed Wrenna's search, granting her entrance into this unholy space they lived in. Wrenna's breath shuddered. The hair on her arms stood on end. Their darkness flowed like hot lava into her veins. She pulled back her search. She easily found who these men were and what their intentions were. Her findings sickened her to her core, causing her to slightly buckle at the knees.

Finally breaking the silence, one of the younger looking men stood up from the table. "You are different from your father. We had an understanding with him, one that was fully being fulfilled on our end and his.

I can feel you probing around in my head. Did you find what you were looking for?" The man laughed, his voice raspy and low. He looked to the others. "What do you think, men? Do you wish to continue on with the original plan? The plan that will benefit us much more. Or should we put our trust in this young female creature?"

Chapter Twenty-Seven

Realization quickly came to Wrenna that these men had no interest in helping the humans. They had their own agenda. An agenda Wrenna didn't quite fully understand yet, but she assumed it had something to do with control. Wrenna rapidly thought through what the next step she should take would be, while the pale, skeletal men looked down at her and waited.

"I see you and I have very different goals for the future of mankind." Wrenna began walking backwards, taking small steps, hoping they wouldn't notice.

"We had a very clear deal with your father, one that we see you were not privy to. Would you like to be enlightened, child?" a man with a thinning, gray mustache and bald head muttered from one end of the table.

"Yes, please enlighten me if you will," Wrenna said, allowing a bit of an attitude to creep into her words.

The man coughed into a handkerchief, placing it back into his coat pocket. Wrenna cringed. She didn't understand how these men were even still living, let alone here, running the show for Abel's people.

"Let me just say, he was providing us with very important assets. Unfortunately, there were many casualties along the way. But we are willing to make the necessary sacrifices. You see, we had a good thing going, and now that you have taken it upon yourself to remove your father from this paradigm, it looks like you will be the one stepping in to fulfill our deal."

Wrenna spoke under her breath. "Seems like my father was the king of making deals with scum," she said, directing her words toward Abel and Marrick. She looked back up towards the men. "What if I do not want to partake in this deal that you have?" Wrenna said.

"You do not have a choice. Your father mentioned that you would soon be learning the ins and outs of what it is that he does. Well, now that he is no longer available, it seems it's time for a quick lesson," the man who sat just right of center said.

Wrenna scanned the empty eyes of each man once more.

Her curiosity took over. "I am willing to learn, but first I need to know what it is I'll be required to do," Wrenna said.

The man in the middle, who was still standing, spoke again. "General, please take Miss Thain and her friends down to the lower level. I think she will get a better understanding by seeing the work we are doing."

The general stepped forward and pressed his fingertips to his eyebrow, saluting the men. The general turned towards Wrenna, Abel, and Marrick once again and said, "Follow me, please."

Before Wrenna left to follow the general, she spoke one last time to the men at the table. "Until I see you again, gentlemen." She tried a flimsy salute, mimicking the general.

They followed the general out the large door and back into the corridor. He led them to what looked like another door, but it did not have a knob. He pressed a button outside of the door. It flashed green, and the doors slid open. The general stepped inside the small space. Abel walked into the small space and turned to face Wrenna and Marrick.

"It's an elevator. It will bring us down," Abel said.

"I've never seen a contraption like this in my day," Marrick said, stepping into the elevator.

"Why couldn't my father have gotten this? Oh yeah, he wanted to live simply. What a load of shit."

Wrenna followed the others; the doors slid closed. She felt a tickle in her stomach as the elevator descended.

It was a quick descent to the lower level. The elevator abruptly stopped, and the doors slid open. The general pushed past Wrenna, once again leading the way.

"This way. Let me warn you, what you are about to see is quite jarring," the general said, and he continued walking.

Wrenna looked to Abel, raising her eyebrows. The walls were cold rock, the lighting overhead dim. With each step they took down the hall, another light flickered on. As they walked, they began to hear what sounded like moaning. Wrenna couldn't pin where the sounds were coming from.

Marrick whispered, "This place is bad. It has the same energy as the prison of darkness I was held in for so many years," as he rubbed his arms with his hands.

A reminder to Wrenna's newest learned reality. They continued walking, finally coming to a large, caged door.

The general yelled, "Graves, here. Come open the gate."

Heavy footsteps approached them from beyond the gate. A large creature moved out of the darkness, pulling a ring of keys from his pocket. When he got closer, the creature's features became more visible in the light. He was not human, nor Fae, but something else. Wrenna furrowed her brow, but she kept quiet. This didn't seem to be the time or place to be asking questions about other races of beings. The creature was a manlike being but much larger in size. It looked like a male due to what appeared to be a long goatee on its chin. He had two large, thick horns growing from the top of his head. His face looked like something Wrenna once saw in a book. A once revered animal, one that had not been seen for centuries, at least from where Wrenna was from. She couldn't quite place the name of the animal, but she knew her ancestors held great respect for this animal back some centuries ago. The creature's chest was so wide that it would have had to turn sideways to exit the gate. They were now walking through. Wrenna glanced down toward the creature's feet, seeing his legs were covered in thick hair and his feet were round, bulky hooves, another bit she had seen in a book.

See, those books weren't a waste of time.

She quickly looked to Abel, checking his reaction to this creature before them.

The general turned and spoke once more. "Arban and some of our researchers work down here. They do things that I believe to be very unorthodox and inhumane. That man Arban, he has a true gift of amalgamation of sorts, but not in a good way. I do want to say that these experiments he and Chief Thain have put together here are some of the vilest things I have ever seen, and I do not agree with any of it," he said, looking back at Wrenna.

The large creature followed behind them closely, not saying a word, only towering over them, pulling up the rear.

The smell of the space quickly overwhelmed them as they walked further into the darkness of the cave-like place. Wrenna had never experienced anything like it before. She began to feel vomit rise in her throat.

"Death," Marrick said as he covered his nose.

Wrenna could hear the sounds of moaning even clearer now as they stepped down several stairs, dropping lower into the space. An overhead light flickered on, making a loud clicking sound, causing Wrenna to jolt back, falling into Abel's arms.

"Are you okay, Wrenna?" Abel asked.

She quickly got back on her feet saying, "Yeah, sorry. This place is awful."

Wrenna felt an overwhelming surge of bad energy, like sadness, move into her. It was as if she could feel the energy of the space, and it was staggering. The general kept moving. Another light flickered on overhead, illuminating a giant, open room, filled with tables. On top of each table lay unmoving bodies, some human, some Fae. They were strapped down to the tables around their ankles and wrist. Some were unrecognizable, their bodies mangled beyond recognition. Wrenna's breath shuttered in her throat. This was not the first time she had seen death, but this was different. Just like the room built under the stairs back at the place she had called home much of her life, this space was a torture chamber.

"Why are they doing this?" Wrenna asked the general.

"The chief and Arban do unspeakable things down here, things that I can't even find the words to explain. From what I understand, they have devised a method to extract any dormant powers of the Fae. They are removing the powers and have been experimenting with implanting them inside of the humans. For what reason, I could not tell you. That is not the only method of cross breeding they are doing down here. They seem to believe that Fae-human mutations create a more powerful being."

Wrenna knew exactly the motives as to why they were performing these terrible experiments. Wrenna peered around the room, searching for any signs of life. She began walking to each table, examining each body. Some had clear evidence of being dead, and others were clearly in the beginning stages of experimentation. A moaning came from the back of the room, still covered in shadows. Wrenna rushed to the sound. The bright overhead light clicked on, revealing a body strapped to the table. Wrenna immediately recognized the two thick braids stitched together, with the addition of red blood sprinkled amongst her hair. The face was unrecognizable due to the bruising and swelling around the eyes and mouth, but Wrenna knew who it was.

"Willow, can you hear me?" Wrenna asked.

She could see that Willow was barely breathing, but Willow was able to release another raspy moan. Abel and Marrick came running to her side.

"Willow!" Abel said as he came up next to Wrenna.

He began to loosen the straps around Willow's wrist and ankles, freeing her from the table. Willow didn't move much due to the extent of her injuries.

"She is badly hurt. I don't think we can move her," Marrick said.

By that time, behind them they heard a ruckus. They heard the general yelling and shuffling. Wrenna turned to see the large creature moving towards them, the general following closely behind.

"Graves's job is to keep the prisoners here," the general yelled to them.

Wrenna turned to face the large beast who was now only mere feet away. She pulled from within, allowing her powers to transverse Graves's mind. He stopped dead in his tracks, feeling Wrenna's presence. Wrenna was unable to find any signs of intelligent thoughts within the beast's head, nothing to indicate it harbored its own feelings. It was as if it were an empty shell that was being controlled by something else. What she did feel was a lingering darkness, not of the beast but transferred to it from something else. This darkness moved around within Graves's consciousness, staying just out of Wrenna's reach. It felt like some sort of parasite that had weaseled its way in, that had taken over complete dominance of the beast, blocking out any ownership that it could possibly have of its own mind.

Wrenna could hear Willow's soft breaths as she still lay on the table behind her. Graves stood frozen and stared blankly at Wrenna. The darkness undulated, forming a shadow that pulsated within his mind. Wrenna could feel the presence. It felt like something ancient, something forgotten. She summoned more of her own power, pushing it deeper into the beast's thoughts. She began to crowd the darkness, encircling it with her light. Graves's body twitched outwardly as if it wanted to pull back but couldn't. Wrenna pushed more, forcing the darkness to retreat slightly. As she touched the darkness, she connected with this other thing. She could feel the presence of the thing that had hijacked Graves's mind as if it were a puppeteer and the beast was its puppet. She pushed a finger of light into the darkness, and before her flashed a glimpse of what this thing was.

It was nothing Wrenna had ever encountered before. She could feel an archaic being, one that had many layers of wear. It welcomed her exploration now, luring her into it with invitation. This thing, Wrenna felt, dwelled far from where they were, but its presence was robust and bold. Wrenna kept a rein on her own powers, only giving in just enough to understand that this was what was controlling Graves. The darkness rubbed up against her more as if it liked her presence there.

Wrenna spoke to it from within her own mind. *Who are you? What are you?* She hoped that it would respond.

The darkness moved more like smoke, flowing more freely now, surrounding Wrenna.

You know me, Queen. We have met before, centuries ago. You were in a different form then, a deep, malevolent voice whispered.

Wrenna felt like she recognized the voice. She had heard it before, but she couldn't place when.

It whispered again, *We are old friends.*

She felt an iciness move down her spine as the darkness began to press back, creeping into Wrenna's thoughts and body. Wrenna stepped back, sucking in a breath. She sensed a shuffling behind her, realizing Abel and Marrick were lifting Willow up off the table. Wrenna kept Graves locked down, flooding her light into the beast's mind. Wrenna didn't like the feel of whatever it was reaching out to her, acting as if they knew each other. She just wanted to control Graves and free Willow.

The voice of the general pulled her from her thoughts. "They have my permission to take this prisoner. Stand down, soldier," he said to Graves.

Wrenna shook her head, taking a moment to return to her body and the present moment. She looked over, and the beast peered back at her, his big black eyes empty. He looked at her like he was aware of what she had done, what she had experienced. A witness within his own mind. The beast stoically turned and walked back up the stairs, leaving them. Wrenna wasn't sure if he was just obeying the general or something else. She turned, seeing Abel now holding Willow, keeping her steady.

Marrick looked up at her. "Is everything okay, my queen?" he asked.

"Yeah, no, I'm fine," she said.

Wrenna turned to the general. "We have to get Willow out of here, get her to someone that can help her. My father thought that if human and Fae were to come together, it would create a sort of super powerful Fae hybrid. That's what he was hoping for when he kidnapped my mother from the surface. The Great Oracle told him that half-human and half-Fae blood would result in a power like no other. This was his plan with all this down here," Wrenna said as her eyes traveled one last time over the room.

Wrenna thought about telling him that her father had failed at achieving that with her, but this wasn't the time or place. She reached back, stepping to the other side of Willow. She placed her arm around her, helping Abel hold her up.

"I won't be any part of this. Those men back there, they want me to continue with this monstrosity. I won't do it. They can kill me first," Wrenna said as she pulled Willow forward, leading the others toward the way they came.

"They will not let you leave here," the general yelled after them.

Wrenna stopped; she knew that he was right. She couldn't just leave;

they would eventually come after her. Those men wouldn't ever stop seeking power and control, similar to her father. If Wrenna didn't try to do something now to stop it, it would just continue. She knew what had to be done. She had to start taking action, starting with the pale human men that awaited her in that room.

"Bring them back to the craft. I will deal with them," she said.

"Are you sure, my queen? I don't feel good about sending you off on your own. I am here to protect you. It is my debt to you," Marrick said.

"Thank you, my friend, but now I need you to help Abel get Willow to the craft. I will be there soon, and we will head back to Shambhala. We need to find a healer for Willow as soon as possible," Wrenna said.

"As you wish, my queen," Marrick said.

The general led them back to the corridor where the large room lay.

"I will meet you at the craft. Be ready to leave. If I am not there in thirty minutes, I want you all to try to leave without me," Wrenna said.

"We can't leave without you. I won't, and we need you to power the craft, remember?" Abel said with a mischievous smile.

"Right. Well, I am sure the general can bring you up to speed on how that craft actually works. In the meantime, just get them there. I will try to be there soon. Don't come looking for me. If you have to find another way out of here, do it," Wrenna said.

Willow moaned, her face so badly beaten her words could not come out clearly.

"We will get you help, Willow. Stay with us. I am sorry they did this to you. They will not get away with this, I swear."

And with that Wrenna turned and entered the large door.

Wrenna walked back into the large open room; the men still sat waiting at the table. As if they were bound to their seats like statues, they sat still as if frozen in place. The room was cold and hollow. She could feel only emptiness in the room, the men themselves vacant.

"I have seen what you and my dear father have been working on. What was the plan, to build an army of some kind? You all only have one train of thought, don't you? Conquer and destroy." Wrenna yelled up at the men who sat stone still in their place behind the table.

"Your father promised us an army. Our men are flawed. They are weak, easily killed. We haven't quite discovered the correct formula in our creations. That is where you come in," a tall, frail man said, showing his yellow teeth.

"Capturing Fae and humans, bringing them here for you to experiment on, yeah, that's not something I will ever do. And what makes you think these little experiments of yours will even work?" Wrenna said.

"Well, you are proof of that, of course," another pale man, with bright blue veins spread across his face, said.

The man who sat in the middle of the table, who seemed to have more authority than the others, spoke again. "You are here with us now, Wrenna. You are what it is we and your father have been trying to replicate. Now that you have made it much easier on us and have removed your father from the equation, we can now do things our way. While you were away, bearing witness to what it is we have been doing here, we had time to discuss a new plan."

"And what would that be?" Wrenna asked.

"Well, you, young girl, you are what we are aspiring to create. Your blood. You are the first hybrid, the goal, so to speak. Now that we have you here, now that you are no longer guarded by your father, we can just use you," the man continued.

"I won't help you. Your agenda is vile and disgusting. I won't support you in any way," Wrenna said.

"It is not your support that we desire. It is your blood," the man said.

Wrenna froze, realizing she had walked back into a trap. Doors opened on either side of her, more doors behind the men, doors on the second floor. Beasts like Graves filed into the large room. They encircled the men and Wrenna, blocking any possible escape.

The man stood from the table and spoke. "You are the final key to what it is we need. To take back control. We have been obliging the Fae and Yama for far too long. It is time we take back what is ours."

Chapter Twenty-Eight

The soldiers pulled in closer to Wrenna, fully entrapping her. Wrenna could feel the warmth of their massive bodies pressing in. Panic filled Wrenna's chest; her mind shuffled through possible outcomes to this situation. Images flashed into Wrenna's mind. A soldier gripping her wrist and pulling her down into that hollow place, that torture chamber. Strapping her to one of those cold slab tables. Visions of Arban slicing into her skin, bleeding her out. Wrenna blocked out the images. It wouldn't end like that. Wrenna recalled her meeting with Lord Surya, and an echo of his voice filled her mind.

You, Rayna, are the savior of all of mankind, those who dwell on the surface and to those who reside within. You can even save the lost to the underworld. It will be you that will change the future of all.

Wrenna was reminded of what it was she was created to do. The warmth of her powers pushed out her fear. It swirled deep within her body, moving from her toes to the top of her head. Coolness filled her neck and shoulders, moving to her head. Her light began to pour from her extremities. The membranes of her eyes slid into place, protecting them from the bright light that was soon to come. The pale men all stood from their chairs, peering over the table, taking in Wrenna's display of power. The beast soldiers stepped back. Wrenna could feel the fear emanating off of them now. Wrenna's light shone bright, engulfing the entire room, tendrils of energy echoed from each of Wrenna's finger-tips snaking their way into each soldier. Wrenna searched within each beast, only to find darkness. The same darkness she had felt before. A foreign, ancient darkness, a parasite embedded into each of their minds. Wrenna pulled more from the now endless well of power within herself, using it to explore the depths of each soldier's thoughts. She found nothing but emptiness, only evil. The soldiers were incapable of any original thought other than what had been programmed in them by this foreign darkness. Wrenna expanded her tendrils of light, knitting it amongst the darkness. The light illuminated the space within each beast soldier. The primeval shadow that lurked within them recoiled and cowered back. Wrenna pushed even more light, more energy. Damp-ening the darkness that filled the empty space held within the conscious-ness of each soldier. In a perfectly orchestrated dance, the soldiers dropped to their knees, their chins falling to their chest. It was as if whatever was puppeting the creatures left, giving them their freedom. Each soldier felt Wrenna's presence now, welcoming her light, bowing to her in thanks.

The old, pale men, still standing behind the long table, gasped.

"What an excellent show of your powers, young one," one of the men said. He looked towards the others. "Imagine the capabilities, the potential. Our army would be unstoppable."

Wrenna stepped closer to the men, pressing her hands on the stage and lifting herself up, standing parallel with each of them now. She felt their energy, their excitement. These men could only think of one thing: what Wrenna could do for them. They were not thinking of what Wrenna could do to them. Wrenna scanned each man. Their eyes were hollow, and they had sunken faces and pale, veiny skin. They were weak, frail, only having their words as their defense. Wrenna brightened her light, blinding the men, causing them to sink back into their chairs. She extended her invisible tendrils once again, creeping her way into the minds of each man. She saw their eyes widen; each of them aware of Wrenna's presence. She already knew what their minds and thoughts entailed; she wasted no time. Each tendril within each man's mind began to slither and wrap around their tiny, bleak existence.

One man spoke out. "Killing us will not stop him. Yama will not give up what it is he wants. Let us work alongside you. Creating this army is the only way to defeat him."

Wrenna slowly contracted her powers, feeling their life begin to fizzle out. Wrenna took her time, allowing her tendrils of power to be a vise grip around their swollen, decrepit brains. She slowly constricted more.

Another man was able to say a few words. "He will come for you. He will destroy all that is important to you. You cannot stop him." The men's pale skin began to wither even more as Wrenna took her time extinguishing the life from them, watching as their broken bodies collapsed onto the table, one by one.

Wrenna turned to the beast soldiers, frozen on their knees, stone still like statues. She went to head towards the door to leave when one soldier got to his feet. He looked deep into her olive-green eyes. Wrenna looked back into his black, empty eyes as he spoke.

His voice echoed in the large room. "Daughter of Lord Surya, Queen Rayna, this is a message to you from our lord. If you want to save your people and the humans on the surface, you must submit yourself to him. Bow down to him and pledge your allegiance to him and his cause. If you do not drop to your knees and speak his name, devoting yourself to him, he will destroy all of what it is that you love," the beast soldier said.

Wrenna walked closer to the beast and stood on her tiptoes, bringing her eyes as close to parallel with his as she could.

"I will never bow down to anyone. You tell him that. Never!" Wrenna said.

Another soldier stood from far back in the crowd. He walked through the others, who stayed still, fallen on their knees. Finally, he got closer to Wrenna and spoke, but his voice was like no other. It rumbled within Wrenna's chest, and its depth pressed into Wrenna's soul.

"One last chance, Queen. Dedicate yourself to me now or die here, buried deep within this mountain. If you say no to me, you will never leave this place alive. What is it you wish to do?" The voice came from the beast, but it was not his voice. He was a mere puppet, his puppeteer regaining control.

"Yama, you come to me once again, using these vessels as a way to speak. Are you too afraid to come to me in person?"

Wrenna stepped up closer to the beast, pulling light from within, allowing the energy to encompass her body.

Wrenna continued, "I will free the people of this earth. Those who dwell on the surface and the Fae beings who live within. I will rid this earth of you like my true father should have done a millennium ago. I will not make the same mistake he did. We will no longer do your bidding. We will no longer serve you, bending the knee to you. I am not afraid of you. My true father gave me the strength and power to defeat you, and my mother gave me the courage. Come to me and face me, you coward," Wrenna said.

The beast stood still before Wrenna, only an empty vessel that housed the voice of Yama. He finally opened his mouth, and the foreign voice echoed from its throat. "Wrong choice, Queen. Your people will suffer greatly. Those you love will feel it most. As for me, I will leave you there in that mountain, trapped for all of eternity. So you can think about the choice you made, sacrificing the Fae of Shambhala and the rest of the human race. This earth will be mine. The souls of the beings that dwell here will be mine. The blame will be all yours, Queen Rayna, daughter of the Sun God. I will grant a few of each realm life so they may pass on the story that it was you that failed them. It was you that made the wrong choice and in return, they all suffered or died. You had a chance, just like your father did, and you chose wrong, just like your father. For that, there will be great suffering. You have damned them all," the beast said.

Once he finished his sentence, the soldier fell once again to his knees, along with the other beasts. The floor under Wrenna's feet began to shake. The walls cracked, and dust began to fill the room. Wrenna ran through the kneeling soldiers and exited the door, back into the corridor that led to the landing pad. As Wrenna ran, she saw human military soldiers scramble about, yelling out orders. She made her way to where Abel, Marrick, and Willow waited by the craft. The floor shook, the walls around the large room moved, and rocks dropped from the ceiling.

Wrenna yelled out to Abel and Marrick, "We have to get out of here now!"

The general who also stood near the launch pad yelled out to Wrenna, "The door will not open. Something has jammed it. We have to go down through the tunnels. That is our only way out."

Another officer ran up to the general, telling him something. Wrenna couldn't hear due to the rumbles of the walls shaking around them, the hum of bodies rushing about.

The general got closer to Wrenna and said, "The Nephilim giants, they have surrounded the mountain. They aim to tear it down, with us inside. We must go down into the tunnels immediately, or we will be crushed," he said.

Wrenna turned to Abel, "Get Willow and let's go. It is the only way!" Wrenna yelled.

More rocks fell to the floor around them, some landing atop soldiers, pinning them to the floor. Stairs that crawled up the side of the mountain began to pull free, hanging loosely, swaying.

Marrick looked up to the devastation and spoke. "My queen, can you face the giants like you did before? Can you defeat them?" he asked Wrenna.

Wrenna's initial thought was to retreat, leaving through tunnels and taking her friends with her. After taking in Marrick's question, she was reminded that she had decided to no longer run, to no longer hide. She did have the power to stop the Nephilim. It was time to use that power once again.

"Yes, you are right, I need to stop them." Wrenna knew that if she didn't do something now, they would all be doomed. She continued, "It is too dangerous here. It is too hard for me to focus. You all need to get to safety." Wrenna paused, pulling from her powers, searching outside the mountain. "I can feel possibly ten Nephilim out there. I don't think I can reach all of them from here. The walls are solid rock. There's just too much going on. Marrick, I need you, Abel, and Willow to go head down into the tunnels with the human soldiers. I will find you there. I can stop this. I just need to get to a better spot higher up." Wrenna looked up.

"Yes, my queen. Please be careful. This is your destiny. I believe in you. I will lead them to the tunnels, and I will bring them to safety," Marrick said.

"Thank you, Marrick. I want you to know I forgive you. I wish I had known you were there the whole time, imprisoned inside Isha. I would have tried to free you. I am sorry," Wrenna said, looking down into the small elf's eyes.

"It is not our fault, my queen. Thank you for your forgiveness," he said.

With a quick smile, he turned and headed towards Abel to help lift Willow as much as he could.

"Wrenna, please be safe," Abel yelled out to her. His eyes softened.

All three followed the general down the stairs that led to the entryway to the tunnels built into the base of the mountain. Wrenna watched them go, taking them in as a possibility it could be the last time she saw them. These newfound friends. They each had come to hold a special place in Wrenna's heart. The only family she had left besides them was Zelda.

Wrenna looked up towards the ceiling of the mountain. Dust and debris fell down into her eyes. The lights flickered and clicked off, bringing darkness to the space. Wrenna pulled from within. Her membranes quickly slid over her eyes to protect from the dirt and bright light. Her light spilled forth, filling the space around her with enough light for her to make out her surroundings. She quickly found a staircase still attached to the side of the mountain. It spiraled upward. Wrenna followed it with her eyes, seeing that it eventually led to a platform near the top of the mountain's peak. She couldn't see if there was an exit or what lay atop the platform, but she felt it would get her close enough, allowing her better reach to the attackers outside. The walls shook more as Wrenna ran to the staircase. She dodged giant rock pieces that tumbled down, tripping several times along the way. The landing pad had cleared out. Some bodies lay pinned under fallen rocks. Blood poured from the mangled corpses, unrecognizable underneath.

Wrenna tried not to spend too much precious time looking, setting her sight on the bottom of the staircase. She finally reached the first step. She paused and pulled her power from within. She gazed up at the many steps she was about to take and prayed to the Gods that she would make it. The mountain shook more as Wrenna took off up the stairs, taking two steps at a time. Her lungs began to burn as she pushed forward. She thought to herself how glad she was for forcing herself to go running every day back in her past life, which seemed so long ago. The life she had taken for granted for so long. Living cluelessly to the reality she was now fully submerged in. She pushed herself more as large chunks of the mountain walls plunged towards the landing pad she had once stood upon. She looked down and watched as it collapsed and fell, covering the entryway to the tunnels where her friends had disappeared only moments ago.

I hope they are safe down there.

As Wrenna reached another set of stairs, she heard a loud crack. The brace that attached the stairs to the wall had broken in half. Wrenna gripped the railing, drawing from within herself, searching for bravery to continue on. She jumped, using the energy from within to launch herself to the next set of stairs. She barely made it before the entire lower staircase broke free from the wall and plummeted downward. Wrenna took in a deep breath as she watched. She turned back. Looking up, she was almost there. She pulled more energy from her core. It pulsed from her feet, propelling her up to the next staircase. Surprised by this newfound ability, Wrenna used it to help scale the many stairs, ascending the mountain wall quicker and with better, flawless accuracy.

She finally reached the platform that lay just beneath the ceiling of the mountain. She looked up, seeing a circular handle connected to a small square metal hatch door. Wrenna reached up and began to twist the handle, cautiously pushing on the small door. Wrenna did it slowly, not knowing what might lie waiting for her on the other side. Wrenna peeked her head slowly out, bracing herself for whatever could be beyond the door.

Luckily, she was surrounded by great, green plants. Like the ones she had seen in her vision. The plants had large bases that were brown and rough, rocklike. At the top were large, puffy green leaves. These plants spiraled up into the sky, taller than anything she had ever seen before. There were many of them, covering the entire top of the mountain. Wrenna was pulled from taking in the beauty of her surroundings as she felt the ground rumble beneath her. She slowly crawled through the small metal hole, finding her feet planted on the shaking ground. Wrenna looked up, trying to see if any of the Nephilim could see her or she could see them, but the plants were too thick, camouflaging her. She ran upward, trying to reach the peak of the mountain, wanting to get the best view of what she would face. Rocks slid down past her. Giant plants had fallen all around her, toppling over one another. The mountain shook more and more. Wrenna wondered how much more damage it could withstand before it collapsed into itself.

Climbing further, Wrenna could finally see what looked to be the top. It was bare, nothing available to hide within. Wrenna knew once she stepped out into that open space, she would be fully exposed to the giants that surrounded her. She stopped just within the tall plants, still hidden. She closed her eyes and took in several deep breaths, calming her mind. She thought of all of the soldiers trapped within the tunnels below her. She thought of Abel, Marrick, and Willow, her newfound family. She thought about the humans scattered amongst the debris, the destruction on the surface. The lives they had been forced to live, hiding, scavenging. Fearing that any moment could be their last. Wrenna's heart fluttered with sadness for those people. She thought of her people, unaware of the dangers and evil that pressed upon them. Imprisoned behind the walls of the city, not realizing that they were next to feel the wrath of this, Yama's wrath. Wrenna allowed the images of those who had suffered and fell victim to this evil to fill her mind. She pulled from the energy it created, pulling from deep within herself. With the overwhelming surge of emotion and thoughts, Wrenna began to feel a fire build inside of her. Within that fire, lying in wait, was an ancient power. She felt it simmer and billow over as her mind swept over the many images of the many deaths she had witnessed. Her imagination was the only window to the many other deaths that had come before. This ancient power began to boil up inside, reaching the edge of Wrenna's being. Light spilled from her, bright orange, filling the space of the mountain before her.

Wrenna felt her body become weightless, her toes hovering just above the ground now. She felt her chest begin to grow and expand, the power and energy filling up her heart space. Wrenna had never felt this depth of power before. It was as if something primordial had awakened inside of her. Was it Lord Surya's power, a power that had been hidden within her for so long? Wrenna didn't have time to think it through. She gave it her full permission to reveal itself, rising up from the deepest part of her soul. Wrenna's golden skin gleamed brighter amongst her orange light. The well of power fully generated, Wrenna moved her floating body to the clear patch of space just at the precipice of the mountain. The wind moved her hair in all directions. The fire opal around her neck lifted upward, light exploding from the stone. Wrenna gazed down the mountain, taking in the abundance of Nephilim awaiting below. It was much more than ten, more like twenty. They had all congregated around the bottom of the mountain, making the base their focal point of demolition. Wrenna lifted her body up higher, giving the Nephilim giants below full view of her presence now. The giants ceased their task, taking in Wrenna's form, their eyes gaping.

She spoke out to them, amplifying her voice. "You will stop this destruction and drop to your knees before me or die."

After a moment of complete silence, the giants broke out in laughter. A female giant, one with raggedy black hair, covered in filth, spoke first. "We are sent here by the great God of Death, Lord Yama. His will is ours," she said.

The female giant reached for a behemoth boulder and pelted it towards Wrenna. She dodged the rock easily, allowing it to slam through the plants behind her.

"Your lord will be no more. Your will is meaningless. I am the daughter of the Sun God, Lord Surya. His blood is my blood. If you stand with Yama, you stand against me. Prepare for your death by my hand," Wrenna said.

Her power vibrated under her chest, waiting for its permission to escape. A few of the giants began climbing the mountainside, bringing themselves higher, closer, to reach Wrenna. The others began reaching for rocks and fallen plant debris, even ripping them from the ground and launching them at Wrenna. She felt a living upsurge of power, the ancient residue of her true father, advance to the surface. Her light changed from orange to white, creating a circular, unbreakable shield that now surrounded her. The rubble from the giants bounced off of her shield, falling to the ground around her. She pushed herself higher into the sky, moving out of reach of those ascending the mountain. In the midst of the Nephilim's attack, a great voice echoed from the air around them.

"Stand down, my faithfuls. It is my turn to break her," said the voice.

From a distance, the large plants began to part, an open path appearing as if leading towards something. Down the path stood Lord Yama. He was large, his skin completely black, like charred flesh. He had two colossal curved horns atop his head. The Death God's body was gargantuan in stature, bigger than any man or Fae Wrenna had seen. In one of his clawed hands, Wrenna saw what looked like a frail body trailing behind him. Her heart fluttered, bile rising in her throat as she realized who the lifeless body belonged to. It was Zelda!

Chapter Twenty-Nine

Wrenna gasped as she witnessed Zelda's lifeless body dangle behind Yama, her arms dragging the ground next to Yama's hooved feet. A sinister smile grew on Yama's face, his teeth, piercing white and jagged, becoming visible beyond his lips.

"Looks like I have hit a raw nerve in you, Queen," he said.

Zelda didn't move, showing no sign of life. Wrenna felt her powers flare with anger. She allowed them to boil, to grow, waiting for the right time to release them upon the beast before her. The Nephilim all dropped to their knees, bowing their heads as the Death God moved closer. Wrenna, not holding back, unleashed millions of electrified tendrils of power from her fingertips. They shattered into the air around her, piercing her white glowing shield.

"Impressive, child. You are your father's daughter after all. Are you a coward like your father as well? We shall see," Yama said.

The Death God reached the base of the mountain. Pausing, he looked up towards Wrenna. "I will give you one last chance. Honor the Fae bargain, continue serving me the souls of the impure, and I will let you live. I will let you continue to live your old meaningless life in your city. You can go back to how you spent your worthless time before. Pledge your life to serve me, and it will be as if none of this ever happened. You can return to Shambhala and take your decrepit, dying friend with you," Yama said.

Wrenna whispered one word, "Never." Wrenna prayed to the Gods that Zelda was still alive, that his words meant she hadn't lost her yet.

As the word left her lips, she unlocked the door, unleashing her powers. All at once, the energy surged into the fire opal around her neck. In seconds, every ounce of energy pooled together, forming a cylindrical white beam of light. The power was now unbridled, fully awakened and freed from the well within her. It shot out, aiming straight for the Death God's chest. Yama, sensing the attack, tossed Zelda to the side and leapt from the ground. He landed several feet up the edge of the mountain. Wrenna's beam of light retracted back into the fire opal. She felt it settle back into place, waiting to be freed again. Yama bound up the mountain, rapidly making his way closer to the peak. Wrenna continued to hover, moving further into the sky, away from the mountain top. She hovered in thin air, easily using her powers to drive her movements. Wrenna took a deep breath, concentrating her focus on each leap Yama took as he ascended the mountain. Perfectly clocking the timing of each of his movements, she easily predicted his next landing. She unleashed the white beam of power from her opal once again, aiming for Yama's next step. It landed flawlessly, exploding into the Death God's chest. He fell back, hitting the rock-covered mountain side. He laughed a bold, devilish laugh as he pulled himself back onto his feet.

"You are strong, much like Surya, but I can feel the presence of human weakness within you," Yama said, now fully standing up again.

He began moving once again. Wrenna noticed he was moving much slower than before.

She heard his voice drift into her mind. *You cannot stop me. My will will be done.*

Wrenna replied back telepathically, *You are wrong.*

Every inch of her body was now electrified with energy. She pulled from her emotions—fear, anger, sadness—and moved that energy faster. She felt a steady flow of all of her energy spiral and swirl up her spine, finding a continuous stream into her head, neck, and shoulders. Wrenna bore down, focusing on the build of power. Wrenna felt as if she were becoming a pressurized vessel. A vessel that held such an abundance of energy that the lid could just barely stay on. She took several chest-expanding breaths in, trying to give it more space, to no avail. Yama was moving closer, the Nephilim following him not far behind. It was only a matter of time before Yama would reach the top of the mountain, coming closer to Wrenna. She watched him, giving him time to get closer, hoping to have a better reach on him once she was ready to attack again. In the midst of her focus, she began to feel a sharp, piercing stab in her head. It felt as if something were penetrating her skull, something from the outside. Wrenna quickly reached for her head with her hands, checking to see if a piece of debris had hit her. She found nothing.

Yama let out a brutal laugh. "Not that unstoppable, are you, Queen?"

He continued his climb, stumbling from injuries that had become more prominent now. The stabbing sensation in her head grew sharper, her mind now faltering from its focus. A fog began to roll in, blocking out her consciousness. There was something dark and evil filtering in. Wrenna tried to pull in another breath but felt something lock down on her lungs. Her moving flow of energy was muted by several excruciating probes of darkness. Yama stood from the mountain, turning his gaze up toward Wrenna once more.

"You aren't the only one who can enter the mind uninvited. How does it feel to be played at your own game?" he said.

Thoughts of weakness spilled in. Whispers to give up took over. Her mind began to falter more as the edge of her powers rolled into the wall of dark fog now bewitching her body. At that moment, Wrenna wanted to give up. She felt the urge to give in to the darkness, to give it full permission to enter and take over every cell of her being. Yama was invading and on the verge of conquer. Wrenna wanted to accept that. He was trying to make her a puppet like he had the beast soldiers and so many others. Mere seconds before Wrenna let go and gave in, a memory flashed in her mind. An image of her mother's face, her lush red hair, her beautiful smile.

From her lips came the words, *Don't give up, Rayna. Keep fighting.*

Her mother's image began to fade, shaking her free from the veil of darkness. She remembered that giving up wasn't an option and was not what she wanted. She felt for the fog, allowing herself to taste its sourness. And with the face of her mother still in her memory, she ignited her powers once again. It was as if the words of her mother became an accelerant, feeding and nourishing the energy within. The fog of darkness pulled back, letting out an ear-splitting shriek. Wrenna began dousing her mind with the will of all of her soul, with the joy of the memory. Yama's unholiness couldn't withstand the pureness. She felt his darkness waver to its existence. Wrenna filled her mind with more thoughts, moments in time that made her happy, that made her feel love.

Yama's sinister darkness abandoned its quest to possess Wrenna's body and soul. She no longer detected the unpleasant companion she had inside her just moments ago. Yama was now just a mere being, climbing the mountain below her. Wrenna looked down towards him, feeling already that the battle was won.

"Your will is no more!" Wrenna yelled as she still hovered in the air.

And with those words, Wrenna opened the lid, releasing the pressure of her powers, freeing them from the space between her eyes. The white light explored outward, targeting its opponent without hesitation. Wrenna watched as her powers landed.

She could no longer see Yama, his body surrounded by dust and smoke. She lowered herself closer, keeping out of reach of the Nephilim. There, in the cloud of dust, Yama's body finally came into view. The force of her powers sent Yama's limp body tumbling down the mountain. Quickly building momentum, his body was thrown and tossed about like a rag doll until it finally came to an abrupt stop, slamming into a large boulder, one that had been thrown there earlier. Wrenna waited, watching for any sign of life from Yama. The Nephilim surrounding the mountain stood, their eyes pressed towards where their God now lay. Wrenna looked back towards where her friend's body lay lifeless on the ground below. Zelda... she was like a mother to Wrenna. Her heart broke as she saw her there. She looked back to where Yama lay tangled up, one arm under his body, the other splayed out to the side. His legs twisted together at the ankles. In a brief moment, Wrenna's mind flashed to her dream. The one she had where she found Zelda dead beside her and bright orange lights above her. The world was wrecked, the smell of smoke and blood surrounding her. This moment reflected her dream.

Wrenna told herself, *I have to end it here. It is time to put a stop to the death and suffering. It is time for me to take back this world for all the people and Fae that dwelled amongst and within it.* She had to do this for Zelda and for all the others that fell by the hands of the Death God.

She reached again into the depths of herself, pulling from the well within. She used all of her sadness, pain, fear, and guilt, dredging up the embers of energy that remained. She felt her fire opal vibrate on her chest. The opal's energy siphoned what remained inside of Wrenna. Her mind raced through the different outcomes, the different ways to finish this, coming to one and only one conclusion: she had to make sure Yama would not come back. Wrenna gazed down, watching the giants all begin to climb the side of the mountain once again. They were now trying to reach their God. She knew what to do. She had to send them all to the depths of the earth once again, praying their souls would perish along the way. Wrenna lowered her head, engaging the last little bit of her powers. The white light launched forth, escaping her opal, blasting towards the top of the mountain. On contact, Wrenna's body thrust back from impact. She pushed more, keeping her full focus on the end result she so desired. The rocks of the mountain began to break apart, falling into the chamber below. Wrenna prayed to the Gods that everyone inside had found their way into the tunnels and were now far, far away. She expanded the beam of light to cover more area, busting up the mountain. She soon got to where Yama still lay unmoving. She watched as the rocks around him broke apart, his body sliding into an open crack, gone into the blackness. The mountain rumbled and quickly broke apart even more. The weight of each giant helped the ground to collapse below their own feet. They too disappeared into the dark man-made cavern below. Dust escaped the remains of what once was a great mountain, engulfing and surrounding Wrenna. She looked down at what was left after the dust dissipated. Where the enormous mountain once stood was now a pile of rubble. The mountain had sunk into the cavern below, shrinking vastly in size. Wrenna hovered over the remains, hoping that this now would end the rule of Yama and the devastation he had caused for far too long.

Wrenna lowered herself down to the ground a safe distance away from the now demolished mountain. She stood, peering at the aftermath, when she heard a voice call to her from a distance. Wrenna turned towards the sound, seeing Abel running in her direction.

"Wrenna!" Abel said, calling to her.

Wrenna stood for a moment, allowing her powers to recede, her light to draw back in. Her eye shields retracted from covering her eyes. Wrenna felt the energy within her body begin to calm and return back to a steadier state. Abel ran straight into Wrenna, wrapping his arms around her, embracing her in a hug. Wrenna returned the embrace. She welcomed it.

Abel pulled back, looking into Wrenna's eyes. "Holy shit, you did all of this?" he said as he looked around, taking in the fallout of what Wrenna had done. He looked back at Wrenna, still holding her close to his chest. "What does this all mean for us? Is it over?" he asked, taking a step back, his hands still resting on Wrenna's arms.

"I think it means your people are free," Wrenna said, yearning for him to hold her again.

"What happened?" Abel said as he turned away scanning the area.

"Yama was here, and he had..." Wrenna stopped speaking as she remembered Zelda. She began running towards where her body still lay upon the shaken ground. She could hear Abel's footfalls following close behind her.

He yelled, "Where are you going?"

Wrenna didn't answer. She could only think of her dear friend lying there alone. Soon Zelda's little twisted body appeared, spread across the ground. Wrenna dropped to her knees next to her, rolling her over. Zelda's eyes were closed, swollen and bruised.

Wrenna called out to her friend, "Zelda, can you hear me?"

Realization of the excessiveness of Zelda's wounds sunk into Wrenna as she inspected her body. Abel was soon there, coming to his knees across from Wrenna. She watched him as he searched for a pulse in Zelda's wrinkled neck.

"She still has a pulse. It is very faint, but it's there," Abel said.

Wrenna reached under Zelda's fragile head, lifting her up into her arms. She hugged her close, whispering into her ear, "I am so sorry. This is my fault."

Tears began to fall from Wrenna's eyes. Zelda lay lifeless in her arms. Abel stood as he looked back behind Wrenna. She could hear footsteps coming closer. Wrenna didn't move; she continued to hold Zelda close. Moments later, Marrick was there standing next to her, and his hand fell to her shoulder. Wrenna looked over at Marrick. His short stature allowed their eyes to meet.

"My queen, I am sorry. She was someone you cared for dearly, I see," Marrick said.

"Yes, she is," Wrenna said, blinking more tears away.

Marrick reached for his necklace, the one that held a fire opal, and he moved to place it around Zelda's neck.

"What are you doing?" Wrenna asked.

"I have heard stories of the great power within these stones. They bring to fruition the things we want most in life. I only wish I could have done this for my family, for those I lost in my past. Their bodies were taken and thrown into a pit of fire before I had the chance. So let me do this for you. I owe it to you."

Wrenna took a hand to her own necklace.

Marrick spoke again. "My queen, let me give you this gift. It would be my honor," he said.

He closed his eyes, moving both his hands to Zelda's forehead. Wrenna continued to hold Zelda, lifting her a bit higher, giving Marrick better reach. Wrenna could feel a buzz in the air around them. The wind began to flow and swirl. Marrick stood, eyes closed, deep in a state of concentration. The buzz soon grew greater. Wrenna felt the charge amplify. The fire opal that now rested around Zelda's neck lifted from her chest and began floating in the air. The charge intensified, and the wind picked up. The air around them became so dense, their surroundings becoming invisible. Wrenna's hair lifted with the wind, swirling around her, making things hard to see. A blast came from the opal. An energizing light shot straight into Marrick's forehead. Then an incredibly loud pop happened, a sound so deafening it caused Wrenna to recoil back. She lost her hold of Zelda's body and fell backwards onto the ground. Within seconds, the surge of the wind came to a sudden halt. Wrenna pressed herself upright, finding Zelda lying before her, still lifeless. She looked towards where Marrick had once stood, but he was no longer there. Wrenna quickly scanned the area, seeing Abel now coming back into view but not finding Marrick anywhere on site.

"Where is he?" Wrenna yelled up to Abel.

"I don't know, I couldn't see through the cyclone of wind and air that was around you all. I couldn't get closer. It was as if the air created a wall, keeping me from reaching you," Abel said.

Then a small moan escaped from Zelda's mouth. Wrenna moved onto her knees once again and bent over Zelda.

"Zelda, can you hear me? It's me, Wrenna," she said.

Zelda moaned again as if responding.

Wrenna kissed Zelda on the forehead. "Oh, thank the Gods," Wrenna said.

The fire opal necklace still rested around Zelda's neck.

Wrenna pulled Zelda's head and shoulders back into her arms. "I am here, Zelda," Wrenna said.

"Namaste, my child," Zelda whispered as she peeled open her swollen eyes.

"He did it," Wrenna said, looking up at Abel.

"Who? Marrick? What did he do?" Abel asked.

"He put his opal around her neck and said that the stones can bring to life what it is we want the most. Then he was gone," Wrenna said.

"Once a Fae is bound to an opal, it is theirs until death," Zelda said softly, struggling to release the words. She took in a long breath and continued, "It is said the stone allows its bonded soul to give its life force to another. I guess it is true." Zelda strained to speak.

Wrenna looked up to Abel once more. "He gave his life force to Zelda to bring her back to me. He did that for me!" Wrenna said, tears now pouring down her golden cheeks. Wrenna pulled Zelda in tighter, hugging her close.

"Easy now, my child. This old body is pretty sore," Zelda said as a brief smile crossed her mouth.

Moments later, the general and many human soldiers began to surround them. Zelda was now sitting upright on her own, Wrenna and Abel supporting her.

"How did you guys get out of the mountain, out of those tunnels?" Wrenna asked Abel.

"There was an escape hatch. The general led us there. We all climbed out just as the mountain collapsed," Abel said.

"What about Willow, where is she?" Wrenna asked.

"She is with the army doctor, back with the rest of the soldiers. They are setting up camp," Abel said.

Wrenna looked to Zelda and Abel and said, "Now what?" as she let out a small laugh.

"Let's go home. I miss my books," Zelda said. Wrenna and Abel lifted Zelda to her feet.

"What about you, Abel? What's next for you?" Wrenna asked as they followed the soldiers towards the camp.

"I'm not sure. I'll stay here and help with search and rescue. We have a ton of work ahead of us," he said, looking around. "I do hope this isn't the last I'll see you. You have begun to grow on me kind of," Abel said with a smile.

Wrenna's broken heart fluttered slightly. "Oh, you aren't getting rid of me that easily, Abel," Wrenna said, trying to give him a reassuring smile back.

Wrenna stopped walking, taking a moment to breathe. Abel, sensing Wrenna's need, continued helping Zelda walk forward, leaving Wrenna time alone. She stood there, her feet grounding down into the earth as her mind shuffled through what was left, through what was no longer. Yama was gone. The Nephilim were gone. Marrick was gone. She had freed the humans from the darkness caused by a bargain made by someone she once had called father. Her city was left, her people still there, unaware of the threat she had saved them from. She thought of Marrick again, letting herself grieve his loss. She thought of Felix and all the others whose lives were destroyed. Wrenna looked up into the sky just as a bright light peeked over the horizon. Yellow light spread across the ground by her feet, shining onto the broken earth. Wrenna felt a smile pull across her face in spite of all that she had been through. She moved forward once again, taking steps towards their future campsite, when something tugged at Wrenna's mind. Anxiety and worry that there was still something not right. This feeling told her that this battle she faced was not over.

As her feet fell upon the ground, she felt a breeze graze her skin, and with that breeze came a voice. "I will ascend once again. I will exalt my throne above the stars, above the highest of clouds. My return will once again blacken out the sun. And you, Queen, will be mine."

A chill ran down Wrenna's spine. Her body became covered in goosebumps as she recognized the hollow voice she just heard.

"Hey, Wrenna, are you coming?" Abel yelled.

Wrenna jolted back into reality from the effects of what just had happened. She looked towards Abel where he stood just feet from her.

"What's wrong? You look like you have seen a ghost," Abel said.

"Oh, yeah, it's nothing. I'm fine. Just tired, that's all," Wrenna said.

Abel reached out for Wrenna's hand as he led her towards the others now enthralled in building their makeshift camp. She couldn't bring herself to tell him what had just happened. She wanted to give them their moment of being free. She wanted to let them think that it was over for just a day. But Wrenna knew it was not.

* * *

Coming Soon

Book Two

The Savior Series

Radiant Queen

About the Author

Katie M. Lebleu is a debut Indie author. She plans on writing many more books in the future, including the second book to The Savior Series. Katie already has a dystopian sci fi novel in the works and hopes to publish in 2024. If you enjoyed this book please share with friends and family. She would appreciate any and all reviews to Goodreads and Amazon.

Thank you for reading.

www.ingramcontent.com/pod-product-compliance
Lightning Source LLC
Chambersburg PA
CBHW031212020726
47499CB00002B/555